PENGUIN BOOKS

Support and Defend

Thirty years ago, Tom Clancy was a Maryland insurance broker with a passion for naval history. Years before, he had been an English major at Baltimore's Loyola College and had always dreamed of writing a novel. His first effort, *The Hunt for Red October*, sold briskly as a result of rave reviews, and then catapulted on to the New York Times bestseller list after President Reagan pronounced it 'the perfect yarn'. From that day forward, Clancy established himself as an undisputed master of blending exceptional realism and authenticity, intricate plotting and razor-sharp suspense. He passed away in October 2013.

Mark Greaney has a degree in international relations and political science. He is the author of the Gray Man novels, the most recent of which is *Dead Eye*. In his research for those novels, he travelled to a dozen countries and trained alongside military and law enforcement in the use of firearms, battlefield medicine and close-range combat tactics.

www.tomclancy.com

facebook.com/tomclancyauthor

By Tom Clancy

FICTION

The Hunt for Red October
Red Storm Rising
Patriot Games
The Cardinal of the Kremlin
Clear and Present Danger
The Sum of All Fears
Without Remorse
Debt of Honor
Executive Orders
Rainbow Six
The Bear and the Dragon
Red Rabbit
The Teeth of the Tiger
Dead or Alive
Against All Enemies
Locked On
Threat Vector
Command Authority

NONFICTION

Submarine: A Guided Tour Inside a Nuclear Warship
Armored Cav: A Guided Tour Inside an Armored Cavalry Regiment
Fighter Wing: A Guided Tour of an Air Force Combat Wing
Marine: A Guided Tour of a Marine Expeditionary Unit
Airborne: A Guided Tour of an Airborne Task Force
Carrier: A Guided Tour of an Aircraft Carrier

Into the Storm: A Study in Command
with General Fred Franks, Jr (Ret.) and Tony Koltz

Every Man a Tiger: The Gulf War Air Campaign
with General Chuck Horner (Ret.) and Tony Koltz

Shadow Warriors: Inside the Special Forces
with General Carl Stiner (Ret.) and Tony Koltz

Battle Ready
with General Tony Zinni (Ret.) and Tony Koltz

Tom Clancy's
Support and Defend

MARK GREANEY

PENGUIN BOOKS

PENGUIN BOOKS

UK | USA | Canada | Ireland | Australia
India | New Zealand | South Africa

Penguin Books is part of the Penguin Random House group of companies
whose addresses can be found at global.penguinrandomhouse.com.

First published in the USA by G. P. Putnam's sons 2014
First published in Great Britain by Michael Joseph 2014
Published in Penguin Books 2015

001

Text copyright © Rubicon, Inc., 2015

The moral right of the author has been asserted

Set in 12.5/14.75pt Garamond MT Std
Typeset by Jouve (UK), Milton Keynes
Printed in Great Britain by Clays Ltd, St Ives plc

A CIP catalogue record for this book is available from the British Library

B FORMAT ISBN: 978–1–405–91929–6
A FORMAT ISBN: 978–1–405–91930–2

Principal Characters

Dominic Caruso: operative, The Campus

Ethan Ross: deputy assistant director for Near East and North African affairs, National Security Council

Eve Pang: computer network systems engineer, Ross's girlfriend

Darren Albright: supervisory special agent, FBI Counter-intelligence Division

Nolan and Beale: investigative specialists, FBI Special Surveillance Group

Adara Sherman: director of transportation, The Campus

Harlan Banfield: journalist, member of the International Transparency Project

Gianna Bertoli: director, International Transparency Project

Mohammed Mobasheri: Iranian Revolutionary Guard

Kashan, Shiraz, Isfahan and Ormand: operatives, Quds Force

Arturo: Venezuelan General Intelligence officer

Leo: Venezuelan General Intelligence officer

Rigoberto Finn: polygraph examiner, FBI

Gerry Hendley: director, The Campus/Hendley Associates

Arik Yacoby: former operative, Shayetet 13, Israeli naval Special Forces

David: Israeli intelligence agent

Phillip McKell: computer network expert

Prologue

The coast of India appeared in the moonlight. There wasn't much to it, really, just a narrow strip of sand that emerged from the darkness a few hundred meters off the ship's bow, but the first sight of land in four days told the man standing on the foredeck two important things.

One: the ingression phase of his operation had succeeded.

And two: the time had come to slit the captain's throat.

The man on the foredeck drew his knife and moved toward the stairs leading up to the navigation bridge. Two of his men fell into step behind him, but they were just along to watch. Responsibility for killing the captain fell to the leader and, in truth, he considered it no burden; in fact, he welcomed the opportunity to once again put his commitment to this mission on display for the others.

The leader and his team of six had spent three days on board an Omani fishing trawler on the open water of the Arabian Sea. Last night they came abreast of this eighty-foot dry-goods vessel and waved a shredded fan belt in the air. In Hindi they asked for help, but when the cargo ship drew even with them, the leader and his men scurried aboard like swamp rats and overran the small crew; they slaughtered all save the captain, and ordered him to head due east with a course set for India's Malabar Coast.

It had taken the leader half a day to convince the terrified captain he would not suffer the same fate as his crew. Killing him would make a lie of this, of course, but as the leader climbed the steps up to the dark bridge, he wasn't troubling himself about going back on his promise; his mind was already off this boat and on to the objective phase of the operation.

The leader was a lieutenant in the Ezzedeen Al-Qassam Brigades, the militant wing of the Palestinian political organization Hamas. He'd been sent on this mission to target a single man, but he had known all along that many others, the captain and his crew, for instance, would necessarily be sacrificed in the action.

So far he had been in total control of his operation. The next phase, by contrast, was in the hands of someone else, and this worried him greatly. Everything now hinged on the competence of a local contact. A woman, he had been told in his mission brief, who had verified the presence of the target and the disposition of the local police and had also, *Inshallah*, delivered a vehicle to his landing point and, *Inshallah*, remembered to leave the keys under the driver's seat.

The leader lost his balance momentarily at the top of the stairs on the outer bridge deck, and he reached out to steady himself. The men behind him were still climbing, they had not seen him stumble, and he was glad of this. They might wonder if it was a show of nerves on his part, and this he could not allow. Actually it was just a slight sway to starboard that unbalanced him, and it stood to reason his sea legs would falter. Born in the Gaza Strip, the leader had grown up within sight of the ocean but had never set foot on anything larger than a fishing skiff with an outboard motor before this week.

He had been chosen because of his intelligence, his ruthlessness and his resolve, but certainly *not* for any maritime prowess.

Up here on the bridge deck, the leader stopped to scan the night in all directions. There were few signs of civilization onshore except for some wooden shacks, but an electric glow hung in the haze over the huge coastal metropolis of Kochi just forty-five kilometers to the south.

Satisfied no one was around to hear a scream across the open water, he reached for the door latch.

The middle-aged Indian captain did not turn as the leader entered the bridge. He kept his hands on the wheel, looking straight ahead, his chest heaving from dread.

He knew.

The leader continued forward with his knife shielded down behind his thigh; he'd planned on asking a question as he approached, something nonchalant to distract the man, to put him at ease for the moment, but instead he kept silent, raising the blade in his right hand.

At three paces he rushed the man's back, reached around in front of his body with the knife, then thrust the blade into his neck and pulled it back across the bare throat. He withdrew the knife and took a single stride back. The Indian spun, blood spewed across the bridge, catching the leader's trousers and sneakers though he leapt back the length of the small room to avoid it.

The other two watched through a portal by the door, clear of the arterial spray.

The captain dropped to his knees, air hissed and gurgled through the bloody wound for a moment. Then he died. Mercifully quick for everyone, the leader thought.

'Allahu Akbar.' He said it with reverence, and he stepped over the body, tracking through the blood because there was no way to avoid it, and he put his hands on the wheel.

But for only a moment – he was no captain. In fact, none of the men on board knew how to bring the cargo ship safely into port, the captain had even told them there *was* no port where they were going, so the leader just pulled the engines back to idle and ordered his men to move to the tender that had already been packed with gear and lowered into the black water on the port side.

Twenty minutes later the seven men climbed out of the small tender and into gentle shoreline surf, then pulled the boat on to the sand, beaching it just clear of the licking waves.

Leaving the boat here in the open would be no problem. They would not need it again; the leader's exfiltration route would be overland to the east, into Madurai and then out on an aircraft with forged papers. Plus, the boat would not stand out and jeopardize the mission, as several other small watercraft lay unattended around this spit of sand. Net fishermen had left them for the night, having first removed their outboard motors and taken them back to their thatched-roof homes to protect them from thieves.

The men pulled black canvas bags from the tender and donned their gear. Three strapped heavy vests under their large black windbreakers; the other four hung small rifles on slings around their necks along with pouches of extra ammunition. The guns were micro-Uzis, a nine-millimeter machine pistol of Israeli manufacture, but any irony in the choice of firearm was outweighed by the gun's undeniable reliability.

In three minutes they were off the sand, running up a dark beach road lined with palm and coconut trees.

The local contact had left her vehicle just off the road alongside a narrow ditch, exactly where she had been instructed to do so. True to the leader's brief, the vehicle was a large brown panel truck that delivered milk from a local farm to the residents of Kochi. The refrigerators had been removed from the back, and this created barely enough room for the five men who climbed through the side door.

The keys were there, under the seat, and the leader found himself both pleased with and surprised by the woman's competence. He slipped into the front passenger seat, his second-in-command took position behind the wheel, and the others sat in the back without a word spoken among them.

They drove east, away from the beach and down a narrow paved road through the backwater, a system of both natural and man-made brackish lakes and canals where the Arabian Sea and the Periyar River meet. Coconut trees lined the road on both sides here, and thick haze diffused the headlights.

The leader checked his watch, then consulted with a handheld GPS device, loaded with coordinates given to him by the local agent. Their first stop was the cell phone tower on Paravur–Bhoothakulam Road. There were no landlines at the objective, so disabling the tower would cut off their target's line of communication with the local police.

The leader conferred with his driver, then turned to face the men behind him. He saw only dark silhouettes.

He had known two of the five men for years; they, like the leader and the driver, were *fedayeen* from the territories. He could make them out by their posture even though he could not see their faces. The other three men he'd met at the camp in Yemen only shortly before setting sail. He focused on these foreigners exclusively, and even smiled at them like a patient and benevolent uncle.

The smile was a ruse; he thought the men fools; he refused to arm them with guns because he didn't trust them as competent soldiers. These men would not wield weapons, the leader had decided, because they *were* weapons.

His smile deepened, and then he spoke to the fools in Arabic. 'The time draws near, my brave brothers. You must prepare yourselves for martyrdom.'

I

Dominic Caruso was only thirty-two years old, and by any fair measure physically fit, but still he found it difficult keeping stride with the fifty-year-old man running several paces ahead of him. In the past hour the pair had done five miles of roadwork broken up by a half-mile swim, and the conditions here weren't helping. Dom sucked as much of the fetid air as he could get into his lungs just to keep going. It was the middle of the night and still hot as hell, and the jungle path was dark save for a little hazy moonlight that filtered through the palms above.

Dom's running partner seemed to be having no trouble finding his way in the darkness, but Dom caught the toe of his shoe on the exposed root of a jacaranda tree, and he fell headlong to his hands and knees.

'Son of a bitch.' He said it under labored breath.

His trainer looked back at him but kept running. Dom thought he detected a smile on the older man's face. His voice was low and heavily accented. 'Do you need an ambulance?'

'No, I just –'

'Then get the fuck up.' The older man chuckled, then added, 'C'mon, D, soldier on.' He turned away and picked up the pace.

'Right.' Dom climbed back to his feet, wiped warm mud on his shorts, and took off in pursuit.

A month ago there was no way in hell the American could have run 10K in eighty-five-degree heat and ninety-five per cent humidity, especially not in the middle of the night after a full day of training in martial arts. But since his arrival here in India he'd made advances in his physical and mental strength faster than he could have imagined, and he owed this all to Arik Yacoby, the man now forty feet ahead of him.

The muddy jungle path ended at a paved road, and Arik turned to the left and began sprinting along it. Dominic gave chase even though he thought they should have been going to the right; he was the visitor, after all, and he trusted that Yacoby knew his way around these roads better than he.

Yacoby wasn't a local, but he'd lived here a few years, and by his elite physical condition it was obvious he'd run these trails and roads hundreds of times.

Dom knew very little about Arik Yacoby's past: only that he was Israeli, an émigré to India, and he had once been a member of the IDF, the Israeli Defense Forces. Dom had no trouble picturing Arik as an elite soldier; his fitness and discipline and the confident and determined glint in his steely eyes announced this fact to anyone who knew what to look for.

Dom had come here to India to train with the man for six weeks. Yacoby held a fourth-degree black belt in Krav Maga, a martial art developed for the Israeli military. Dom's hand-to-hand training with Arik had been intense in and of itself, but these additional nighttime PT sessions had added another facet to the grueling experience.

They'd swum, they'd run, they'd climbed – often all in

the same night. It seemed to Dom as if Arik felt it his duty to impart not just the skills of hand-to-hand combat, but every physical and mental aspect of serving in the Israeli Special Forces.

Everything short of the use of firearms, that is. This was India, and although Arik Yacoby was now a permanent resident of Paravur, he was no cop, and no soldier, and he therefore could not obtain a gun legally.

But Dom didn't think Yacoby's lack of a firearm made him in any way less dangerous.

This India quest to study Krav Maga was the third evolution of five in a four-month training course for Dominic Caruso. Just before coming here, Dom had spent three weeks mountain climbing in the Yukon, led in one-on-one tutelage by a veteran Canadian alpinist. And before that, he'd spent two weeks in Reno, Nevada, studying sleight of hand and other applications of misdirection from a master magician.

After his Krav Maga training in India, Dom was slated to fly to Pennsylvania to work with a former U.S. Marine sniper on his long-distance shooting, and then from there he would go straight to Sapporo, Japan, to learn from a master in edged-weapon combat.

At each of these evolutions Dom tapped the experience of his expert trainers in the one-on-one courses and peppered them with literally thousands of questions. The trainers, on the other hand, didn't ask him much of anything. They didn't know his real name – Arik just referred to him as D – they didn't know his organization, they didn't know his background. All they knew, all they *needed* to know, was that Dom came with the blessing of important people connected to the U.S. intelligence community.

There was certainly an assumption by the trainers that Dom was CIA or DIA or JSOC or some other acronym that meant trouble, and Caruso himself did nothing to dispel that notion. But he was none of these things, nor was he an employee of any official government agency. Instead, Dominic Caruso was an operations officer for an entity known as The Campus. It was an off-the-books intelligence organization with a direct-action arm. Only a few in official government ranks knew of its existence, and these few made the connections to the one-on-one elite training cadre around the world, so Dom and his fellow Campus officers could learn from martial artists, mountain climbers, snipers, divers, extreme athletes, language and cultural experts, or masters in any other discipline that might be necessary for them to succeed in their black operations.

Before his time in The Campus, Dom had been a special agent in the FBI. This gave him a tremendous amount of practical training, but the FBI Training Academy at Quantico didn't send its recruits up mountains or have them skulking through tropical swamps.

Caruso had learned much at each of his stops on his extracurricular training circuit, but his time here with Arik Yacoby had been the best of the evolutions so far, thanks, in large part, to Yacoby and his family. Arik's yoga-instructor wife, Hanna, had taken him into her home like a long-lost relative, and their two young boys, Moshe and Dar, aged one and three, had treated him like a human jungle gym, playfully climbing over him each night as the adults sat in the living room of Arik's rustic village farmhouse and talked over dinner and beer.

Dominic was an unreformed bachelor, and he was surprised by how much he had enjoyed this glimpse into family life.

This evening, Dom had finished dinner with Arik and his family, and then retired to his room to do his 'homework,' reading up on the philosophies of Krav Maga. He'd nodded off before eleven, but just after midnight Yacoby appeared at his door and told him he had three minutes to put on his swimming shorts and running shoes and to get outside.

These night ops, as Yacoby called them, were designed to help condition Caruso's body to adapt to working on command, even when he'd had little sleep or his biorhythms were telling him it was time to shut down.

Dom's body had adapted to this regimen, although reluctantly, while Arik himself seemed to genuinely enjoy the late-night runs and swims.

Three minutes after Yacoby woke Caruso up, the two men began their run. They headed away from the house and up a road that led out of the cluster of farms and bungalows in the Jewish neighborhood, and into the palm trees. They turned west toward the ocean and then north, away from the closest village and along a jungle trail that at times turned nearly impossible to negotiate because of the complete darkness of the double canopy of coconut palms and banana trees.

They reached the banks of Paravur Lake and Yacoby stepped into the water with hardly a break in stride, and then he began a relaxed but powerful breaststroke that

Dom could keep up with only by pumping his arms and legs in an Australian crawl.

Dom wasn't a fan of this lake. The first time he'd swum in it he'd climbed out on the far bank only to find himself twenty-five feet from a pit of cobras. Arik had laughed at Dom's panic, and told him the cobras, like most dangerous creatures on earth, just wanted to be left alone, and they wouldn't start anything if Dom didn't.

Tonight Dom saw a massive python in the reeds near the water's edge, but he didn't bother it and, true to Arik's promise, it just slithered away, and the two men finished their swim without incident.

From here they ran on a levee along a large cassava paddy, then entered the backwater jungle, running for two miles along the second dark trail of the evening.

Now back on paved road, they re-entered the village of North Paravur. A small tuk-tuk buzzed past them on the otherwise empty road, the two-stroke motor coughing as it stopped at a house to pick up a woman heading to the local bus station for an early ride to work down in Kochi. Arik and Dom waved to the woman and the driver as the tuk-tuk made a U-turn in front of them.

Finally Arik slowed to a walk. He spoke through slightly labored breaths. 'Two kilometers home, we'll relax the rest of the way. I'm going light on you tonight.'

Dom panted as quietly as possible; he could barely speak at all. Between gasps of air he squeezed out, 'Appreciate it.'

'You'll really appreciate it in the morning. We will begin with some full-contact work in the dojo, and follow this with a long swim before lunch.'

Dom just nodded as he walked, gulping the hot, wet air.

The lights of another vehicle appeared behind them seconds later, and the two men moved off the road as a large brown milk van passed on its way south.

Arik cocked his head at the sight of the vehicle, but he said nothing.

A minute later Dom and Arik walked by the local synagogue in the dark, and Arik said, 'I have ancestors in the cemetery around back. The oldest Jewish community in India is right here, you know.'

Dom just nodded, still too winded to talk, and he fought a smile. Arik had mentioned this fact a half-dozen times in the past month, after all. Yacoby traced his roots all the way back here, to the western shores of India, before his family had been uprooted and resettled in Israel. He had returned here to explore his past while on leave from the IDF several years ago, and as he toured the old synagogue and walked the streets of North Paravur, he decided someday he would come back here to live, to fortify the small Jewish community and raise his children on the same land his ancestors had walked generations earlier.

Dom liked this about Arik. He was strong of character and purposeful of thought.

The Yacobys' small farm was at the end of a long cul-de-sac off Temple Road, in an area near the synagogue and the local Jewish community. Thick jungle ran down both sides of the paved road, and the farm backed up to a massive Pokkali rice paddy. The neighborhood was cut off from the rest of the village, and for this reason both

Arik and Dom noticed the vehicle parked off the side of the road ahead of them when they were still fifty yards away.

It was the milk truck they had seen passing them ten minutes earlier.

Yacoby took Dom by the arm and slowed his walk. 'That doesn't belong.'

They approached from behind, more curious than concerned. They looked in the windows and saw it was empty.

Arik looked down the road in the direction of his farm.

Dom said, 'I've seen it around.'

Arik pulled his phone out of a waterproof case in his cargo shorts. As he did so he said, 'Yes, but not here. It delivers from a farm north of town to Kochi, in the south. We are two kilometers east of its daily route.'

Caruso was impressed Yacoby knew the movements of an individual local vehicle with such precision, but he didn't yet share his trainer's obvious concern.

Yacoby dialed his wife as he began walking up the road, with Dom following close behind. After a moment he looked down at his phone.

'No service.'

'Does that happen around here?' Dom asked.

In a whisper, Arik replied, 'Occasionally. But I don't believe in coincidence. Something strange is going on.'

Dom thought Arik was jumping to conclusions awfully quickly, but Arik knew the area better than he, and he also knew the threats. Dom said, 'Let's go, then,' and started walking on the road.

'Not that way,' Arik countered. 'We can approach my farm

from the west by going through the trees.' Arik turned and headed into the thick flora, and Dom followed.

Once inside the jungle, Dom realized it wasn't as thick as it appeared from the outside. Each banana or coconut or jacaranda or mango tree occupied its own space, there was just enough room to move between the trunks, and there was very little light let through to allow for much undergrowth. Arik had a tactical flashlight with him, but he left it in his pocket and instead used the glow from his cell phone to lead the way so as not to reveal his location. By the dim light the men moved quickly enough, spurred on by the desire to find out who had cut the cell service and left the van by the side of the road.

They came to the edge of the jungle behind a wood-shed that sat next to the gravel driveway on Arik's farm. The two men knelt down and surveyed the property, taking advantage of their excellent night vision. They had spent the last hour and a half outside in the dark, after all, so their pupils were conditioned to take in every last vestige of available ambient light.

The little farm was only four acres, with a two-storey bungalow in the center, a long single-storey building that Arik had turned into his dojo and Hanna's yoga studio, and a large chicken coop next to the vegetable garden in the back. A work truck and two jeeps, all belonging to the Yacobys, were parked in the driveway on the near side of the bungalow.

Caruso reached out slowly and squeezed Yacoby's arm, and the Israeli followed the American's gaze. In the dark he could just make out movement on the far side of a small pond in front of the bungalow. It was a human form, this much was certain, but with the darkness it was impossible to tell more.

A few seconds later, both men turned to the sound of scuffling gravel. A second figure moved between Arik and Hanna's jeeps, parked next to each other on the drive, not seventy-five feet from where the two men knelt in the palms. This man stepped up to the other man by the pond, and together they seemed to peer toward the house.

Dominic had thought Arik was overreacting to the sight of the unoccupied vehicle, but now his heart started pounding and he felt the dull ache in his lower back that always accompanied danger. Something ominous was happening right here and right now, and he was painfully aware both he and his trainer were unarmed and dressed only in cargo shorts.

Arik pulled Dom back a few feet into cover and whispered to him, his eyes still searching ahead. 'That's two in front. I'll try to see if they have any weapons. Make your way through the trees so you can get a look at the rear of the house. Meet me back here to report. Go.'

'Arik, if this is some kind of a test or –'

Yacoby turned to Caruso. His eyes were tight with worry and his jaw was forward and flexed. 'No drill, D. This is real world.'

'Understood.' Dom moved off.

It took Caruso less than a minute to get a line of sight on the rear of the property. At first he detected no movement other than an occasional shuffling in the chicken coop and a large lizard scurrying along the top of a wooden fence by the vegetable garden. But just as he was about to head back to the woodshed, he sensed motion in the dark closer to the house. He moved a few feet to the right and craned his neck farther to see what was there.

He saw them now in the night. One hundred feet away stood two figures; at least one of them was armed with a weapon hanging from a sling over his shoulder. They both wore dark clothing and stood close to each other in the center of the backyard, facing Arik's home.

Dom thought one of them might have been wearing a mask, because no moonlight reflected off his facial features. He couldn't tell anything about their ethnicity or their intentions, or even the make of the one weapon he saw. He tucked himself back into the palms and headed back to the Israeli, careful to move as silently as possible.

When Dom arrived back behind the woodshed he almost passed Arik without seeing him.

'Report,' Arik said, revealing himself in the near total darkness.

'Two men. I saw one gun. SMG or some sort of little machine pistol. Couldn't tell what kind. They are watching the house from the far side of the chicken coop. Are the guys in front armed?'

'Micro-Uzi on one. He's got a mask. Other one might have a pistol, but can't see his hands clearly.'

Dom's mind was racing. 'Shit. Any chance they are Indian police?'

Yacoby shook his head.

'What do you think?'

'Two-man fire teams. It's a classic *fedayeen* configuration.' Caruso knew *fedayeen* meant Islamic fighter.

'Lashkar?' Dom asked. Lashkar-e-Taiba was a Pakistani-based terrorist organization that had been active in India for years.

'Maybe,' replied Arik, but he didn't sound convinced.

'You think they will hit the house?'

Before Arik could reply, a woman's shout cut through the hot night air. It was Hanna, Arik's wife, Dom recognized it instantly. She sounded more confrontational than afraid, but her raised voice in the otherwise silent night was bone-chilling.

Yacoby lurched up, ready to run to the sound of his wife's cry, but he caught himself and knelt back down. He whispered, 'They already have. These are perimeter security. There are others inside. At least two. Could be more.'

Dom looked to the Israeli with horror. He noted the relevant calm in Yacoby's voice. He was intense, but there was no panic. He had to have been thinking about his wife and kids, but he somehow had the ability to push that aside and concentrate on the problem before him.

Getting past the four men outside.

Caruso asked, 'How do you want to do it?'

Arik kept his eyes on the bungalow. He spoke quickly but softly. 'It would take a half-hour to get the local police here, and I have no confidence they won't just make the situation worse. None of my neighbors have a landline or a firearm. I have to deal with this situation myself.'

'Right.'

'Hanna and I have a plan in case of trouble. If she had time, she would have put the kids in the bathroom off our bedroom. That's where I'm heading. I'm going straight for the house. Side door to the kitchen off the driveway.'

'And me?'

'You stay here. Watch the men in the back and sound an alert if there is trouble.'

Caruso shook his head. 'Not happening. I'm in this with you, all the way. I can cover you better in the house.'

Arik did not turn his head to look at Dom, he gave only a slight nod, his eyes still riveted on the scene in front of him. 'Good. We go for the side door together. Once inside, I'll grab a kitchen knife and try to make it to my family on the first floor. You grab a knife and be ready to engage these four out here if they come in.'

This sounded to Dom like a suicide mission, but he saw no other choice.

Yacoby stood slowly, readied himself to move forward, but then he leaned closer to Caruso. 'If something happens to me, and you can get to it, I have a Tavor rifle and six mags in a locked chest under my bed. The combination is one, nine, six, six, four.'

Dom knew Arik wasn't supposed to have a gun here in India, but it was no great shock he did.

'One, nine, six, six, four. Got it.'

Quickly, but still in a whisper, Arik said, 'There will be no time for hesitation. You must show these men no mercy.'

Dom stood up. 'Just get to your family.'

The two men moved toward the woodshed as Hanna Yacoby cried out again, her voice cutting through the sweltering night.

2

Arik and Dom crossed the crushed-seashell driveway between the cars in a low crawl, both men scraping their knees and hands in the slow and painful process. Dom was in the rear, his eyes shifting between Yacoby in front of him and the little he could see of the backyard of the property, hoping like hell neither of the men back there heard the noise and came to investigate. Arik was trying to keep some awareness of the men at the front of the property, but his main attention was on moving as quickly and as quietly as possible on his way to the house.

They made it to the side door, Arik rose just enough to get a hand on the latch, and he turned it slowly. A third shout emanated from upstairs in the bungalow, but this time it was a man's voice, and Arik could not understand the words. He used the yelling to mask his movement, and he slipped into the dark and empty kitchen.

Caruso moved in behind him, then he and Yacoby both pulled carving knives out of a rack on the counter. The men did not speak, Arik just disappeared down the dark hallway toward the main living area with the staircase to the first floor, and Dom moved to the one place in the kitchen where he could see both entrances. He was thirty feet from the front door, fifteen from the kitchen door, and, frankly, in no good position to engage armed enemies at either entrance if it came down to it. The best he could do was prepare himself and hope Yacoby made it to his family, or to his gun, without generating enough noise for the enemy to send reinforcements into the house.

Weighing his options, he moved back to the knife rack and pulled a second weapon – this one a well-balanced high-end paring knife – and he returned to his post.

This still might be a suicide mission, but Caruso wasn't going down without a fight.

Arik Yacoby had no idea how many opposition forces he was up against, but he'd come to the conclusion that the downstairs was clear. He could hear only the one man above him, shouting questions at his wife, who now shouted back just as angrily.

At the bottom of the stairs he kicked off his sneakers, then he began moving silently up by ascending close to the wall, where the boards would not creak.

When he reached the top of the stairs he could barely see down the hallway that traveled the length of the first floor like a spine. An open bathroom door half-way down on the right allowed some moonlight to filter into the hall, and by this he could tell that his bedroom door was open at the opposite end of the hall. There were no moving shadows in the moonlight, indicating to him that either the bathroom was empty or anyone in there was perfectly still. Ahead on his left, the two doors were also open, and the rooms beyond them were pitch dark. The first was his private office, and the second was his kids' room.

His blood ran cold, but he began moving up the hall with the knife at the ready.

He heard the man questioning his wife in the bedroom now. He spoke English, asking, not for the first time, apparently, where her husband had gone. He sounded frustrated, nearly desperate, and the crack of an open hand across flesh and a cry from his wife told Yacoby the intruder wasn't getting any answers from Hanna.

Arik again checked the light in the bathroom for signs of a presence there, but still there was no movement. He had to clear the two rooms on his left before making it down the hall, but just as he began moving to check his office, a man appeared out of the black, stepping into the hallway. He wore a black ski mask and was several inches taller than Yacoby. Their eyes met for an instant, Arik sensed a weapon in the man's hand, but he didn't take time to focus on it. Instead, his own hand shot out like a piston, he stabbed the man in the arm but lost his grip as his victim spun away. Yacoby recovered by lunging forward with the dexterity and skill of a Krav Maga master. He pushed the slung machine pistol away from the masked man, then ripped it out of his hands and turned it around, pointing it high in his adversary's face. The masked terrorist tried to raise his hands to defend himself, but Yacoby thrust the short-barreled rifle forward, shoving the flash hider into the man's eye socket, knocking his head back again. As the gunman stumbled back into the office, the Israeli leapt on him, covered his mouth with his hand, and flipped him around on the floor. He snapped the man's neck with a wrenching twist, severing his spinal cord.

The Israeli lowered the body the rest of the way to the floor, then quickly unfastened the Uzi from its sling and turned to check the room for other threats.

The office stood empty, but when he looked back up the hallway a figure appeared in the doorway to the master bedroom. Arik could barely make it out in the moonlight, but it was clearly an adult male, and he saw the man's arm rise quickly in front of him.

In that instant Arik knew he'd have to fire the Uzi, and this would alert every one of the armed men on his property. He aimed and squeezed off a single round, and the armed intruder in the doorway spun away with a cry and grabbed his neck as he fell.

Arik began running up the hallway now, knowing he was racing against time to get to his family. He held the smoking Uzi out in front of him as he spun toward the last darkened doorway on the left, checking for any movement. This was his children's room, and he was glad to find it empty. That they weren't here meant to Arik that his wife had had time to move them into the bathroom off the master bedroom.

He had just started to turn back to check the hall bathroom behind him when he heard a man scream. Before he could turn around, a figure flew out of the bathroom, crashed on to his back, and pitched him forward, slamming him into the wall of the hallway.

The machine pistol spilled out of Arik's hands as he went down.

Dom assumed the gunshot above would bring at least some of the men from outside into the house, but he had no idea which door they would come through. His eyes shifted back and forth between the kitchen door and the front door down the hall. He was certain he was about to engage the enemy, but not quite sure how he would go about it.

It was quiet for only a couple of seconds, and then came a wild scream and the crashing thuds of men slamming into one another in the hallway directly above.

As Dom kept an eye toward the living room, the front door flew open and a man burst through. Dom could see little more than a single figure; he didn't have time to register if the man was carrying a weapon, but he wasn't going to take that chance.

He threw the paring knife in his right hand overhand as hard as he could, aiming high at the man's face, because he knew a thirty-foot throw would take a lot of power off the strike.

The steel blade buried itself into the intruder's torso, just below the collarbone, and the man stumbled back, out through the doorway. Dom saw him collapse in a heap in the front yard before the door shut on its springs.

Now the kitchen door creaked behind him. Dom had just turned to the noise, ready to check this attacker for a weapon, but a burst of automatic fire settled the question for him. Dom dropped low to the ground, dove behind the island in the middle of the kitchen, and then he crawled across the floor, trying to keep the island between himself and the man in the doorway.

Another long burst of gunfire told him the intruder had not moved from the doorway, so Caruso stayed low, came around the island to the man's left, and then rose with the carving knife in his right hand. He covered the last five feet in a headlong dive, plunged the blade handle-deep into the man's side, burying it between two floating ribs, and body-checked the armed man into the open pantry by the door, using his hip and arm to keep the Uzi directed away from himself.

The man cried out in pain; as Dom's face pressed against his nylon mask, he could smell the fear and the sweat, and he thought he could smell the sea in the fabric of his clothing. Almost instantly, Dom felt the taut muscular body begin to soften as the armed attacker's brain went into shock. Dom knew the blood loss would take some time to kill the masked intruder, but already he was able to pull the Uzi out of his weakening hands. The gun was slung around the man's neck, however, and Dom had just begun to unfasten it when the kitchen door opened again, less than five feet behind him. He looked over his shoulder and saw a man in the doorway silhouetted by the moonlight. He held an Uzi high in front of him toward the room and was clearly surprised to find a target just feet away on his right. He swung his gun in Dom's direction.

Dom gave up on getting the Uzi off the man he'd stabbed; there was no time. He reached back behind him for something he could throw. This was his training taking over. He had been studying Krav Maga, living it for the past month, and he'd learned from Arik to use whatever tools he had at his disposal to disable an imminent threat.

Krav Maga is not a classically attractive martial art, but its beauty lies in its cold efficiency.

Caruso was hoping to get his hand on a knife. Instead, his fingers closed on the rim of a metal pot, and he swung it around, threw it through the air, striking the Uzi and the hand holding it, and knocking the shooter off target.

He rushed to the attacker, drove a fist to the man's mid-section, and then tried an elbow to the face that glanced off and did no damage.

The armed man tried to back away to raise his gun again, but he was blocked by the island in the middle of the room.

Dom threw another punch at the man's torso. It connected, but now the attacker managed to get around the edge of the island and back up and away.

Caruso flung a rolling pin from the island at the figure in the dark, striking him in the chest and knocking him back on his heels into the refrigerator on the far side of the room.

He knew he'd bought himself no more than a second, so he fell back into the pantry now, on to the man with the knife in his ribs. Dom grabbed the Uzi, spun it around, pulling the dying man by the sling around his neck, managing to get the gun out in front of him at hip level. He squeezed the trigger. Flame filled the pantry and the kitchen as he fired fully automatic, a long burst toward the space the armed man by the refrigerator occupied. Sizzling ejected cartridges bounced off cans of vegetables in the pantry and then rained back down on Caruso, singeing his bare torso, but he kept firing. He'd spent the past two hours in near total darkness, so the sustained flash of the short-barreled weapon felt to his eyes as if he had been enveloped by the sun. He could see nothing of his target, so he kept the gun up and the trigger pressed and the bullets spraying until the weapon emptied.

Dom's eyes were completely whited out by the muzzle

flash, he rubbed them with his free hand, and he shook his head in a futile attempt to battle the ringing in his ears. It took him a moment to find the target through his burning pupils, but he was happy to see the masked man lying dead on his back on the floor.

Dom knew he had to get upstairs to help Arik, and he also knew he needed a loaded firearm to do it, so he started to kneel down to take the Uzi from the dead man, but just as he did so, another man burst through the kitchen door.

This man wore no mask, he was clean-shaven, young, and he looked wild-eyed and terrified. But he was close, contact distance to Caruso, who was kneeling with his back against the kitchen counter.

Caruso rose and punched the man in the midsection with his empty hand, and his fist slammed into a surprising hardness there. It felt like the intruder was wearing a chest rig of ammunition for a rifle under his jacket, presumably as a way to keep it hidden from view.

Dom punched again with his other fist, but he didn't make the same mistake twice. This time he went for the young man's face, striking him in the jaw and knocking him back on to the island in the center of the little kitchen.

Dom knelt quickly, scooped up the Uzi, and fired a single round into the forehead of the man lying on the island. The machine pistol barked in his hand and the room lit with the flash, then all was dark and silent again. He started to run for the hallway to the staircase, but he stopped himself, turned, and looked back at the dead man.

It only now registered. This man had carried no weapon, but he'd worn something heavy and solid on his chest.

Why the hell would he have a chest rack full of Uzi mags if he didn't have an Uzi?

Dom rushed back to the body, ripped open the zipped windbreaker, and then backed away suddenly, slamming his hips into the kitchen counter behind him.

In front of him in the dim light lay a dead man wearing a suicide vest. Long, fat rows of explosives had been stitched into gray canvas. Loose wires crisscrossed the entire apparatus.

A gasp passed Caruso's lips. 'Arik.'

While Dominic had been fighting for his life downstairs, Arik Yacoby had been doing exactly the same in the upstairs hallway. The man who'd jumped him from behind was now dead, his neck, jaw and skull a wreck of shattered bones. Yacoby was hurt, too, his lips and nose dripped blood, but he pushed away the pain and exertion of the fight in the tight space, and he felt around to find the Uzi in the dark. He grabbed it with his left hand.

Behind him, his wife screamed in Hebrew. 'Arik! *Neshek!' Gun!*

Yacoby dove to the floor of the hallway, spinning as he dropped, and he landed on his back as a burst of fire from his bedroom sent supersonic lead up the hall in his direction. The rounds went over him; he was flat on his back holding the tiny machine pistol pointed between his bare feet and up the hall. He focused on the flash and, careful to fire only aimed semi-automatic rounds from the fully automatic weapon to avoid hitting his family, he shot at the light.

He felt his own Uzi being ripped out of his hands, and realized a round from the gunman up the hall had struck his weapon and knocked it away, probably damaging it as well. But the gunfire from his bedroom ceased and, through the ringing in his ears, Arik thought he heard the unmistakable sound of a micro-Uzi hitting and bouncing on the wooden floor.

Below him, he heard ferocious fighting. A long spray of automatic rounds, the cries of a man and the crash of bodies, but his mind was on his bedroom and what he would find there.

He leapt to his feet and ran for his family.

Dominic Caruso sprinted into the living room, heading for the stairs. As he passed the open front door he looked to the ground, expecting to see the first man he'd taken down in the engagement with the thrown paring knife. But the ground in front of the door was empty. Caruso spun into the stairwell, hoping against hope the man with the knife in his chest was not now heading upstairs, *and* wearing a suicide vest.

The stairwell was clear. Dom began taking the steps three at a time. As he climbed he shouted, 'Arik! Bomb vest!'

Yacoby had made it into his bedroom, where he found his wife tied to a chair in the center of the room, her tousled hair hanging over her face. She looked up at him in the dark.

'The kids are hiding in the linen closet. They're fine.'
She gestured with her head toward the en suite bathroom near where he stood.

Arik was relieved that his family was alive, but he needed to get downstairs to help his student. He knelt down to grab the micro-Uzi on the floor next to the dead man.

As he knelt he heard a noise behind him. He looked over his shoulder up the dim hallway, and saw a young, clean-shaven man staggering toward him. Through the faint glow from the moonlight coming from the bathroom, Arik could see a knife protruding from the man's upper-left chest, but still he managed to move quickly. Arik spun toward the man, raising his gun as he did so.

From the staircase behind the man he heard a scream from D, his American student: 'Arik! Bomb vest!'

Yacoby had put the sights on the center of the man's chest, but knowing he was wearing a vest changed everything. He shifted his aim to the man's head as fast as he could and, while doing so, he shouted, 'Hanna!'

Dominic had almost made it up to the first floor when a wave of light and heat engulfed him from above. His brain registered the fact he was airborne, he felt weightless for a moment, and now the incredible noise overtook him. He knew he was falling backward; his bare back made glancing contact with the wooden staircase, and his legs flew up above him, and he did a reverse somersault and continued his roll all the way down, crashing chest-first through the wooden banister and then flipping to the ground floor, where the back of his head slammed down on the teak floorboards.

Stunned by the impact, he needed seconds to regain an understanding of where he was and what was happening. He choked on smoke and his eyes burned, but he pushed away the pain and focused on getting back in the fight.

He squinted in the thickening black air and pulled himself up to his feet, then moved toward the staircase again, but his legs gave out and he dropped on to the lower steps. As he tried to pull himself upward by his arms he looked up and saw roaring flames pouring out of the second floor, and above the flames, the night sky.

It looked as if the entire roof of the stairwell and hallway had been blown from the bungalow in the explosion.

Dom slid back to the floor, collapsed unconscious on to his back, fingers of black smoke enveloping his prostrate body.

3

Caruso awoke to jolts of pain and waves of nausea, convincing him only after significant delay that he had not burned to death.

He opened his eyes, looked down, and found himself in a hospital bed. This wasn't the first time he'd regained consciousness since passing out in Arik Yacoby's burning home, but each time he only managed to lift his head, to catch a quick glimpse of the ambulance or the hospital hallway or the room he was in, and then drop his head back before drifting off again.

He didn't know if this process had been going on for a couple of hours or for a couple of weeks.

As his eyes cleared a little more he realized a doctor was standing at his bedside. A dark-skinned Indian with gray hair and a youthful face, the doctor wore scrubs, not a white coat. He took Dom's pulse, placing his fingers on Dom's left wrist while he checked his watch. When he finished he looked up at Dom's face and seemed surprised to find his patient looking back at him.

'Well, hello, sir. I'm surprised to see you awake. You are still under sedation.'

To Dom, the doctor's lilt sounded almost musical, but he wondered if this was just the effect of the drugs in his system.

The Indian began listing a litany of injuries. 'You have

suffered a slight concussion. Not serious, but expect head-aches for a few days. Maybe weeks.' He looked down at his clipboard. 'Otherwise, bruises and cuts, mostly. A few significant. Eleven stitches on your forearm. A small piece of shrapnel from the bomb, we suspect, but it passed all the way through, so we don't know for sure. A puncture to your right pectoral. It was a metal screw. We got it out. Not deep. We've cleaned you up, shouldn't be an infec-tion, but you'll want to watch those injuries. There is significant bruising across your –'

The patient interrupted the doctor. 'The Yacobys?'

The doctor did not answer him directly. He only stepped to the side, revealing to Dominic the presence of another man in the room, sitting on a cheap recliner by the door with his legs crossed. He was middle-aged, with slicked-back black hair and a full mustache, and he wore a dark suit and tie.

'Hello, John.'

Caruso did not reply.

'John Doe. That is your name.' He eyed the American with an expressionless, almost tired face. 'Unless you would like to give me another. No? John Rambo, perhaps?'

'Who are you?'

'I am Detective Constable Naidu.' He stood up. 'And I am here to ask you some questions.'

'The Yacobys?'

Naidu shook his head back and forth; there was an obvious lack of sensitivity in the gesture. 'Dead.'

Dom closed his eyes and shook his head. 'No.'

'Yes,' Naidu corrected. 'All four of them. Along with seven others at the scene. Nearly a dozen dead bodies, and you, my young American friend, were the only sur-vivor.' He leaned forward with eyebrows raised. 'Miraculous, wouldn't you agree?'

Dominic didn't answer. His mind was on the Yacobys. *Dar. Moshe.*

'You were pulled out of the burning building by neigh-bors, at great personal risk to themselves. You did not ask who saved you, but I thought you would care to know.'

Caruso stared off into space. *Arik. Hanna.*

'We know from the neighbors you were a guest in the home of the Yacobys, they saw you coming and going, but you had no identification on you when you were found. They said they thought you were American, and by your accent, I agree. But that is all I have. If there was any-thing in the home . . . passport, visa, U.S. driver's license, it was burned in the fire.'

Caruso fought the images in his head, did his best to push them away just as he did his best to ignore the pounding headache that grew with each word out of Naidu's mouth. The sedation seemed to be wearing off by the second.

'I need to make a phone call.'

'And *I* need *you* to answer my questions. Why would anyone want to kill your friend and his family? On his visa he said his occupation was personal trainer. His wife was a yoga instructor.'

Dom did not answer. His forearm stung under the dressing now.

Naidu raised his voice. 'We found the rifle. Who was Arik Yacoby?'

'He was my martial-arts instructor. That's all.'

'Pakistani terrorists do not often go to such great lengths to kill martial-arts instructors.'

'They were Pakistani?'

Naidu looked at Caruso with genuine surprise. 'This is India. Who else would they be?'

Caruso laid his head back on his pillow. This was to be a hostile interview, that much was clear. And Dom was not in the mood. 'I have no idea. I'm not the detective constable. If I were you, I'd look into the dairy truck parked at the end of the street.'

Naidu replied, 'I have already taken care of that. The woman who drove it is being sought. She has left the village, but we will find her.'

Caruso looked around the hospital room, then said, 'Pretty sure she's not in here.'

'You are more interesting to me than she is.'

Dom closed his eyes. 'Then I'd say your investigation is fucked.'

Naidu ignored the insult, and instead he looked down at his notepad. 'Let's not waste time with games. We know Yacoby was a former member of the IDF. If he was something more, I need you to tell me.'

'Something more?'

'Was he a Jew spy?'

Dom fought to control his urge to rail at Naidu. Instead, he said, 'I want to make a phone call. I will not say anything else until I do.'

Naidu's jaw flexed. Slowly he said, 'You don't want to find out who is responsible for your friends' deaths?'

Nothing from the man on the bed.

'You show no respect for our investigation, but perhaps you should. You are not a suspect. We know you fought against the attackers. The blood of one of the men found in the kitchen was all over your hands. I am not going to charge you with murder for that, you might be pleased to know.'

Dom rolled his eyes. He wasn't thinking about the implications for himself.

'I just want you to help me understand why they came for Arik Yacoby.'

'I can't help you. I don't know.'

Naidu sighed. 'Pakistani terrorists. The threat of nuclear war. New conflict with China. Crime. Corruption. Disease. You don't think my nation has enough problems without armed Jews coming to our shores and encouraging new enemies?'

'Do I get my phone call or do you want an international incident when I leave?'

'You get a phone call when I say you get a phone call. You leave when I say you leave.'

'Do you always treat guests to your country with such warmth?'

Naidu laughed. 'I am not from the tourism bureau, Mr John Doe. Maybe you can arrange an elephant ride with them when you get out of prison, but I am here to extract information from you.'

Prison? Naidu was flailing. Dom knew almost everything there was to know about interrogation tactics – he'd been trained by the FBI, after all. He could tell there was something missing from the detective constable's bluster. The bark was there, but Dom sensed no bite.

He smiled thinly. 'I can hear it in your voice. You are bluffing. You don't have the authority to do a damn thing to me.'

Naidu deflated a little. Though he kept his chin up and his voice strong, Dom saw weakness in his eyes. After a long staring contest, Naidu broke his gaze. 'I would like to keep you here. You would open your mouth, eventually, I promise you this. But someone thinks you are important. A plane has arrived from the United States. My superiors have ordered me to put you on it as soon as you are fit for travel.'

With that, Caruso threw off the sheets and kicked his legs out over the side of the bed. He began sitting up, but he'd only flexed his abdominals when he recoiled in pain. It felt as if all his ribs had been broken or, at least, very badly bruised.

He dropped back flat on the bed.

The detective constable cracked a slow smile as he noticed the young American's agony. He stood and walked to the door, then turned back, still with a smile only half hidden under his mustache.

He said, 'Forgive me, John Doe. In this situation, I must find my satisfaction in the little things.'

4

Ethan Ross ran late for work almost every Monday, and today was no exception. He would never admit it, but arriving fashionably late was by design; he found punctuality to be beneath his station, and chronic tardiness nothing more than a harmless passive-aggressive way to protest the inflexible rules of his organization.

He'd slept in a little this morning, not at home in Georgetown, but at his girlfriend's place in Bethesda. Last night he and Eve had gone out to a bar to watch a Lakers game that didn't end till after eleven here on the East Coast, and then they'd stayed for one more round that had somehow turned into three.

They'd finally made it to bed at one, and to sleep at two after Ethan's amorous mood overpowered the five greyhounds he'd consumed. He'd planned on going home to spend the night at his own place, but after sex, all he wanted to do was roll over to the edge of the bed and crash until morning.

At eight-fifteen Ethan awoke suddenly, roused by a panicked and shrill rendering of his name.

'Ethan!' The voice was Eve's, and his eyes opened and fixed on her alarm clock, because she was holding it in front of his face.

'Calm down,' he said, but she was up and running for

the bathroom, because punctuality was more her thing than it was his.

He made it downstairs to his red Mercedes coupe a few minutes later, cranked up some music and drove south to his town house on 34th Street, where he indulged in a long, leisurely shower and then took all the time he needed styling his blond hair with molding clay. He dressed, then stepped in front of his full-length mirror so he could check the fit, cut and sheen of his gray Ralph Lauren sharkskin suit. Satisfied that his purple polka-dot tie wasn't too much with the sharkskin, he slipped on a pair of cherry loafers and gave himself one more long appraisal in the mirror, assessing and then approving his style and looks.

At nine he sauntered down the front steps of his row house, still unhurried and unstressed, and he climbed back into his warm Mercedes and headed off to work, music blaring again.

Traffic on Wisconsin Avenue wasn't too bad, but he hit his first snag of the day when he found Pennsylvania to be mired in gridlock. While he crept forward he sang along with his Blaupunkt stereo. Neil Young's *On the Beach* was a 1974 release that would have been a unique listening choice for most thirty-two-year-olds, but Ross had grown up with it. Revolution music, his mother used to call it, although Ethan realized there was a certain dissonance to the concept of singing along with anti-establishment songs while driving his luxury car on his way to his government job.

No matter. Ethan still considered himself something of a rebel, albeit one with a more realistic worldview.

He'd been listening to his old albums since he got off work on Friday, both alone and then with Eve. She didn't much care for them, but she didn't complain, and he didn't really give a damn. Eve was a brilliant but hopelessly submissive Korean girl who would walk on glass for him if he told her to do so, and sometimes Ethan liked to unplug on the weekends, to go from 5 p.m. Friday to 9 a.m. Monday without checking his phone or his iPad or watching any TV. He didn't do it often, but there were times when his job was too stifling: endless boring meetings and conference calls and lunches with people he didn't want to eat with or trips with people he didn't want to travel with. He'd had a few months like this, his work was frustrating him and interfering with his well-cultivated self-image as a D.C. power player, and only detoxifying himself from work and inoculating himself with the music of his childhood could refresh him and get him ready to face work again on Monday.

Eve didn't complain; Ethan was certain she was just happy to have him to herself for two full days.

He checked his hair in the rearview, turned up Neil Young even louder, and sang along, pitching his voice in and out of key and fighting the power the only prudent way to do so at present.

Ethan Ross liked to tell people he worked at the White House, and it was true, with a caveat. His office was in the Dwight D. Eisenhower Executive Office Building, next to the West Wing, and while the Eisenhower EOB housed many offices for White House personnel, it wasn't, strictly speaking, the White House.

West Wing employees distinguished themselves from Eisenhower Building employees by saying they worked 'inside the gates', while the EOB staff worked 'outside the gates'. Ross didn't see any distinction himself. He was a White House staffer to anyone who asked, or anyone who would listen, for that matter.

He had spent the last three years here, spanning two administrations, serving as deputy assistant director for Near East and North African affairs in the National Security Council. He prepared policy papers for the President of the United States, or at least he coordinated the preparation of policy papers for the national security adviser, who then determined if the President should see a summary of them. The papers came from the work of the Department of State and the U.S. intelligence community, as well as a series of domestic and international think tanks and academic institutions.

His job, as he described it, was to give POTUS the best information available for him to conduct policy.

But his job, as he *actually* saw it, was to push paper while others made key decisions.

Ethan worked closely with the U.S. intelligence community, getting data from most all of the sixteen agencies related to his region. Not just the CIA, but also the National Reconnaissance Office, the National Geospatial-Intelligence Agency, the Department of State's Bureau of Intelligence and Research, sometimes even the military intelligence agencies. Coordination was his role, he wasn't a decision-maker himself, but he did have his finger on the pulse of happenings in his region.

It was a moderately high position for someone his age,

although, as far as Ross was concerned, it was far beneath him. He had considered the work just barely impressive at twenty-nine when he was put in the post, but now, two weeks before his thirty-third birthday, each and every day he lamented what he saw as his slow rise to the ranks of the power players.

His work no longer pushed him. Ethan thought he was smart enough to phone it in, and so that's exactly what he had been doing for some time.

He hoped to advance out of this job soon – not into something higher at NSC, this had just been a place-holder for him. Rather, he wanted to make his way into the U.S. delegation to the United Nations. He had been bred for a life of high-level work in an international organization. His father had worked as a staffer in the UN for twenty-five years before becoming an international-studies professor, both at universities abroad and then back home in Georgetown. His mother had served in the Carter administration as an under-secretary in the United States Mission to the United Nations, then as ambassador to Jordan during the Clinton years, before herself becoming a professor at Georgetown and a best-selling author of political biographies.

Just like every workday, Ethan parked his red E-Class coupe in a parking facility a block away from the Eisenhower Building, and just like every workday, it pissed him off when he walked to the EOB and saw open parking spaces in the lot. His position did not merit a reserved parking space; only the highest-ranking two dozen or so execs had such privileges.

He stepped through the gate at the 17th Street entrance,

then pulled his badge out of his coat. He was late enough that the security line was short, so in under a minute he left the drab gray outbuilding and headed up the steps into the main building.

The Eisenhower EOB used to be known as the State, War and Navy Building, and it had been the nexus of American foreign power at the end of the nineteenth century and the beginning of the twentieth century – the era when America emerged as a world leader. It had been constructed over a seventeen-year period in the late 1800s, and crafted in the ornate architectural style known as French Second Empire. The elaborate symmetrical iron cresting, balustrades and cornices were meant to portray permanence and character, and many felt the huge structure, in many ways, overshadowed its next-door neighbor, the White House.

Ethan wasn't as impressed with the architecture as others were, because he knew the Eisenhower Building wasn't the power center it used to be, and certainly nothing like the building next door at 1600 Penn.

He made it into the third-floor NSC wing at 9:39, entered his small office, hung his coat on the rack, and frowned. His secretary, Angela, always had his coffee ready for him, a Venti mocha from Starbucks that she picked up on her way into work and placed on his desk next to his telephone.

Angela was here, he had seen her sweater hanging over the back of her chair in his outer office when he entered, but his coffee was nowhere to be found.

Ross sighed. *You had one job, Angie, and you dropped the ball first thing on Monday morning.*

A moment later he heard movement outside his office, and he called out as he sat down. 'Angie?'

His fifty-four-year-old secretary appeared in the doorway a moment later. 'Good. You're here.'

With both a look and a tone crafted to convey just a hint of displeasure, he said, 'Did you forget my coffee?'

'No, sir. I put it at your place in the conference room. Everyone else is waiting.'

Ethan jerked his head to his morning agenda lying on his blotter, worried he'd forgotten a meeting. Rarely did he have any planned events so early on a Monday. But his agenda confirmed he was free. 'I don't have anything till ten-thirty, and that's off-site.'

'They said they were calling everyone on their way in. I thought you'd gotten the message.'

Ethan had heard his phone ring through the sound system in his Mercedes, but he'd muted the call without looking at it. The speakers had been pouring out Neil Young, after all, and by the time the last smoky notes of 'Ambulance Blues' drifted away, he'd been pulling into the parking lot and he'd forgotten about the call.

'What's going on?'

'I don't know, but it must be a big deal. Everyone was supposed to be in the conference room at nine-thirty.'

Ethan looked at his watch. It was 9:41.

He sighed again, and headed off for the conference room.

5

Ethan entered the open double doors of the NSC conference room and saw a full house looking back at him. The U-shaped table was completely occupied, and it was standing room only against the walls. He knew the table could accommodate sixteen, so he estimated there were at least twenty-five in attendance.

His Venti mocha was right there on the table, but sitting in front of it was Walter Pak from the South and Central Asia desk, and Ross couldn't muster the gall to push his way through the crowd and grab his drink when all eyes were on him.

As he headed for an open spot by the wall, he scanned faces quickly in an attempt to discern the reason for this morning's emergency meeting.

He saw the deputy directors and assistant deputies for all the other regions: Europe, Russia and Eurasia, Asia, South Asia, Central Africa – even the Western Hemisphere. Whatever new problem had popped up seemed to be impossibly wide in scope. Ross half smiled to himself, wondering if NASA had gotten word that aliens were poised to attack.

He also noticed several men and women from the IT department. This he considered odd, but not especially so, as they were higher-level system administrators and they found their way into many staff meetings when questions about access and networks came into play.

He located a spot on the wall and then turned to face the front, and now he noticed someone who didn't belong. A fit-looking male in his late thirties wearing a dark blue suit stood at the front of the room behind Madeline Crossman and Henry Delvecchio, who were positioned side by side at the lectern and had obviously been addressing the group.

Ethan didn't know blue-suit guy, but he did know Delvecchio and Crossman.

Delvecchio was the deputy for regional affairs, the head of all the regions. He worked directly for the national security adviser, and that made him one of the top men in the NSC.

Crossman, on the other hand, was not a big deal as far as Ethan was concerned. Any worries Ethan had that this was something of major import vanished the instant he saw Maddy Crossman standing at the lectern. She was a compliance and security director, an administrator in charge of making sure everyone filled out requisition forms correctly and didn't leave their key cards at their desks when they went to the john.

Ethan gave a contrite half-wave at Crossman and Delvecchio and said, 'Sorry, folks. Car trouble.'

Henry Delvecchio gave an understanding nod and returned his attention to the room. 'Again, I apologize for rushing everyone in first thing, but we have an issue that needs your attention. I trust you all have heard about the events in India last night.'

Ethan looked around to other faces. There were nods, clear indications of understanding.

Ethan Ross, on the other hand, didn't have a clue what had happened in India. Suddenly he felt like he was back in his undergrad days, walking in late to class with a hangover only to find out there would be a pop quiz, and he didn't have any idea of the topic of the test.

The good news, as far as Ross was concerned, was that this wouldn't have a damn thing to do with him, as India wasn't his turf.

Instinctively, he swiveled his head to Joy Bennett, assistant deputy director for India. That was her neck of the woods. He felt a little schadenfreude. He couldn't help it. He'd never thought much of Bennett.

Let's see how she deals with whatever dustup is going down over there.

He found it strange, though, that Joy Bennett was looking back at him.

Delvecchio continued, 'The attack on the Jewish citizens on the Malabar Coast was the first border incursion over water by terrorists since the massacres in India two years ago by Pakistani terrorists. And while the loss of life this time was just a small fraction of the earlier attacks, there are reasons to suspect this was not an attempt at a mass-casualty event that failed, but rather, this was a targeted killing of an Israeli national with key ties to the special-operations community.'

There were a few gasps of surprise around the room.

'The perpetrators, and this has not made the news yet, were a mixture of Palestinian *fedayeen* and Yemeni jihadists, working together, which is as unusual as it is troubling.'

In Ross's mind, alarm bells began going off. Israel,

Palestinian, jihadi, attack. *Christ.* The fact he had spent the weekend away from his phone and computer had suddenly gone from smart to stupid in his mind, and Ross considered himself anything but stupid.

Fuck!

Delvecchio looked at Ethan's boss, the deputy director of Near East, who in turn looked to Ethan.

He cleared his throat, nodded slowly and thoughtfully, and then bullshitted. 'It is something we are looking at closely.'

'Anything you want to add right off the bat?'

Ross affected a distant look that was intended to portray thoughtfulness. Then he shook his head slowly.

Delvecchio threw Ross a lifeline. He said, 'You probably haven't had a chance to read the report from CIA. Just came over from Langley about thirty minutes ago.'

'I was just about to pull it up when I heard we were meeting.'

Delvecchio filled in the pieces. 'Maybe a dozen dead on Indian soil. Seven attackers. Three attackers wore suicide vests. One vest detonated. It would be interesting even if the victims were nothing more than Israeli expats. But one of the victims was Colonel Arik Yacoby, a former Israeli Defense Forces officer.'

The assistant deputy director of combating terrorism strategy spoke up. 'Henry, there are tens of thousands of ex–IDF officers. Presumably thousands are outside Israel at any one time. All respect to the dead, but what's so damn interesting about this retired colonel?'

Delvecchio answered, 'Colonel Yacoby was the former leader of a group of Israeli naval commandos.' He looked down to a sheet of paper on the lectern in front of him. 'Shayetet Thirteen.'

The ADD of CTS nodded thoughtfully. 'Got it.'

Delvecchio said, 'Most of you remember the attack on the Turkish aid flotilla off the coast of Gaza four years ago. Shayetet Thirteen was the unit that boarded the Turkish freighter, the SS *Ardahan*. According to the CIA, Colonel Yacoby led the boarding party. If you remember, nine Palestinians were killed in the raid, including three combatant commanders of the Al-Qassam Brigades.' Delvecchio paused for effect, then added, 'Which is the same unit the CIA believes orchestrated the attack in India over the weekend.'

He paused to shuffle some papers on the lectern and, while he did so, the ADD of combating terrorism strategy asked, 'How does CIA know Yacoby was part of the IDF raid on the Turkish ship?'

'Our friends at Langley had a paid informant on the SS *Ardahan*. This agent passed crucial intelligence about the security of the ship to his handler and then, after conferring here with the NSC, POTUS ordered the CIA to feed the intelligence on to the Israelis. In the back-and-forth of this communication, a meeting occurred in Tel Aviv between CIA officers and Shayetet Thirteen commandos, including Colonel Yacoby. His name made it into the CIA database after the meeting. After the flotilla raid by Shayetet Thirteen, the CIA wrote up an after-action review for internal dissemination.' Delvecchio paused. 'Colonel Yacoby's name was put in the AAR.' He added, 'In error.'

Someone – Ross thought it was Pak from South and Central Asia – said, 'That is a significant error.'

'Agreed,' Delvecchio said. 'It should have been redacted and code-worded. It wasn't our file, we didn't do it.' He hastened to add, 'Not that it matters to Colonel Yacoby and his family.'

Madeline Crossman, the compliance and security director, said, 'We have serious concerns the Palestinian terrorists learned Mr Yacoby's name from the CIA report.'

Beth Morris spoke up. She was assistant deputy director for Western Hemisphere. 'I'm sorry, Henry. Madeline. Is there some linkage here with NSC that I don't understand?'

Henry Delvecchio nodded. 'Beth, we have reason to believe there has been an insider compromise.'

There were soft gasps throughout the room.

When they subsided he said, 'The complete CIA file on the SS *Ardahan*, including the name of the Shayetet Thirteen team leader, was accessed on the network here in the NSC office four months ago. The files were copied and moved into a file-sharing section of the server. From there, we can only assume they were printed out or downloaded.'

Morris asked, 'They were accessed by *who*?'

Crossman said, 'We do not know. There was a breach of forty-five documents classified at the secret level or above. Whoever moved the files disguised the electronic fingerprint of the breach.'

Morris's voice rose in indignation. 'And you think one of us stole the files and gave them to the Al-Qassam Brigades?'

Crossman replied, 'Beth, there was, without question, anomalous behavior. That's all we know at this point for sure. We need to rule out any nefarious actions.'

Morris looked over to the IT staffers in the room, who were all more or less sitting together. 'It had to have been someone who knew how to disguise the electronic fingerprint, whatever the hell that is.'

The entire IT department bristled at the comment, but they were generally quieter than the regional staffers. One of them said, 'These files were taken off JWICS?' JWICS was the Joint Worldwide Intelligence Communications System, an Internet of sorts for America's intelligence agencies.

'Yes, that's correct,' confirmed Crossman. 'Specifically, the files were accessed on Intelink-TS.' This was a top-secret network that ran on JWICS.

'How many people had access to the TS files?'

'Including staffers and IT administrators, and adding in those outside contractors with access to both the TS files and the NSC terminals . . . thirty-four.'

Ethan Ross looked around the room, but while he was counting heads, Beth Morris spoke up again.

'Is everyone who could have accessed it here?'

'Thirty-one are here, actually. One sysadmin called in sick today, and two are on vacation. One is traveling abroad. I don't have to tell anyone here that we take this breach incredibly seriously. More so now that it is quite possible lives have been lost due to the compromise.'

The room came alive with cross talk.

Pak, the ADD from Asia, asked, 'Do we know it was our leak that caused it? How do we know the Israelis don't have a compromise of their own, or that the information about Yacoby could have been obtained some other way?'

Delvecchio said, 'No, we do not know our leak led to

the deaths in India. But it doesn't look good. Another file in the cache taken was a follow-up review of the CIA's involvement in the raid, done just last year. This file did not mention Yacoby by name, but it stated the Shayetet colonel who led the raid had retired and moved to Paravur, India.'

One of the staffers shook her head in disbelief. 'Why the hell would they put that in the file?'

'Apparently, CIA's National Clandestine Service contracted the retired colonel for training purposes. He was some sort of a martial artist. The file said he could be reached to contribute to the review, although in the end he was never contacted.' Delvecchio cleared his throat. 'The two pieces of the puzzle the Palestinians would need for yesterday's assassination . . . those being the man's name and his location, were both in the digital breach from the NSC. Again, we don't know that's how the Palestinians got the intel, but the President has been notified, and he has already made the decision to tell the Israeli prime minister about the compromise, so we need answers immediately.'

Ethan Ross spoke up now. 'Henry, you can be certain my department will conduct a full security review. I'm sure the other desks will conduct their own reviews.'

Crossman spoke up before Delvecchio could answer. 'That won't be necessary.'

'It's protocol,' said Ethan.

'It *is* protocol, but for a matter this delicate, where there is a possibility of a high-level leak of classified information, the security review will be conducted by DOJ. This flies way above desk level, Ethan.'

There was some shock, a fresh din of indignant comments around the room.

One of the IT guys mumbled something about the computer system's antiquated architecture and weak safeguards against an inside attack. Another systems administrator tried to ask technical questions about the breach, but Crossman shut him down, saying the ongoing investigation precluded her from answering specifics.

After several moments the murmurs in the conference room rose, and neither Henry Delvecchio nor Madeline Crossman seemed able to take back control. The fit man in the dark blue suit who had been standing silently behind them stepped to the lectern. Ethan thought he had a Clark Kent hairstyle and a build like an amateur bodybuilder.

Under his breath, Ethan muttered, 'Oh, shit. It's a G.'

Beth Morris's tone was almost derisive as she asked, 'And who are you?'

'Supervisory Special Agent Darren Albright. FBI Counterintelligence Division.'

'CID? Oh my God,' mumbled Morris. 'We are being treated like criminals.'

Albright shook his head calmly. His voice was soft but powerful, like a man indulgent of others, but barely so. 'No, ma'am. You are not being treated like criminals. Trust me.' He eyed the room. 'This isn't how we treat criminals. I am working with Director Delvecchio to organize the polygraphs we've ordered in a manner that is least intrusive to the important work everyone here is doing.'

Morris snorted. 'If you aren't treating us like criminals, what do you call dragging us into FBI polygraphs?'

Albright spoke politely, but he didn't smile. To Ross he

didn't seem the smiling type. 'I call it treating you like suspects. Criminals are cuffed and frog-marched to jail.'

The room flew into a barely controlled and sustained rage at the comment. Beth Morris was the most vocal of the group. Albright conferred with Madeline Crossman softly, but Ethan could hear him ask her Beth Morris's name. Unsurprisingly to Ethan, Crossman gave it with a little sneer. She was the office hall monitor, after all.

Albright said, 'Mrs Morris. Forgive me for saying so, but you certainly have a lot of concerns about this polygraph. Would you like to talk to me in private after the meeting breaks up?'

Beth glared at both Albright and Crossman. Finally she said, 'I have no problem taking another poly. We all hold security clearance, and that goes with the territory. I do take issue with the fact we're sitting here with the FBI. NSC has its own security protocols.'

Albright just smiled at Beth Morris, then he addressed the room. 'Don't mind me, folks. I'll be poking around a bit for the next few days, but you won't even know I'm here. You will have your polys, then everyone can get back to work.' He added, 'Almost everyone, that is. The person responsible for the data breach will have some questions to answer.'

The meeting broke up soon after this, and Ethan returned to his office, passing his curious secretary with neither a glance nor a word. He immediately pulled up the CIA report on the India attack on his computer, and spent several minutes reading it over and over and over.

Twenty minutes later he passed through his secretary's office again, this time on his way out the door. He wore his overcoat and his car keys were dangling from his hand, even though he had a ten-minute walk back to his car.

He noticed Angie looking at him with surprise. It was only ten-thirty, after all, early for lunch, even in Washington.

'Running out for my ten-thirty meeting. Coffee with a consular official up in Dupont. Hold my calls.'

6

Dominic Caruso arrived at Kochi's Cochin International Airport in the back of an ambulance. It was the middle of the night, and traffic was light both on the highway to the airport and on the grounds, which worked to the advantage of both the Indian government and the people who sent the plane to pick him up.

Dom spent the ride prone with his wrist handcuffed to the arm of his gurney. He assumed he had Detective Constable Naidu to thank for his jewelry. It was a last show of displeasure and passive aggression from the law enforcement officer who'd been ordered by government superiors to send his one witness to a terrorist act on his way without any semblance of a proper interrogation.

Dom didn't think much of Naidu personally, he was, at least, an asshole, and it seemed to Dom that he was an anti-Semite as well. But Dom did have to allow for the fact that he understood the Indian policeman's frustration with losing his witness. Dom had been an FBI agent, was still officially in the FBI – on paper, anyway – and he knew that had he been in Naidu's shoes, working a crucial case with an eyewitness in his hands, and then received a call from some shadowy and powerful superior telling him to ship said key witness out of the country immediately, it would piss him off no end. And Dominic also knew he was not above a little payback, perhaps in a manner similar to how Naidu treated him.

Dom rattled his handcuff a little, but then let his hand drop back down to the gurney.

The ambulance stopped and Dom was wheeled out and pushed along a hot tarmac glowing and buzzing with electric lighting. He could hear the whine of finely tuned jet engines, and he thought that he knew exactly the make and model of the aircraft here to take him home, though he could not be certain.

Soon he heard voices, but from his vantage point he couldn't see who was talking, nor could he hear what was being said. A police officer uncuffed his wrist; then he saw another figure approach from behind.

An attractive blonde with her hair in a tight bun leaned over him. Dom was relieved to see Adara Sherman, the transportation director for his organization, and immediately he felt like this ordeal in India had come to an end.

Adara did not speak directly to Dom, but this was no surprise. Dom had been around Adara regularly for more than two years, and he knew her to be polite, but he also knew her to be all business, all the time. Their boss, Gerry Hendley, had warned Dom and the other young single men in the organization that Adara was off-limits. Even so, Dom and his mates, on occasion, had tried to at least establish a friendly camaraderie with her. But whenever Dom or the others attempted to establish a rapport with her, even in the most jocular and non-threatening manner, their efforts were met with stark professionalism.

She wasn't cold, really . . . but she was most definitely not warm.

Adara Sherman looked Dom over in a manner that seemed to Dom like she was checking to make sure she had the right piece of luggage. She gave a quick nod to the two ambulance personnel and the two policemen and said, 'I need you to put him on the plane, if you will. There is a sofa I have prepped as a bed in back.'

'Yes, ma'am,' one of the attendants replied.

Dom started to sit up on his own, but Adara put her hand firmly on his shoulder and pushed him back down flat without saying a word. He knew he could have gotten up and walked on board himself; it would have hurt, but he'd prefer it to being carried up on a gurney. Still, he wasn't going to fight Adara Sherman to do it.

He had no doubt these locals thought she was just the good-looking stewardess on a ritzy corporate jet, but Dom knew something these boys didn't know. He knew where to look on her blue blazer to see the very faint imprint of a .40-caliber SIG Sauer pistol in her waistband. And he knew she kept an HK MP7 Personal Defense Weapon stashed in a hidden spring-loaded locker just inside the galley opposite the door, and she was trained to deploy the weapon and address threats to the aircraft in under three seconds.

Sherman was both a flight attendant and a transportation coordinator, but she was a hell of a lot more than that, and Dom knew better than to go against her wishes.

Adara stepped out of the way and Dom felt the gurney being lifted and carried through the hatch of the Hendley Associates Gulfstream G550.

The medics deposited him on the sofa, they weren't particularly gentle with him, and his rib cage felt every jostle and twist. They let his legs hang off to the side, then they left the aircraft after a quick look around at the beautiful high-end furnishings. Dom noticed one of the police officers had boarded as well, and this man stayed behind.

After the men from the ambulance had deplaned and Dom was alone in the cabin with the cop, the Indian leaned over the American and said, 'Naidu wanted me to tell you to give him a call sometime. If you ever have any information.'

Dom shrugged; it hurt his bruised ribs to do it. 'You tell him I appreciate his hospitality.' And then he waited for the man to leave. The cop deplaned behind the medics and stood outside on the tarmac talking to Sherman for a moment. Dominic took the time to pull himself up to a sitting position. He grunted and groaned with the sharp pain in his ribs and the dull aching in his head, but in no time he was on his feet, heading for the galley at the front of the plane.

He wanted to fix himself a drink.

He was halfway up the length of the cabin when Sherman entered the aircraft. She saw him standing and pointed to the sofa bed. 'I need you on your back right now, please.'

'Can I grab a quick –'

'No, you may not. Lie down. I'll take care of everything once we're airborne. Right now we need to go.'

Dom reluctantly returned to the couch, but he found he had more trouble sitting back down than he had standing. Sherman was by his side immediately, helping him down on to his back. She then lifted his legs and put them on the sofa, covering them with a blanket.

He breathed a long, relieved sigh. Having his feet up reduced the pain in his ribs considerably.

'Thanks.'

She did not reply. Instead, she buckled him into the sofa bed, moved quickly to the hatch and shut it, then conferred with the pilot and copilot for a moment. Within a minute the aircraft was moving and Adara was back in the cabin, buckling herself into a jump seat by the door.

As Dom lay on his back during takeoff, it occurred to him that this was not the first time he'd been injured and strapped down to this exact same sofa. He'd been shot in Pakistan a couple of years earlier, and the long flight home had been an uncomfortable one. This time his wounds were not as severe, but there was another key difference between the two events. Back then the mood on the flight home had been ebullient: he and his teammates had just prevented a nuclear detonation, and it seemed his wound had been a small price to pay for the success of the operation.

This time he was going home knowing a family of four, people he had come to care for a great deal, had died a fiery death, and he had a feeling he would be second-guessing his every action and reaction during the fight for a long time to come.

The Gulfstream leveled off over India, heading east toward the Bay of Bengal. Their flight plan would take them over Thailand and Taiwan, then over the Pacific

Ocean, to the U.S. West Coast. They'd stop in San Diego to refuel, and then fly the rest of the way back to the aircraft's home base of Baltimore, arriving sixteen hours after departing Kochi.

Five minutes after takeoff, Adara returned to Dominic, who continued to feel like a piece of luggage. In an attempt to push the image out of his mind, he decided to press the issue of getting a drink.

'Adara, I could use a Maker's Mark on the rocks.'

She knelt down and unfastened the restraining straps on the sofa, then began unbuttoning his shirt. 'Sorry. It will have to wait. You don't need a stewardess right now as much as you need a medic. I'm going to check you out, see what we need waiting for us back in D.C. I had the Indian hospital e-mail me your films and assessment, and I looked them over during takeoff. Nothing broken, but I want to look at the bruising on your chest.'

Dominic reacted with restrained anger. 'I'm fine, Sherman. I've spent an entire day in the hospital. I've been evaluated.'

'Not by me, you haven't.'

'All I need is a drink and to be left alone.'

But Adara Sherman did not back down. 'If you are going to be an asshole about this, it will only take longer for me to do what I need to do.' She paused, and her tone softened slightly. 'This is my job, Dominic. Now be a big boy and let me check you out.'

Dom realized he was taking out his frustrations on Adara. He slowly sat up enough for her to get his shirt off.

'I'm sorry. Tough couple of days.'

She looked at his bruised torso. The right side of his rib cage was black and blue. 'Yeah, I'd say so. What happened here?'

'Fell down some stairs. Think I might have hit something on the way down.'

She cracked a little smile. 'What gave you your first clue?'

After unwrapping the bandage on his chest and cleaning and debriding the puncture wound there, she did the same with his bandaged forearm. She then directed her attention to cleaning some smaller cuts and scrapes on his chest with antiseptic.

'You don't trust the Indian doctors?'

'I trust them fine. But one thing I learned in Afghanistan: wounds can't be too clean.'

Dom knew the woman had been a Navy corpsman, which in her case had not meant sitting on a ship passing out Dramamine. She had served in both Iraq and Afghanistan, treating U.S. Marines, sometimes under fire herself. Dom had seen a lot of action in his years with The Campus, but he thought it was possible, even likely, that the attractive 'flight attendant' had seen much more.

Dom asked, 'You still think about it? The war?'

He was almost certain he would get some sort of professional non-response, but instead she stopped cleaning his wound for a moment. The cotton swab remained motionless, just barely brushing the damaged flesh on his chest.

She looked him in the eyes. 'Only every day.'

Her eyes flicked away from his quickly, he could see her admonishing herself for her breach of professional distance, and she continued cleaning the abrasions without speaking.

He winced with pain from time to time, but mostly he sat there quietly.

When she finished the examination and the recleaning and rebandaging of his wounds, she left for a moment and returned with some painkillers and a bottle of water.

'No, thanks,' Dom said.

'Are you hurting?'

'Headaches. Not bad.'

She held out the pills again, and Dom shook his head. 'I need to think. Can't think on those.'

'How 'bout I make you that drink?'

He cracked his first smile in twenty-four hours, though it wasn't much. 'If you insist.'

Ten minutes later Adara moved up the darkened cabin and stood over Dominic, who now reclined on one of the leather captain's chairs in the rear of the cabin. She used the light from a satellite phone to illuminate his face, expecting to find him already sound asleep. Instead, his dark eyes were wide open and full of intensity, and they looked up at her.

She held the phone out. 'It's Mr Hendley.'

Dom took the phone and checked the time on a clock by the chair. 'Hey, Gerry.'

Gerry Hendley, director of both Hendley Associates – the financial management firm that served as the white-side front for The Campus – and The Campus itself, was a former South Carolina senator with a deep southern drawl. 'How you holding up, Dominic?'

'I'm sure Ms Sherman gave you the complete rundown of my injuries.'

'She did. I'm asking *you*.'

'I feel like I've been run over by a bus, but I'll be fine.' He paused. 'You have any intel on what went down?'

'Figured that was all you'd care about, so I've been digging. 'Fraid I don't have too much just yet. I talked to some friends at Langley. We know at least some of the terrorists were members of the Al-Qassam Brigades. They set sail from Yemen five days ago and hijacked an Indian cargo ship to move unmolested through Indian waters.'

Dom leaned his head back on the leather couch and closed his eyes. 'Al-Qassam? *Fucking* Hamas.'

'That's right.'

'Do we know why they targeted Yacoby?'

Gerry said, 'No, but I'm reaching out to my sources here in the U.S. and abroad to get an answer. All I know at this point is that Yacoby had served until fairly recently as a commander in Shayetet Thirteen.'

'An Israeli naval commando? That explains a lot of the training he was putting me through.' He had a thought. 'Al-Qassam is Hamas's army. They are more or less conventional forces. When did they start using suicide vests?'

'Never. Due to the fact their op began in Yemen, we're entertaining the possibility the guys with the vests were Al-Qaeda.'

'Yacoby was one man, living abroad with his family, basically a soft target. Why would Al-Qassam use suicide bombers along with their gunmen?'

'There is a lot of speculation about that. One theory,

and it does make some sense to me, is that the plan was to assassinate Yacoby and then go take hostages at the synagogue or some other place where the Jewish people in the community congregated. The Al-Qaeda in the vests would martyr themselves, take as many Jews as they could, and the Palestinians would escape.'

Dom nodded. 'And this would mask an assassination.'

'Exactly. They could make it look like Arik and his family got caught up in a jihadist attack on Jewry in the area, and not targeted specifically by the guys from Gaza.'

Dom thought about it for a moment. 'Make it look random to protect whoever passed the intel about Yacoby and his whereabouts?'

'Possibly. I don't know. Let's not overspeculate.'

'Fair point.' Dom picked at the bandage on his arm, then said, 'The more important question is, how *did* they find out about him?'

Gerry said, 'Unknown at this point. I wonder if the Israelis have a traitor on their hands.'

'Shit,' mumbled Dom. Then he said, 'You know what, Gerry? I was about two seconds away from getting a gun sight on the back of the suicide bomber's skull. I could have prevented their deaths.'

'Don't think like that. I know you did a hell of a job. The report from the Indians is you killed multiple attackers yourself.'

Dom wasn't listening. His mind was back at the Yacobys' farm. 'Arik had two boys.'

'I know, son. I know.'

'If I'd made it upstairs a little faster, I just might have —'

Hendley's southern drawl boomed over the sat phone.

'You just might have been blown to bits with the rest of them! Look, Dom. I can't tell you how to get past this. I'm sorry, but I don't know.' After a pause he said, 'You've been through this sort of thing before.'

Dom *had* been through this sort of thing before. His twin brother, Brian, also an operative for The Campus, had died in his arms more than two years earlier. Dom knew he had changed since his brother's death, and he feared the changes weren't for the better.

'With Brian, you mean?'

'Yes. I was the one who sent you and your brother to Libya. That weighs on me every day.'

Dom countered without reservation, because he'd never blamed Gerry for what happened. 'You made the right call. What we were doing needed to be done. Brian just got the short end of the stick.'

'And so did Arik Yacoby and his family. There's nothing you can do about it, and no sense replaying that night over in your mind for the rest of your life.'

'Yes, sir.' Caruso forced the thoughts of the dead family in India out of his head. 'What's the fallout going to be for The Campus on this?'

'Hard to say. We don't know how Al-Qassam knew about Yacoby, so we can't gauge your exposure yet.'

Dom knew what Hendley was thinking. 'Until you know how the intel got out about him and his location, you don't know if I've been burned as well. For now I need to stay away from The Campus. From the guys.'

Gerry said, 'Shouldn't be hard to do. The rest of the team is spread out around the world. I'll keep everyone where they are, but you take some time off. Just take it easy.'

Dom chuckled into the sat phone, but his heart wasn't in the chuckle. 'I was already on stand-down before this happened. Now you're telling me to get lost.'

'No. I'm telling you to get better. Ms Sherman tells me you'll need some recovery time. While you're doing that, this situation will subside. I can instruct the pilots to take you wherever you want to go. You want Adara to find you a resort hotel somewhere in the Rockies? A beach house in Hawaii? Someplace you can take it easy until everything blows over?'

'Honestly, Gerry, I just want to go home. Back to D.C.'

'Fair enough. Get some rest. Adara will take care of you.'

7

Harlan Banfield was a print journalist by trade; he'd been at it for more than forty years and he certainly looked the part. He was small and frumpy, with permanently messy silver hair and bright gray eyes that conveyed kindness and empathy even when they were locked on a politician he was interviewing for the purposes of writing an excoriating hit piece.

Harlan's day had begun in College Park, Maryland, at a morning meeting for an association of foreign correspondents. He'd been a foreign correspondent himself, with bylines from places as far away as Ho Chi Minh City and Montevideo, and even though he had settled down much in the past few years and rooted himself firmly to the D.C. area, he still liked to get together with other current and former globe-trotting reporters at the monthly breakfast.

The meeting broke up at 11 a.m., and soon after Harlan climbed into his nine-year-old Volkswagen and made the drive down to his one-room office in a high-rise on K Street, deep in the District's downtown Golden Triangle. He had a morning of phone calls ahead before he had to head back out to lunch with old colleagues at the *Washington Post*.

Banfield's career began working the city beat for the *Philadelphia Inquirer* in the seventies. He served in New

York with UPI in the eighties, before finally taking work as a foreign correspondent for *The Washington Post*. He was based in Europe and the Middle East, primarily, but he was both an excellent journalist and a single man without a family, so he was sent to all the hot spots for twenty years before returning to D.C. to work at the *Post*'s office on 15th Street in the twilight of his career.

Banfield was sixty-six now, but he had not retired. He still did some freelance work around town, writing mostly for various electronic media outlets.

In addition to his work for hire, Banfield also authored a blog about D.C. lobbyists from a decidedly anti–D.C. lobbyist perspective. His blog got him some small attention inside the Beltway, but he wasn't doing it for the mainstream, because Banfield's blog, like his sporadic freelance work, was, by and large, a front.

In truth, Harlan Banfield was much more than a journalist. He was also the U.S. liaison of an organization that called itself the International Transparency Project. The ITP's website put their mission statement succinctly, identifying the group as a loose worldwide consortium of philanthropists, journalists, lawyers and activists who endeavored to support government openness and accountability. They did this by seeking out, encouraging, funding and protecting whistleblowers.

The homepage of the ITP's website displayed a picture of a sunrise over Washington, D.C., with the phrase 'Truth vs. Power' in bold type above it. There was something telling about having D.C. on the homepage of the website. The organization was – ostensibly, anyway – designed to expose government malfeasance in every country on the globe, but in truth, ITP focused the vast bulk of its efforts on what it saw as the evil empire, the United States of America.

Banfield didn't hate America, though he thought it probable some of his foreign colleagues in the ITP did. Banfield just liked a good story, and nothing gave him a bigger thrill than unveiling closely guarded secrets. High-level government leaks were the coin of the realm around Washington, and Harlan Banfield loved serving as a clandestine clearinghouse for the biggest leaks in the Beltway.

Banfield felt there existed in the United States, a Deep State, a shadow government, wealthy and well-connected members of industry who were the true power behind the scenes. And working as the U.S. liaison to the ITP was his way of peeling off the superficial layers of government secrecy, in hopes of someday digging deep enough to find the truth about this shadow government.

He wasn't in it for any attention – members of the Project did not reveal their identities to the world at large. It was an attempt to minimize exposure to government surveillance, and in Banfield's case, it had worked. As far as most people knew, he was just an aging foreign correspondent who'd long since been put to pasture, but he loved unlocking the secure doors around D.C.

He pulled into his building's underground garage a little before noon. It had started to drizzle, and he was glad to have a dedicated spot under cover. He'd just locked his Volkswagen and begun walking toward the elevator when he sensed a figure in the dark on his left moving between the cars along the wall of the garage.

He stopped, clutching his keys in his hand as if they might be some sort of adequate protection against a mugging.

The figure came closer, but remained out of the light. He faced Banfield but said nothing.

'Hello?'

The man stepped into the light now. He wore a trench coat with the collar up and a knitted cap on his head, pulled down just above his eyes. He looked instantly familiar to Banfield, but it took him several seconds to identify him.

'Ethan? Is that you?'

'We need to talk.'

'*Christ*, son! You scared the living shit out of me.'

'Where can we go?'

'Why the dramatics? You could have just e-mailed me. Come upstairs. We'll go to my office.'

'No!' Ethan Ross said, lurching forward as he spoke. Banfield recoiled a little, but it was in surprise, not fear.

'What the hell is going on?'

'Your office might be bugged. Your phone, too.'

'Why would they be bugged?'

'Let's take your car. I know a place we can talk.'

At Ross's direction, they drove through Georgetown and crossed the Francis Scott Key Bridge into Virginia. Here they merged into the northbound lanes of the George Washington Memorial Parkway, which ran northwest away from the D.C. metro area.

'Shall I cancel my lunch meeting?' Banfield asked.

Ross did not answer.

'Do I need to stop for gas? How far are we going?'

'Not much farther.'

Banfield pressed his luck, doing his best to engage Ross in conversation, but the younger man just stared out the window of the car and did not reply.

The rain was light but steady, and the only sound inside the Volkswagen was the soft whine of wet tires and the slow cycle of the wiper blades.

After only a few minutes on the winding, hilly road, Ross told Banfield to take the next right, and immediately the sixty-six-year-old reporter realized they must be heading to Fort Marcy Park.

The park was a wooded and secluded location, across the river and northwest of downtown D.C. It had been a real fort back in the Civil War, on a hill with sweeping views of both the Potomac and open farmland, and thoroughly fortified with earthen walls, dugouts and trenches, many of which could still be discerned as unnatural-looking undulations in the landscape.

Now the park was little more than a highway rest stop, there were no buildings of any kind, but a couple of cannons stood on the earthen berms above trenches filled with tall bare trees.

Banfield parked in the small lot and immediately turned to Ross for answers, but the younger man opened his door and began walking away from the car, up the hill and into the woods. Banfield grabbed an umbrella out of the backseat and followed him.

They walked for several minutes, until Ross sat on a wet wooden bench next to a lone cannon out of view of the parking lot behind them. Banfield sat next to him; they faced the Potomac but couldn't see the river through the foliage on the hillside in front of them. Banfield winced as a wet, cold breeze stung his face. He had been deferential to Ross over the past fifteen minutes, but his patience diminished quickly while they sat there, staring off into the woods. 'Ethan, I am an aging city dweller with bursitis in his hips and an allergy to almost everything, and you've brought me out into thirty-eight-degree rain and walked me into the woods. What the hell is going on?'

Ross ignored the rain. He stood from the bench and began pacing back and forth on the berm next to the cannon. 'It's fucking India, Harlan, *that's* what is going on.'

'India?'

'The attack yesterday. You heard about it, right?'

'Well, yes. Sure. It was on the news. But I don't know why –'

'It was a Palestinian assassination of an ex–Israeli commando.'

The blank look on Banfield's face showed he had no idea what Ross's point was. 'I didn't see that on the news,' he said, 'but . . . sorry . . . why do I care?'

'The guy killed in India was the on-scene commander of the Turkish peace flotilla massacre.'

Banfield blinked hard, a show of surprise. Ross stared into his eyes, searching for clues that he knew this already.

'Oh,' the old man said softly. His shock seemed genuine to Ross. 'I see what this is all about. Even so, we don't know that –'

'We *do* know. I'm telling you, the FBI was waiting for us all this morning when we got to work. They are saying they know about the unauthorized download of the flotilla files. They say the dead Israeli in India, Colonel

Yacoby, was mentioned in the files, as well as the fact he was living in that little village.' He stopped pacing and leaned down over Banfield. 'He was referred to by name in the CIA docs!'

'I don't remember that. There were a lot of pages in those files.'

'I don't remember, either, but the G's seem *fucking* certain!'

Banfield himself stood now, and he looked off over the trees. 'When did you deliver the files to me? It had to have been three months ago.'

'It was four.'

'And only now do they reveal the breach was detected? Why is that?'

Ross answered in a whispering shout. 'Because somebody got *fucking* killed! When I gave you that data you swore to me anything that could put lives in danger would be redacted, and the only people who would get the intel would be the media. You said you'd give them to an ITP-affiliated reporter at the *Guardian*, and he would reveal the fact the U.S. gave covert help to the Israelis in the attack on the flotilla. It was supposed to embarrass the White House, maybe nudge us away from covert ties with Israel. Maybe pro-Israeli hawks in the administration would get fired. And the next time some shit like this went down in Israel, Washington would be less eager to spy on behalf of a criminal regime.'

Ross pulled off his soaking knitted cap and ran his hands through his sticky wet blond hair, then said, 'Nobody said a goddamned thing about terrorists blowing up a family of four.'

Banfield positioned himself in front of Ross, blocking his ability to pace. He held his umbrella high enough for the taller man to fit under it, but Ethan did not come that close. Banfield said, 'Listen to me carefully. The files you passed to me did not go to anyone in Palestine.'

'Where did they go?'

'We still have them.'

'Why haven't you given them to the *Guardian*?'

'Remember what I told you when you gave me the information? If we released it so close on the heels of the breach, it could put you in danger.' Banfield squeezed Ross on the shoulder. 'I'm not going to let anything happen to you. My organization has refined the art of whistleblower attribution masking. You are safe.'

Ross sat back on the bench slowly. He wanted to believe, but wasn't sure.

'I'd feel better if you told me the ITP doesn't have contacts in Palestine.'

'Of course we have contacts in Palestine. We have contacts all over. But we didn't pass this on to anyone. We would never be a party to such a brutal act. Our partners in Palestine are as far removed from the personality types that committed this crime as you and I are from the thugs who run around D.C. knifing people for their wallets. There are bad apples out there. We just aren't working with them.'

Banfield sat down next to Ross, and the rainfall blew in from the river on to their faces. The umbrella served no purpose, but Banfield held it anyway.

'You've done nothing wrong, Ethan, and you are one hundred per cent in the clear. This thing in India was unrelated to the whistleblowing you did four months ago, I'm sure of it.'

'Well, the FBI is *not* sure of it. They are conducting polygraphs later in the week.'

Banfield did not show any surprise. 'That's to be expected. It's just a fishing expedition.'

'Perhaps, but they will be thorough.'

'You've never had any problems with polygraphs in the past.'

Ethan sighed, doing his best to regain composure. 'Of course not. I went to Harvard – I'm not going to be out-smarted by a fucking state college grad with a box of wires and lights. But my other polys were just annual security recerts. A second-rate investigator with no presumption of any deception. I *knew* I would ace the box, so I aced the box. This time will be different. It will be a single-scope poly, the best FBI investigators in CID, and they will know what questions to circle back to. It won't be a cake-walk this time.'

Banfield tried to calm the younger man down. 'The polygraph is a stage prop. It's bullshit. The key to the poly-graph is understanding the equipment is a hoax set out to intimidate the guilty into a confession. The examiner will interrogate you, and he will use the polygraph as a pretext to say he does not believe you. It is his tool to draw out a confession. Don't confess, stay relaxed.' Banfield smiled. 'And *believe* that which is true.'

Ethan glared at Banfield. 'You aren't telling me any-thing I don't know.'

The older man put his hands up. 'I'm sorry. Of course

not. But just know this: you are not to blame for the attack in India. The information you gleaned from CIA files is as secure right now as it was when you downloaded it. We are just holding it for the right moment.'

Ethan looked off in the distance and mumbled, 'I can beat the box.' He didn't sound sure, and Banfield registered this.

'You *can*.' Banfield put his arm around Ross. 'I'll get you some medications to take. It will help.' He leaned down to look into Ethan's face. He gave him another squeeze on the shoulder. 'Listen to me. We work with a lot of patriots like you. Probably once a month someone gets pulled into a surprise polygraph. Nothing has ever come from it. *Ever.*'

'Don't lie to me, Harlan.'

'I wouldn't dare. And I'm not just kissing your ass here when I say it, but you are a hell of a lot sharper than some of the other whistleblowers out there.' He smiled and rolled his eyes, indicating the level of intellect of the others.

Ethan nodded, conceding the point without a hint of self-consciousness, and he lightened up a little. He took a moment to look around the park, as if for the first time. He and Banfield were the only two people in sight.

'Okay. I'll spend the next couple of days prepping for it. But I'm not going to trust any technology in the meantime. Who knows how wide and how deep this security review will go? We need to be careful. The FBI could get a court order to tap every one of us with TS clearance in the EOB. No phones or e-mail.'

'A phone is okay in a pinch if you buy a new one. Just go to a convenience store and get a cheap mobile. Only use it in an emergency. I'll do the same.'

'Okay, but I'd rather meet in person.'

Banfield thought for a moment. 'Do you still go running in the mornings?'

'Some mornings,' Ross said. And then, 'Why?'

'Buy some chalk.'

'Chalk?'

'Yes. For the next few days, go for a morning jog down Wisconsin Avenue. Turn east on N Street. On the southeast corner there is a green fire hydrant by the road. If you want to meet me here, drag a small piece of chalk on the top of it, just three inches or so, big enough so I can see it as I pass by on my way to work. If you put it there I'll show up here at 8 a.m.'

'And if you need to talk to me?'

'Same thing. I'll mark the hydrant.'

Ross nodded slowly. 'A little old-fashioned, but okay.'

'The old ways are the best ways, son. Phones are tapped. Unsecure e-mail is read. Nobody out there is looking for chalk anymore.'

Banfield dropped Ross off at his car, which was parked several blocks away from Banfield's office in Thomas Circle, then he drove back to the parking garage under his building. He had his eyes open for any surveillance, but as near as he could tell he was in the clear. He considered himself something of a proficient amateur on matters of surveillance, and this stemmed from some training he received early in his career. In the seventies a young Harlan Banfield had enrolled in a five-day corporate security class in London. It was put on for executives and journalists traveling abroad, and Harlan found the course to be a mixed bag. The self-defense portion of the curriculum, in Harlan's estimation, was silly and naive. He took the program before heading over to Lebanon to cover the civil war there, and he thought it unlikely any armed Shiite manning a roadblock he ran into would be much impressed by his ability to twist someone's thumb or apply a knife hand to the groin.

But there were some very helpful aspects of the training, none more so than the instruction on the basics of how to identify a tail and to spot other types of surveillance operations.

Since London, Banfield had supplanted this training with decades of real-world experience, and in his years working secretly for the ITP, he'd fallen back on his training and practice to keep an eye out for anyone following him.

He made it up to his eleventh-floor office confident no one was more interested in him this day than any other, and he locked himself in. He didn't bother removing his coat or his fedora before sitting down at his computer; instead, he immediately logged on to an encrypted instant message service called Cryptocat, then typed a long alphanumeric code that he had committed to memory. This led him to a screen where he could select from a buddy list, but instead he typed in a recipient address from memory because he had not saved it into his list.

Almost instantly the two-party encryption was authenticated. His fingers hovered over the keys. After a moment he typed: *We have a problem.*

The response came back thirty seconds later. *Which is?*

Ethan Ross.

Yes.

Banfield cocked his head. He typed: *Yes? Yes, what?*

I only just learned the details of the attack in India. I expected to hear from you about our friend.

He thinks we provided the information.

He's wrong.

That's what I told him. Please confirm I was correct in telling him we haven't passed it on to the Guardian *yet.*

You are correct.

He will be polygraphed.

How is his mood?

Concerned. I'd say very concerned. I gave him the song and dance about how we do this all the time. I think he bought it. I will provide him with a cocktail to defeat the poly, but frankly, I don't know if he can beat it.

He doesn't have to.

Harlan Banfield did not understand the message. He typed: *What do you mean?*

There was no reply for more than a minute. Banfield fought the urge to send a question mark over the messaging service. Instead, he cracked his knuckles and forced himself to wait.

Finally a new line appeared on his screen.

I'm on my way.

Banfield sat up straighter at his desk and his chest heaved. He had no idea what was going through the head of the person on the other end of the encrypted chat, but his concerns that ITP leadership would not see the importance of the event dissolved instantly, because Banfield knew the director of the ITP was in Switzerland.

If she was on her way, then clearly she understood the magnitude of the problem that Ethan Ross had become.

8

Dominic Caruso rolled slowly and gingerly out of his bed and pulled himself up to his feet with the aid of a belt he'd wrapped around his bedpost for just that purpose. He walked on legs that felt lethargic from lying down for an extended period of time, and the bright bulb in his bathroom made his head pound.

Since arriving home he'd climbed out of bed only a few times to answer nature's call or to grab a water bottle or some canned food from his kitchen. Adara Sherman had called him just hours after she dropped him off at his place; she offered to come by with some groceries because she knew Dom wouldn't have anything fresh in his condo. Dom thanked her for the call, but he told her his next-door neighbor was running errands for him right then.

It wasn't true. Dom just didn't feel like having any visitors.

Yesterday afternoon he'd got up and moved around a little more. He took the elevator downstairs to the tiny market in his building, and he came back up to his place with two plastic bags full of canned food, yogurt, sodas and beer.

He picked at a can of tuna and another of peaches in sugary syrup, drank a beer, and went back to bed.

Dom was determined to do something productive today, despite the aches and pains. He started his shower, then took the bandages off his chest and forearm. He stood there with his sore body pressed up against the cold tile next to the shower for several minutes, until finally he stepped into the water.

The hot spray stung his wounds, but it went a long way toward making him feel human again. After the shower, he changed the bandages on his forearm, drank coffee, and went into his living room. He had all the lights off in his place now because the lights added to his headache, so he sat on his couch in the dark with his laptop and spent the early part of the morning reading everything he could find online about the attack in India. Much had been written on the subject, but the vast majority of it was sensationalized, editorialized, or simply conjecture, and so much of it – he knew because he had been there and seen it firsthand – was dead wrong.

He had to turn his computer off after an hour or so. The images from the event and the speculation about it only forced his brain to relive everything that had happened, to experience the moment again as a virtual after-action report.

With this 'hot wash,' Dom inevitably analysed his own actions in the most critical way possible. He told himself now he should have gone upstairs with Yacoby from the beginning, covering the stairwell and keeping the other attackers downstairs instead of splitting their access points. He should have dispatched the poorly trained attackers in the kitchen more quickly than he had. He should have anticipated that the terrorist with the knife in his chest would not have died quickly, and therefore remained a threat.

There were a lot of things he could have done differently, and now, as he sat on his couch in his fifth-floor D.C. condo, he wished he'd done them all.

The more Dom thought it over, the more certain he became of one thing.

He had failed Arik and his family.

The death of Dom's twin brother, Brian, played out in his mind in much the same way. He'd spent the intervening years dissecting every aspect of the event, judging himself to be responsible. He could have been faster, if not in the gunfight itself then at least in his treatment of Brian's gunshot wound. He could have saved him.

Dom knew he had done his best, but both in Libya and in India, his best just hadn't cut it.

A little after nine he shook the images and anguish out of his mind long enough to pour himself a fresh cup of coffee, his third of the morning. He'd just lowered himself back down to his sofa with his laptop when his phone chirped. He looked down and saw it was Adara Sherman calling, no doubt checking up on him again. He let the call roll to his voice mail.

Soon after this, his doorbell rang. The chime made his head throb. He rolled his eyes, thinking it must be Sherman, which would mean she was efficient as hell in her efforts, though he expected nothing less. But when he opened the door to the bright hallway, standing in front of him was a fit-looking man in a suit and tie under a trench coat, wearing a perfect part in his dark hair. He was taller than Dom by several inches, with big round shoulders that his coat could not conceal.

The man said, 'How ya doin', Dominic?'

Dom knew this man, though he hadn't seen him in several years. 'It's Albright, right?'

Darren Albright nodded. 'That's right. Good memory. I'm impressed.' They shook hands.

'It has been a while.' Dom's mind began racing. He remembered Albright from Quantico, the FBI Training Academy. To the best of Dom's recollection, Darren had been a cop for several years before joining the FBI, and was several years older than Dom.

'Special agent?'

'Supervisory special agent, for what it's worth.'

Dom was impressed, he had obviously played his cards right at the Bureau.

What in God's name is this guy doing here?

Albright said, 'Good to see you.' He stood there a moment, obviously waiting to be invited in.

Caruso shuffled.

The FBI special agent said, 'Can I have a few minutes of your time?'

'Sure.' *Shit.*

They stepped back into the condo and Dom flipped on a couple of lights. He looked around at his disheveled place. The only company he ever had around here was female: usually brief intense flings whom he would bring over to impress with a bottle of wine and a beautifully cooked Italian meal. In these instances he usually had plenty of time to make his place presentable.

In the time he'd been home from India, on the other hand, romance had been the last thing on his mind, and his condo looked the worse for it. 'Sorry about the place,' was all he could say.

'It's no problem. I was a bachelor myself until last year.'

'Oh yeah?' Dom said, feigning interest in his old class-mate's love life. 'Congrats.'

'Thanks. Got a baby on the way in August.'

'Awesome.' He thought of Dar and Moshe, and he steered the conversation in another direction in hopes the images would drift away. 'So, you got the field office here in D.C.? That's a hell of a good deal. I got Alabama as a first office of assignment.'

'I know you did. That thing you did down in Birmingham, punching the ticket of that child killer. That was a righteous piece of work. I told myself I'd buy you a whiskey the next time I saw you.'

Caruso stood in the middle of his living room. 'It's nine-fifteen in the morning. I'm guessing that's not why you're here.'

The big man shook his head. 'No, it's not, but I'd settle for a cup of that coffee I smell.'

A minute later the two men sat in Dom's kitchen at a table adorned with a month's worth of unopened mail and unread newspapers.

They sipped coffee, or, more accurately, Albright sipped coffee while Caruso sat anxiously behind his undisturbed cup, doing his best to feign nonchalance.

Albright tracked back to something Caruso had said earlier. 'Actually, I'm not at the D.C. office. I got assigned Houston right out of the Academy. Hot as hell, all the time.'

Caruso said, 'Before the Academy, you were a cop, weren't you? SWAT from some local PD force?'

'Yeah. Saint Louis.'

Dom said, 'I'm surprised you didn't go for HRT.' HRT was the FBI's vaunted Hostage Rescue Team, the top tactical officers in federal law enforcement.

'I did. Unfortunately, I busted my foot in a training accident. It's okay now, but it knocked me out of HRT. After three years at the office in Houston I was assigned back up here to CID.'

If Dom had been concerned about the fact an FBI special agent had come calling on him, now he was doubly so. What the hell was a G from their Counterintelligence Division doing in his apartment?

Nothing good, he was certain.

'CID?' Dom said. 'Interesting work?'

Albright replied, 'Has its moments. Like now, for example. I have a few questions about what happened the other day in India. Do you mind?'

Dom rubbed his forehead. He'd been more concerned Albright would be here to ask some questions about The Campus. Although a few well-connected senior members of the FBI and other organizations knew the existence of Dom's off-the-books employer, Albright wouldn't be on this select list.

The fact that Dom was in India, on the other hand, could easily be known to the FBI at large. He relaxed a touch, but still remained on guard as to what he could and could not say. 'Yeah. Okay.'

'I heard you got a concussion.'

'Just a mild one.'

'How do you feel?'

'I'm okay, thanks.'

Dom was nervous, and he could see that Albright was

aware of it. Albright said, 'You were over there training in Krav Maga with Colonel Arik Yacoby, ex of the IDF?'

Dom shrugged. He didn't know where Albright was getting his information. 'That and some other PT stuff. I didn't even know he was a colonel. I did a little yoga with his wife, too.'

'Yoga.' Albright raised his eyebrows. The incredulity on his face was obvious.

'Yeah.'

The FBI agent nodded, not taking his eyes from Caruso to write anything down.

'You seem edgy, Dom.'

'Not at all.'

'No?'

'You must be misreading my confusion about your presence in my kitchen.'

Albright sipped. 'Fair enough. Let me help you, then. I'll lay my cards on the table. This morning, when I was in the office before heading over here to interview you, I got a call from Anthony Rivalto. You know who that is, don't you?'

'Yeah. He's the director of the NYC field office.'

Albright cocked his head. 'That was years ago. Now he's the assistant director of CID.'

'Your boss, then.'

'My boss's boss, but yeah. He called me directly to let me know to tread lightly with you. I can talk to you, ask you if you want to volunteer anything, but you have some sort of force field around you that precludes me from digging too hard.'

Dom did not respond.

'You have connections, is what I am saying.'

Still nothing from the dark-haired man across from Albright at the kitchen table.

'Of course at first I figured it was just because your uncle is the President. That ought to be good for the white-glove treatment. But I looked into you, to see what you were doing, where you were assigned, any news about you at all.' Albright held his empty hands up. 'Nothing. After Birmingham, you went black. To the dark side, I mean.'

'The dark side?'

'You're FBI still, I got that confirmed through personnel. But only on paper. In real life you're some kind of spook. I know you aren't CIA proper, or at least nothing anyone wants to fess up to. I guess you could be seconded to one of the other intelligence agencies, or maybe you are affiliated with the military somehow, but I know you didn't serve in uniform yourself. You might be with some secret spook fusion cell, but I don't expect you to confirm any of this. Anyway, AD Rivalto basically said that if I walked in here and saw a tactical nuke on your kitchen counter I couldn't do jack squat about it.'

Dom gestured to the one appliance on his small kitchen counter. 'For the record, that's a juicer. I'd prove it, but it's broken.'

Albright didn't smile. 'I know the drill. I've been working around here for five years. I've run into a fair number of guys who couldn't say shit about what they were doing, who they worked for. I just wait for the dreaded wink and nod from my higher-ups, and then I move on.'

'And the call from AD Rivalto was the wink and the nod?'

'It was. Still, you and I are buds from way back, so I told Rivalto I'd drop in on you for a cup of coffee and a chat, and I'd stay within bounds.'

Dom said, 'And here we are.' He played with the bandage on his arm absentmindedly. He and Albright had never been friends. Just classmates.

Albright asked, 'Did you notice any surveillance on Yacoby or yourself when you were in India? Anything out of the ordinary at all?'

This was more comfortable territory for Caruso than talking about himself. He said, 'My guess is the Palestinians were using a local for intel. Someone who blended in. They were traveling in a dairy truck that I'd seen around the town a few times in the weeks before. I know the Indians are looking into that.'

'I heard you killed three of the tangos.'

Dom replied with, 'It's the four that slipped by me that really count.'

Albright still wasn't writing anything down. Dom noticed this because special agents normally don't interview a subject involved in an investigation without writing up an FD-302, an official form, and to do this they need to keep some sort of record of the conversation. Dom found the absence of a pen and paper comforting, although he wasn't about to let his guard down.

'Colonel Yacoby didn't say anything to you about any enemies in the U.S., did he?'

This surprised Caruso. 'In the *U.S.*? No.'

'Any enemies at all? Anywhere?'

'No, although it was obvious he was ex-IDF. You do that for a while and you piss some people off. Especially Palestinians.'

'Yeah, I imagine so. Good guy, this Yacoby?'

'Good? No, he was more than that. He was a great man with a great family.'

Albright nodded, drummed his fingers on the kitchen table while he thought about his next question.

Caruso furrowed his eyebrows. 'I've got to ask. Why is U.S. counterintelligence involved in this? What, exactly, are you investigating?'

Albright put his cup down. 'A leak.'

'A leak?'

'Yep. A digital breach. Arik Yacoby's name and location were on a CIA file that was part of a cache of documents improperly downloaded from a terminal in the Eisenhower Building a few months back.'

'What kind of files?'

'The file with Yacoby's name on it was an after-action report about the IDF raid on the Turkish freighter in the Gaza flotilla a couple of years back. Classified TS. It named him as the leader of the team that fast-roped down to the deck and killed the Al-Qassam operatives. Another file made reference to the fact the colonel was now living in Paravur.'

'Are you suggesting someone in the U.S. government ratted out Yacoby's name and location to the terrorists?' Caruso all but shouted the question.

'Take it easy. We don't know that. We know his name was in the files, and we know someone brought up the files on a terminal on the third floor of the Eisenhower

Building, which is where the National Security Council staff works. Whoever downloaded the data obfuscated things in the system so we can't tell who did it. We don't know, as of yet, anyway, if they communicated the contents of the files to anyone, much less to the Palestinian terrorists.'

Caruso was barely listening. The Eisenhower Building was less than a half-mile from where he now sat in his kitchen in Logan Circle. His blood boiled as he considered the possibility that someone in *his* town, in *his* government, had been involved in the killing of the Yacoby family. He wanted to leap out of his chair, to grab the Smith & Wesson pistol on the top of his bookshelf by the door and storm down Vermont Avenue to demand answers.

Instead, other than a slight flexing of the muscles in his jaw, he showed no evidence of the depth of his emotions. 'What are you doing to find the traitor?'

'We've whittled it down to thirty or forty people who had access and opportunity. Starting the narrow-scope polygraphs tomorrow. I'll do secondary interviews if anyone flags after they get boxed.'

'What else?' Dom was challenging Albright now, almost accusatory, but Albright let it go.

'We've got some computer forensic people on it, trying to cut that number down a little more by digging into the skill set necessary to pull off the breach.'

'That's it?'

Albright leaned back and crossed his arms. He was the one under interrogation now. 'I've run leak cases before. When we do find the culprit, odds are we'll learn the leak wasn't executed with malice aforethought. Instead, we'll find some system administrator who cut corners because he wanted to leave early for the weekend, so he used unauthorized means to move some data around without going through protocol, then covered it up after the fact. If not that, it will be a well-meaning dolt who screwed up and moved the wrong files on to the file-sharing portion of the server, and then they made it out into circulation without his or her knowledge.'

'What are you saying?'

'I'm saying, Caruso, that I expect to learn that the intel slipped out negligently, maybe even purposefully, but not maliciously. The chance there is a mole in the government working for Palestinian terrorists is next to nil.'

Albright saw this was doing nothing to calm the fiery man sitting across from him.

'Having said all that, I take this shit seriously. Whatever the reason for the unauthorized access, it happened, and I'm going to find out why.'

Caruso said, 'You'd be doing me a hell of a favor by giving me a call if you learn anything after the polys.'

'Sorry, Dom. It's a need-to-know kind of thing.' Albright stood up from the kitchen table.

Caruso stood up as well, only faster. 'I need to know.'

'You making this personal?'

Dom shook his head. 'Of course not. Shit doesn't get personal with me. I'm just asking for a little professional courtesy. I *am* FBI, after all.'

'On paper.'

'In the flesh.'

'Right. If you are working in some sort of fusion cell

93

within the CIA, which I suspect you are, you know they can make a formal request for information. There are channels.'

Dom shook his head. 'It's just me, Darren. It's just *me* asking *you*.'

Albright seemed to consider this while he walked back through the living room. At the front door he turned around. 'All right. You have my word. I'll give you a shout if something turns up with this, but only if you promise me you'll let me and my team do the work.'

'You got it. Thanks.'

The men shook hands and Albright said, 'In the meantime, here's a little advice. You need to take it easy for a while. The dark side can get along without you for a few weeks. No offense, but you look like shit.'

Albright stepped out into the hall, and Dom shut the door behind him.

'I wish everyone would stop telling me to take it easy.'

Dom reached Gerry Hendley at his seaside home in Myrtle Beach, South Carolina, where he went from time to time to get away from the pressures of Hendley Associates, The Campus and Washington, D.C., in general. Dom reported his contact and conversation with FBI special agent Darren Albright, which both he and Gerry, after some discussion, determined to be both good news and bad for The Campus. Yes, Gerry agreed, it was good news that the leak that exposed Arik Yacoby to the Palestinians didn't look like it had anything to do with Dominic Caruso or The Campus. But now the FBI at large was aware of and interested in Dominic. This could, and probably would, draw more attention to him than usual, even if it was only that he was witness to a crime. Already Albright had dropped in, and as the investigation into the leaked documents progressed, it was possible more Feds with more questions would dig deeper into the day-to-day life of Dominic Caruso.

Gerry decided Dominic needed to continue his hiatus from all Campus activity and contact with the rest of the team. It was just temporary, he insisted to his frustrated operations officer.

Hendley ended the conversation by soliciting from Dominic a promise to continue to take it easy and recover from his injuries.

Dominic wasn't happy, but he saw no alternative to Gerry's logic, so he reluctantly agreed. 'What else am I gonna do, boss?'

He hung up his phone and reached for the television remote, hoping he could find something to take his mind off everything going on, because he knew he didn't possess the personality type to sit on his ass for very long.

9

United Airlines flight 951, a Boeing 777 flying from Brussels, touched down at Washington Dulles International Airport at 1 p.m. in a driving rain. The first to deplane were the first-class passengers, and within this group was a small man with short black hair and a boyish face.

If any of the deplaning passengers noticed him at all they would have presumed him to be a foreign exchange student, perhaps from Turkey or Lebanon or Saudi Arabia. His backpack was sleek and trendy, his jeans were designer, and he certainly looked no older than twenty-three or so.

In truth he was thirty-five, and he'd not come to America to study.

The man's name was Mohammed Mehdi Mobasheri, but the documents he presented at immigration control said something altogether different. They claimed him to be a young Lebanese diplomat, flying from Beirut via Brussels. A call to the Lebanese embassy in the Woodley Park neighborhood of D.C. would have confirmed his travel and his bona fides, but no call was necessary because his diplomatic visa appeared to be in order.

But while it was true his flight had originated the day before in Beirut's Rafic Hariri Airport, the Lebanon-to-Belgium leg of his journey was, in fact, the second leg, and not the first. He had flown into Beirut early the previous morning from Tehran on a military transport, and he'd received his Lebanese documentation only in a guarded room at Rafic Hariri a half-hour before wheels up to Belgium.

And now he was in the immigration line in Dulles. He stood with a pleasant, if somewhat tired, smile on his face while he was cleared for entry into the United States. He passed through quickly, and then he breezed through customs with nothing to declare.

During the flight over, Mobasheri had sat by himself in the first-class cabin, but four more men tasked with serving him were on board UA951. The four had traveled all the way from Tehran as well, though they had stayed apart from one another since deplaning the military transport in Beirut. They flew in coach, carrying Lebanese identification; their documents claimed them to be businessmen and not diplomats.

Mohammed left the airport terminal on his own, and he was met by a limousine from the Lebanese embassy in the arrivals queue at Dulles and whisked away. The other four were picked up in a Chevrolet Suburban with tinted windows.

Mobasheri had earned the privileges bestowed upon him. He was a member of a special elite unit within the Iranian Army of the Guardians of the Islamic Revolution, more commonly known as the Revolutionary Guards. The four men who traveled with him in a clandestine fashion were Quds Force, Iranian foreign intelligence operations. They had all come from Iran via Lebanon because Iranian intelligence used the Shia-run Lebanese government as a proxy when necessary to pass men and matériel into nations where teams of declared Iranian government agents might otherwise raise red flags.

The five reunited one hour later in a safe house in Falls Church, Virginia. Here they met with more Iranians, two operatives who lived and worked in D.C. These were official cover intelligence officers from the Iranian embassy, and they worked for yet another group in Iranian intelligence, MISIRI, the Ministry of Intelligence and National Security of the Islamic Republic of Iran.

The two MISIRI men were known to American counterintelligence, and the FBI did their best to keep tabs on all Iran's spies here in America, but these MISIRI officers were professionals. This stood to reason; only Iran's very best intelligence operatives were sent to work in the land of Iran's greatest foe, and only after they had proved themselves in many other hostile stations abroad. The two MISIRI officers here in the four-bedroom suburban Falls Church home were experts at shaking surveillance, and they'd arrived here free and clear after a several-hours-long surveillance-detection route.

Mohammed Mobasheri and his four subordinates sat for a briefing from the two 'local' officers, information integral to their mission here in the United States. Not that the MISIRI officers knew anything about these new men or their mission. They knew the young-looking Revolutionary Guards officer only as Mohammed, which was more common in Farsi than John was in English, and all they knew about his operation was that he was traveling here with four Quds Force 'body' men on a special task, and he was to be extended every courtesy and afforded every resource he needed.

All on the orders of Tehran.

The spies from the embassy knew this to be highly unusual. They didn't much like the fact that this stranger from another organization was working on their turf, but it didn't much matter what they liked, because he had sanction from the Supreme Leader, the highest level of Iranian government. That they weren't read into his mission was bewildering, but that really wasn't the strangest part of their day.

Mohammed himself was the strangest part.

The MISIRI spies had worked with many Revolutionary Guards officers in their careers, of course, and they knew them all to be, by necessity, strong and confident and powerful alphas. No one could rise through the ranks of Iran's military in any capacity whatsoever without possessing leadership prowess and intrinsic personal dominance.

But immediately upon meeting Mohammed they thought him to be something of a strange bird, not a typical Revolutionary Guards officer at all. He was clearly highly intelligent and intellectual, and he seemed to be in fair physical condition, but he was smallish, somewhat baby-faced, and his demeanor was shy, introverted, and almost pathologically mild-mannered. His voice was thin, and he seemed unsure in his actions around the MISIRI officers, almost as if he were intimidated by their presence.

He asked relevant questions, so he wasn't a bumbling fool, but he looked to the experienced MISIRI men like a grown-up kid who'd never left his parents' house before being sent to the U.S. on a mission of obvious national importance.

What the fuck was that all about?

During a cigarette break in the backyard, one of the D.C.-based MISIRI officers said to the other, 'If he is fucking scared of us, his own countrymen, what the hell is he doing here around real enemies?'

The other quipped, 'That little lamb has flown a long way just to go to the slaughterhouse.'

The men who arrived with Mohammed, by contrast, were typical Quds. While they dressed like businessmen and would pass as such to the uninitiated, to the MISIRI officers they appeared to be ex-military, special operations forces, perhaps commandos from Takavar, elite hand-picked operators who then endured a special twenty-month training program before being put into the most danger-ous combat and missions around the Islamic Republic.

These men would have made the cross-border runs into Iraq during the war there, bringing matériel and expertise, training Iraqi Shiites to engage coalition forces and destroy them. They would have fought Israelis in Lebanon, they would have worked with militias in Paki-stan and insurgent groups on the Afghanistan border.

The Iranian spies knew enough about Quds Force to recognize they were in the presence of some seriously scary dudes.

But the four stood in stark contrast to their mild-mannered leader, who looked like he'd probably not held a gun since his mandatory Army service, which would have begun on his eighteenth birthday.

The embassy spies were correct on all counts. Moham-med Mobasheri was not an ex-commando like the rest of his team. He'd been a young computer geek, the son of well-connected government employees, when he went into compulsory military service. There he was trained how to stand and march and use a weapon, but then he'd left infantry operations and moved into something that utilized his existing skill set, a special program for computer operations.

As the MISIRI men had guessed, this was Mobasheri's first time in the United States, but he spoke English well. His father was ex-MISIRI himself, a general in the Ministry of Intelligence and National Security of Iran, and these D.C.-based MISIRI would have all but bowed down to this boy-man if they'd known his true identity and his parentage.

Young Mobasheri learned English in school in Tehran as a child, then spent several years living abroad in Australia and in Ireland and in the United Kingdom, following his father's cover postings as an agricultural official.

It was his father who pushed him into computer operations in the military, mostly to protect him from the dangers of combat but also because Mohammed had shown interest and aptitude with computers as a child. Moreover, General Mobasheri was a forward-thinking spy, and he knew much of the espionage of the future would involve computerized information systems, and he wanted his son involved in a growth industry that also served the Islamic Republic.

After compulsory military service Mohammed was sent to study computer science at Imperial College London. He returned to Iran with a doctorate and ideas about the future of IT and its application to intelligence, and by his late twenties he was a chief strategic planner for the Revolutionary Guards' fledgling offensive cyber-ops division.

Over the next few years he developed offensive cyber-ops capabilities for his nation, and he started a unit called the Markazi Digital Security Team, one of the most elite offensive cyber-hacking groups in the world.

Most Americans are unaware that Iran's military has such robust computer-hacking capabilities, but Mobasheri had been one of the leaders of this all-but-unheralded success of the Islamic Republic. He and his team of hackers had broken into American defense networks, and had placed infiltration-agent programs into U.S. wireless companies that had taken years and tens of millions of dollars to clean out.

His power grew in the Revolutionary Guards, and the Supreme Leader himself took a special interest in young Mobasheri's operations, clearing the way for him to expand into plans that were more and more audacious.

Which led him all the way to Falls Church, Virginia. Now, after months of preparation and groundwork, Mohammed Mobasheri was here in the U.S. on a special operation with a powerful sanction.

Mohammed was disarmingly calm and polite, even shy, especially when compared with the hard Takavaran around him. But he'd not made it this far in his organization by exhibiting weakness. He was a man with big ideas, high aspirations, and he was certain he'd be reaching out to Tehran via encrypted means soon enough, asking for – no, demanding – approval to add to his mission parameters.

The MISIRI men from the embassy thought their support of this team working out of Falls Church would be limited to information, perhaps some vehicles, and documentation. But Mohammed made it clear, in an offhand and almost apologetic manner, that he would require a surveillance team first thing in the morning, and they might be put to work for several days straight.

And guns. The little man who looked like a college student gave a handwritten sheet of paper to the MISIRI officers, and on it was a list of pistols, shoulder holsters, ammunition and sound suppressors.

The MISIRI officers were not happy, but they were compliant. This mild-mannered oddball had the backing of the Supreme Leader, after all, so they had no choice but to do whatever the hell he demanded, as if the Supreme Leader himself were standing before them giving the orders.

Ethan Ross spent the entire afternoon piddling around his office, doing everything within his power to portray relaxed confidence. Normally this wouldn't be hard to manage – it was his default state of being, after all – but since the meeting in the conference room, his world had been knocked off-kilter and he could do little more than sit quietly with a distracted gaze on his face.

At lunch the talk in the dining room had been, not surprisingly, on the data breach. Ethan remained quiet while most of the rest of his colleagues speculated that some IT geek had accessed the files and then covered it up, either because he'd screwed up in the first place or, just maybe, because he was spooking for a foreign power.

Ethan's only comment on the subject was a hope that his poly didn't interfere with either the staff meeting in the West Wing on Wednesday afternoon or his appointment to get his teeth cleaned on Thursday afternoon. He forced out the words, knowing he'd look guilty as hell if he didn't bitch about the intrusion along with everyone else.

He'd attended a directors' meeting just after lunch, and he'd strolled with other staffers to a conference room on the north side of the Eisenhower Building, their voices echoing up the ornate marble corridor as the topic of conversation remained on the investigation. At the meeting there was more small talk about what most of the staff saw as the FBI's heavy-handed encroachment on the NSC, but Ethan said little. He only thumbed through pages of a briefing booklet he'd been working on, and did his best not to show any signs of concern.

By mid-afternoon he was back at his desk; in front of him was a printout of a letter he'd written requisitioning a paper on popular opinion in Jordan of the new U.S. ambassador. It was something to get his mind off his situation – busywork.

Except it wasn't working.

Every time someone passed his office he felt a tightening in his stomach, and his hands, already dry and papery, burned at the palms. He had visions of G's like that Albright character he'd seen marching into his office, storming around his desk, and telling him to stand up and put his hands behind his back.

Ethan felt nauseated about the possibility his breach could be uncovered, but more than this, he was disoriented. He knew he had done everything right. His breach *should* have gone undetected.

What the hell went wrong?

It is said there are four major motivations for committing espionage, and in the intelligence realm the collective is abbreviated as MICE: money, ideology, compromise, ego. In Ethan's case, money and compromise were not relevant. His mother was wealthy and she shared her largesse with her adult son, and Ethan had no real skeletons in his closet that could have led to his being compromised.

Instead, his motives could be best characterized as a combination of one part ideology and four parts ego. To those very few who really knew him, this would come as no great surprise, because Ethan Ross was somewhat opinionated, but he was most definitely a narcissist, and if these predilections were built into him by nature, his nurture certainly did nothing to help him overcome them.

Ethan's parents, like all parents everywhere, were convinced their child was brilliant and special. Unlike most parents, their conviction was confirmed by outsiders when, at the age of four, young Ethan earned a Very Superior classification on the Stanford-Binet Intelligence Scale IQ test. After this verification of his excellence, he became the family prodigy and was forever after treated as such. He was placed in the best schools, tutored in math and science and language, and told regularly that he'd have a future not just of importance but of power as well.

Ethan grew up like a member of royalty, living first among socialist Europe's upper class when his parents were in government and education abroad, then as the child of tenured professors in academia here in the U.S. His parents' core political beliefs in the strength, power, and certitude of UN resolutions, multinational peace treaties, and international law ensured that Ethan was brought up with the conviction that a benevolent governing class should rule over those incapable of making decisions for themselves.

And Ethan was raised as an heir apparent to this ruling class. He thought nothing of the fact both the vice president of France and one of the Belgian princesses were close family friends. He skied in Zermatt and beached in Monaco, and the home in Georgetown Heights where he spent his teenage years was in the same cul-de-sac as homes owned by a senator, three ambassadors, a Pulitzer-winning playwright, and one of the best-known national television anchors.

Even before he left home to pursue an Ivy League education, he was introduced to world leaders at parties as a future secretary of state, or even as a future President, and Ethan Ross grew into manhood believing his own hype.

At Yale he studied with an eye toward the family business, diplomacy, so he majored in international affairs, but like many his age, he'd developed a passion for computers as a teen, and his keen intellect advanced his love for technology to a level far beyond most. He sought a minor in computer science at Yale, much to the chagrin of his parents. They thought it pedestrian of him to spend so much time with his head in the minutiae of computers instead of on the big macro issues that would lead to the betterment of society. His father called computer scientists nothing more than glorified blue-collar workers. His mother treated his obsession as a fad and a fancy, as if he were spending his time playing Grand Theft Auto instead of what he actually was doing, learning Linux-based programming and developing his own software.

But he did well at Yale in both of his chosen disciplines, and then, to his parents' everlasting relief, he attended Harvard's Kennedy School to focus exclusively on statecraft.

After university he took a job with the Department of State in the Foreign Service. He spent the bulk of his twenties in consular affairs, but where most foreign service officers had to do their time in the lower rung of consular postings like Djibouti, Haiti or El Salvador, Ethan Ross's family pedigree and a few calls from senators who were good friends of Mom and Dad steered him away from the hardship areas, and instead his three foreign postings were at three of the diplomatic corps' most sought-after locations: Vienna, Amsterdam and Paris.

At age twenty-eight he left State to work in the Democratic presidential administration as a junior foreign policy adviser. Soon he had his eye on a position under the U.S. ambassador to the United Nations, but the job prospect fell through, so he moved laterally from the White House into the National Security Council to get some practical training under his belt before taking the next high-ranking United Nations post that came along.

But his career path hit speed bumps when his personality clashed with both hawkish NSC staffers with military backgrounds as well as members of the new Republican administration in power, and with his darkening prospects came the darkening mood common with those who feel their work beneath their abilities and their talents unappreciated. Staffers he considered inferior took plum UN postings, while Ethan stayed at his desk in the Eisenhower Building, watching life pass him by.

By his early thirties, Ethan's narcissism was on full display. His self-confidence had morphed into cockiness, and then finally what a few in his department considered unbridled arrogance. By his third year in his position at NSC he had become indignant about what he considered his small role in the U.S. diplomatic realm, and this, partnered with his feelings of superiority, made his working relationship with many of his colleagues particularly icy.

All that said, no one had any suspicions he was responsible for passing secrets.

Ethan Ross's first foray into the nebulous world of intelligence trafficking began above board, when he was selected by the deputy director for the Middle East region to pass a small piece of information on background to an acquaintance, a reporter at *Politico*.

Authorized government leaks are a common tool in statecraft. Officials speaking on background to a friendly reporter often relay an item of coveted information, careful to secure a promise from the reporter that he or she understands no attribution should go along with the nugget.

Ethan's leaked item to *Politico* made the paper the next day. It wasn't interesting enough to extend beyond the Beltway or even outside the conference rooms around downtown D.C. and Foggy Bottom, but he appreciated the laserlike impact of the well-timed chat with a compliant member of the fourth estate.

After this successful tipoff to his *Politico* acquaintance, he was used by NSC staff on other occasions to pass further items of interest, most of which amounted to little more than gossip.

But Ethan began to get a taste for it. A feel for how to leverage secure information for low-risk impact, and a hunger for the feeling of power that came from pushing policy through his own actions.

It was his ego, ultimately, that convinced him he didn't really *need* supervisory approval for his disclosures, he was more than competent to make the decision about what to spill himself. And it was his ideology that gave him the desire to drop specific bits of intelligence to the media. He believed U.S. foreign policy had become too meddlesome and overbearing since the new administration had come to power. He saw too many violations of international law under the guise of national security, too many American soldiers and spies working together with too many foreign soldiers and spies. The institutions he truly believed in – the International Court of Justice, the United Nations, and other large world institutions – could never flourish as long as world powers like America continued to act in the shadows to tip the scales in their own favor.

Ethan had the means and the motive to make small gestures to combat such imperial overreach. But he knew he could no longer use the reporter at *Politico* for unauthorized disclosures, because it would be only a matter of time before Ethan was outed as the conduit of the intelligence.

He needed to find himself a new cutout.

He first learned of the International Transparency Project after reading an article translated from *Der Spiegel*. The German magazine produced a series of investigative reports into the U.S. military-industrial complex and its purchase of weapons of war from German companies such as Diehl BGT Defence and Atlas Elektronik. Using confidential memoranda from inside the companies, *Der Spiegel* revealed precise budgets, specific weapons capabilities, and exact delivery dates. As evidence, they showed the leaked e-mails between the defense contractors and the U.S. Department of Defense.

The ITP was credited in the article for finding and then protecting the whistleblower who passed the intelligence to *Der Spiegel*, though ITP made no formal announcement itself.

This was but one of many 'gets' attributed to the ITP over the next few months, and the more Ethan looked into them, the more he liked what he saw. He was fascinated by the anonymous nature of the organization and the impressive list of successes ascribed to them, though he was skeptical at first of the claims that the organization kept whistleblowers safe through encryption that even the American National Security Agency could not hack.

Still, Ethan had to admit, the Project seemed to be getting things done.

He learned more about the ITP in an award-winning documentary film with the sanctimonious title *The Future of Truth*. The movie portrayed the loose consortium of whistleblowers, investigative journalists, and ethical hackers (the film used the laudatory term 'hacktivists') as a group of citizen world police, a league of idealists who were the last line of defense between corrupt national governments and the common man.

Around this time, Ross was in Berlin for a NATO conference and he saw, just by chance, that the director and producer of *The Future of Truth* would be speaking at the nearby Berlinische Galerie about her film. On the spur of the moment, Ethan walked over to the event. As an American government employee with TS security clearance, this could have raised a red flag had anyone known about it, but he simply bought a ticket to the gallery and slipped into the back of the room as the filmmaker gave her presentation.

The director's name was Gianna Bertoli; she was a

forty-five-year-old Swiss who'd learned filmmaking at UC Berkeley and spoke perfect English. She talked at length about the ITP, fawning over both the integrity and the technical prowess of the organization. The one skeptical reporter in the room asked her about rumors of foreign sponsorship of the group, but Bertoli dismissed the allegation out of hand, saying in the year she spent researching and filming her documentary, she never once caught even a hint the Project was anything more than a well-meaning cadre of egalitarians who were sponsored by wealthy progressives, mostly in the United States and Europe.

Ethan was as impressed with Bertoli as he was with the subject of her film, and by the end of the evening he decided he would reach out to the ITP.

Ross contacted the organization via their website using Cryptocat messaging, and within weeks he and Harlan Banfield were meeting face-to-face in a greasy-spoon diner in Chantilly, Virginia. It was Ross's idea to meet in person. He had no intention of passing intelligence off to another country, and he had to at least entertain the possibility the website and the film were all part of some elaborate false-flag scheme to get American government employees to reveal secrets to the Chinese or the Russians. But by meeting with Banfield face-to-face, and by looking into his past history and affiliations, he satisfied himself that the Project was just what it claimed to be: a clandestine clearinghouse where whistleblowers could share information in safety with journalists.

During that first meeting, Banfield was on guard much the same as Ross. He had worked sources since before the man in front of him had been born; he knew better than to press this confident and intelligent NSC staffer for information. Instead, he let Ross talk about his philosophy, and his desire to work in the shadows against policies he disagreed with. Banfield listened quietly and carefully, and he took note of the fact Ross had some grievances against his coworkers who did not appreciate him and an administration that did not share his worldview or beliefs about international law.

Banfield had been around the block a few times, especially with whistleblowers, and although he loved them for the product they passed, he didn't hold the individuals themselves in much regard. Ross, in Banfield's estimation, was full of grandiose ideas about diplomacy and politics. Some of them the veteran newsman actually agreed with, but as he sat there quietly in the diner listening to Ross talk, it occurred to him that if this handsome young man did someday run for political office, Banfield wouldn't vote for him.

The guy was a pompous-assed narcissist.

Still, Harlan Banfield said all the right things and he told Ethan Ross he hoped they could work together to make right some of the current administration's many wrongs.

There was little risk to Banfield in this endeavor. He knew no one was ever prosecuted in the United States for publishing classified data, only for leaking it. Even though Banfield would serve as a channel for the intelligence breaches and not as a publisher himself, he was a respected member of the fourth estate, and because of this he knew he was safe. Ross wasn't there to entrap him, although he still might have been a government plant, and this could have been a ploy to get Banfield to reveal himself as the ITP's U.S. liaison. There was little Banfield could have done to prevent this, but if he was outed by the U.S. government, he wouldn't be arrested. He would simply pass the baton to someone else and end his formal relationship with the Project.

At their first meeting, Ross handed Banfield a single typewritten sheet of paper in a plastic bag. The paper wasn't an original document; it was instead a piece of classified intelligence Ross had typed himself, and the bag was to keep his fingerprints off it during transport.

This first leak was small; it was his notes of a transcript of a top-secret NSA SIGINT intercept between two executives of an Israeli bank. In their conversation they went into some detail about their practice of not lending to commercial accounts that had supported a candidate in the Labor Party.

Ross provided no documentary proof this conversation ever took place, but Banfield promised to get the intelligence to the right person to have an effect.

More than a month after he passed on the information, Ethan received a secure e-mail from Banfield. Attached was a short article from that day's copy of *Haaretz*, an Israeli left-of-center daily, exposing the bank and its politically motivated lending practices. The executives denied the charge, but they were equivocal, obviously because they didn't know what information *Haaretz* had managed to uncover.

Banfield followed up the link with a note.

'Good job! No smoking gun, but the bank is on notice, and the eyes of the world are upon them!'

Harlan was stroking his ego, this Ethan could plainly see, but Ethan did feel a jolt of power nevertheless, a confirmation of his ability to effect outcomes. His own disclosure had made a positive difference. Not in any great way, but he felt the risk had been minimal, and very much worth the reward.

The *Haaretz* article became a proof of concept. Ethan Ross was now an ITP whistleblower. Ross and the ITP were a perfect match. Neither was in it for any fame or notoriety, and both felt they knew better than the U.S. government what should be classified and what should be revealed to the world.

His early successes as a whistleblower were impressive. He slipped Banfield information about a CIA/Mossad operation to discredit an outspoken opponent of the U.S.-backed government in Jordan, and this led to harsh criticism of the policy in the world press. Next he outed a Cayman Islands–registered enterprise that was, in actuality, a front company set up by the Mossad to pay off journalists in Latin America who ran stories promoting Israeli business interests. This revelation created a minor firestorm in Argentina as a right-of-center television station was exposed as a shill for a foreign power and the leftist government revoked its license.

For more than a year Ethan continued in this vein with the Project. Every two months or so he'd either meet Banfield in person for a chat or forward something via Cryptocat. The process was going well for both parties, and although Ross remained frustrated by what he saw as his stalled career in government, he truly believed he now possessed more real power than even those with the dedicated parking spaces at the Eisenhower Building.

Then Ethan learned about the U.S. involvement, a few years earlier, in the Israeli attack on the Turkish ship SS *Ardahan* taking part in the Gaza peace flotilla. He had sat in on a morning meeting with some White House staffers, CIA execs, and senior military advisers. The subject was funding for political opposition parties in Lebanon, something Ethan knew quite a bit about. He was there to quietly advocate for pushing U.S. dollars to a UN program to educate Palestinian refugees through a Hezbollah-supported organization, but his position wasn't getting much traction. One of the CIA men made an offhand remark about the secondary benefits of direct CIA funding of some of the smaller Lebanese factions in areas where the Palestinian camps were located. A White House staffer seconded this line, adding, 'We saw how beneficial it can be to have people inside the camps during the so-called Gaza peace flotilla attack. Beneficial for us as well as the Mossad.'

Immediately one of the CIA execs put a hand up and reminded the staffer that not everyone in the room was cleared for that code-word operation. The staffer apologized sheepishly – these things happened – and the conversation moved on.

Ross spent the rest of the meeting wondering what the hell the staffer was talking about. He knew nothing of any CIA involvement in the Mossad attack on the SS *Ardahan* – an event that dominated the news cycle for more than a week and nearly brought the Middle East to the brink of war – but he damn well planned on finding out. When he got back to his desk, it took Ethan only minutes to find the relevant data about the CIA involvement in the affair. The primary documents were located in a code-word-access database on Intelink-TS, but Ethan was able to gain access to a brief summarizing the operation with his SCI access.

The CIA had an informant on the boat, the informant had a CIA sat phone, and the CIA passed Mossad all the tactical intelligence necessary to take the ship. They did this not by giving primary access to the source via the sat phone. No, they kept their informant's identity secret from the Israelis. Instead, a CIA officer with military experience met with the Shayetet 13 commandos on the day of the raid and gave them all the details of the armed Palestinians on the Turkish-flagged freighter.

After the raid, Tel Aviv went out of its way to stress that the United States had not been involved in the operation. Ethan bought the line, and now he realized he'd been tricked.

Ethan fumed. The simple knowledge that the CIA had passed the intel to the Israeli commandos before they dropped down to the boat and started shooting peace activists made him furious.

He'd gone into government service to follow in his mother's footsteps and make the world a better place, not to bolster a hegemonic America by helping its shills around the globe kill peace activists.

There was no turning back now. Ethan decided to act.

He passed his limited and unsubstantiated information in an e-mail to Banfield, who promised to get it to the *Guardian*.

Ethan woke each morning to check the website of the *Guardian* for any news about the flotilla raid. After a week of nothing, he received a Cryptocat chat request from Banfield. The older journalist told Ethan the *Guardian* dismissed Ethan's tip because he'd provided nothing to substantiate such an incendiary charge.

Ross was furious the British paper did not publish on his anonymous assertions alone.

Banfield did what he could to calm Ethan in the chat, saying the SS *Ardahan* allegation had simply proved to be too much for the *Guardian* to swallow without proof. He then helpfully suggested that if Ethan could somehow safely get documentary evidence, then they could pass this along and get some real traction for the story.

Ethan thought it over, enjoying the mental challenge of devising a plan to leak the information without getting caught. He knew if he downloaded the documents off Intelink-TS, it would leave a digital fingerprint of his doing so. As soon as the news came out about the U.S. involvement in the *Ardahan* attack, computer security officials at CIA would be able to track the user who accessed the information and moved it from the database portion of the network to the file-sharing portion of the network, a necessary step for items downloaded to pass through. Even if he just printed out the files, he'd still leave a trail.

The more Ethan wrestled with the problem, the more his ego told him he *had* to come up with a solution. He decided to resurrect his interest in computers to try to find a way to cover his tracks to get the documents he needed.

He began spending his evenings studying computer science with vigor, reading everything he could about the security of the systems on which he worked every day. At work he pestered IT employees with made-up problems involving his logons and access, careful to adopt a constant look of confusion and bewilderment on his face so everything they explained was explained two or even three times.

He volunteered for projects that required him to have his access levels temporarily boosted so he could use the networks in the building that gave him some access, via JWICS, to deeper regions of the classified CIA databases.

But Ethan soon came to the realization that despite his incredible intellect, there was just too much even he did not know. The problem, as he saw it, wasn't his intelligence; rather, it was that there existed no way for a man in his position to delve any deeper into the inner workings of computer security without raising eyebrows.

Then Ross found a serendipitous answer to this problem – her name was Eve.

I I

Ethan pulled into his driveway just before 6 p.m. A light freezing rain fell, so he held his leather folio over his head while he ran to his front door and put the key in the lock, but before he could turn the knob the door opened suddenly. Eve Pang reached out and grabbed him by his tie and pulled him inside, and then she kissed him deeply.

He shut the door behind him and she pulled his tie off, her lips did not unlock from his as she completed the feat, and then she pushed him up against the door and went to work on his coat.

Ethan caught a quick full-body glimpse of her in the mirror against the wall by the hallway. She had already changed from work, and now she wore one of his white pinpoint oxfords that matched the color of both her panties and her thick wool socks.

Eve pushed his overcoat off him and tried to let it fall to the floor, but he caught it behind his back and laid it on a chair by the door. She began removing his suit coat, but he fought her attempts to pull it down.

Finally, she removed her mouth from his. 'Is something wrong?'

'Tough day at work, babe. Can we talk?'

Surprised, she said, 'Yes. Of course.'

'Good,' Ethan said, and he headed upstairs to change while Eve hung up his coat for him in the hall closet.

Eve Pang was Korean American, a senior network systems engineer for Booz Allen Hamilton, a government contractor. Ross had met her six months earlier, after a presentation she gave at a training conference for government employees with TS security at her corporate offices in Tysons Corner, Virginia. He had signed up for the daylong class just to meet her. He knew she was one of the nation's top classified network administrators, and while most of the other NSC staffers in attendance couldn't wait to get out of the mind-numbingly boring training and back to D.C., Ross, on the other hand, was captivated – primarily by the classes on secure network infrastructure, and secondarily by the Asian girl with the nerdy glasses who administered a portion of the course. She was attractive, but more important, it was obvious to Ethan she possessed incredible knowledge about the architecture of the U.S. intelligence community's most classified systems, and he wanted some of that knowledge.

Eve had worked on the security infrastructure of JWICS since she received her doctorate at MIT at the age of twenty-five. Now, at thirty-two, she was a highly paid Booz Allen systems engineer based at Fort Meade, but she worked all around the D.C. area on security protocols for the U.S. intelligence community's VPNs, or virtual private networks, remote-access systems that allowed government employees to log on to some of the intelligence community's most highly classified databases from outside of the confined networks.

Ethan Ross asked her out the day he met her, and she agreed with wide eyes and a thumping heart. She was flabbergasted by his advances – she'd dated only other computer geeks, and most of them had been Korean, but he was an attractive, charming and well-groomed White House staffer, who seemed as interesting as he was intelligent.

Ethan knew he was using her, but he wasn't bothered by things like that, because he'd never possessed much in the way of a conscience when it came to relationships.

Their early dates involved a lot of talk about work. Eve had lived computer science for her entire life, she essentially *had* no other hobbies apart from her work, so networks and code were the easiest topics for her to talk about. And since her new and inquisitive boyfriend possessed top-secret clearance, she did so freely. Sure, there were aspects of her job she knew she shouldn't and couldn't discuss, even with her boyfriend, but little things slipped out here and there, especially after a glass of wine, and she saw no great harm in that.

They were on the same side, after all.

Ethan never even gave so much as a hint to Eve that he was leaking classified information to the International Transparency Project. And he passed his computer security infrastructure questions off as both his own personal interest in computer science and a desire to ensure the NSC was safe from both outside hacks and inside breaches.

Ethan liked to war-game scenarios with Eve while they ate dinner or sat in front of the fireplace in her condo. She knew he was extremely intelligent, just like she was, and he possessed orders of magnitude more curiosity about her job than she did about his.

It didn't hurt that he plied her with wine while they talked, and her lips loosened by the glass. But she actually found the war-gaming fun and intellectually challenging. Eve fielded his questions, proud that her genius boyfriend took a real intellectual interest in her work. She joked with him on more than one occasion that even though she was an IT security professional, he was more obsessed with security than she was.

One night they sat on the sofa discussing vulnerabilities to the system, after a second bottle of claret lay empty on its side on the coffee table and a third was newly opened. Between sips from her glass, Eve explained that the weakest aspect of network security was at the default domain administrator level. The default domain administrator was the first account created on a network, and it had sweeping privileges. IT professionals often disable the DDA after setting up other users with lesser authority, but, Eve explained, in the case of Intelink-TS, the CIA's top-secret network, the DDA was up and running, though the password for it was known only by a few highly placed administrators, all of whom were thoroughly vetted.

Eve claimed that anyone who logged on as the DDA had virtual godlike access to all aspects of the Intelink-TS; it was virtually the keys to the kingdom. An administrator with bad intent could dig around in secret corners of the system, and even exfiltrate data and erase the history of the transaction.

Ethan's interest was piqued, but he needed more

information. 'Wow. Those people given that logon must be very reliable.'

Eve smiled and winked with an eye already half-mast from drink. 'I have it.'

'You *don't*.'

Her smile widened. 'I *do*.'

'And with it you can go anywhere and no one would know?'

'If I wanted to. I never have. Why should I?'

Ethan still found this all hard to believe. 'There is an audit trail for everything we do. Madeline Crossman, the security compliance officer in my department, is always checking on us via audits to make sure we don't try to pull unauthorized access.'

Eve replied, 'There is no audit for the DDA that I can't get around, which means, when I'm logged on as the DDA, there is no audit for me.' She giggled. 'Ethan, at my level, I *am* the audit.'

'So your password makes you untouchable?'

'Not exactly untouchable. I work with the virtual private networks that access Intelink-TS via the JWICS, and this requires two-factor authentication.'

She walked over to her purse and pulled out two small identical fobs the size of key chains with LCD screens on them. On the screens were a half-dozen numbers. One of the devices had a red tag on it that said *Pang* and the other said *Pang-DDA*.

'I use these. I can access the CIA's network via my laptop by putting in my logon and then adding the number on the screen, which changes every thirty seconds. But if I wanted to log on as the DDA, I would do the same thing and use this fob. These fobs and the numbers on them track back to me.'

Before Ethan's eyes, the six numbers on each device changed to six new numbers.

Ethan looked at the fobs closely. 'But you are saying someone who isn't logging in remotely, like someone inside CIA or somewhere with direct access to the network, wouldn't need these things.'

'Exactly right. Someone on the network itself only needs the DDA logon, and then they can do whatever the hell they want. I've written papers about it, it's a real vulnerability, but no one listens.' She laughed, dropped the fobs back in her purse, and reached for her wineglass. 'The best IT people in the business aren't working for the government, and we contractors are given a lot of access power, but not a lot of decision-making authority.'

Ethan mumbled to himself. 'Incredible. You're almost untouchable.'

She reached out, took Ethan's hand, and slipped it under her button-down oxford shirt. She placed his hand on her small breast. 'I am touchable. See? But with my password and my fob, you are the only one who can touch me.' She laughed at her joke, and in her laugh Ethan could tell just how inebriated she was.

He decided to push his luck. 'Don't you ever worry you'll forget your password?'

She shook her head. 'My password? No, because I use it every day. But I only use the DDA credentials every few months, so I have it written down.'

'What? That's not smart, Eve. Even *I* know that.'

She kissed him. 'Don't worry. I'll show you.'

She left the room for a moment, and Ethan sat there, gobsmacked. *No one* in IT handed over their password, even drunk lonely girls trying to impress their boyfriends.

He scrambled to refill her wineglass.

When she returned she opened a single sheet of paper. He tried not to snatch it out of her hands, because he knew its importance to his mission.

But when he saw it, he realized he didn't have the keys to the kingdom he thought he did. It was a page full of handwritten characters that looked like Asian script of some sort.

'It's in Korean?' Ethan said. 'That's not exactly secure, babe.'

'It's not Korean. It's Idu. A thousand-year-old script that was used in Korea. Not many people can write it. But the best part is, it looks like traditional Chinese. Like Kai-shu, which was around at the same time. If someone tries to translate the words and numbers here, they will get it wrong, because they will think it is traditional Chinese. Idu is forgotten.'

Ethan was impressed, and he told his girlfriend so. She beamed, she swooned, and ten minutes later, she passed out.

Ethan photographed the page of chicken scratches with his phone.

While Eve slept, Ethan spent the rest of the night congratulating himself on his incredible intellect and social engineering skills, and wondering how the hell he was going to translate characters from Idu.

Ethan found a translator after some Internet searching, a professor of ancient East Asian languages at the University of Chicago. The professor did it for free; it took him just minutes to e-mail back a fourteen-character series of letters and numbers. Ethan then used the DDA access credentials to log in on a JWICS terminal in the NSC's secure administration wing. He found the docs on the SCI code-word-access flotilla operation. He didn't read every page of every document himself; that would have taken hours, and he had only minutes.

He pilfered the files using the techniques Eve had outlined to him over dinner, and sent the files to Harlan Banfield. Banfield looked them over, then told him they would sit on them until they knew the breach had gone undetected, perhaps as long as six months. Ethan was impatient, he was certain he'd executed the breach perfectly, but Banfield insisted the ITP would nevertheless use its own tried-and-true security protocols.

And then nothing. For four months he'd seen nothing in the news on the flotilla raid. He'd held off pilfering more documents from JWICS because he wanted to see how the *Guardian* exploited this first batch, but the fact that Banfield and his group hadn't even sent the files on to the media infuriated him.

And now this. The FBI running around the NSC, claiming a data breach, and alleging the breach got some ex–Israeli commando and his family killed.

Something went wrong with his exfiltration of the data. He'd managed to obfuscate his involvement; he'd logged in as a DDA, so they couldn't have known it was him, after all, but somehow they had still noticed the transfer into the file-sharing location.

*

Tonight Ethan and Eve sat at his house, not hers, but they drank claret and talked about network intrusions, much like that evening four months ago. Eve knew all about the NSC breach; even though it didn't involve her or one of her virtual private networks, she would have been briefed on it first thing this morning.

Ethan talked about the meeting with the FBI man the day before and the possibility there was some sort of a mole at NSC, but this was all just to set up his line of inquiry, because he desperately wanted to know what went wrong. He didn't think for a second he had made a mistake himself. No, he was certain Eve Pang had screwed up in her explanation of the DDA logon's omniscience over the network. This angered him, but he wouldn't let it show.

Between sips of wine and while gently stroking Eve's hair as they sat facing each other on his couch, he asked, 'What do you think happened?'

'I know exactly what happened.'

This surprised Ross. 'You do?'

'Yes. The government IT hacks are fools. They let the intrusion happen, but then they got lucky. It was nothing more than that.'

Ethan forced himself to take a sip of his wine. His fingers wanted to crush the glass in his hand, but he forced an air of calm. 'How did they get lucky?'

Eve smiled. 'A spot audit for anomalous behavior was done on the network. This happens less than five per cent of the time. Even then, the audit records were never reviewed. They were just stored automatically on the server.

It picked up the files being moved to the file-sharing server in the National Security Council office.'

'I see,' said Ethan. 'Can they tell if the files were downloaded or printed?'

'Most likely downloaded. The printers themselves would have recorded the job if they were used. I assume even the government IT security people are competent enough to check that out.'

She added, 'Someone should have begun investigating this four months ago. Instead, it wasn't till the thing happened in India when the system administrators at Langley were asked to review the files on Intelink-TS to make sure they were secure.' Now she laughed out loud. 'They must have pulled up the logs and shouted "Oh, shit" when they saw they were accessed and exfiltrated.' Then she added, almost as an aside, 'They'll never find out who did it.'

'Why not?'

'Do you remember that night when I told you about domain administrator access?'

Ethan looked off into space for a long moment. 'Vaguely.'

'I'd bet anything someone logged on as a DDA to do it. I can't prove it. That's the problem with DDA credentials, but that's what I think happened. They'll never know who broke in that way, so they might as well give up looking.'

'How about that,' Ethan said. He wanted to put his hand through the wall.

Just as he'd expected, he'd done everything exactly right. It had only been a stroke of very bad luck.

His intrusion likely never would have been noticed if not for the completely coincidental death of the Israeli in India.

Eve tried to make another move on Ethan, but he wasn't in the mood. She went to bed early, and he sat in his living room with a glass of wine in his hand, staring at a movie on TV that he didn't give a damn about.

His entire focus now was on beating the polygraph. If he did that, he'd be fine. He told himself there wasn't a single FBI agent in the world who could outsmart him. The investigation would fizzle out, or else that bitch Beth Morris at the Western Hemisphere desk would be suspected of the breach.

The only thing left for him to do was ace the box.

I2

Dominic Caruso stood at his stove, stirring diced tomatoes into a saucepan full of fat shrimp, olive oil and herbs. The smell of garlic and oregano was prevalent, and the crushed red pepper made his eyes water. The heat from the stove created a thin sheen of sweat on his forehead, which he blotted away with the towel on his shoulder. When his forehead was dry again he left the towel on his shoulder, keeping it at the ready. This was shrimp *Fra Diavolo*, after all. He'd really start sweating only when he ate it.

Dom had always loved to cook; when he was young, it brought him closer to his mom and grandmother, and now it brought him back to his childhood, and with that came some happy thoughts. And that was the plan this evening. He wasn't cooking because he was hungry. Tonight he thought it might be a good idea to do something productive to occupy his mind for a couple of hours. So he'd climbed off the couch, ignoring his bruised ribs and his slight headache while he struggled to get his coat on, and then he ventured out for groceries.

Fixing a real dinner wasn't much, but it beat ordering a pizza, and it beat sitting in his dark condo and brooding.

Dom turned down the heat on the saucepan and stepped away for a moment to open a bottle of Trebbiano he'd found tucked in the back of his refrigerator. He swigged right out of the bottle while he went back to the stove, then splashed a little into the *Fra Diavolo* and ducked the steam that roared up out of the bubbling dish.

While he cooked, his mind drifted, thinking of the last meal he'd prepared here in his place. It had been the evening before his flight to India and, unlike tonight, he had not been alone, because Dom did not, as a rule, cook for one.

Her name was Abbie; she was a bartender at an upscale saloon in Georgetown. He'd been a regular at her bar, though he was quiet and preferred sitting in the dark to interacting with her other regulars. One night he stayed till closing and the two of them then went to a local late-night watering hole for a nightcap. They sat talking for an hour over beers.

He'd told her he was in corporate security, and other than 'cool,' she'd made no comment about his job again.

They'd made love at her place first, but after a couple more nights of meeting for drinks before the inevitable late-night hookup, Dom asked her over to his condo for a home-cooked meal. He prepared an authentic veal-and-ricotta meatball dish and served it by candlelight with one of his favorite Chianti Classicos. She seemed pleasantly surprised he could actually cook, but she hadn't come over for the veal, so soon after their plates were stacked in the sink and the bottle of Chianti was empty on the coffee table, Dom and Abbie disappeared into his dark bedroom and the meal was all but forgotten.

Dom enjoyed that last night before India, but he'd barely thought of Abbie at all during his trip, and she hadn't e-mailed or called once while he was gone.

So that was that. Dom decided he'd have to avoid her bar for a while, so they could both move on.

Dom plated his dinner and headed into the living room, grabbing the Trebbiano along the way. In stark contrast to the candlelit dinner with Abbie, tonight he sat alone on his couch with his feet up on the coffee table; the TV was tuned to a poker tournament, but he wasn't paying attention to it. He sipped his wine and ate his shrimp and sulked. He was proud of tonight's dinner, it had the right balance of flavors: the buttery sweetness of the shrimp, the heat of the red pepper, and the zing of the citrus. But he was in a dark mood, partly because he didn't have a woman here to eat it with him and fawn over it, before he could take her to his bed.

Dom was Italian, after all. He was well aware of the seductive power of food.

His mind drifted off the food, off the women, and he thought of the Yacobys and the meals they'd shared, and he thought of the kids, and he thought about the American son of a bitch who sold them out to the terrorists as if their lives meant nothing.

This train of thought brought him yet again to his own responsibility in their deaths. Try as he might to remain objective about his actions, he continued to second-guess himself for being unable to save them.

Dom wrestled with the images in his mind throughout dinner. When his plate and his bottle were both empty, he considered checking his refrigerator again to see if there was another cold bottle of Trebbiano tucked in there somewhere. He thought he might try to watch TV and drain another bottle before bed.

No. He couldn't sit here all night drinking alone and thinking dangerous thoughts.

He looked at his watch. 10.30 p.m.

He came up with a new plan for the evening, and instantly his mind drifted away from the Yacobys. He knew it was temporary, just like cooking the *Fra Diavolo* for one had been.

But it beat sitting here brooding.

'Don't do it, Dom.'

He didn't know why he talked to himself like that. He knew he was going to do it. His body ignored his inner voice. He stood, went into his bedroom and changed into a pair of jeans and a brown leather jacket. Slipping his left arm in the sleeve felt like someone was twisting one of his ribs with a pair of pliers, but he fought through the pain and got it done.

Before walking out his front door he took five minutes to straighten his place, because even though he wasn't sure where he was going, and he had no idea who he would meet there, he had no intentions of returning alone.

By 11 p.m. Caruso sat on a bar stool at a 14th Street gastropub called The Pig. He'd been here a dozen times in the past, each time looking for food, drink, and perhaps something more. As he sipped his beer he scanned the dark and lively establishment, his eyes tracking over dozens of tables, each one with a cluster of patrons enjoying themselves.

And Dom identified several potential targets.

This always felt to Dom a little like the fixed-position

surveillance ops he did with The Campus. Except he wasn't tailing terrorists or Russian mobsters or keeping an eye out for enemy countersurveillance.

No, he was here to pick up a girl.

Dom's phone contact list was crammed with other hookup opportunities, but they all would entail a certain amount of familiar conversation that would involve, inevitably, a high level of compassion and concern. Dom was rough and ragged, mentally and physically, and all of his female friends, even the most peripheral, would attempt to mother him, trying to find out what on earth was wrong.

Dom wasn't looking to be mothered tonight.

He didn't notice the woman just down the bar on his first examination of the room, but that wasn't because she was unattractive. On the contrary, she was a striking brunette, his age to a few years older, with almond eyes and full lips. He hadn't noticed her at first because she was surrounded by three young and very large men. One sat on either side of her at the bar, and the third stood close behind her. One of the men laughed loudly and put his arm around her, while the other two drank whiskey out of rocks glasses and glanced around the room with sly grins on their faces.

Dom's eyes moved on. His radar scanned for targets of opportunity, after all, and this particular potential target was lost in the signal interference of testosterone.

He finished his beer and ordered another. A redhead sitting with a friend at a two-top near the back wall caught his eye, and he hers. Dom scanned for a wedding ring on her ring finger like a seasoned pro, and saw her finger was unadorned, but then he noticed the woman's dramatic mannerisms in her conversation with her friend, and her ragged fingernails were evident even from halfway across the room. He pegged her as more frazzled and emotional than he was prepared to deal with at the moment, and he resumed his scrutiny of the room.

A tall athletic blonde in a business suit glanced his way through a large group of both male and female coworkers, but her dress and the gang around her told him she worked on the Hill. Dom knew a few congressional staff members. He had nothing against them personally, but he wasn't really in the mood to listen to either inane party politics or cynical gossip from the congressional cloakroom, so he moved on, continuing his slow study of eligible women in the pub.

Dom sighed inwardly while he searched. The older he got, and the better he became at reading people, the tougher it was to find someone he was compatible with. He wondered whether or not he really wanted to ever get married, since he found it so damn hard to connect with someone mentally even for a single night.

After another long pull off his beer, Dom recognized the real impediment to a connection was his own frame of mind. India had fucked him up, even for something as callous and momentary as sleeping around.

C'mon, D. Soldier on.

He ordered his third drink of the evening, and when it arrived he thought about making his way toward a table of three good-looking college-aged women in the middle of the dining room, but his plan was derailed when he heard the beautiful brunette just down the bar from him raise her voice in annoyance at one of the three big men surrounding her.

'I said no!'

Dom's eyebrows rose. He'd all but discounted the woman during his initial scan because she was in a group of men, but now he tuned his ears into the conversation between the brunette and the young men, and he looked them all over more closely.

The three dudes looked to Dom to be about seven hundred and fifty pounds' worth of trouble. Their muscles strained in tight T-shirts emblazoned with eagles and skulls and wolves and other nonsense, tattoos ringed their forearms, and their leather coats lay haphazardly on three chairs at a table nearby. He scrutinized their eyes and postures and confirmed all three were either drunk or at least well on their way.

Dom sized up the situation quickly. The beautiful woman didn't know these guys; she was several years older and much better dressed than they, and she looked impossibly small and painfully uncomfortable as they towered over her.

Dom used his practised powers of observation to determine the woman had arrived alone; she was on business here in D.C., perhaps, maybe staying at one of the big four-star chain hotels in the neighborhood. She'd dropped in for a late dinner and a glass of wine, and then had apparently fallen prey to a crew of steroid-addled horny jackasses.

This is not your night, honey.

Dom focused on the barrel-chested blond-haired man with a goatee who seemed to be doing the talking. He was the one incurring the wrath of the small brunette. He said something to her, Dom wasn't able to pick it up, but she answered him with a roll of her eyes and a shake of her head.

Now the man said, 'You don't got to be a bitch about it.'

'I'm not being a bitch. I was trying to be nice, but you weren't listening.'

'I sent you over a drink. The least you can do is be friendly and join us at our table.'

'I'm sorry, I shouldn't have accepted it. I've got an early flight tomorrow and –'

'One more drink! What's it gonna hurt?' he shouted, and he loomed over her ominously.

No one else at the bar had taken any interest in the conversation except for a well-dressed gentleman at the far end, who looked on with idle curiosity. The bartenders were out of earshot, laughing it up with some other patrons.

The two friends of the blond with the goatee kept their mouths shut as he and the woman argued. Dom gave this a moment's consideration and determined any real friends would have hustled their buddy away from this confrontation and told him he was acting like a jerk, so the fact that these two were holding their tongues indicated to Caruso the blond was the alpha of the trio.

The brunette tried to ignore the young tough. She flipped her bill over, then pulled out her wallet and put a couple of twenties on the bar. She attempted to push her bar stool back to stand up, but the man behind her didn't move. The blond with the goatee put his hand on her back, keeping her right where she was.

He said, 'Where you goin'? You gotta do a shot.'

Dom swigged the last of his beer, threw his own cash on the bar, and then stepped forward into the fray.

13

Dom placed his hand gently on the bearded blond's chest, and leaned in close as if to shout over the music and the din of the crowd.

He kept a faint smile on his face as he said, 'Hey, buddy. You asked. She answered. Let this one go. Don't sweat it, you'll catch the next one.'

Dom's demeanor was unsettling, confusing to the bigger, younger man. Was this stranger threatening him? With a smile on his face?

Who the fuck was this guy?

'Who the fuck are you?'

Dom thought he detected Michigan in the man's voice.

'Nobody. How 'bout you let me buy you a whiskey? What are you drinking? Evan Williams? Big spender.' Dom held his hand up for the bartender and flashed a quick look at the brunette. He was hoping she'd understand that his look meant 'Go. Now.'

But she just stood there.

One of the other big men grabbed Dom by the shoulder and spun him around. Dom found himself looking straight ahead into the muscular chest of the young man. His eyes tracked up and he smiled. 'Take it easy. I was just telling your buddy that I'm picking up this round.'

The woman backed away from the bar now, and she put her purse on her shoulder, but she did not walk to the door. She just stared at the dark-haired man who'd come to her rescue, unsure what to say or do.

The blond man with the goatee spun Dom back around to him, using Dom's shoulder again as if it were a door handle and causing his bruised ribs to spasm in pain. 'Nobody was talking to you, asshole. Stay out of this.'

Dom sighed a little. He knew he should disengage. These people meant nothing. This wasn't some back alley in a Third World hellhole. This woman wasn't in real danger; if she started yelling, surely some other man would eventually get off his ass and come over to defend her honor.

But Dom couldn't help himself. He stood his ground.

The blond said, 'Seriously, bro? You wanna piece of me?'

Dom knew the question was asked as a provocation, but he considered it carefully. *Do I want a piece of you?* he asked himself.

He had to be honest. *Yeah.* A piece of this jackass was exactly what he wanted. It wasn't mature or professional, but Dom was in that kind of mood.

As much as he knew he could get himself out of this without resorting to violence, he did not disengage.

The blond man smiled, showing teeth stained with chewing tobacco. To Dom he looked like a guy who realized he wasn't getting laid tonight, but was just as happy, if not happier, to discover he was going to at least get to punch a man in the face.

A nice conciliation prize for a guy like him.

Dom added, 'She and I are walking out the front door. You boys *should* stay right here.'

The blond said, 'You walk out that door with her and I'm going to follow you out and break your pencil neck.'

Dom didn't think he had a pencil neck, but he didn't dispute the point. Instead, he just turned, took the brunette by the arm, and said, 'Let's go.'

As he walked by the two big men who'd been standing close behind him, one of them jolted at him suddenly, his fist up and high like he was about to pound Dominic in the jaw. He threw the fist, but stopped it an inch from Dom's face.

Dom didn't even flinch. He knew this guy wouldn't sucker-punch him because the alpha of the group had already claimed him as his prize. He just gave the man a little smile and kept walking.

The big man with his fist held in the air was taken aback. He was used to smaller men cowering under his threats. He recovered quickly, and turned to bluster. Gleefully he said, 'Shane's gonna kick your ass. It's gonna be a one-hit fight, bitch.'

Dom just continued toward the door with the girl in tow, and the three big men rushed to grab their coats.

As Dom walked past the end of the bar he noticed the distinguished gentleman in the nice suit sitting alone. He had turned away, he stared down into his Manhattan, though Dom was certain the man had seen and heard everything.

From behind him he heard the big man call out again. 'A one-hit fight!'

Moments later, Caruso, the girl and the three tattooed men in leather jackets were standing on the dark sidewalk in front of The Pig. A few couples passed them by, uninterested in or unaware of the impending trouble. The blond with the goatee squared off in front of Caruso, his nostrils pulsating as the adrenaline rush of the moment sped up his breathing.

The girl said exactly what Dom expected her to say: 'Please. Don't do this for me.'

Caruso did not reply, he only smiled at her a little. It wasn't about the girl anymore. He faced the big man, while the other two stood behind their leader.

'One-hit fight!' The guy said it again. Dom wondered if he ever said anything else.

'Shut up, Doyle! You too, Joey. This asshole's all mine,' replied the blond with the goatee.

Dom maintained a relaxed exterior. On the inside he was already chastising himself for not de-escalating this situation. He forced himself to make one more half-hearted attempt. 'So, Shane, any chance you want to just call it a night?'

'I'm gonna beat the fuck out of you.'

Dom did not reply. He knew Arik Yacoby would not have been proud of him at all, and this only made him madder at himself.

Shane was going to suffer for Dom's anger.

Shane ambled forward nonchalantly, and Dom saw that he was trying to close the distance he needed to take him down with a single punch. Dom let him close, kept his hands down to his sides and his shoulders relaxed. Even when the big blond adjusted his stance, stepping one foot out and the other back, getting himself ready to throw a jab, Dom continued to portray the air of one oblivious to what was about to happen.

Dom wasn't oblivious, however. He was reading all the tells. Shane was clearly a trained boxer, right-handed, going for a headshot, and his plan was to drop his opponent, no doubt with one shot to the jaw to impress his buddies.

Dom took a half calming breath, his eyes unfixed on anything, but all his senses primed for the attack to come.

Doyle shouted once again. 'A one-hit fight!'

Shane's right hand was down by his side, but Dom noted the instant it morphed into a massive, square fist. When the fist fired up at Dom's face he was prepared to bob away from it, but instead he used his speed to bring his left elbow up to the side of his head as he swiveled his torso. The punch glanced off the high elbow and was deflected by Dom's spin, knocking Shane's arm across his own body and causing him to lose his balance since he'd thrown all his weight behind the jab.

Dom continued his spin by stepping across his body with his left leg, picking up speed as he rotated in place, whipping his own right arm out away from his body and launching it in a three-hundred-and-sixty-degree arc, a blur of knuckles and leather jacket that fanned through the night air.

Dominic's spinning back fist struck perfectly against the big bearded man's jaw, the wet splat of bone on bone with flesh caught between echoed off the front windows of the pub. Shane's head jacked to the left and his legs gave out, as if a switch had been thrown and all muscles holding him upright had just been shut down for the evening.

Shane crumpled to the sidewalk awkwardly as his two big friends stood stupefied.

Dom looked up at Doyle. 'Whaddaya know? You were right.'

As Dom expected, Doyle was the next to attack. He telegraphed his movements as he charged. He was a lefty, he planned a hook as soon as he got in striking distance, but Dom stepped diagonally into the hook, parried it with his forearm, and then backed up into Doyle's advance. Dom drove his head back into Doyle's face, then took his left arm and used it to throw the big man over his back, slamming him down on the sidewalk with incredible force.

The air bellowed from Doyle's lungs with the impact, and he gasped like a fish on a dock, desperate to fill his lungs back.

The third big man, Joey, hadn't said much of anything. He seemed to be in some shock that his two friends were lying on their backs in front of him, but he kept his focus on the man who had put them there.

He raised his hands into fists and moved closer.

Dom said, 'You don't have to do this, Joey. Shane's your boss, isn't he?'

'Yeah.'

'Construction?'

'Large-appliance delivery.'

'Large-appliance delivery,' Dom repeated, as if this should have been obvious. Then, 'He's going to be off work for a couple of weeks. Doyle, too. He'll be pissed you didn't stand up for him after he and Doyle went down, but at least this way you can generate some income for him while he's out.'

Joey seemed to consider this; he actually weighed the pros and cons. Finally he gave a half-shrug. 'He won't see it like that. He's not that great a businessman.'

'Then find a new boss,' Dom said.

'Tough economy.'

Dom regarded the statement. 'True. I guess you better just let me pound the shit out of you.'

Before he got the last words out, Joey charged forward. Dom was surprised by the man's sudden speed and intensity, and the attacker managed to get inside of Dom's punch and wrap his arms around Dom's arms, pinning them high over his head.

Dom's bruised ribs cried in agony and the muscles around them seized, his back spasmed from his shoulder blades to his tailbone.

The big man lifted him in the air with ease. Dom had no doubt he was one hell of a large-appliance deliveryman.

As Dom felt himself go inverted behind Joey's head he pushed out of the hold, then kicked harder, away through the air behind his attacker. He landed on his feet, unsteady and in pain, but perfectly positioned when Joey turned to find the man he had just tossed like a rag doll an instant before now facing him in a fighting stance.

Dom punched the man hard in the nose. His head snapped back but quickly returned to neutral. His nose was red, but he showed no sign of any physical deficit from taking a hard jab to the snot box.

Joey smiled at Dom as if to say, 'That's all you've got?'

Dom answered the unasked question by firing out another jab, but this time he extended his fingers, turning his fist into a spear, and he gouged into the big man's solar plexus, then followed with a spear from his left hand into Joey's throat, just enough to put him on his back, rolling in the street in a coughing fit, five feet away from Shane, who was still out cold, and Doyle, who had rolled onto his hands and knees but was still gasping in search of air to replenish his empty lungs.

Dom stood in the middle and regarded his handiwork. He knew Arik wouldn't have been proud of his student's inability to move away from an avoidable threat. But Arik couldn't have faulted his fighting skills. He'd taught Dom a lot in a month of daily grappling and training.

And Dom had put it to use.

After a moment, however, he remembered this altercation had involved a woman. He looked around for her, and found her standing by the curb. This wasn't his first bar fight over a female. He knew the brunette would either be repulsed by the fight, and think as little of Dom as she did of the men he was trying to protect her from. In that case she would walk away quickly, now that it was over. Or else she would be drawn to him. She would latch on, and she wouldn't be going anywhere without her brave defender.

He looked up the sidewalk to see which one this girl was going to be. He saw her standing there in the night, her arms crossed tightly over her body, shielding herself from the fight in front of her.

She said, 'That was honorable, what you did. Trying to talk the one guy out of it.'

'He didn't want it any more than I did. He was just obligated. Boys' rules.'

She nodded. Said, 'Thank you.'

'Don't mention it.'

'I really thought chivalry was dead.'

'It's in intensive care. Occasional signs of life.'

She smiled, batted her eyes. He saw what was going on behind the eyes. She was sizing up this situation. Bar fights and strangers coming to her aid weren't the sort of thing that happened to her.

'I'm Monica.'

'Dominic.'

They shook hands. Dom turned to head back to his place, doing his best to hide the fact his ribs and back were killing him, but she didn't let him get twenty-five feet before she caught up to him.

'I hate to sound trite, but would you let me buy you a drink? Seems the least I could do.'

Dom jerked his head toward The Pig. The windows were full of patrons and employees staring at the three big men on the sidewalk and the smaller man who'd put them there. 'I'm going to go out on a limb and say I'm not welcome back in there tonight.'

'We can go to the bar at my hotel. I'm at the Loews Madison. It's right around the corner.'

Dom sighed a little, but he didn't let it show. His designs on mindless sex tonight had fallen by the wayside the moment the bear-hug flip aggravated the pain in his badly bruised ribs. As beautiful as the woman in front of him was, at the moment he felt more passionate about going home for a short-term relationship with a bag of ice.

'I'll walk you back to your hotel,' he said. 'Just in case those guys manage to put themselves back together and hit the streets looking for mischief. But then I'm going to call it a night.'

Monica seemed a little crestfallen; she just nodded without replying. Dom figured it upped his cachet with her even more. Once she got over the embarrassment of rejection, she would take his rebuff as chivalry.

14

The Economy Inn in Richmond, Virginia, was a locally owned and operated establishment, although it did its best to trick travelers passing under its sign on Interstate 64 into thinking it was part of a well-known and similarly named national two-star chain. Anyone fooled into stopping for the night, thinking they would find some standard of at least minimal quality, would be disappointed as soon as they were buzzed in to the tiny lobby. The bait-and-switch sign over the interstate had clearly been the main marketing focus of the owners, because the property itself was an unapologetic dump. Cheap furniture, old and threadbare carpeting, and a sour smell greeted anyone entering the three-storey motor-court-style hotel's common area, and the rooms themselves were no better.

The inn was less than fifteen per cent occupied, but two middle-aged men sat together on a lumpy bed in room 309, anxiously smoking cigarettes and looking at their mobile phones. Both men were big; one was an ex–tight end at Virginia Tech, though that had been twenty-two years earlier, and since then his job at an auto parts retailer required him lifting nothing heavier than the occasional car battery. And the other man was just fat. He'd never done much of anything sports-related. Just a young nerd who'd morphed quite naturally and comfortably into a middle-aged sloth.

The tight end illuminated the screen on his phone for the twentieth time in the past thirty minutes. 'Ten fifty-eight. Where the hell is this mother –'

A soft knock at the door caused both men to sit bolt upright. The fat nerd stood and took a step back away from it, and the tight end stood and looked through the peephole in the door. He nodded to his cohort, then slowly opened it.

A small, young-looking man stood in the dim of the third-floor landing. He was alone; his dark eyes seemed wide and terrified as he looked up to the man filling the doorway. 'Uh . . . You are Mr White?' His accent was French.

Behind the tight end in the doorway, the fat man by the bathroom door said, 'That's me. You are Mr Black?'

The small man on the landing looked back and forth quickly between the two men. He seemed like he might turn around and run away. Instead he said, 'I . . . I do not understand, Mr White. We had an agreement. You were to be alone.'

The tight end grabbed him by the collar and led – not quite pulled – him inside the room. He kicked the door shut behind him.

Mr White said, 'Relax. I brought a friend just in case you brought anyone with you or tried anything funny. He's going to search you for a wire.'

The tight end had the young man against the wall a second later, and he pulled off the man's backpack and tossed it on the bed, then felt under his jacket, raking his hands all over.

The young foreign man said, 'A . . . wire? What does

this mean?' His voice cracked as he spoke. He looked and acted petrified, and this relaxed the two Americans considerably.

'Just calm down,' White said. 'You understand my predicament here. I have to make certain you aren't a Fed.'

'But you *know* me. We have been communicating for over a year.'

'And you know *me*, Black. I'm taking a big fucking risk meeting you like this. I don't know this isn't some kind of a sting. My buddy is going to make sure you're legit, and then we can get down to business.'

The tight end lifted the man's shirt and realized the foreigner couldn't be one hundred and twenty pounds soaking wet. He turned around to face White. 'He's clean.'

'C'mon, man. You forgot to check his bag.'

'Oh, right.' He opened the backpack, pulled out a thin Toshiba computer, a mobile phone, and some power cables. He turned the bag upside down and shook it over the bed, but nothing else came out.

'Good,' said White. 'Have a seat.'

The foreign man sat down at the little chair by the desk and White sat back on the bed. They were less than five feet apart in the tiny room.

The tight end stood by the door, looking down on both of them.

Mr Black put his hands on his knees as if to steady himself or to fight off a wave of nausea.

'You okay?' asked White.

'Would it be okay if your friend waited outside while we conduct business? I am sorry, but I am a little nervous about this.'

White just smiled, lit another cigarette, and nodded to his friend. 'Eddie, go out and have a smoke.' He looked at the small foreign man in front of him. 'I'll shout if I need something.'

Eddie said, 'I'll be right outside.' The big tight end left through the door, pulling his cigarettes and lighter off the table as he exited.

Mr White's name was not White, it was Phillip McKell. He was a systems infrastructure analyst for L-3 Communications Corp., a government contractor that worked, like Booz Allen Hamilton, on the U.S. government's classified intelligence networks. He was an expert on JWICS infrastructure, and he held a top-secret security clearance. He'd met Black, in the virtual world anyway, in an online technology forum a year earlier. The relationship started with a few comments under each other's postings, but soon McKell realized the two shared many interests. At first the man he came to know as Black claimed to be a university student interested in all things related to America and computer science, but over time Black revealed during private encrypted chats to McKell that he was, in fact, a French national and, most interestingly to McKell, he was a member of Anonymous, the largest and most infamous worldwide hacktivist group.

McKell was disbelieving at first, but when Black told him, again privately, about an upcoming Anonymous computer denial-of-service attack on the websites of the British government, and then the attack actually happened, McKell realized he was in communication with the real deal: an actual Anonymous hacktivist.

McKell knew he shouldn't have continued the online relationship. He was already violating company regulations by having an online identity and communicating with others on technical forums; if L-3 found out he'd engaged in private chats with an Anonymous member, he'd be fired on the spot and stripped of his security clearance. But McKell saw in Black a potential payday. There was a reward for information leading to the arrest of members of Black's organization, and McKell knew people collecting the reward could remain nameless. This was an attempt to protect traitors to the Anonymous organization, but McKell thought he might be able to collect a reward for turning Black in to the authorities, so he remained in contact with the Frenchman. Early on he realized he had nothing tangible whatsoever on the man, and attempted to cultivate more of a friendship in the hopes of learning real information about his identity. That, he felt certain, would earn him a big payoff.

Unfortunately for Phillip McKell, however, his priorities changed when he lost his job at L-3 and his coveted security clearance, after a surprise spot audit of his home computer turned up a record of his online forum postings. McKell argued that he did not share classified information about government networks, and all his correspondence online was kept to a general open-source level. But the investigators didn't see it like that. Sharing any details about his work was a violation of his security clearance and then, with the pulled clearance, came the loss of his job on secure networks.

He was actually told by the chief government investigator on his case, 'You'll never work in this town again.'

After he lost his job he quickly became desperate for money. He tried harder to get Black to reveal his identity so he could collect the reward; he even shared information about himself – it hardly mattered now that his clearance had been yanked. But when Black didn't budge, McKell decided he'd earn money by working the opposite end of this equation. The out-of-work American actually made a proposal to Black. He told him he could give Anonymous information about the inner workings of U.S. government networks. His thinking was that Black's organization might pay for technical help in designing its own direct denial-of-service attack on Washington, D.C.

Black promised he'd ask his higher-ups what they thought it was worth, and then, a few days later, he came back to McKell with a shocking counterproposal.

Anonymous wanted to conduct an actual infiltration of the JWICS top-secret Intelink-TS network, and wanted McKell to build the infiltration agent software to do it.

McKell laughed when he read Black's request, and he quickly typed back it was impossible, since the top-secret network was not accessible via standard Internet access unless one had access to a virtual private network. McKell wasn't on a VPN when he worked for L-3, and he sure as hell wasn't now. Someone would have to physically breach the network by sitting at a computer on the system to load the software. Anonymous hackers couldn't do it from some basement in France or Germany.

Black replied, quite simply, 'That's our problem, not yours. If you build the infiltration agent, we'll find someone to upload it. For your work you will be paid three million dollars.'

From that second on, McKell thought of nothing but all that money and how he could get his hands on it. He set up an account in Dubai and gave the account and routing numbers to Black, and within hours $100,000 had been deposited into the account as earnest money. Satisfied he was dealing with people who could and would fulfill their end of the bargain, Phillip McKell locked himself in his house and ate nothing but pizza delivery for nearly six weeks while he worked on his code for the infiltration agent.

McKell knew the U.S. intelligence infrastructure back to front, and through this knowledge he was aware of the physical drive locations where top-secret information was kept. The key to his infiltrator program was its 'crawler' function, which went into the location, then both copied and categorized the data before downloading it.

After his weeks of constant work and never-ending pizza, McKell's task was complete. He contacted Black, and the delivery date was confirmed.

And now Mr Black sat in front of him. But just as White's name was not White, Black's name was not Black.

His name was Mohammed Mehdi Mobasheri. He'd arrived from Tehran via Beirut the day before for this meeting, after having spent the past year cultivating McKell on the technology forums, while simultaneously confirming his position and access with L-3 Communications.

This was just the first step of Mohammed's plan, approved by the Supreme Leader, but the rest of the plan hinged on the obese, amoral, and obviously godless American seated on the dirty bed in front of him.

*

As soon as Eddie left the room to stand on the mezzanine and smoke, Mohammed said, 'Thank you. Now, do you have the infiltration drive?'

'Do you have the money ready to wire?'

He tapped his laptop. 'I can do it myself instantly as soon as I have the device.'

McKell nodded, crossed the little room, and reached behind a lamp on the table next to the TV. From behind it he pulled out a yellow thumb drive and held it up.

Mohammed looked at it closely. On it were several block letters in different colors. He cocked his head. 'I'm sorry. What does this mean? NASCAR?'

'Yeah, didn't figure you Frenchies would know about the National Association for Stock Car Auto Racing.'

'No.'

'It's just a decoy. Somebody sees this dumb-looking thumb drive, and they're not going to think it's got anything important on it.' McKell grinned at his own cleverness. 'Right? But the truth is, this isn't some little thumb drive. This is a one-point-two-terabyte HyperX drive. It's got the infiltrator loaded on it, and the downloaded files are stored right on board. You can get hundreds of thousands of files on a TB of drive space.'

'I see,' replied Mohammed.

McKell said, 'Okay. I've said it before and I'll say it again. Truth in advertising and full disclosure and all that shit. With this device you won't be able to do a damn thing. You'll need to be on the network. I'm talking physically. This drive needs to go into a port in a node that is already past the firewalls. Then the program will go out, round up and categorize the data, and exfiltrate it.'

'This is not a problem.'

McKell kept talking. He was a computer scientist; precision was paramount to him, even in a situation like this. 'Only other thing you could do, theoretically, I guess, would be to find someone with access to a VPN. That's a virtual private network. If they could get past all the extra security steps to log on to Intelink from outside the wire, then you could use this remotely.'

Mohammed took the drive in his hands and looked at it more closely. He ignored what McKell said, and asked a question of his own. 'You have been away from your position for several months. How do you know they have not changed things in a manner that will make this program obsolete?'

McKell shook his head with another grin. He was supremely sure of himself. 'That's the beauty of the government, kid. The contracts for L-3 and the other companies have been renewed, and they're a matter of public record. I know what systems are in place, because they are the only systems that can do the job. Sure, they'll change passwords and access codes and protocols for admittance, but they can't change the nuts and bolts of data retrieval.'

'And what about encryption? If you pull data off the servers, how can you be certain it is readable?'

'The data is not encrypted at rest, meaning where it is stored. If you have the key to get into the data, then the data is readable. It's as simple as that.'

'I see.' Mohammed opened his computer and slipped the drive into the port. 'I will evaluate your code. If it looks good, I'll authorize the wire transfer right here and now. We will conclude our business.'

'Sounds good to me.'

For the next thirty minutes McKell watched while Mr Black scanned through the directories. Mohammed's technical know-how was insufficient to create this himself. It would take someone like McKell and his years of experience building and maintaining the architecture. But the Iranian knew logical code when he saw it, and he searched down to the source code level for red flags that would indicate McKell had cut corners or left out necessary bits that would keep his program from actually working.

He asked a few questions of the American, who answered helpfully.

Finally, Mohammed ejected the device from his computer and said, 'I am satisfied. Thank you.'

'No, Black. Thank *you*. It was a hell of a lot of work, but now comes the fun part. Go ahead and wire the rest of the money.'

Mohammed closed his laptop, put everything in his backpack, and stood from the desk.

'The money,' McKell repeated.

Mohammed held his hands up in apology. 'There is no more money.'

The fat man on the bed seemed genuinely confused. 'What do you mean there's no money? There better be a fucking *lot* of money.'

'I do hope you spent the hundred thousand doing something enjoyable. There will be no further transfer.'

McKell's eyes went wide now. He did not sense danger, only a double cross. 'Look, Black. You seem to forget. I brought backup. Don't fuck with me or things are going to get ugly.' He turned to the door. 'Eddie!'

The door to the room opened quickly, and the big ex—tight end filled the doorway to the landing, but only for a moment. McKell saw the ragged hole in his friend's forehead just as his head drooped, and then Eddie fell face-first into the room. The back of his skull was all but gone. Brain matter and blood were matted in the hair around another ragged hole, but this one was ten times larger than the one in his forehead.

McKell looked at the body, then up in the doorway. Eddie had been held up by two men who now stood on the landing. They were much smaller than Eddie, but they were still much larger than Black, who now stood right next to Phillip McKell.

The two new men stepped into the room. While McKell sat on the bed, still disoriented by the quick turn of events, one of the two men reached under his black leather coat and pulled out a long pistol with a silencer on the end of it. He lifted it to McKell's forehead.

Mohammed did not know the actual names of his four Quds body men. There was no official reason for this; their identities were not above the security clearance of a major in the Revolutionary Guards. Instead, Mohammed had told the men when he met them in Tehran to give him the name of the city of their births, and he would call them by the city. It was easier for him to remember, he explained.

So Mohammed knew the four men only as Shiraz, Kashan, Ormand and Isfahan. They, in turn, knew him only as Mohammed, which was quite easy for them to remember, as two of the four Quds men were named Mohammed themselves.

Mohammed nodded to Shiraz and Kashan, then moved from his chair at the desk, and he sat next to the fat American on the bed. 'Phillip. Yes . . . I know who you are. Phillip McKell. Age forty-three, unmarried, unemployed. Now is the time for you to realize your situation. You will not be paid, but you can still choose to walk away from this with your life. I truly hope that is the choice you make.'

McKell's face had gone white.

In Farsi, Mohammed spoke to Shiraz. 'We wait a moment and he'll die on his own.' The men remained stone-faced, not laughing at the quip.

McKell heard the words, then coughed out a hoarse question. 'You're an Arab?'

Mohammed looked at the other two men. In English he said, 'Americans. No cultural understanding.' He turned back to McKell. 'I am from the Islamic Republic of Iran. Not an Arab. A Persian.'

'You . . . you are not with Anonymous?'

Mohammed shrugged, smiled in apology. 'Sometimes I am. When it is convenient to my work. They, and other groups like them, are . . . what is the term? Useful idiots.' Mohammed threw another big shoulder shrug, a show of contrition. 'Not unlike yourself.'

'What do you want?'

'Oh, actually, I have what I want. You already gave it to me. I only now need to know that it will work. We expect to attempt the breach in the next forty-eight hours. You will be kept right here. My friends will stay with you. If there is any problem with the breach . . . *any* problem, they will be ordered to punish you, and to take their time doing it. I hope it doesn't come to this.'

'Oh my God.'

'I will leave, and when I know if your software worked as described, I will contact my friends here and give them one of two orders. You live on, or you die so very slowly and unpleasantly.'

McKell's eyes clouded and his lips trembled.

'So you see, I am leaving now with the drive, and this is your last chance to tell me if you left anything out, put anything in, or did *anything* to it to render it ineffective.'

Now Phillip McKell began crying.

Mohammed looked on uncomfortably for nearly a minute.

Eventually McKell spoke, between sobs and gurgles of mucus in his throat. 'It's not a trap. I swear to God it will work!' He put his head in his hands and began blubbering openly. 'Please. *Please* let me go.'

Mohammed just winced in discomfort, then he glanced to Shiraz. In Farsi he said, 'I believe him.'

Shiraz nodded, stepped forward, and pressed the tip of his Glock's suppressor on the top of the seated man's head. McKell pulled his hands away from his face quickly and he started to scream, but the Quds Force operative shot him at point-blank range.

He dropped dead on to the floor at the foot of the bed, blood dripped from his mouth and nostrils, and the Iranians began their work. Shiraz and Kashan collected the personal belongings of the two dead Americans, removing anything that could be used to identify them. Then they lifted both men off the floor and laid them on the king-size bed.

While this was going on Mohammed stood close to the wall by the bathroom, his eyes fixed on the bodies. While he gazed at the dead men he used his mobile phone to call in Isfahan, who appeared in the doorway with a pair of two-litre soda bottles in his hands. He opened the first bottle and began pouring gasoline on the bed, and handed off the other bottle to Kashan, who took it and poured it all over the bodies, taking care to thoroughly soak every stitch of clothing.

When they were finished with their work, Shiraz addressed the commander of the operation. 'Mohammed, you should go to the car. Ormand is waiting. We will be right behind.'

Mohammed shook his head, still looking at the bodies. 'Give me the lighter. I want to do it.'

'Sir, there are a lot of fumes. It will go up quickly. Better you –'

Mohammed reached a hand out. 'Please. I want to do it.'

Shiraz looked at the others. With a shrug he said, 'Sure. Of course. But stand in the open doorway and throw it in. The flames can be unpredictable.'

The three Quds Force operatives went out on to the landing and checked the area, then they looked down to make sure Ormand was still there, behind the wheel of the running Chrysler four-door. When they were satisfied everything was in order, Shiraz pulled his Zippo lighter from his pocket and held it out to Mohammed.

'Are you sure?' he asked.

'Of course. Why not?' Mohammed took the lighter with a quavering hand, and he did as the Quds Force operative suggested, standing in the doorway, then tossing the burning lighter on to the bed. It erupted in flame and light, and Mohammed stood there watching for several seconds, as the bodies were engulfed in the inferno.

'Sir?' Shiraz said from behind. 'We must leave immediately!'

Mohammed observed the fast-moving fire, the death and the destruction he had wrought, up until the moment Shiraz put his hand on his arm and pulled him gently out of the doorway. Then the Quds officer shut the door to the room – already fully engulfed from the bathroom at the back to the curtains in the front window – and he pushed the little Revolutionary Guards major toward the stairwell, the other two body men leading the way.

15

Ethan Ross jogged through the high-dollar streets of Georgetown in a frigid predawn, passing town homes and chic stores and coffee shops not yet open for the day.

There were several runners on the pavement with him, even now at 6 a.m. Like Ethan, most wore expensive running shoes and cold-weather compression pants and base layers and gloves. Virtually no one was over forty, and virtually everyone had earbuds in their ears. But as far as Ethan was concerned, the similarities ended there. He doubted any of them had Joan Baez pumping through their headphones like he did. He also seriously doubted any of the other runners here in Georgetown planned on going by a predetermined point in the neighborhood to hunt for a secret signal indicating that the meeting in the woods for later in the morning was a go.

Ethan had not slept well at all. His polygraph was set for 3 p.m., and although he knew objectively he had the skills he needed to beat it, his armor had always been his impenetrable confidence. His armor had been administered a hell of a blow, and this unfamiliar insecurity resulted in his bout of nerves and poor sleep.

At ten minutes past six he passed the green fire hydrant in front of the Gap Kids on the corner of Wisconsin and N Street. He glanced at it quickly as he jogged by. He thought he saw the telltale chalk mark, but he wasn't certain, so he pulled up his run and came to a full stop. He stood there, feigned an air of nonchalance as he pretended to stretch his calves by leaning against the hydrant, and while doing so he leaned down and examined it carefully.

Yes, a distinct white chalk mark had been made across the top of the iron device.

His plan had been to continue up N Street and make a big loop back to his place, but now that he knew he had to meet with Banfield before work, he cut his run short and turned to head back up Wisconsin.

It was laughable tradecraft, but no one was watching, and he got away with it.

Ethan arrived at Fort Marcy Park at 8 a.m., and he parked in the little lot a few spaces down from Harlan Banfield's Volkswagen. He climbed out of his Mercedes, then marched quickly through the frosty morning up the hill with his hands deep in the pockets of his wool trench coat. The trail to the rendezvous point wound up and around a thick copse of trees, so it wasn't until Ross rounded the turn that he stopped dead in his tracks.

Harlan Banfield was there, standing by the cannon, and he was not alone. With him was a woman with long, curly black hair. She wore a black coat and stood with her hands deep in her pockets. Vapor from her breathing hung around her face, obscuring her appearance.

Ethan felt a quick twinge of panic, and his face reddened with anger and confusion. His first thought was that the FBI was here, in the trees, and they were going to knock him to the ground and drag him off. He looked around, half expecting the ubiquitous Hollywood-generated sound of the clicking and clanking of guns as they were pointed at him.

But there were no sounds save for the rumble of a big truck rolling along Chain Bridge Road fifty yards on through the woods.

Banfield called out to Ross, his hand up and waving him forward. 'It's okay, Ethan. Everything is fine. Come over here, I have someone I'd like you to meet.'

Ethan wanted to turn away and run back to his car, but he saw no chance of escape if this was a trap. He forced himself to continue to the cannon and the two people waiting for him there.

He was all the way up to the woman before he recognized her. He'd seen her on TV and on the Internet, and he'd once seen her in person in Berlin.

She extended her hand and Ethan shook it. 'My name is Gianna Bertoli.'

'I know who you are.' His anger subsided quickly, but his concern remained. As he looked once again into the trees he said, 'I saw your film. I admire the work you do for the cause.'

She smiled. 'Thank you, but it is you who deserves admiration.'

After an uncomfortable silence the three of them sat down on the small bench.

Ethan coughed nervously. 'I hope to hell you haven't come to film a documentary about all this.'

She shook her head with a smile. 'No. Of course not. I just arrived from Geneva last night. I'm here to personally assure you we are going to take care of you throughout this investigation.'

'Then I guess that makes you the head of the International Transparency Project.'

Her smile widened and she nodded. 'While working on the documentary I got an intimate look at every aspect of the Project. I met all the players. I grew to respect the work they did. As it happened, I was asked to take over the reins after the former director fell into ill health, and it was an honor to do so.' She beamed. She was as charming as he remembered her from Berlin. 'It's a role that is both eased and complicated by my film work.'

Ethan breathed vapor into the cold morning. 'You are here because Harlan told you about the polygraph.'

She smiled. 'He mentioned it. And I know he also mentioned that you will beat the polygraph as soon as you realize you have nothing to hide.'

'With apologies, Ms Bertoli, I *do* have something to hide.'

'But it is not guilt and it's nothing to be ashamed of. You had no role in what happened in India. I am here to guarantee you of that. It was just bad luck. Bad luck for everyone.'

Banfield reached into his coat and pulled out three small and plain plastic bottles, each one containing several pills. He said, 'These will help. The first two are sertraline and clonazepam. They will relax you. You'll want to take the pills this morning, as soon as you can, to see how they affect you. Test your speech. A good polygraph examiner can tell if you're doping up to beat the box. Just take one each. This should *not* overly sedate you. Take one more of each a half-hour before the exam.'

'And the other bottle?'

'Glycopyrrolate. It will inhibit your ability to perspire.

Take two pills now, and that should cover you for the rest of the day.'

Ethan took the pill bottles from Banfield and slipped them into the pocket of his wool coat, but his eyes remained on the Swiss woman. 'You wouldn't have come if you weren't concerned. You think I'll fail, don't you?'

'On the contrary, if you get arrested, you will be a lost cause to me. If I thought you were a lost cause, I wouldn't be here. I have every intention of getting you extricated from this short-term problem and back to the important work you are doing. We have much invested in you at the Project. We have a lot of whistleblowers working for us.' She gave him a half-wink. 'But you are our rock star.'

Ethan considered himself impervious to the charms of others. Working as a diplomat, he'd dealt with hundreds of people in his career who attempted to use their charisma to captivate and thereby control him.

Such tactics rarely worked on Ethan.

But Bertoli was different. She conveyed at once an air that was sexy, motherly, intelligent and compassionate. She transmitted an appearance of calm control. Ethan found himself drawn to her magnetism.

She said, 'I want you to know we are prepared to go to whatever lengths are necessary, with no restrictions at all, to protect you. Whistleblowers like you merit our services for as long as you need them.' She added, 'You will be safe.'

'Thank you.'

'However, there is something you can do to help yourself.'

'What is that?'

'Create an ace in the hole.'

'I don't understand.'

Bertoli smiled at him. Sympathetic. Compassionate. 'Yes, you do. I am talking about you taking some information of a sensitive nature from the files where you work. Something damning. And then you encrypt it and keep it ready to use as a get-out-of-jail-free card if the need arises.'

Ethan Ross looked off into the woods. 'You are talking . . . you are talking about a scrape.'

Banfield looked back and forth between the two of them. 'A scrape?'

Ross said, 'She wants me to pull every bit of classified data I can get my hands on. Store it on a portable and protected device of some sort.' His voice cracked. 'And then run with it.'

'No,' she said. 'You don't need to run now, but you need to be ready. It is the only way, Ethan. Obtaining something from the files of a classified nature that, if revealed, could be more trouble to the American government than they are prepared to deal with. I'm not talking about sharing it with anyone. Not even me. No, this is just for you. Just for your own safety. If you need to protect yourself, you can have it ready to wave under their nose.'

'I'm not that naive, Ms Bertoli. If the FBI finds out about what I did, then I am fucked.'

'It's Gianna. And it's naive to think the FBI doesn't turn the other cheek when a target creates more trouble than he's worth. I've seen it happen. They keep it quiet, of course. No one admits they dropped an investigation because a target held something over their heads, but it does happen.'

Ethan said, 'I don't even know how to scrape.'

Gianna reached into her purse. 'I brought something with me from Europe.' She held up a yellow thumb drive, just a small plastic rectangle with a USB connector. On it was written *NASCAR*.

Ross didn't understand why it was marked with advertising for stock-car racing, but he knew exactly what it was, and his cockiness meant he needed to tell her.

'That's a crawler.'

The Swiss woman nodded her head solemnly.

Banfield was still out of the loop on this. As a journalist, he dealt with sources and leads. Not computer hacking. 'What does it do?'

Ross answered. 'Ms Bertoli wants me to sneak this into NSC, plug it into a port on my computer. It will send a spiderlike program out there and scrape data. It will then pull it all into a file on the server and exfiltrate it out. How much data?' he asked.

'That is one-point-two terabytes.'

Ethan whispered, 'Holy shit.' He looked the thumb drive over more closely. 'You know it will work?'

'It will work. It was created by ex-employees of the NSA. People who know how to exploit the Intelink-TS network, but people without access to the system any longer.'

Banfield said, 'So anyone who can get at a White House computer can plug that in and –'

Ethan cut him off. 'No. You need the right administration access.'

Gianna said, 'And we know you can get that access. We've been very impressed with your computer skills.'

Ethan sighed. 'You will insult my intelligence if you pretend you don't know I am dating an IT security expert working for a government contractor.'

Gianna's smile now turned apologetic. 'I am sorry about the façade. I was not sure how you would take it if you knew we looked into you. Not much, just a little.'

'It just makes your organization look competent. That is important to me, especially at present.' He sighed again, still thinking about the potential for a scrape. 'I have a way to do this, but if I'm discovered, they will assume she helped me.'

Gianna softened. 'Of course, Ethan, I am biased because I am fond of you. But you need to be thinking of your own self-preservation here. Eve will be fine. If you should need your get-out-of-jail card, it will only be because you have been discovered. If you have been discovered, that means they know you accessed the network. Not Eve Pang.'

'What is the crawler designed to exfiltrate?'

'U.S. intelligence proxy assets around the globe.'

'All over the world?'

'Correct.'

Ethan shook his head emphatically. 'You don't understand my motives. The intelligence I have passed has been done for ideological reasons. Causes I believe in. I am no enemy of the state. I'm not some zit-faced hacker who wants to vacuum all the secrets out of America to put them on the Internet. I have specific grievances with the administration in power, and I am working against specific targets. Not America itself.'

'As I said, this is your decision. But I do have some

experience in protecting brave patriots like you, and my suggestion comes from many years of this experience. Nine times out of ten it is completely unnecessary, but I felt it wise to make the suggestion nevertheless. Just remember, if you decide at a later date that you might need to flee, it might well be too late for you to gain entry to the data you need. The government will block your access to secure networks if they have any suspicions of your whistleblowing.'

Ethan's face darkened and he leaned toward Bertoli. 'Is that why you came? To have me pull more information off the network before I get arrested? To get one more piece of intelligence before I am worthless to you?'

'Your imagination is very vivid. No, Ethan. That is not why I am here. I am telling you, I do not want the information you take.'

Ethan stood, a way of ending the meeting. 'I won't need the crawler, because I won't need an ace in the hole. I'm going to beat the box, the G's are going to move on to something else in a few days, and the entire matter will be forgotten. Trust me, I remain in control of this situation.'

If Gianna was disappointed, she did a good job of hiding it. 'Of course, Ethan. And we are here at your service.'

Ethan shook hands with the two and then he left them there in the trees. He retraced his steps back to his vehicle and drove back to D.C. He popped several of Banfield's pills, swallowing them down a throat that had gone dry for some reason.

16

Dominic Caruso woke at nine, late for him. Instantly he felt his pounding head, the stiffness in his ribs, and lingering stinging from the wound on his arm.

He sat up and rubbed his face. His disposition, if anything, was worse now than it had been before he left his condo last night. More than anything, he was mad at himself for engaging the three assholes in the bar. Not because they didn't deserve it, but because his commitment should have been to his clandestine work with The Campus, and instigating bar-room brawls was listed nowhere in The Campus's mission statement.

What he did last night was a potential compromise to his organization; it was as simple as that.

He felt like he deserved some pain and penance for his behavior, so after a quick shower he dressed for a morning run, and he headed back out the door into the cold.

He ran west on Rhode Island; all around him morning pedestrian commuters filled the streets, along with other joggers. Vehicle traffic was congested, and he had to run in place at almost every streetlight for the first several blocks.

He took M Street for a while, and then New Hampshire down to K, and then he continued west into Georgetown.

Dominic's first run since his injury in India wasn't a

complete disaster, but he realized quickly he wasn't going to be able to push himself. His legs were fine, he wasn't tired, but the heavy breathing that came from even this light exertion was hell on his sore rib cage.

He ran through Georgetown and picked up the Chesapeake and Ohio Towpath trail, and he took this west, along the Potomac River. There were other runners out on the trail here, and although he was surely in better physical condition than the vast majority, he moved slower than many to keep his breathing measured and calm.

In the bright blue sky on his left one aircraft after another lined up over the Potomac River and followed the turns of the river on the way to Ronald Reagan Washington National Airport to the south. This, Dom knew, was the River Visual Approach to runway 19, and as long as aircraft were landing from the north and conditions were VFR, these planes would slide down through the clear sky all day long. He watched them come in on their approach, and it took his mind off his troubles all the way to the Georgetown Reservoir.

Here he turned around and began heading back home.

Running to the east, he didn't have the planes to occupy his thoughts, and his mind drifted. He was back in India, sucking the oppressive night heat, with the mud sticking to his ankles and the lake water in his nostrils.

Then he and Arik came upon the dairy van.

He shook his head in a vain attempt to vaporize the images, and he picked up the pace to add burning lactic acid in his thighs to the mix to help him focus his thoughts on the here and now.

Dom left the towpath and headed north on to the

campus of Georgetown University. He was pumping along at speed now, trying to push for a few more minutes despite a chest heaving and hurting. He ran the streets around the football field, planned on one more lap before slowing to a walk, but up ahead of him the Georgetown University pep band appeared. They began crossing the street in front of him to load into a line of buses by the field. Dozens of young men and women in their street clothes carried their instruments and music and backpacks and rolling luggage. They were a slow-moving operation, so Dom pulled up his run, not wanting to fight through them, and he turned and headed back the way he came.

Almost immediately he noticed the car.

A gray Mazda four-door, a few years old and completely nondescript, had been turning on to the two-lane university road fifty yards behind him. Just as Dom looked up at it, the driver of the vehicle seemed to change his mind, and instead turned left along the tennis courts.

Dom was trained to notice things like this. He kept jogging toward the intersection, but while doing so he considered the possibility his change of direction had led to the car's abrupt maneuver. He wondered if the car had just seen the band clogging the road, and that was why it had turned around. Dom looked over his shoulder to check this, and he saw the band was shielded from the intersection by the line of buses parked on the curve along the fence to the football field.

With nothing else to go on, the car remained little more than a curiosity to him, and he ran on to the east.

Five minutes later he finished his run on Wisconsin. He

knew he didn't have the steam to make it all the way back to his condo, so he began walking through Georgetown. He decided to grab a latte and a croissant at a bakery, and then catch a cab back home.

He stepped inside the bakery and got in line behind a dozen hipsters. While he waited he looked out the window into the street. Thomas Jefferson was all but empty of traffic at the moment, but on a whim he craned his neck back and forth. He cocked his head in surprise when he saw a gray four-door Mazda pull to a stop on the other side of the towpath a block to the north, just barely in view through the window. It looked like the car he'd seen at the university fifteen minutes earlier, but he wasn't sure. He chastised himself for not being on his game and paying closer attention.

He left the bakery with his breakfast, still thinking about the gray Mazda. It was no longer parked near the towpath, but he decided he'd check whether or not it was tailing him by walking along the towpath to see if it appeared on the next street ahead. He walked slowly on Thomas Jefferson while he sipped and ate, then turned into the towpath and disappeared from the street. This shielded him for a block, so he knew if he was under surveillance anyone watching him would have to reposition somewhere in advance of his direction of movement. He tossed his latte in a garbage can and broke into a run with the croissant in his mouth, hoping to get ahead of anyone while they repositioned to a static overwatch.

When he arrived at 29th Street he saw nothing out of the ordinary. There was no street parking here, and he saw no vehicles idling by the side of the two-lane road. A few pedestrians passed, but a quick glance at them effectively ruled them out as obvious surveillance.

Dom crossed 29th and continued on the towpath, he ate a few bites of the croissant – even if he was under surveillance he still had an appetite – and he was halfway to the end when he quickly stopped and reversed his route. He all but rushed back to 29th, stepped out into the street from the east, and saw the gray Mazda idling there at the curb, facing south. The two men in the car, both in the front, had their eyes facing to the west down the towpath.

They had judged his timing by the speed he'd been walking on Thomas Jefferson, and by running on the towpath he was able to sneak up on them from behind.

Dom knew he should have observed them for a few minutes to see if he could get any ideas as to who they were, but he was outraged by the tail, and his impetuous nature won out. He sprinted across the street and rapped his knuckles on the driver's-side window, startling the two men looking in the opposite direction. Slowly the window came down. A middle-aged driver with salt-and-pepper hair and a Mediterranean complexion stared back at him with tired hangdog eyes.

Dom asked, 'Why are you following me?'

'I don't know what you're talking about.' His accent was heavy and somewhat familiar, but Dom couldn't immediately place it. Dom reached in quickly and pulled the keys out of the ignition. As he withdrew his hand with the keys, the driver reached up and put Dom's hand in a surprisingly strong and confident wristlock.

Dom realized he was still holding the croissant in his

left hand. He dropped it and reached under his sweatshirt and unsnapped a small, hooked Ka-Bar knife from a locking sheath that hung on the waistband of his underwear and shorts. He brought the fat, matte-black blade to the man's thick throat. His own right hand was still held tight in a wristlock inside the car.

The man in the passenger seat reached to his own waistband now. Dom thought he was going for a gun.

Dom pushed the knife harder against the driver's throat with his left hand.

'You draw and I cut him!'

The passenger lifted both hands away from his waistband and into the air. With an accent similar to the driver, he said, 'Not necessary, Mr Caruso. We are friends.'

'I know my friends, and I don't know you. Who are you, and why the hell are you following me?'

The middle-aged driver let go of Dom's arm. 'We don't have authority to speak to you.'

'Then who does?'

'I do.'

Dom spun around at the sound of the man's voice close behind him. Standing there on the sidewalk was the same distinguished-looking gentleman he'd seen having a Manhattan at The Pig the night before. Now he wore a full-length camel coat and a driving cap.

'You?'

'Please, Dominic. Put the knife away before someone around here calls the police.'

Dom sheathed the Ka-Bar reluctantly and covered it with his sweatshirt.

'Very good. Why don't we go for a short walk along the towpath? You seem to like this route. I will answer your questions while we stroll.'

They walked back to the west, silently because a track club with two dozen runners passed by in ones and twos. When the runners disappeared around a bend ahead and the two men had the towpath to themselves again, Dom said, 'Okay, we're walking. Start talking.'

The older man said, 'My name is David. I work for the Israeli government.'

'You mean Israeli intelligence.'

'Yes.'

'You mean Mossad.'

'Perhaps.'

'You've been watching me since last night?'

'Yes. You were very impressive.'

Dom stopped walking. 'What did I do that impressed you?'

The Israeli snorted out a laugh. 'The three men you dispatched with your knowledge of Krav Maga, of course. We were not terribly impressed when you took the lovely young woman named Jennifer back to the Loews Madison, and then said good night to her in the lobby so she could go to bed alone.'

'Not that it's any of your business, but her name was Monica.'

David broke into laughter. 'No, it was Jennifer Hartley. She gave you a fake name. That's rich. I guess you two really don't have much of a future.'

'She was with you?'

'No. But we looked into her.'

Dom considered this. 'So you didn't set that up last night? Some kind of an altercation to test my abilities, and then a honey trap to use against me?'

'Set it up? Of course not. We are not fight promoters, and we are not a dating service. We were watching you, and then looking into her, trying to figure out who, exactly, you work for. We already knew you knew how to fight, because we know you trained in private tutelage under Colonel Yacoby.' He shrugged. 'But trust me, Mr Caruso. We could not care less whether you know how to make love.'

'Okay,' Dom replied uneasily, still clueless as to what was going on.

David began walking again, and Dom followed his lead.

David said, 'Your altercation last night raised more questions than it answered. You don't seem like you are trying to maintain any sort of cover. From a tradecraft perspective, you made some terrible decisions.'

Dominic hung his head, shamefaced, but did not reply.

David continued. 'So I don't think you are working here in D.C. I think you have been told to take some time to yourself. In fact, I suspect your leaders, whoever they are, have mandated it after what happened in Paravur.'

Dom wasn't going to confirm anything about his employer, but he didn't challenge the comment. 'Sorry to disappoint you with my tradecraft.'

'I am not disappointed. I am relieved. It helped me come to a helpful conclusion.'

'What conclusion?'

'My conclusion is this: You are angry. Furious about what happened to Arik. It is consuming you. You turn to other outlets to channel your rage, but only one thing will provide you with any real comfort.'

'You were a friend of Arik's?'

'An old colleague.'

'He was Mossad?'

'I did not say that. *I* was IDF. *He* was IDF.'

'You were Shayetet Thirteen?'

David smiled. 'I did not say that, either. You ask a lot of questions. Just as I will not ask you any more about who you work for, I will require you do not ask me anything more about me.'

'I'll ask this. What is it you want?'

'In short, I want . . . *we* want, what you want. We want the person who leaked the intelligence about the operation against the SS *Ardahan*.'

Dom stopped again. A jogger passed by, so he waited to speak for a moment. Finally he said, 'How do you know about the leak?'

'Your government told my government. We've asked to be updated in their investigation. We want a name, and we don't have one.'

'I don't know who did it. The FBI doesn't even know who did it.'

'I am aware of this. We are hoping that might change. We are hoping the culprit will be identified.'

'And then?'

David shrugged, started walking again, and Dom followed.

David said, 'Your government is seeking answers. That

is good. But we hope you, Dominic, are seeking vengeance. Vengeance is what we want. Unfortunately, we can't do anything to jeopardize our relationships here in Washington by targeting an official of the United States government. We're tremendous fans of the President of the United States, your uncle, and we hope he is a fan of us, as well. That makes our actions here delicate, to say the least.'

'So you want to use me?'

'We want *you* to use *us*. Logistics, information, planning, equipment.'

Dom walked in silence, and he thought about the extraordinary offer being made to him. His mind switched suddenly.

'What happened on SS *Ardahan*?'

David clearly expected this question, and he had an answer ready. 'The *Ardahan* and three other vessels were heading to Gaza, supposedly with relief supplies. We knew the other three were decoys, loaded with food and medical supplies, but the *Ardahan* was also carrying rockets for Al-Qassam. Colonel Yacoby and his team arrived by helicopter. They fast-roped to the deck but they were set upon instantly, attacked with knives and iron pipes while they were still on the ropes. The peace activists, if you want to call them that, beat the shit out of several of Yacoby's guys. Many broken bones. They knocked one commando unconscious and tossed him overboard. Our Navy fished him out alive, but barely.'

'And then?'

'Colonel Yacoby was authorized to use deadly force only in response to deadly force. He and his men fought back several attackers with nothing more than fists and rifle butts, but when his man was thrown unconscious into the sea, and a Palestinian pulled the commando's rifle off the deck, Yacoby saw this, and he gave the command to his team to engage with deadly fire.'

Dom had seen grainy video footage from the event, taken by the protesters on board the *Ardahan*. Black-clad frogmen with short-barreled rifles opened fire on a deck full of men and women in civilian clothing. In the end nine lay dead, and twenty-two were wounded.

David said, 'I am not going to say everything went to plan. It did not. But it wasn't the massacre of innocents that the world press made it out to be. Arik Yacoby showed restraint until he realized such restraint would get his entire team killed. The ship was carrying rockets and bomb-making matériel for Hamas, hidden in stores of baby formula. Seizing the equipment on the high seas was in our nation's national security interests. We are . . . *comfortable* with what happened.'

Dom thought about Arik. He believed he would have done his best to execute his mission without any loss of life. But he also believed Arik would have done anything to keep his own men safe. Dom said, 'Look. I'm a fan of Israel, as far as that goes. And I would love to get my hands around the neck of this traitor. But I'm not spying for a foreign government.'

David was taken aback. 'Spying? Who said anything about spying?'

'Actually, you haven't said much of anything about anything. What is it, exactly, you want me to do?'

'The culprit is an employee of the U.S. government.

That much is obvious. We will not engage in direct action against an American U.S. government employee, especially not here in Washington.'

'But I *will*?'

'You *might*. We planned on taking some time to find out if you could be useful to us. We would not have spoken with you today if you didn't outsmart my surveillance detail. We planned on watching to see if you were operational. We know all you did in India to try to save Arik, and we thought it might be important to you that a measure of justice is done.'

Dom nodded.

David said, 'You are alone. We know you are isolating yourself so you don't expose your friends right now.'

'And you want to be my new friends?'

David smiled. 'Friends with benefits. But with no strings attached. Kind of like the opportunity you passed up in the Loews hotel last night.'

'I don't believe that's considered a friendship. That's called a one-night stand.'

'Well, then. I am sure that is a phenomenon about which you have some knowledge.' David reached into his pocket and pulled out a business card. He put it in Dom's hand. 'Call us if we can be of any help.'

Dom looked at the card. It was blank other than a handwritten phone number with a D.C. exchange. He said, 'I'm not promising anything.'

'I don't want promises. I just hope you call sometime.'

Dom rolled his eyes. 'Your one-night-stand metaphor is straining.'

David chuckled a little. 'I think that is a good metaphor

for what we are thinking. When some evidence comes out against whoever stole the data, use us for your needs.'

Dom said, 'I'm going to need to check you out. Some guy walks up to me on the street and –'

'Of course. You know other Mossad officers. Talk to your friends. They will vouch for me. They don't know me. But they can establish my bona fides by calling the number on the card. I will put them in contact with the right people in Tel Aviv, and they will call you back and say I am exactly who I say I am.'

They had reached Wisconsin Avenue by now, so they left the towpath. David stepped into the street and a white Taurus pulled up next to him. Dom faintly remembered noting the car when he ran along the Georgetown Reservoir, but he'd not flagged it as suspicious. Behind the Taurus was the gray Mazda.

The two vehicles with the Mossad men rolled off into the morning traffic. As the Mazda passed by Dom, the middle-aged driver with the hangdog expression flipped him the bird.

17

From the moment Ethan Ross arrived at the Eisenhower Building at 9 a.m., right after his clandestine meeting at Fort Marcy Park, he'd remained closed up in his office, pretending to work while keeping as much distance from his secretary as possible. While he thumbed through briefing books and scrolled through drafts of policy papers, he all but ignored the words and ideas in front of him, and instead used his fertile brain for other endeavors.

Of primary importance was his need to test the effects of the clonazepam and sertraline on his central nervous system before his polygraph this afternoon. After an hour to let the meds dissolve into his bloodstream he felt they were stabilizing his mood significantly, and he also felt reasonably certain no one would be able to detect he had taken meds to alter his disposition. To doubly confirm this, he made an impromptu call to his mother on the West Coast and chatted with her for several minutes. He knew she would detect any slur to his voice or change in his normal speech patterns, and he decided it would be better to test his coherence on her than on his secretary or other National Security Council staff.

His mother made no mention of his speech during their conversation, so he felt at least somewhat confident the clonazepam and sertraline would do their job today without threatening to reveal themselves by making it seem as if his mouth was full of marbles.

And the glycopyrrolate was unquestionably doing its job. While he would have no reason to perspire here in his cool office, he could tell his mouth was uncomfortably dry, and he presumed this to be due to the effects of the drug. He'd take another dose of pills before the test, just to be certain, and this would add to his completely calm and unfazed appearance.

While closed in his office he also spent his hours before the poly strategizing how he would beat the test. He had given this a great deal of thought in the year he had been passing intelligence to the Project, and he actually found it enjoyable to concoct mental games and thought processes to alter his brainwaves.

During the time he had been whistleblowing, he'd undergone two routine polygraphs, and he'd had no problem with either. That said, today would be several orders of magnitude more challenging, and he knew he'd have to up his game because of the specific nature of today's questions.

Ethan took his second dose of the meds at half past two, another glycopyrrolate, another clonazepam and another sertraline, and then left for his polygraph ten minutes early. He decided to leave his suit coat on his chair and head down in his shirtsleeves. It might show him to be more relaxed and comfortable, and that might help him during the exam. As he walked down the marble hall he took stock of his disposition and his situation, and he realized he actually felt pretty damn good.

No state college grad in a bad suit was going to out-smart him, Ethan told himself, and he looked forward to the challenge ahead.

The exams were being held in an office suite on the third floor of the Eisenhower Building, and Ethan couldn't help noticing that the examination room was right next to the administration office computers where he'd slipped in to access the Gaza flotilla files four months earlier. He suspected this was just coincidence – this office suite was the logical place for the examination – so it didn't cause him any real consternation.

He waited on a sofa in the outer office of the suite while another NSC staffer underwent his own exam, and while waiting, Ethan chatted with the secretary. FBI supervisory special agent Darren Albright, who was him-self now working out of an office here in the Eisenhower Building, dropped by to introduce himself, and he and Ross exchanged brief pleasantries. Ethan tried to ingratiate himself a bit to the chiseled and ramrod-straight G-man, but Albright was all business; other than an insincere thanks for Ross's showing up for the mandatory poly, he didn't have much to say and he left the room soon after.

A few minutes before 3 p.m., Walter Pak, assistant deputy director for South and Central Asia, exited the examination room. He was himself in his shirtsleeves, Ethan was relieved to see, and Ethan also felt more com-fortable when Pak gave him a relaxed wink as he left the room.

Ethan winked back, then he stood from the sofa when the examiner leaned his head out of the inner sanctum of the suite.

'Deputy Assistant Director Ross. Are you ready?'

Ethan flashed a wide grin. 'Ready and waiting.'

The examiner was an FBI special agent with the ethnically confusing name Rigoberto Finn. He looked to be near sixty years old, but he was in good shape, and Ethan was unable to tell if the thick gray hair on his head was his own or an excellent toupee.

Ethan had planned on identifying aspects of the examiner to make friendly conversation before the test to curry favor with the man, but the contrasts in Special Agent Finn threw Ross off-balance from the start.

Finn walked Ethan back to a small windowless office, sat him down in a wooden chair with a square black pad on the seat, and then spent the next few minutes wiring him up with all the sensors used in the exam.

Finn attached a pair of wired tubes around Ethan's torso; one measured upper respiratory function and the other lower respiratory function. Three sensors were placed on his index and ring fingers to record his EDR, the electrodermal response, or galvanic skin reflex, a measure of sweat secretion.

As the FBI examiner tightened the Velcro in place, Ethan fought a smile. Because of the glycopyrrolate, Special Agent Finn could lock him in a sauna and Ross wouldn't do any sweating today.

Last, Finn attached a blood pressure cuff to Ethan's upper left arm.

Ethan also sat on an activity-sensor seat pad. This device recorded both major and minor body movements, ensuring the examiner had a computerized record of how the examinee's body reacted to the questions asked.

Finn went to work behind his computer, monitoring the signals to make sure everything was hooked up properly and operational. He stepped back around the desk twice to adjust the fingertip straps. Ethan wondered if Finn was surprised how little perspiration he detected on the EDR sensors even before the test began.

'Everything okay?' Ethan asked.

'Just fine,' Finn answered distractedly as he returned to his computer.

While Finn spent a moment behind the laptop on the desk, looking over some of the questions, Ethan tried to engage the older man in some small talk. He asked Finn how long he'd been doing this and he did not look up from his work as he replied, 'Long, long time. Shall we get started?'

'Be my guest.'

Ross realized this grizzled old bastard was not going to play around.

Whatever, Ethan told himself. *Let's do it.*

The drugs were relaxing him, he was sure, and this belief fed on itself, helping him keep his anxiety level low.

Special Agent Finn began the pre-examination with a baseline interview, a series of simple and even inane questions that were designed to see what the examinee's typical physical response would be when showing indications of either truthfulness or deception. These baseline questions were always similar. The first few were given to elicit responses Finn would know were truthful.

'Is your name Ethan Ross?'

'Yes.'

'Do you work at the National Security Council?'

'Yes.'

'Do you live in the USA?'

'Yes.'

After a few more of these, Finn asked questions he knew would elicit a nervous response, even if the subject told the truth. 'Have you ever told a lie?'

Ethan hesitated a moment. 'Yes.'

'Have you ever cheated on a test, even as a child?'

Another hesitation. 'Yes.'

'Have you ever viewed pornography?'

'Who hasn't?'

'Yes or no, please.'

'Yes.'

Last, some questions were put in specifically to elicit a 'No,' to see how a truthful negative answer would look on the computer.

'Is your name Archie Bunker?'

'No.'

'Do you have a pet snake named Simon?'

'No.'

Each time Finn asked a question, Ross kept his face calm and passive, but he clenched his toes and even his sphincter as hard as he could, doing his best to hide the strain visually from Finn while at the same time hoping to spike his sensor readings on the computer. At the same time, he let his mind drift back to his past, and he thought of embarrassing and painful memories.

Finn asked another battery of baseline questions, Ethan

answered in the same manner, but after the tenth question Finn's eyebrows furrowed, then he looked up at his subject. 'Please try and relax.'

Ross instantly realized he was overplaying it. The sensors were reading too much distress on the questions where there should have been none. He was trying to muddle the baseline, but instead he realized he ran the risk of waving a red flag at the examiner. The last thing he wanted was for Finn to have reason to suspect him of gaming the test. He smiled, nodded and said, 'I was like this in school. Always got a little antsy on test day. I'm sure you see a lot of people like that.'

Finn looked over the top of his laptop at Ross. 'I see a lot of everything.'

Ethan smiled, but the FBI agent had turned his attention once again to his computer and he didn't catch it.

Finn finished the baseline interview and went into the pre-test, talking to Ethan for a few minutes about the questions to come. One by one, he went down the actual list of questions he would ask when the real polygraph was under way. Ethan knew the examination questions were given before the test for two reasons. One, an innocent person would relax somewhat knowing everything that was to be asked of him or her beforehand. And two, a guilty person would only become more anxious knowing what was to come, and the sensors would record the heightened reaction to the question preceding their deception.

Once he'd gone through all the questions, the exam began.

Finn spoke in a slow and measured tone. 'Do you plan on responding truthfully during this examination?'

'Yes.'

He went through many of the baseline questions again, then asked, 'Did you download the unauthorized CIA files in question?'

For the first time in the sixty or more questions asked by Agent Finn, Ethan did not clench his toes and his sphincter when he answered the question. Instead he tried to channel the most peaceful relaxed thoughts he could. He'd planned for this, so the calm imagery of a yoga retreat on the beach in Thailand he'd visited with his mom and an old girlfriend a few years back entered his head quickly and easily. He imagined himself lying on the yoga mat, the sound of wind chimes and a soft breeze cascading over him.

'No.'

Finn remained hunched over the computer, he made no outward reaction, but he did not ask the next question immediately.

The room was perfectly quiet. Ethan fought the desire to shift in his seat, and he did his best to keep his breath measured. He glanced to a spot on the wall so the stress of trying to gauge Finn's reaction would not cause him to move and thereby spike his readings.

Nothing. Agent Finn still seemed to be looking at his computer. Ethan fought to keep the peaceful images in his mind while he waited for the next question.

Finally, Finn asked, 'Do you know who was responsible for the unauthorized use of the CIA files relating to the Mossad attack on the SS *Ardahan*?'

Again, Ethan tried to find a Zen thought. Waterfalls. The beach in Phuket. Yoga music.

'No.'

Another long pause. Then, 'Is your name Ethan Ross?'

Gone went the yoga retreat, and back came the clenching and the stressful imagery.

'Yes.'

Finn went on to other questions, but circled back to the interrogatories regarding the CIA files several more times. Each time he took longer and longer before he seemed satisfied he'd read all the sensors, and then he would move on to other questions, before coming back again and again to the subject matter under investigation.

Ethan was gaming this exam, but he was pretty sure Finn was gaming it as well. He seemed to be trying to get a sense of Ross's anxiety about the pertinent questions, and keeping him on the hot seat a little longer was one way he could do it.

Twice Finn stopped the test, closed the laptop, and left the room. Once for five minutes, once for fifteen. Each time he returned he asked Ethan if he was applying countermeasures to defeat the polygraph.

Ethan was, in fact, very much using countermeasures, but he did not find these questions terribly panic-inducing, because he'd been asked this on every poly he'd ever sat for. Finn was going through the motions, Ethan told himself, and he concentrated on continuing to obfuscate the results.

Roughly ninety minutes after Ethan sat down, Agent Finn announced the examination was complete. Ethan thought back to his earlier times on the box, and thought this one might have been a little longer than average, but not alarmingly so. He half worried he might have given himself a hernia with all the clenching, but he fought the urge to show even the slightest sign of relief that the test had ended.

Agent Finn seemed more polite now as he unhooked the perspiration sensors from Ethan's fingers, the respiratory monitors from his chest, and the blood pressure cuff from his arm. He offered Ethan a bottle of water and Ethan took it, then Finn went back behind his desk.

Ross knew that this was the real examination. The post-exam interview. Now Agent Finn would try and trip Ethan up, and Ethan was ready.

Finn looked Ethan over for a long time, then said, 'We had a little trouble with that one, didn't we?'

'Trouble? Trouble with what?'

'The computer's readings on your questions showed some level of deception. I don't think you are being untruthful, per se, but I need to try and clear up the deception.'

Ethan just shook his head. 'I told the truth.'

'Yeah, I hear you, but there are a million shades of the truth. Even the grayer shades are one hundred per cent benign, well meaning. The computer has trouble discerning the different shades.' Finn smiled a little. He was all smiles now. 'It just smells trouble. It takes a human being to resolve that trouble so we don't get any false positives.'

Ethan knew exactly what was going on. Finn was playing a good cop/bad cop routine with the machine itself. He'd apologize for the machine's distrust in him and played himself up as the good actor in the equation.

Ethan just shrugged. 'I don't know what to tell you. I am very comfortable with all my answers.'

'Look, Mr Ross. I know how it is working in a government office. There can be a hell of a lot of good reasons to pull a file off a network. We didn't come over here thinking anyone was a . . .' Ethan thought he was pretending to hunt for the word. 'A spy or anything like that. This is a clerical mistake. Don't worry anyone is going to make this more than it is.' He hesitated. 'Unless we can't resolve the deception. Then we'll have to dig a little deeper.'

Ethan tried to keep a measured tone. 'Honestly, Agent Finn, I can't think of any reasons to access an unauthorized file. My work is too important to me. It's really not worth losing a security clearance.'

'I can see you are holding back a little. Coming clean on the truth will keep Albright and his team from working you a lot harder than they need to. If you downloaded the file with someone else's logon, then you might get your clearance yanked for a month. Just maybe a note in your record. But if your poly comes back deceptive and you don't resolve that, then CID is going to be looking at you as a potential intelligence officer for a foreign power. Espionage stuff. The whole big enchilada. Nobody needs that.' Another smile, apologetic.

Ethan couldn't help himself now. He laughed. If he thought he was truly imperiled he would have clammed up and gone into self-preservation mode, but this guy was insulting his intelligence by using some goofy playground psychology. 'Really? This is your ploy? Does this ever work? Is this the point in the polygraph where a small mind just bursts out a full confession because they think they are going to get charged with a one-hundred-year-old law and spend the rest of their life in Leavenworth? Seriously?'

'Are you saying you *would* confess if you weren't so darn smart?'

Another chuckle. 'As I said, I've got nothing to confess.'

Finn said, 'I've been doing this a long time.' He let the statement hang in the air in the still room.

'Yes?'

Agent Finn stood and extended his hand. Ethan was surprised by the suddenness of the act. He stood himself and shook it.

Finn said, 'Thanks for dropping by. I think I have what I need.'

As Ethan turned to walk out the door, Finn called after him. 'One more thing, Mr Ross . . . the exam is over. You don't have to answer if you don't want to.'

Ethan smiled. 'As I've said, I've got nothing to hide.'

'Are you, by any chance, a hyperhidrotic?'

'I'm sorry?'

'I'm just curious if you suffer from palmar hyper-hidrosis?'

'I'm afraid I don't know what that is.'

'It's a medical condition. Excessive sweating of the hands.'

'What? No. Of course not.' Ethan touched his hands together. Smiled confidently. 'I'm not sweating at all.'

'That is precisely my point. Your hands. They are paper dry. Either you have some sort of damage to your sympathetic nerve trunk in your thoracic region, or you are taking an anticollagenic to reduce sweating. There are a few different pills out there to combat it, which will make you dry as a bone if you take too much. But all these meds require a prescription. We can check your medical records.

We have the authority to do that, you know. But I already know what we'll find.'

'You won't find anything.'

Finn's smile grew so wide the hairpiece on his head revealed itself by moving as a unit. 'I know we won't.'

'Then . . . what is your point?'

Agent Finn said, 'Never mind. Thanks again for coming in.'

Ethan cracked a little smile for show, but he couldn't quite hold Finn's gaze as he turned to leave.

This did not feel like a ploy to Ethan. Agent Finn seemed genuinely suspicious.

18

In contrast to the previous evening, tonight Dominic Caruso wasn't out on the prowl for strange women or blundering into fistfights. For dinner he sat on his couch, eating leftover *Fra Diavolo* that he'd warmed in the microwave, and he washed it down with a glass of water.

He had other things on his mind now. The food was just fuel.

Adara Sherman had called him yet again, shortly after he'd returned from his morning run, and again she asked if she could come over to check his wounds or run errands for him. Dom appreciated the gesture, although he was almost positive Gerry Hendley had asked Adara to do some drive-by wellness checks on him to make sure he was behaving himself and convalescing quietly at home.

Dom told Adara he was fine and she'd not pressed him too hard. Gerry had probably orchestrated that as well, telling her not to push Dom right away.

Gerry would see Adara as the one member of The Campus who could serve as a conduit between the rest of the force and Caruso. She wasn't an operations officer, she was an employee of the shell company that operated the Hendley Associates Gulfstream, which provided her with a secondary layer of detachment from The Campus.

Dom knew he'd have to interact with Sherman sooner

or later, otherwise he'd get a call from Gerry. But for now, his mind was elsewhere.

Dom's conversation with the Mossad officer in Georgetown had determined his actions for the rest of this day. As soon as he got off the phone with Adara he called an ex–Mossad man he knew living in Maryland, who agreed to call the phone number on David's card to see if this man was, in fact, representing Israel. An hour later Dom's friend called back and verified David's identity. He was, according to Dominic's Israeli friend, an ex–IDF colonel now working for Mossad here in D.C.

Satisfied he was not at risk of getting sucked into some sort of false-flag situation, Dom then reached out to FBI special agent Darren Albright, leaving two messages for him during the course of the afternoon. Albright hadn't called him back yet, which pissed him off, but in the brief and fleeting moment when he put himself in Albright's shoes he recognized the supervisory special agent in the Counterintelligence Division was probably busier than a one-armed fan dancer at the moment with the leak investigation at the NSC.

Dom didn't let him off the hook for not calling him back immediately, but he did force himself to hold off on leaving a third message on his voice mail.

Now it was late evening, Dom was back in his bathroom, changing his bandages. He stripped a length of medical tape off a roll with his mouth, then he used it to secure a small square of white gauze over the stitches on his forearm. He repeated this once more, fixing the gauze in place with a second strip of tape. He was pleased with his work, and doubly so that he was healing quickly enough that he no longer needed the larger dressing on his arm.

He'd just dropped the tape and gauze back into a drawer in his bathroom when his mobile phone rang. He snatched it off the vanity and answered on the first ring.

'Hello?'

'Caruso? Albright here. I'm returning your call. Your *calls*, I should say.'

'Hey, man. I appreciate it.'

'Awfully busy. What can I do for you?'

'Just wondering if you learned anything from the polys?'

'I thought I told you I'd give you a call when I had something.'

'You did. I'm just a pushy son of a bitch. Sorry about that.'

'Right.'

'Anything?'

Albright hesitated before saying, 'Not really. A couple of soft possibilities.'

'Tell me about them.' Dom added, 'Please.'

After a long sigh, the special agent replied, 'One of the NSC senior staffers, female. When I met her the other day she seemed agitated about the investigation. The examiner pressed her pretty hard, and the test came out inconclusive. I'm not too hopeful – even the examiner said she might just be so damn high-strung the machine had a hard time figuring her out – but I thought I'd circle back with a surprise visit to her office tomorrow, maybe shake her tree and see if anything falls out.'

Dom thought that might be a good idea, though it

didn't sound like a promising lead. 'You mentioned two possibles.'

'Yeah, there is another NSC staffer who might warrant a closer look. Nothing definitive, but we'll do some digging. No clear deception on the poly, another inconclusive. But on this guy the examiner thought something was fishy.'

'What do you mean?'

'The examiner is the best in the Bureau. He thought the subject was playing the system. You know, doing the old butthole clench, biting his cheek, taking meds to control his perspiration, shit like that.'

'Does that work?'

'Believe it or not, sometimes it does. We've caught guys at CIA and FBI and DoD who spied for decades and beat their annual polys the entire length of their careers. All people are different, the gadgetry can only do so much to account for the individual, but in the end it's looking at a statistical mean. You can beat the exam by being different from the mean.'

'And this character who tried to skew the box? What is his role at NSC?'

'He's assistant deputy in the Middle East and North Africa Division. His background is solid. Not a single red flag, although he's not terribly well liked around the office. It doesn't look too promising, but there is one thing about him that makes me a little more interested.'

'What's that?'

'He's dating a woman who works for a government technology contractor. She's in the classified network security infrastructure field.'

'Is she getting a poly?'

'No. She had no access to the Eisenhower Building, and she is as clean as they come. It's just worthy of note that this assistant dep at the NSC might have gleaned a little technical know-how from his girlfriend. Whoever moved those files to the file-sharing server knew how to hide their identity.'

'What's this deputy assistant's name?'

'Ross. Ethan J. Ross. His mom is Emily Ross.' That didn't ring a bell with Caruso, and Albright registered this from the silence. 'She's a well-known biographer. Wrote a bunch of books about First Ladies and such. Can't say I've ever read any. She's got political clout, which means her boy might have gotten some preferential treatment along the way, but again, all his previous polys and security checks have been stellar.'

Dom walked over to his couch and leaned over his laptop. He typed in 'Ethan Ross' while he talked.

'Did you meet this guy?'

'I introduced myself. That's all.'

'What's your take on him?'

Albright snorted into the phone. 'Caruso, if I could spot a spy by his handshake I'd be a fucking rock star. I don't know.'

'He's going to get a tap and tail?'

Another snort. 'Hold your horses. Nothing like that yet. I don't know how you boys do things in spookland, but we don't put a package on everybody who raises an eyebrow. The examiner thinks he's shady, but he didn't fail the exam, so I can't make him a person of interest until I find something else. I've already started digging into his work history a little more, pulling up earlier polys to look for anomalies. We'll talk to his superiors about his attitude and watercooler talk. That sort of thing. I'll stop in his office tomorrow and give him the stink eye, see if he shits his pants.'

'That's it?'

'If he warrants more attention, he'll get it. Plus, I've got a hell of a stink eye. Believe me, I'll tap the guy if he needs to be tapped.'

While they spoke, Caruso had already Googled the man, and he found a bio and a picture of him from his days working at the White House. He enlarged the picture and stared into the eyes of a young, thin man sitting in front of a U.S. flag on a flagpole. He had blond hair and a nice suit and a little smile that Dom read as somewhat smug.

'One more thing,' Dom said. 'The polygraph examiner. You said he was the best in the Bureau.'

'I did.'

'That must be Jim Barker.'

Albright whistled into the phone. 'Damn, Caruso. You need to update your Rolodex. Barker moved out to L.A. three or four years ago. No, I'm talking about Rigoberto Finn. He's in the Baltimore office, and he's as good as they come. CID brings him down to D.C. regularly.'

'Finn. Right,' Dom said, although he'd never heard of the man. He scribbled the name down on a pad next to his computer, along with the word 'Baltimore.' Then he said, 'And Finn says you need to work this Ross?'

'He did, and I will. But I told you, it's going to take some time.'

'Then I won't keep you on the phone. Darren, I really appreciate the call. If you get anything else –'

'If I get anything else, *I'll* call *you*. I promise I won't forget about you out there in spookland.'

'This isn't spookland. This is my condo. It's just me.'

'Right.' Albright hung up.

Dom continued looking at the photo slowly and carefully.

Ross was a good-looking guy, Dom had to admit. He had his own Wikipedia page, too, but Dom found an article about him in the *Post* that looked more reliable. He was thirty-two, he was in Mensa, the organization for people with genius IQs. This article showed a picture of the man standing next to his mother, Emily Ross, and it identified her as an ex–U.S. ambassador and a longtime tenured professor at Georgetown who had recently retired and moved to the West Coast.

Caruso focused again on Ethan Ross. He looked into his eyes.

'Are you the guy? Are you the fucker who got the Yacobys killed?'

Dom had no idea if Ross was responsible, but at the same time, he had no other real suspects. On a whim, he looked up Special Agent Rigoberto Finn's mobile number on an FBI internal phone list. It was nearly 11 p.m., but he dialed it anyway.

After enough rings to where Dom was certain it would roll to voice mail, a gruff- and tired-sounding man answered.

'Finn.'

'Special Agent Finn, I'm very sorry to bother you so late. This is Special Agent Caruso calling from D.C.'

After a couple of coughs to clear his throat, Finn said, 'Dominic Caruso?'

'That's right.'

'I'll be damned. The President's nephew.'

'At your service.'

'I remember you smoked that child killer down in Georgia a few years ago.'

'Alabama. Yes, nasty business.'

'That was a damn good shoot. What I would have given to be in your shoes just once in my career.'

Dom cleared his throat uncomfortably, not sure what to say.

Finn asked, 'What can I do for you?'

'I'm calling about Ethan Ross. I understand you boxed him this afternoon.'

'Yep. You working with Albright?'

Dom waffled for a moment, looking for the least untrue thing he could say. 'You know Darren. 11 p.m. and I just got off the phone with him. I'm doing a little follow-up on Ross.'

'Yeah, that Albright's a ballbuster. I'm still at the Hoover Building. He's got me filing reports from today's exams. I'll be back at NSC first thing tomorrow, boxing another group of staffers.'

'I hear you. About Ross . . . Darren said you liked him as a suspect?'

'Maybe not a suspect, but a person of interest, for sure. Intelligent as hell, I could read that off him instantly, but he was gaming the shit out of me.'

'You sure about that?'

'I told Albright, and I'll tell you. Ethan Ross went into

that exam ready to obscure all relative physiological indices. People don't go to that much trouble just for kicks. I don't give a damn what the box says about the results. I had to mark it down as inconclusive, because Ross did a good job hiding his deception, but I'd bet my soon-to-be-relevant-and-insufficient pension that he was hiding something significant.'

Dom thanked Finn for his time, and he hoped like hell the examiner would have no reason to mention this phone call the next time he spoke with Special Agent Albright, then he hung up. Dom next decided to spend the rest of the evening planning his one-man operation to look deep into the life of Ethan J. Ross.

19

A steady sleet hissed on the streets of Georgetown, but Ethan jogged right through it. Anyone looking out a row-house window or driving by on this early morning would surely think the man in the orange windbreaker an exceptionally dedicated runner, but the truth was quite different. Rising an hour early to run through the streets had been hell on Ethan this morning, and now traipsing through sleet that burned his eyes and cheeks seemed insane, but he told himself he had to make the predawn check of the green fire hydrant on Wisconsin. He could have driven by, of course, but it would have been completely out of character for him to do so, and even with zero real tradecraft training, Ethan knew that would have raised red flags in the unlikely event he was being watched.

He passed the hydrant and saw no telltale mark from Banfield. He wondered if it could have washed off in the weather, but he thought that unlikely, as the hydrant itself was dry. He continued on, jogging up 29th and leaving no mark behind himself. Although he wanted to talk to Banfield and Bertoli about yesterday's polygraph, he decided to give it a day for things to quiet down before leaving a signal and heading back out to Fort Marcy.

He continued alone through the sleet, lost in his thoughts. He was still apprehensive about the poly, even though he'd worked hard to convince himself he was just being paranoid. Even if Agent Finn had suspicions about his truthfulness, Ethan knew the best thing he could do for himself was remain calm and continue acting as if all was normal, both at home and at work.

Finn had nothing, Albright had nothing, and if he just chilled out, Ethan told himself, he'd be fine.

In an effort to play it cool, he'd had Eve over the previous evening, they'd gone out for dinner at a Korean barbecue in Adams Morgan, and then they returned to his place to watch a movie until heading to bed. Eve made it clear halfway through the movie she wanted sex, but Ethan begged off. Again, he wasn't in the mood.

Eve was a little disappointed, but not too surprised. Ethan was normally the aggressor, but he'd seemed distracted lately.

She spent the night, but went home early in the morning while Ethan was out on his run. Before she left she brewed him a pot of coffee and pulled his cup out of the cabinet, staging it for him next to the coffeemaker. On top of the cup she left a Post-it note with a heart on it that she drew with a Sharpie.

Ethan returned from the run to the empty house, walked into his kitchen, crumpled the Post-it and tossed it in the trash. Then he poured himself a cup of coffee and headed upstairs to start the shower.

At 8.40 a.m. he stepped out the front door of his Georgetown row house. By now the clouds had moved on and the sky was bright and blue. He buttoned his wool coat against a cold breeze as he descended the stairs and headed down to his Mercedes in the driveway.

A moment later he fired up both the engine and the stereo. He was in a Rage Against the Machine mood this morning, so he selected a playlist on his phone and then rolled off down 34th Street in the direction of work.

Dominic Caruso watched him go.

He stood in a small grove of trees across the street in Volta Park, his hands in his pockets to protect them from the cold wind. His head and face were covered with a wool hat and a neck gaiter, and he wore gray coveralls and black sneakers. A white hard hat was tucked into the crook of his arm, and a small black backpack hung over a shoulder.

He looked like a laborer who'd just climbed off a bus from one of the poorer sections of town, down here in fashionable Georgetown to work on the roads or an exterior home-remodel project.

After Ethan Ross's Mercedes disappeared down the street with some sort of thundering rap music Dom couldn't identify blaring through its closed windows, he turned his attention back to Ross's home: 1598 34th Street was a narrow, whitewashed brick two-storey row house with a driveway on one side and steps in front that led both up to the tiny porch and down to a basement entrance. It wasn't a large building at all, maybe fifteen hundred square feet or so, but in this ritzy neighborhood Dom put its value at north of two million dollars. Dom doubted the average NSC staffer would be able to swing a mortgage here, which meant Ross's wealthy mom was probably footing the bill.

Dom didn't know if this guy was the traitor or not, but he'd already built up some biases against him.

From his position in the neighborhood park Dom could see the fronts of all the row houses up and down the other side of 34th Street. He took a few minutes to make sure none had security cameras on their porches that were angled to pick up the sidewalk in front of Ross's property. He knew exactly where to look for them, and he found nothing that gave any indication that an approach of 1598 would be recorded for posterity by a neighbor.

He then spent a few minutes analysing several other crucial features about Ross's property and the neighborhood from his viewpoint here in the quiet little park. When he had all the intel he needed he turned away, headed back up the street to Wisconsin Avenue. His mission for right now was to get out of the cold and to enjoy a leisurely cup of coffee. He wanted to make certain everyone in the neighborhood heading to work or to school this morning had cleared out, so he decided to time his entry for 10 a.m.

Last night after he got off the phone with Albright, Dom read through Ross's bio and CV and a few articles he had written for *Foreign Affairs* and other publications. He'd found nothing in his writings of note other than a bias against Israel, which wasn't at all uncommon in U.S. diplomatic circles. He then looked up Ross's name and birth date in a D.C. real estate records database and found his address in Georgetown, pulled up the neighborhood on Google Maps, and used Street View to virtually walk the area. This gave him a basic understanding of the layout and style of the buildings, and he was even able to use his computer to look over a fence in the side yard that showed him the rear of his target's property.

Dom knew there was much Street View could not

reveal – the map was not the territory, after all – but he also knew spending a few minutes on his tablet looking at the area was a hell of a lot safer than spending the time physically wandering the streets around his target location and climbing fences.

No neighborhood-watch busybody was going to call the cops on him while he sat on his couch looking at Ross's house virtually, even if he spent all night doing so.

There was another program on Dom's computer that did much the same thing, although in higher detail. EagleView Technologies had a satellite mapping service that was similar to Google Maps, but it had more coverage with higher resolution in places where Google Maps did not bother to provide data, which made it a great resource for military and intelligence purposes. Dom could have used EagleView to research Ross's home, but for his needs – a view of a street in Georgetown – Google Maps was just fine.

Dom appreciated technological advances like this. His uncle had been a spy, sort of, back in the old days – the 1980s. Dom couldn't imagine what that was like, operating against the Soviet Union without a smartphone and worldwide satellite imagery.

He thought it must have been exhausting.

After spending a half-hour on Google Street View and the property-records search of Ross's home that gave him the basic layout, he decided he could, with some tradecraft and planning, pay a covert visit to Ross's home to look for more information.

It was a decision he did not take lightly. After all, this was B&E, breaking and entering. One hundred per cent against the law, even for a guy with a badge that said he was FBI. But Dom was driven by the death of the Yacobys and the faint sense that he was on the scent of one of the people responsible for their deaths, and if the Bureau's best polygraph examiner suspected Ross was hiding something, Dom decided that was good enough for him to poke around into the man's affairs.

Albright, on the other hand, would have to go through channels, which meant he'd have to jump through a maddening array of bureaucratic hoops. Dom told himself he'd dig into Ross a little, and if he turned out pure as the driven snow, Dom would back away quickly and discreetly. He'd be chastened by his impetuous behavior, but there would be no harm, no foul. On the other hand, if he found evidence that this White House wonder boy with the model looks and the multimillion-dollar house had anything to do with the deaths in India, then he knew exactly what he was going to do.

Dom was going to ask Gerry for lethal authority to kill him.

Ethan Ross got lucky with the traffic this morning and he made it to work a little early – a rare enough occurrence that one of the security guards in the entrance shack to the Eisenhower Building made a joke about him vying for a promotion. In his office Ethan took off his coat, grabbed his waiting mocha off his desk, and stepped out into his secretary's office. He chatted with Angie for a few minutes, well aware of his need to appear cool and casual, and quite impressed with his ability to do so. Angie asked about the poly and he remained relaxed, going into little detail but assuring her it was nothing more than a nuisance.

He actually got some work done in the first part of the morning. The national security adviser himself had an appointment in the Oval that afternoon, and Ethan's direct boss had sent him a couple of questions to answer about a dispute in the Knesset that might or might not come up during the meeting. Ethan did some research in his files and on the Intelink-TS system, and he called a colleague at CIA. He sent his answers back to his boss before 9.30 a.m.

Everything was going smoothly today, and Ethan's feigned relaxed demeanor morphed into authentic composure as the morning wore on. He could see the light at the end of the tunnel; the FBI investigation would fizzle out in days, and this would all be behind him before he knew it.

He took a long break after sending his work to his boss, grabbed a cup of coffee in the dining room and chatted with some other staffers, then he returned to his desk. He'd just sat back down when he heard Angie talking to someone out in her office and he glanced up. There, just outside his door, stood FBI special agent Darren Albright.

The FBI agent looked huge and menacing as he loomed in the doorway, his eyes locked on Ethan and his broad shoulders squared toward him.

Ethan felt his head recoil, just an inch or two. He clenched the sides of his desk with both hands.

What's going on? Was he under arrest? Was Albright going to tell him to stand up and turn around?

Ethan relaxed a little when Albright said, 'Don't get up,' but Ethan stood on shaky legs anyway.

The special agent said, 'I just stepped in to see your secretary to check your schedule. Wondering if you have time for a quick interview.'

'An *interview*?'

'It's routine,' Albright said, but the blank expression on his face remained, and Ethan read it as ominous. 'You have a few minutes?'

Ross then bent over his blotter to look at his agenda for the week. He kept his hold on the edge of the desk as he did so, worrying his hands would shake.

'Actually, we'll have to do it another day. I'm taking the afternoon off. I'm out of here in a few.'

'Going somewhere?'

'To the dentist,' Ethan replied flatly, careful to hide any defensiveness.

Albright did not blink. 'This won't take but a minute.'

Ross looked back up from his blotter. He shrugged, a nonchalant gesture that he wondered if he had overbaked. 'Well . . . I'm right in the middle –'

'Five quick minutes. Just a couple of questions.'

Fuck. He wished he'd taken Harlan's pills this morning. He *should* have taken them, should have been ready for an impromptu questioning like this. He wouldn't sweat – the glycopyrrolate would last for several days, but he regretted not taking the mood-stabilizing meds.

Ethan motioned to the chair in front of his desk, and he and Albright both sat back down. He folded his arms in front of him and put his elbows on his blotter. He pushed down hard into them, now virtually obsessed with the idea of avoiding displaying to Albright the anxiety he felt by exhibiting tremors.

The FBI man pulled out a notebook and a pen, then began flipping through the pages, as if looking for something. 'Your girlfriend.' He tossed another page to the side and scrolled down some more. 'Eve Pang.'

Ethan clenched his jaw and straightened his back slightly. 'What about her?'

'She is an information systems security manager at Booz Allen.'

'That's correct.'

'Working, I see, on firewalled and VPN platforms.'

Ethan narrowed his eyes and looked over Albright's shoulder to a spot against the wall as if he was thinking. 'Not sure. We don't talk about work too much, but I think that sounds about right.'

Albright cocked his head. Ethan couldn't tell if he was genuinely surprised or playing a role. 'You don't talk about work?'

'Not really.'

'You got your B.A. in computer science, didn't you?'

'Yes.'

'So you probably have a lot to talk about.'

'Not really. What she does is light-years beyond my knowledge.'

Albright smiled. Ross realized he'd never seen the man make the expression. 'How would you know what she does if you two don't talk about work?'

'Well. I mean . . . I know in general what she does.'

'You do? How so?'

Ethan felt his blood boiling. Albright's leading and provocative questions were quick and terse and designed to make him ramble, perhaps to incriminate himself. Ethan didn't know if all this was due to Finn's suspicions yesterday, or if everyone here on the third floor was getting the same treatment, but he felt genuine fear sinking into the pit of his stomach. Yesterday he'd had time to plan for his polygraph, and he'd been ready, more or less. This impromptu inquisition had caught him completely off guard. His mind raced with doubt and worry. *Why the hell did I tell him I could talk? Would it have looked worse to refuse to speak? What can I say to stop this interview right now?* 'Really, Special Agent Albright, I don't think it's appropriate for you to bring Eve into this. She doesn't even work here, and –'

'I mean . . . it's only natural to discuss work. I talk about the job with my wife, general stuff, mind you, because she doesn't hold a security clearance. I would imagine Eve probably told you all about the unauthorized breach of the *Ardahan* files as soon as it happened, four months ago. There wouldn't be anything wrong with that. You're cleared TS.'

Albright went silent again. Ethan felt him trying to pull words out of his mouth.

Ethan only shook his head slowly.

Another G is trying to get you to confess. Shut the fuck up.

Albright sat patiently.

At last, and only to break an interminable silence that Albright seemed content to let last forever, Ross said, 'No. She didn't say anything about it. Of course she wouldn't, would she?'

'Wouldn't she?'

The two men looked at each other for a long moment in dead silence. Finally Ethan said, 'No. Delvecchio said even though the breach was months ago, it was only identified after the attack in India last weekend.'

'Oh, right. That's correct.' Albright coughed and looked down at his notes, an affectation that made him look uncomfortable. 'My mistake.'

Nailed him, Ethan thought. This son of a bitch thought he was going to win a battle of wits with Ethan Ross. Bolstered now, Ethan said, 'You are thrashing around, Special Agent Albright. I get it. You need to catch the culprit. I honestly hope you do. But you are barking up the wrong tree.'

Albright shrugged, his big shoulders heaved in his suit. 'Maybe so. Maybe not.'

'Do I need to bring my lawyer into this?'

Albright furrowed his brow like he was genuinely confused. 'Your lawyer? I don't know, Mr Ross. I guess if you are in some kind of trouble then *yes*, you might need a lawyer.'

The room went silent again.

Albright let the tension build before he spoke. 'I'm going to interview Ms Pang. You might want to take this opportunity to get out in front of anything she says.'

'Interview her? She doesn't have anything to do with the network here.'

'Yes, but she has a lot to do with you. We won't box her, but we'll ask her about your conversations. If there was anything at all that she let slip in her pillow talk, anything that you might have used to facilitate the download of the *Ardahan* files, well, you won't be the only one in trouble.'

'That's outrageous.'

'What's outrageous is the fact that someone in this

office, someone entrusted with classified information, violated that trust. It would also be outrageous if someone's girlfriend helped him, either wittingly or otherwise. She'd lose her clearance for certain, she'd lose her reputation. If I could tie an indictment on to her, I would do just that.' Albright leaned forward. 'I'd drag her through the coals, just to fuck with the guy who betrayed his nation.'

Ethan kept a poker face. 'Is there anything else, Special Agent Albright?'

Albright nodded. 'That's right, you need to be running along so you can go get your teeth cleaned.'

'And I assume you need to move off down the hall to the next office to try and scare Walter, and then move from him to Beth's office to terrify her. Interesting job you have. Must be a blast.'

The FBI man headed to the door, but he stopped, turned, and looked back. 'Actually, this part of the job sucks. But the best part, the part I fucking live for, is that moment when I Mirandize some arrogant prick who thought he was going to get away with it.'

'Well, then, I wish you luck with that.'

Albright said, 'Yeah, see you around,' and he left the office without another word.

Ethan sat quietly for several minutes, his elbows still on the desk, pondering the conversation with the FBI special agent. Then he lifted his coat off the rack, grabbed his briefcase, and headed for the door.

20

Dominic Caruso returned to Volta Park at 10 a.m., and he stood behind a fence, watching 1598 34th Street NW on the other side of the road. He was still dressed in his gray coveralls, and now he wore his hard hat and his sunglasses.

Dom fitted into the fabric of the neighborhood perfectly; no one walking their dog or driving by would notice him at all, not that there was much automobile or foot traffic on the street at 10 a.m. on a Thursday.

Most home break-ins happen in daylight because that's when people aren't home, of course, but there is also something about the middle of the day that causes natural defenses to diminish. People who look like they belong are rarely noted and almost never suspected.

Dom crossed the street at the corner, then he walked down to 1598, and he stepped on to the property as if he had every reason and right to be there. He took the steps down to the basement entrance, and here he stood shielded from the street and anyone who passed.

Dom seriously doubted Ross had a tenant in a private apartment down here, but he knocked nonetheless, then rang the doorbell. When no one answered after a minute, he repeated the process upstairs, and only after he was certain no one was home did he go back down the steps and move around to the tiny narrow driveway.

Next to the electric meter on the side of the house Dominic found the telephone junction box. He used a screwdriver from his backpack to open the panel, and then he simply unplugged the outgoing phone line.

If the security system had been wireless, he would have had more difficulties, but the little sign sticking out of a planter on the front stoop told him all he needed to know. This particular company did not offer wireless home security in this area, so Dom felt comfortable he could defeat the system with ease.

He went back down to the basement entrance, where again he was invisible to the street. He did not pause, he did not second-guess himself. Instead he pulled a lock-picking set out of his backpack, knelt down and went to work. He defeated the old door's deadbolt and knob lock in eighty seconds.

He opened the door extremely slowly. Immediately, the burglar alarm began chirping. This notified the home-owner that he or she had sixty seconds to disarm the alarm before it sounded and, under normal circumstances, contacted the monitoring station.

But Dominic had prevented the outgoing call, so the alarm was more an annoying noisemaker than a security device.

He kept his shades on and his helmet low on his head as he entered the house, still holding on to the door and moving at a glacial pace. At this stage he was on the hunt for motion-detector cameras, the type Ross might have attached to his wireless router. These would work independently of the home security system.

Dom pegged Ross as a techno buff. He had a background

222

in computers, after all, so he could easily set up his own enhanced home-monitoring system using his wireless network.

Dom walked slowly now, his entire body moved less than three inches a second, meaning each step through the house took ten times longer than normal. Off the shelf, motion detectors were typically set to notice movement that tracked faster than three inches a second, so Dom and his teammates at The Campus had spent many silly yet laborious hours of training to defeat motion sensors by walking through hallways like wind-up toys whose springs had sprung, giving them little energy for movement.

This required patience and care. If Dom bumped something on a table here in Ross's home, if he dropped something out of a pocket, if he kicked something on the floor, or if he simply moved one inch per second faster than planned, the camera would notice him, and Ethan Ross would get an urgent text message on his phone alerting him to a disturbance at his home. A motion-capture photo would be sent along with the text, displaying Dom in his residential-construction worker getup, and real-time video would be recorded at a website run by the security camera's manufacturer.

The alarm began sounding loudly throughout the house after a minute, but Dom ignored it, knowing it was a small risk anyone in the area would even hear it, a smaller risk anyone would call the police if they did, and an infinitesimal risk the police would show up in time to catch him in the act.

He found what he was looking for three minutes after entry. He'd taken the stairs up to the main floor and entered the kitchen from a rear entrance to the hall. A small camera was on the kitchen peninsula, facing the living room and the front door. Dom approached the camera from behind, so he moved at a normal pace, and he simply flipped a switch on the back that turned it off.

Free to move around the ground floor at will now, he found the locked security system box on the wall in the hallway and had it open in ten seconds. He unplugged the alarm, stopping the shrill siren. He left the box open and the wire dangling from it while he resumed his hunt throughout the house for electronic eyes.

He expected to discover another wireless security camera facing the back door, so he was not surprised when he found it overlooking a glassed-in back porch, but this cam was trickier than the first, because Ross had hidden it at the top of a pantry closet with a small hole cut through the door. He considered flipping off the entire wireless system in the house, but there would be a record of that in the router's memory, so after spending a minute trying to figure out how he could defeat the device without opening the door and triggering it, he simply decided to avoid the entire back porch altogether, even though in front of the camera's lens stood a wicker settee and a coffee table full of loose papers that appeared to contain some handwritten notes.

Dom took the stairs to the second floor, where he found another motion detector, but this one was linked to the home security system, and had therefore already been disabled.

He looked at his watch. His breach and clear of the premises had taken seven minutes, twelve seconds.

For step two, the security evaluation, he did a quick walk through the home, looking for evidence of a roommate who was not home but might return, a dog out for a walk with a walker, a live-in girlfriend who might pop home for lunch, kids who needed to be brought home from school early, or any indication that others came and went. From the closets he determined Ethan lived alone, although it was clear two people had slept in the bed the previous evening.

Dom knew from Albright that the man had a girlfriend, but the only photographs he found around the home were either of Ethan himself or of Ethan's mother.

Next Dom focused on the file cabinet in Ross's small home office. He thumbed through the meticulously indexed files until he found a tab that said Home Security. He pulled out the file, shuffled through some papers, and located an index card containing the password for the system's key panel. He put the paperwork back where he found it, hurried downstairs, plugged the power back into the wall box, and shut the case. At the key panel by the front door he typed in the password and disarmed the alarm, putting it in a dormant mode that would not activate if the doors were opened or closed.

Stage two was complete twelve minutes and twenty seconds after he entered through the basement door.

Still looking at his watch, Dom felt he probably had several hours before Ethan would return from work, but he didn't have any information about a possible housekeeper, so he gave himself only thirty minutes to do what he needed to do inside the home.

Now came stage three: the SSE, or sensitive site exploitation.

He began upstairs in the bedroom, where he found a mobile phone by Ross's bed, which surprised him. Most people have only one phone, and they keep it with them. For a brief, horrifying second Dom worried Ross was still somewhere in the house, but the thought quickly disappeared as Dom realized he'd already checked every room at least once. This guy simply owned more than one phone, for some reason. Dom checked the phone quickly for any telltales, anything Ross might have set up so he could know if it had been tampered with, then carefully confirmed the device was password-protected.

Yep. Damn.

Pulling intel off the device would take hacking equipment Dom did not have, but finding this phone was not a complete strikeout. He looked it over closely and decided it was new: the buttons were stiff and the case was pristine. He then carefully opened the back of the phone with a small screwdriver and photographed the number on the SIM card. Dom knew, with the right equipment, the subscriber identity module number could be used to track the phone or trace its usage.

He checked the living room next. It was rather stately for its small size, with high ceilings and antique bookcases. Dom set his phone to record video of everything out in the open, paying special attention to handwritten phone numbers, parking stubs, receipts, and other items that Ethan generated in his day-to-day life that might be able to attach him to either a person or a place.

Dom spent the next several minutes looking through the wastepaper baskets, thumbing through mail and receipts, and filming everything as he went.

He didn't have time to go through everything, but this was exploitation, not analysis. When he got back home he would feed the video file through analytical software that would identify, evaluate and categorize words and numbers pulled from each image.

Dominic filmed a stack of books on a shelf, and a similar stack on the coffee table. Every last one of them had to do with computer security.

Of course, Dom knew that Ross's girlfriend was a computer security expert, but these looked like textbooks, not something she would need, since she had earned her doctorate years ago.

So they belonged to Ross? Was this guy a policy wonk, or was he a computer programmer? Dom realized he was looking for reasons to be suspicious of the man, and this proved nothing in itself, but it was at least a little curious.

He kept searching.

A MacBook Pro sat on the living room couch. Dom checked it quickly for any obvious tamper-detection traps, such as a hair attached to the lid and base that would break if someone opened it. Just like with the phone he found no telltales, which made Dom think Ross behaved just like most normal people, and he had mistakenly put his faith in a home security system that could be defeated by anyone with a screwdriver and a little knowledge.

Dom opened the laptop and confirmed it was, in fact, password-protected. He imagined there were answers to be found on the hard drive, but he didn't have the resources to uncover them. He thought about David and his promise for logistical support from the Mossad, but he couldn't think of a way to exploit the hard drive in the time he had to do so without Ross knowing someone had been snooping around his place.

No. That wouldn't work. Dom would have to find clues somewhere else.

Five minutes later he was back upstairs in Ross's office, flipping through the paper on his desk, then digging inside the drawers. In a file folder he found a copy of Ross's clean title on a 2013 Mercedes Benz E-Class coupe. Red. Dom took a picture of the VIN. If he could find it later, either here at Ethan's house or in a parking lot near the Eisenhower Building, he would attach a slap-on GPS locator under the bumper so he could then track the vehicle with an app on his phone.

On a whiteboard on the wall by the desk Dom saw Ross had written a few notes to himself, and he sucked these up into the video recording.

His watch chirped, alerting him he had ten minutes remaining of his allotted thirty. He went downstairs for a quick check of the kitchen, and here he looked through drawers and cabinets and at cans and jars. He recorded matchbooks, pens and notepads with logos, even the names and vintages of the wines in his wine rack. He found small plastic pill bottles in a drawer, and they stood out because unlike most prescription medication, there were no markings on any of the bottles. Inside each he saw several pills, with each bottle containing pills of a different color and shape. Dom photographed them carefully, and then put them back where he'd found them.

He had just started to check for trace markings on a blank notepad attached to the refrigerator when he heard a noise, like a footfall, on the small brick porch outside the front door of the row house, just twenty-five feet from where he now stood. He was understandably startled at first, but within a half-second he deduced it must have been the mailman.

Dom stood there for a moment, watching the mail slot, expecting his assumption to be confirmed, when a stack of letters and ads fell to the floor. While he watched, he reached over and flipped back on the wireless security camera covering the entrance and the living room.

But just as he flipped the switch, Dom heard the unmistakable and panic-inducing sound of a key sliding into the lock of the front door. The door latch clicked instantly, and a shaft of light from outside raced toward him along the hardwood floor.

21

Dominic dropped flat on his chest in the kitchen behind the peninsula, shielding himself from the entryway. He spun himself around to face the doorway at the back of the kitchen, which led to the hallway that ran along the northern side of the first floor. He began pulling himself forward with his hands so his sneakers didn't squeak on the polished floorboards, using his cotton coveralls to slide silently.

Behind him, he could hear the front door close and someone in the living room walk over to the wall security system keypad and punch a couple buttons.

A male voice muttered, 'What the fuck?'

Dom suspected this was Ross, and he'd obviously just noticed the security system was disarmed, meaning either someone had changed it or else he had forgotten to set it this morning when he left for work.

Dom kept pulling himself across the floor, slowly but surely. While he did so he thought Ross would have to be either incredibly switched on or a complete obsessive-compulsive to have no doubts he had remembered to alarm the system.

There was an entrance to the hallway to the back stairs from the living room, and another from the back of the kitchen. Dom hoped like hell Ross would bypass the kitchen altogether, but he heard the creaking footfalls on the hardwood as Ross began moving in his direction.

Dom picked up the pace, moving along the floor. He kept his legs up and pulled himself with his forearms, using the low friction of the slick surface to slide along on his chest and hips. It took all his upper-body strength to accomplish this, and doing so without grunting with effort was difficult.

He pulled himself into the hallway out of view, and he'd just kicked his legs out of the kitchen when the kitchen light snapped on. Ross was just fifteen feet behind him at the light switch, and very possibly still heading his way toward the stairs up to his bedroom.

Dom launched to his feet and moved straight back down the hall, making his footsteps as soft as possible and doing his best to keep them in perfect cadence with the louder steps of Ross behind him. Dom passed the staircase on his left and ducked through the open doorway of a tiny laundry room on the right. The dark space was barely enough room for a stacked washer and dryer, but Dom pressed himself hard against the appliances to stay out of view from up the hall.

He heard keys dropped on a counter, and the footsteps behind halted for an instant, but then they started up again.

Looking directly ahead, Dom could see the stairs in front of him. If Ross climbed the stairs he would only have to glance down and to his right to see a man in gray coveralls and a white hard hat leaning back into his washer and dryer.

Ethan Ross entered the hallway on Dom's left and began climbing the stairs.

Dom pushed himself against his backpack with all his might, backing himself up another inch or two. He was furious for allowing himself to get into this compromised and dangerous position. He had a pistol in a shoulder holster under his coveralls, but he wasn't about to pull it. So far, Dom had enough evidence to suspect Ross only of being a rich mama's boy. If Ross saw him, Dom could do little more than run for the front door.

Ethan climbed the stairs toward the first floor, slowly and distractedly, in great contrast to his movements since leaving his office a half-hour earlier. He'd all but raced home, intent on getting in touch with Banfield and Bertoli as soon as possible, but this all changed the moment he entered his house and tried to turn off his home security system only to find it had already been disarmed. He was out of it today, not nearly as confident as he needed to be, but he couldn't believe he hadn't armed the security system before he left this morning.

He thought back and was nearly certain he remembered doing so, but he had to admit to himself that, despite his sharp intellect, for mundane repetitive tasks it wasn't hard to get one day confused with the next.

Ethan pushed the alarm system out of his mind as he headed into his bedroom, and immediately he returned to his main worry. Special Agent Darren Albright. Ethan had left work shortly after Albright left his office. He wasn't concerned about appearances, he told Angie he was heading out for lunch before his dentist appointment and would be gone for the rest of the day. And although he was certain she'd heard at least part of his conversation with the special agent, he knew Angie wouldn't suspect him for an instant of being a whistleblower.

He changed out of his suit and then stepped into his closet to grab a pair of jeans and a cashmere sweater. All the while he thought about how he would get in touch with Banfield. He had to be sharp now, sharper than he'd obviously been so far. Making contact with Banfield without using the fire-hydrant signal was a danger, of course, but he thought it so important now it was even worth risking a phone call, although he knew he had to use some sort of code in case either he or Banfield was under surveillance.

When he was still in the process of getting dressed he picked his home phone out of its cradle by his bed, then brought it to his ear. As he did so he noticed the mobile Banfield had convinced him to purchase a few days earlier, and it occurred to him it would be foolish of him to use his landline to make the call.

He cradled the home phone and snatched up the mobile. While he dialed the number with one hand, he struggled to pull his head through his cashmere sweater.

Directly downstairs, Dominic slipped off his sneakers, then tied the laces together quickly so he could hang them around his neck. In his stocking feet, he scooted along the floor of the downstairs hallway so as to stay as quiet as possible, and he moved to the back of the house. He entered the covered porch – he was in front of the lens of the security camera in the pantry, but he knew it wouldn't matter now that Ross was home. The wireless camera wouldn't send an alert to his phone if his phone was connected to the same network, because it would know he was home.

Dom first planned to make his way out the back door, climb the fence and clear the scene, but the fact Ross was home gave him an opportunity Dom could not pass up.

He knelt down by the messy coffee table on the closed-in porch and he recorded all the paperwork there with the video function of his camera phone. He found more papers in a magazine rack next to the couch, and this he pulled out and sifted through quickly, careful to record each sheet.

While he worked he kept his ears tuned to the footfalls directly above him. He could hear Ross moving into and out of his closet, and then he heard a muffled voice.

It was only Ross speaking, so Dom presumed he was talking on the phone.

Dom didn't know if he was using the mobile phone by the bed or another mobile, but he sure as hell wasn't using the landline in the house, because Dom had disconnected the wire in the box outside.

Dom couldn't make out anything said until the very end of the one-sided conversation, when Ross all but shouted, his voice agitated, 'I mean today! Right the fuck now!'

Dom thought this sounded highly suspicious. He finished his work on the porch and headed for the door. It had a serious exposed slide lock and a massive deadbolt. Dom unlocked the deadbolt, but just as he reached for the sliding lock, he jerked to a stop. Behind him in the hallway came the sound of creaking stairs – Ethan Ross was on his way down.

Shit.

On the other side of the back door was a screen door, and Dom imagined it would be a noisy proposition to open this in a hurry. He turned away from the exit and scooted in his stocking feet back to a hallway closet by the entrance to the porch. He pushed himself inside, hiding behind the array of thick coats hanging there. He just needed a place to stay out of sight until Ross left the house. He'd peeked in the closet earlier, and now he decided it was his best possible option.

But Murphy's Law kicked in. He heard Ross's shoes squeak on the hallway floorboards when he turned at the stairs and began walking in Dom's direction. Dom realized Ross was heading for this very closet. Dominic rolled his eyes, pushed his backpack hard against the wall, and fought the urge to yank his Smith & Wesson out of his shoulder holster.

The closet door opened, Dom remained pressed flat against the cedar back wall, he didn't move a muscle, and he held his breath.

Ross fumbled with his coats for what seemed to Dominic to be an eternity. He yanked out a suede riding jacket, then put it back in favor of a camel-wool three-quarter-length coat, and then finally he settled on a high-tech red North Face synthetic down ski jacket. When he pulled it out Dom was exposed at the back of the closet, but Ross had already turned away. He shut the door and headed toward the front of the house, and Dom blew out a long, silent sigh.

As Ross entered the living room, his mobile phone rang. Dom heard him answer, and he managed to pick up the majority of the conversation because Ross's voice carried down the hallway.

'Hey, Mom. No, I left early. I told you. Dentist appointment. Taking the rest of the day off.'

Next came some grumbling from Ross that Dom couldn't understand, then he said, 'I'll do it later. I don't have time right now.'

After several more seconds of frustrated complaining, he said, 'I'm walking out the door. It's up in my office. I'll call you later and –' A long hesitation and an almost childish sigh Dom could hear even through the closed closet door. 'All right! Wait a minute.'

Dominic heard Ross running back upstairs; he sounded annoyed and hurried. When Dom knew Ross had stepped into his first-floor office, Dom pushed his way out of the closet and walked in his stocking feet to the back door. There he carefully unlocked the wooden door and opened it, then slowly pushed open the screen door. As he suspected, it squeaked upon opening, but Ross was talking on the phone upstairs, giving his mother someone's name and e-mail address.

Dom walked through the tiny backyard, staying close to the wall of the house on the off chance Ross was looking out a first-floor window. He made it to the driveway, knelt to put his shoes back on, and then he turned to head around to the front of the property.

Dom found the red E-Class parked in the drive. He reached into his backpack as he walked up to it, and he barely broke stride when he knelt down and placed a slap-on GPS receiver under the rear bumper.

He reattached the phone line at the junction box, and then closed it up and moved toward the street. With a quick glance to the front door of the row house to confirm he was in the clear, Dom stepped out on to 34th and began walking north.

As he headed away he heard Ross open and then shut his front door. Dom didn't look back, even when the Mercedes pulled out of the drive into the street and screeched off to the south, again with heavy music blasting from its speakers.

Dom relaxed for the first time in an hour. He didn't think he'd gotten much for his troubles, but he had collected some data he could analyse, and he had a way to see where Ross was heading. He suspected he was not going to the dentist. Whoever he was meeting with, Ross seemed to think it was an emergency.

Dom wouldn't try to track him to his meeting, it was too risky. Instead, he decided he'd go home and sit at his laptop to watch Ethan's movements in real time while he loaded all the data he'd picked up into the analytical software.

Ethan found himself back in Fort Marcy Park for the third time in four days. He hadn't driven here himself; instead, he'd parked his car in a lot near Washington Circle, and from there he took a cab into Arlington/Shirlington. He walked through The Village at Shirlington, an upscale outdoor mall, then caught a bus that took him to within a half-mile of the park, and he went the rest of the way on foot.

The long transit wasn't his idea. Harlan Banfield instructed him to take a circuitous route during their brief phone conversation, after first telling him to leave his primary mobile phone at home. This all seemed like a lot of silly spycraft to Ethan, he'd looked over his shoulder several times and hadn't noticed anyone tracking him, but Banfield had insisted, and the old newspaperman seemed like he knew what he was talking about, so Ross reluctantly tossed his main phone on his bed, took his new phone, and left his house to begin something Banfield dramatically referred to as a 'dry-cleaning run.'

He'd run around for forty-five minutes, it was the noon hour now, and as soon as he walked into the park Ethan saw that he and his collaborators would not have the place to themselves as they had on their earlier meeting. In addition to Banfield's Volkswagen, several other vehicles were parked in the little lot, and Ethan saw men and women eating packed lunches behind the wheel of their cars. A school group of twenty-five or so fourth-graders skittered around the Civil War–era gun emplacement, led, more or less, by a teacher and a park ranger, and a young couple wearing military fatigues – after all these years in the NSC Ethan still had trouble distinguishing the different branches by their utility uniforms – walked hand in hand on the trail.

For a moment he worried that everyone in the park – with the possible exception of the fourth-graders – was working for the FBI and was here only to catch him in the act. But he pushed this out of his head. He didn't have anything incriminating on him, and Banfield had told him he'd wave him off if he didn't feel comfortable with their level of privacy when he arrived.

Banfield and Bertoli stood by the cannon, in the exact same spot he saw them standing in before. Ethan looked for a signal from Banfield – he had a newspaper under his arm that he would drop to the ground if he wanted Ethan to pass them by and keep walking, but he kept the paper under his arm as Ethan approached.

Banfield spoke as soon as Ross was close. 'Do you absolutely *know* you weren't followed?'

'Of course I don't know. I mean, I don't think so. I didn't notice anyone, but I'm a White House policy maker, not some low-rent private detective.'

Bertoli waved the worry away. 'What has you so upset today, Ethan? The polygraph?'

Ethan said, 'The poly seemed to go okay, but the examiner asked me if I was taking medicine to keep me from sweating.'

Banfield winced. With a grave expression he said, 'You told him no, of course.'

'Of course I did. But I don't think he bought it.'

'Might just be a fishing expedition,' announced Banfield, but Ross couldn't tell for sure if he believed it.

'And then today. Special Agent Albright. He just showed up and questioned me, over and over. I asked if I needed to lawyer up and he backed off, but they are suspicious. At least I think they are.' He ran his hands through his blond hair. 'I mean . . . shit. I don't know. Maybe I'm just losing it.'

Banfield said, 'They might be doing this to everyone who had access to the file.'

'Maybe. But he said he was going to interview Eve to see if she might have told me about techniques in passing that were used in the peace flotilla download. She would never betray me intentionally . . . but Albright is good. He could twist her up. Get her to say something that makes him more suspicious.'

The three of them stood quietly in the park for a moment, weighing the situation. Banfield said, 'We can find out if you really are a person of interest, or if the FBI agent was just trying to rattle your cage.'

'How?'

'If you are a POI, they will put a surveillance package on you. Hopefully they haven't done so already, but the dry-cleaning run I sent you on would have shaken them off if they *were* tailing you.'

'Again, I didn't see anything.'

'It wouldn't be obvious, son. There would be a number

of cars rotating in and out when you are in your vehicle. Half a dozen men and women, probably more than that, when you are on foot. They'll tap your home and office phone, use a court order to get access to your mobile.'

'Jesus Christ.'

'Calm down,' said Gianna. 'Harlan, that would be a worst-case scenario. Let's not make things more stressful than they have to be.' She turned to Ross. 'We don't know that they are watching you yet.'

Banfield said, 'Here is what we'll do. I'll run you around town a little bit, just have you go from here to there without a care in the world.'

'And?' asked Ross.

'And I watch out for anyone following you.'

'Will you be able to –'

'Of course I will. I didn't just fall off the turnip truck. As I told you before, this isn't our first time dealing with this sort of thing. How soon can we run a little test?'

Ross looked at his watch. 'I am off for the rest of the day. I have a dentist appointment at one.'

'Good. You'll buy a headset so we can stay in communication via your new phone, go back to your car, and go to your appointment. If there is surveillance on you and they lost you, they'll know that's where they can pick you back up. Once you're finished, I'll direct you to a location where I'll be waiting to identify any FBI personnel following you.'

Ethan nodded distractedly, but Gianna stepped forward and gave him a hug. 'Hopefully everything is fine,' she said. To Ethan, this was a massive understatement.

'But if there are reasons for concern, we will take the steps necessary to keep you safe. Please, you must relax and trust me.'

Ethan looked into Bertoli's eyes. He thought of his mother, even though Bertoli was twenty years younger. 'I do.'

Banfield said, 'You're going to have to hurry to make your dentist appointment.'

Dominic spent half an hour sitting at his kitchen table, loading data from his phone into software on his laptop that would analyse and categorize his find. It was more work for the computer than it was for Dom, so while everything was loading and crunching he opened his slap-on GPS receiving app on his computer and began tracking Ethan Ross's Mercedes.

He saw from the map display that the vehicle had been parked in a lot in Washington Circle for more than fifty minutes. Just sitting there. Dom took this to mean whoever Ross rushed out to meet either lived or worked in the area. If Ross was indeed the traitor this was seriously bad news, as the options in the area for a man with classified U.S. intelligence and the will to share it with unsanctioned parties were plentiful. Embassy Row was within walking distance to the north, and other embassies and foreign organizations dotted the area. Dom guessed there were more state-actor enemies of America in a ten-square-block area around that parking lot than in any other place in the United States.

But he realized he was getting ahead of himself, making assumptions based on a lot of speculation. He fought the urge to continue with these assumptions without, at least, checking into some competing theories about just what Ross was doing.

He typed in 'dentist offices' in a Google Maps search of the area, and he saw a half-dozen within a couple of blocks of the parking lot where the Mercedes sat.

Shit. For all he knew, Ross had simply gone to get his teeth cleaned.

'No.' He said it aloud. The bits of the phone conversation he'd picked up back in Georgetown made him near certain Ross was meeting with someone else. 'Right the fuck now!' wasn't something someone said to the receptionist at the dentist office. There was an emergency in Ethan Ross's world, and Dom had to figure it involved the investigation into the SS *Ardahan* leak.

Dom knew this wasn't enough evidence for Albright. He wouldn't even reveal what he'd learned because it would only tip the FBI off that Dom was in play and inserting himself into the investigation. He thought about calling David, but he didn't have anything for the Mossad to do at this point. He had a suspicious-acting character demanding a clandestine meeting with . . . someone.

It wasn't much, but right now, it was enough for Dom. He decided he'd keep an eye on Ethan Ross to the best of his abilities. Dom was all alone, and couldn't very well tail him effectively. But he decided he might as well try a soft mobile surveillance. He put his shoulder holster back on, checked the lay of his Smith & Wesson under his arm. He then put on a thick black leather jacket and grabbed his motorcycle helmet and his keys. He turned on his phone's app for the slap-on tracker so he could follow Ross if he left the lot while Dom was en route, and then he headed down to his Suzuki TU 250 street bike.

Dom arrived at the parking lot in Washington Circle as Ethan Ross climbed out of a taxi just yards away from his vehicle.

To Caruso that looked fishy as hell. Why would he park his car and then cab it someplace else? Certainly he couldn't imagine any scenario that involved a dentist.

Dom circled the block to give Ross time to get into his car, and by the time Dom made it back around, Ross was pulling around the roundabout that served as the perimeter for Washington Circle Park. Dom expected him to head west on K Street back toward Georgetown, but instead Ross merged into traffic heading east on K.

Dom pulled into traffic several vehicles behind him. He kept himself shielded by the intervening cars and trucks, even though his smoked visor and the sheer distance would have made it impossible for Ross to identify his face even if he had been looking for surveillance.

Dom followed the bright red and easy-to-track vehicle all the way to Chinatown, where Ross pulled into a covered lot a block north of the Verizon Center, paying eleven dollars an hour for the privilege. Dom got lucky and found street parking a block to the south and he locked his bike while keeping an eye on the exit to the lot. Ross appeared a minute later, but instead of walking into Chinatown, he walked away from it, east on H Street. There were a number of office buildings here, but the NSC staffer just kept walking by entrance after entrance, continuing all the way to Massachusetts. Dom was well behind him and on the other side of the street, careful for any attempts by Ross to detect surveillance. This could have been an SDR – an attempt to see if anyone was on him – but Dom was playing it so soft he felt safe enough for the time being.

Finally, after fifteen minutes of walking through the cold, Caruso realized Ross was heading straight to Union Station. His first thought was that his target would descend into the Metro just outside of the station, which would have certainly made continued surveillance of him difficult if not impossible. But instead, Ross entered Union Station itself. He wasn't carrying any luggage, just a leather messenger bag, so Dom doubted he would be skipping town this afternoon.

Dom assumed Ross was here to meet someone, either for a perfectly aboveboard late lunch or for a clandestine meeting of some sort. If it turned out to be the former, Dom figured he would just go in and find a location to set up a static watch and keep tabs on the man, maybe see who he dined with. If the latter was the case, if he was here to interact with someone surreptitiously, well, Dom was a realist. Union Station was a huge area for one man to cover, with dozens of corridors, shops, restaurants, washrooms, and trains.

Dom wasn't going to stick so close that he would see anything too dramatic. That happened only in the movies.

As soon as Ross entered through the door near the Metro, Dom headed to the Massachusetts Avenue entrance, then entered into the huge, cavernous main hall. It was after 2 p.m. – most people in D.C. took lunch between noon and one, so the area was far from crowded.

Ross entered from the West Hall into the Main Hall, passing forty feet from Dominic without even glancing his way. Dom watched him out of the corner of his eye as he walked around the circular Center Café in the middle of the marble floor, then he headed through a double doorway to the main level mall concourse of the station.

Dom stayed on him, far enough behind that he ran a significant risk of losing him if Ross tried any evasion tactics or 'dry cleaning.' But he remained close enough to keep him in his sights as long as Ross kept things simple.

And Ross unwittingly co-operated. He entered a bookstore and browsed for a few minutes. Dom stayed across the hall in a clothing store with racks of suits high enough to hide himself if need be, and he found a mirror that just picked up Ethan while he stood at a book rack across the hall.

Ross didn't buy anything, and soon he was climbing the stairs to the shops on the mezzanine level.

Dom let him go, deciding instead to wait it out down here on the main level and keep an eye on both stairwells that led up to the mezzanine. If Ross had a meeting planned on the first floor, then Dom would be out of luck, but surveillance was a trade-off, and he absolutely did not want to spook this guy and cause him to raise his defenses.

Dom positioned himself between the two stairwells up to the mezzanine and pretended to make a phone call while he waited for his target to return. He spent his time watching others heading upstairs. Businessmen and businesswomen killing time while waiting for trains that would take them to New York, Baltimore, Richmond or Philly.

Young mothers struggling with strollers on their way to the mezzanine-level shops. An elderly couple moving slowly up the staircase, who were quickly overtaken by two college-aged men wearing tracksuits and backpacks.

Ethan Ross came down the stairs at the opposite end of the shopping hall a few minutes later. Dom fell in behind him as he headed back up the length of the main floor, then passed by as Ross stepped into a clothing store, crossing a large mirrored wall near the front.

As he checked the mirror, Dom noticed for the first time that his target was wearing a Bluetooth headset in his right ear. He didn't seem to be in conversation with anyone, but Dom could not be certain.

He also noticed that Ross wasn't on any real surveillance-detection route, because at no point did he check for a tail, or even look into the mirrored wall for any easy indication someone was following him.

The pieces came together slowly for Dom, but they did come together. The idle wandering around, the utter lack of interest in his surroundings, the headset in his ear.

Ross *was* on an SDR, but he wasn't the one doing the detection. Someone else was here, a confederate of his, watching him or, more accurately, watching for anyone on his tail.

The hairs stood up on Caruso's forearms under his jacket as he thought about enemy eyes on him right now.

23

The more Dom mentally retraced his own steps over the past half-hour, the more he convinced himself he'd played his surveillance correctly so far. He'd not followed Ross up the obvious choke point of the mezzanine stairs; he'd let the man come to him in the mall instead of just walking behind him. If Dom had been pinged by the opposition, whoever and wherever they were, then he was certain he'd just been pegged for closer scrutiny as one of many potential tails. He was sure he hadn't tipped his hand definitively that he was a surveillant.

Ross walked out of the clothing store now – again, he hadn't bought a thing – and he headed back to the staircase, this time descending to the food court in the basement.

Caruso's first inclination was to back off, to get the hell out of Union Station before Ross's fairy godmother, somewhere close by with eyes on him right now, tipped him off that he was being followed by a guy in a black biker jacket. But as he started to walk, Dom decided his best move was to make it obvious he wasn't a tail by blowing his cover on purpose. So he walked to the staircase, caught up with Ross, and then passed him going down, nearly brushing against him as he descended. It was such an overt move that, Dom determined, he would be discounted as a potential watcher by anyone who saw him.

In the food court, Dom got in line at a gyro stand. For

nearly three minutes he willed himself to look straight ahead, hoping that anyone suspicious of him was watching him the entire time, noting his complete lack of interest in anything other than his lunch. He ordered a lamb kebab and a Coke and paid for them, then waited while his order was prepared. All the while he looked ahead at the gyro stand or down at his phone. Only when he had his food in hand and found a plastic chair and a little table by the center staircase did he glance up and out at the big room.

It was just a quick peek, and then he looked back down to his lunch, but Dom had been trained to use a single glance to take a still picture of his surroundings with the camera in his brain. As he began eating, he processed the photo he just took. There were the fifty or so tables in front of him, the food stalls going down the right-hand side, the hallway to the restrooms on the left, and there, facing away and heading toward the restrooms, was Ethan Ross.

Dom looked up again as he took a sip of his Coke, keeping his gaze relaxed and natural. Ethan disappeared down the hall to the men's room. There was no way Dom would follow him, even if he didn't suspect Ross had a spotter somewhere in this room watching his back. The hallway was another choke point the spotter would send Ross down to ID an overzealous tail.

Nope, Dom decided he'd let his target piss on his own.

Caruso ate another bite of food, but stopped chewing suddenly when he saw something curious in front of him. A man in his thirties and wearing a charcoal-gray suit and an overcoat walked toward the bathroom hall to the men's room. There was nothing particularly interesting in that, but Dom noticed the man exchange a quick but unmistakable look with two young men sitting at a table eating pizza. On second glance, Dom realized these were the two college-aged men in tracksuits he'd seen heading up to the mezzanine behind Ross ten minutes earlier.

Charcoal-suit man didn't look like he was with the college boys, they certainly hadn't been together earlier, but the glance was one of insecurity. Concern.

To Dom the look said, 'Should I follow him in?'

After the look the man did, in fact, head down the hallway to the bathroom.

Dom had been on the passive lookout for Ross's spotter, but he knew these guys weren't working with Ross. The glance said something else.

They weren't Ross's fairy godmothers.

This was a tail.

Dom corrected himself. This was *another* tail. This had to be the FBI conducting surveillance on Ross, and this infuriated Caruso. He wanted to punch his fist into the wall next to him, but he fought the urge. He knew good and well that Ross's spotter would have seen the man he'd funneled into the choke point, and this meant Ross would now spook and go to ground, making proving anything against him much more difficult.

Dom took out his phone and dialed a number he'd saved in the memory. After a few rings, a man answered.

'Albright.'

Caruso whispered, though there was no one around. 'Damn it, Darren, your boys are fucking up.'

'My . . . boys? *What* boys?'

'Listen to me. The tail on Ross has got to pull back.

He's running an SDR, but he's got a spotter. Your team is trying to stick too close to him. Shit, I'm ninety per cent sure it's already too late. One of them just got dragged through a choke point.'

'Where are you?'

Dom sighed. 'I'm at Union Station. The food court.'

'You are following Ethan Ross?'

'A hell of a lot better than your team is following him.'

'I told you before, you are to stay out of the investigation. And you agreed to that. On top of that, he's not even a subject of inquiry.'

'If he's not a subject of inquiry why do you have a tail on –'

'We *don't* have a tail on him!'

Dom watched the two young men at the table as they stood and headed for the stairs, drifting through the light crowd. Dom expected they would go up and find a static watch location for when Ross ascended.

Dom asked, 'Then who the hell are these guys?'

Albright did not respond to the question. Instead, he said, 'I want you to go home. I'll come over later and talk to you about this.'

'This tail on him isn't FBI? You're one hundred per cent certain?'

'I am disinclined to discuss any part of the investigation with you at this point, since you obviously haven't held up your end of our bargain. But just so you will back off and not harass any civilians who are presumed innocent, I can positively confirm, on my mother's grave, that I do not have any surveillance package *of any kind* on NSC staffer Ethan Ross.'

'What are you going to do about these guys?'

'I suggest you contact the NSC. If there is a security issue involving one of their employees, *they* need to take care of it.' Albright hung up the phone.

Dom rolled his eyes. Clearly, Albright didn't believe Caruso's concerns were valid.

The two young men were out of sight now, but Dom thought about their appearance. They both had dark hair and somewhat olive complexions, but they could have been from just about anywhere save Scandinavia. The man in the charcoal suit had salt-and-pepper hair and lighter skin, although he wasn't exactly fair, either.

There were really no definitive conclusions he could draw about them from their appearance.

Ross appeared from the bathroom hallway, and Dominic looked down at his food. When he looked up again, thirty seconds later, Ross was gone. He'd apparently ascended the other staircase, on the far side of the basement from where Dom now sat.

Dom did not go after him. There was already too much going on around here for his taste, so he decided he'd just finish his lunch and go home.

He took a bite of the kebab, but realized he'd lost his appetite. Thinking about Ross, the fact he had confederates, the fact he now knew he was under suspicion and he would now act in a way that might well make him safer for it, churned Dominic's stomach. He stood and dumped his leftovers in a nearby garbage can, then headed toward the stairs closest to him.

Just in front of him a thickset older man in a camel-wool

coat turned to take the stairs, and Dom had to slow to let him pass.

Dom had just taken his first step up when he looked above him, past the older man, and he noticed a pair of uniformed D.C. metro police officers descending. One spoke into the microphone attached to his epaulet, and both men moved purposefully, as if they were being dispatched downstairs on a mission.

Almost instinctively, Dom turned around and began walking away from the stairs.

He knew instantly that Darren Albright had called the local police.

Not to grab Ross. Not to grab the guy spotting for Ross. Not to grab the men following Ross.

But to grab Caruso.

'Fucking Albright,' he mumbled to himself.

He walked past the hallway to the restrooms on his left and he continued to the stairs at the west end of the basement. Just before he reached them he turned away quickly and pretended to use an ATM on his right, keeping his back to the stairs.

Two more metro PD came down the west staircase and passed him unaware. After they moved on into the room, Dom spun away and shot up the stairs, then out of Union Station.

Just as Dom had suspected, Ethan Ross's fairy godmother *had* spotted the men on his tail. Harlan Banfield had sat in the food court, at a bench alongside a creperie ahead of Caruso but out of his view on the other side of a support column.

The moment he saw the men, Banfield ID'd them as FBI. This was confirmation bias. Ross thought the Feds were on to him, someone was, in fact, on to him, so Banfield presumed it was the Feds.

He was in constant communication with Ethan, but he did not tell him he was being followed. Instead, Banfield told Ethan to begin walking back to his car in Chinatown, and he would tell him what to do next. Once Ethan was out of the bathroom and taking the stairs out of the basement, Harlan headed to the staircase closest to him, rushed past a young man in a motorcycle jacket, and climbed up. A pair of D.C. police were heading down, but Banfield didn't pay any attention to them. He was already thinking about what to do next with Ethan Ross.

As he headed back to his motorcycle in Chinatown, Dom fished through his pocket and pulled out the card the Mossad officer gave him the previous morning. He dialed the number, and David answered on the first ring.

'Mr Caruso, so good of you to call. How can I be of service?'

'Do you have surveillance on someone here in D.C.?'

David chuckled. 'That is a vague question. Of course we have someone under surveillance. Syrian diplomats. Palestinian radicals. Egyptian military attachés. Your capital city is a surprisingly hostile environment. I presume, however, you are referring to someone specific?'

'Someone who might have been involved in the NSC breach.'

David answered unequivocally. 'Absolutely not. As I told you, we are hoping you might help us with that. We have other feelers out, of course, but so far nothing solid. If you are telling me you already have a suspect, I will be most impressed.'

'Well I *do* have a suspect, and he's got a tail.'

'FBI?'

'The FBI says no.'

'That's interesting. Some other actor is following him?'

'It appears so.'

'What is this man's name? I'll look into it on my end.'

Dom hesitated. No, he wasn't ready to get the Mossad involved in this. They were just one more moving part to a situation that was quickly becoming extremely complicated. Dom decided it was better he kept them at arm's reach – for now, anyway. 'It's just a hunch. I'll let you know if I find out anything more.'

'If you say this man is under surveillance, then that makes him more than a hunch. Involve us, Dominic, and we can use our resources to vet him.'

'I'll call you back.' Dom hung up the phone and kept walking. David was right, Ethan Ross was more than a hunch. But for now, all Dominic could do was try to think of a way to convince Special Agent Albright of this fact.

24

After an hour of Ross's browsing through several malls and chain stores in a very natural-looking dry-cleaning run, Banfield saw no more sign of any surveillance on his whistleblower. Still, it was clear to Banfield that the FBI was, at least, attempting to monitor Ross's movements.

At three-thirty in the afternoon he called Ethan and told him to go to an underground parking garage in Columbia Heights. Here, Ethan climbed into Banfield's car, and together the two men drove through rush-hour traffic to the Ritz-Carlton on 22nd Street, where they parked in the underground lot below the hotel.

While Ethan waited in the car, Banfield went alone up to Gianna Bertoli's two-room suite, checked the area and the route up a back stairwell, and then returned to shepherd Ethan up with him.

The three turned the volume on the television high and they ran the water in the bathtub and the shower and then sat close together on chairs in the living room of the suite. Bertoli had no real suspicion she was under surveillance, but as the director of the International Transparency Project, she'd learned to take a number of necessary steps to ensure her privacy.

Only when they were all seated with wine from the minibar in their hands did Banfield inform Ross he was, without a doubt, under surveillance by the FBI.

Ross's eyes glazed over.

Bertoli asked, 'You're certain, Harlan?'

'Yes. I identified at least three men following him through Union Station. We slipped away from them after that, and he was clean by the time I picked him up. But the tail was real.'

'Shit,' mumbled Ethan.

Banfield turned to Ethan and brightened a little. 'That's the bad news. The good news is I checked with another of my whistleblowers, and this person has access to U.S. federal employee files. I had her look into NSC employee records, and there are no new flags or security holds on badges or computer access of any staff member. That makes me think the surveillance on you is very preliminary. They are suspicious, and they'll keep digging, but for now they don't have enough to go on to do anything more than put a tail on you.'

As far as Ethan was concerned, Banfield was just sugar-coating it. Ethan felt his entire life slipping away from him. His family would not understand. While his parents would be sympathetic with the ideological reasons behind his actions, they were ex–government hacks, and they would think him a traitor like the rest of the world.

He leaned back in the chair and stared into space.

Bertoli knelt on the floor next to the young NSC staffer, hugging him in sympathy, as if the two had known each other for years.

Ethan spoke into the softness of her curly hair. 'What am I going to do?'

She put her arm on his shoulder and held it firmly. 'For now, you need to act naturally.'

257

'Albright is going to talk to Eve, and he is going to lean on her. She'll tell them she told me about specific system vulnerabilities, and then they will arrest me.'

Bertoli said, 'You are in a serious situation, I do not want to minimize it. But it is not dire. Not yet. The problem is, when it *becomes* dire, it will be too late for you to help yourself.'

'What does that mean?'

'There is something you need to do, and you need to do it now.'

'You are talking about the damn scrape again?'

'Yes. Harlan just said you still have access to your system. Go in to work tomorrow morning and download the files, then secure them whatever way you think is best. Just in case you need your ace in the hole.'

He shook his head. 'I'll just dig my hole deeper. Better I take my chances now. If they arrest me, I'll get the best lawyer money can buy, and I'll make as much noise as I can. Maybe if I'm lucky –'

Bertoli put her hand on Ethan's cheek. 'My poor, naive Ethan. If they catch you, you won't be famous. There won't be a big trial for you to air your grievances.'

Ethan said, 'This is America. They'll *have* to put me on trial.'

She shook her head. 'No. They will psych you.'

'*Psych* me?'

'Deem you a security risk, and then put you in a psychological facility, fill you up with meds, give you sort of a chemical lobotomy. They will forget about you. Everyone will forget about you.' With a rueful smile she said, 'The worst part is . . . *you* will forget about you.'

Ethan had heard rumors along these lines, but he'd never believed them. But Bertoli seemed utterly credible. He found it impossible to doubt her.

'What do you propose?'

Banfield said, 'You make your scrape, then you get out of town. Someplace far away so you can avoid arrest and set things up on your terms. Not theirs.'

'I could go to my mom's in San Francisco.'

Bertoli shook her head. 'No, Ethan. I am talking about going abroad. I'm talking about asylum.'

He put his head in his hands. '*Asylum?* No. *God,* no.' He mumbled to himself, his eyes distant like a victim of shock, as the weight of his predicament crashed down upon him.

The NASCAR drive appeared in her hand, and she folded it into his. He did not resist. Once again she said, 'If you wait until you need it, it will be too late.'

Banfield leaned closer, too. 'Through my contact, I will know if your access is blocked. That will be our indication that the FBI is planning on making an arrest. But again, it will be too late then.'

Ethan put the crawler in the pocket of his jacket and stood up. 'I don't know. I need to think about it.'

Bertoli let the worry on her face show, but she said, 'Okay. I understand.'

Harlan and Ethan left Gianna a few minutes later, slipping out the back stairs and down to the parking lot.

As the two men drove out of the neighborhood on the way to drop Ethan at a taxi stand in Petworth, Ethan decided he would talk to Eve to get a feel about just how bad things were. If she had been interviewed by Albright, if the situation seemed utterly hopeless, then he would go to the office tomorrow morning and steal secrets to use as a bargaining chip.

But he'd do it only if he had to. He told himself *he* was still in control, not Banfield, not Bertoli, not Albright. He would do what was best for him. Ethan believed in nothing more than he believed in his own intellect, and he still thought he could game this seemingly hopeless situation into something else. Not a victory for him, perhaps. That was too much to hope for. But maybe a draw. A détente between the parties.

Ethan Ross had faith in his brilliance. He'd get through this somehow and come out on the other end intact.

Dom Caruso sat on his couch with a half-empty bottle of Harp beer in his hand. The TV was off, his computer was shut down and in another room, and he'd straightened his living room to some small degree, because he expected company soon.

In the quiet of the moment he made a mental survey of his injuries. The headaches had gone away, he was thankful for that. He felt the tightness in his rib cage still; the pain had lessened greatly, but the spasm remained constant, and the ache of bruised tissue rose and fell with every breath. The cuts to his arm and chest were healing, he'd probably not rebandage them after his next shower, even though they would look pretty nasty for a few more weeks.

Dom had a little experience picking up knocks and dings. He was tough enough to shrug them off mentally long before they disappeared physically.

The knock at his door came about when he expected it to. Even the nature and temperament of the knocks, four thundering angry bangs, sounded just about as he had imagined they would. He didn't get up from his couch at first. Instead he sipped his beer, leaned back on his sofa, and waited for the next set of furious knocks.

No sense in rushing what was to come.

After several more bangs he heard, 'Caruso!'

'It's open,' Dom answered back.

Darren Albright entered a moment later; he wore a dark blue suit with no overcoat, and his hands were empty. He shut the door behind him, saw Dominic sitting on the sofa, and all but stormed over to him.

'Have a seat.' Dom pointed to a leather chair, but Albright ignored it.

'We had a deal.'

'I thought of it as more of a gentlemen's agreement.'

'And you're not a gentleman?'

'There's a time for that, sure. This just isn't it.'

Albright heaved as if summoning the strength to continue talking to a disobedient child. He sat down and leaned forward. 'I can't have you interfering with the investigation. Ethan Ross is just one of many potential subjects in this. It's going to take some time and some good fieldwork to narrow down the actual culprit. Anything that can jeopardize a good arrest is going to –'

'I think he's your man.'

'If you know something that leads you to that conclusion, I'd like to hear it.'

Dom opened his mouth to speak, but Albright held a hand up quickly. 'Unless, of course, what you say might compromise this investigation or make a successful prosecution impossible. I can't know what you and your spook buddies have done to violate Ross's Fourth Amendment rights, for example. If it's inadmissible in court, which I guess is probably the case with every goddamned thing you guys do, then do me the favor of keeping me the fuck out of it.'

Dom closed his mouth. He had nothing to say now. Albright noted this. 'Great. That's just fucking great. I'm going to just play like I don't know you and your people conducted some sort of unreasonable search and seizure.'

'"Unreasonable search and seizure"? Reciting buzzwords from the Fourth Amendment isn't going to help you catch your man.'

Albright launched out of the chair. 'But it will help me convict the guilty party! That's all that matters to me. I can see it in your eyes, Caruso. This is personal. Very personal. But when an off-the-books spook makes things personal, law and order are the first things tossed out the window.'

'Who says I'm an off-the-books spook?'

'I've looked at the books! You aren't on them. I'm an FBI agent. I draw conclusions. Look, you and I swore the same oath when we joined the Bureau. We affirmed that we would support and defend the Constitution of the United States against all enemies, foreign and domestic. Last time I checked, the Fourth Amendment was still part of the Constitution.'

Dom said, 'Yeah, well, our tactics are different, but we're both after the same enemy.'

Albright fired back. 'You're after Ross. I don't know that he's the enemy.'

'You still have no idea who was tailing him in Union Station?'

'I do know.'

Caruso brightened up quickly. 'Who?'

'You!'

Now Caruso dropped back on the sofa and rolled his eyes. 'Are we going to get past that? I'm telling you, someone else is interested in Ross.'

Albright seemed to take the idea seriously for the first time. 'If he did have a tail, then maybe it's the Israelis. They've got feelers out around the Hoover Building. They want answers. Maybe they found out he was one of the people we were looking at, so they are doing their own surveillance.'

Caruso shook his head. 'No.'

'No?'

'You'll have to trust me on that.'

'Right now I don't trust you on much of anything.'

Dom thought about what he should say, and what he should leave out. Finally he spoke slowly, with obvious care. 'The Israelis approached me the other day, asking questions. They lost a good man, and they are pissed. They wanted to see if I had any intel. I didn't, but it was clear they didn't, either.'

'How do you know they haven't found out about Ross some other way?'

'Trust me, they are flailing. They don't know about Ethan Ross. Whoever is following him is working for someone else. I don't know who it is, but unless one of the other thirty or forty potential leakers in the NSC both gamed their polygraph *and* have a mysterious entity on their tail, then Ethan Ross just might be your best bet right now.'

Albright conceded the point with a slow nod. He said, 'All right. Here's what I'll do. If you back off, and I mean back all the way off, then I'll put a surveillance package on Ross.'

Dom asked, 'When?'

'You are a pushy son of a bitch. I can get it in place by a.m. tomorrow.'

'Why not now?'

'Because it takes time! You are FBI, or at least you pretend to be, so you know that. If I was absolutely certain Ross was the man, if I *knew* he was in play with fresh intel, then yeah, I'd pull resources from everywhere and get surveillance set up in nothing flat, but I don't know any of that. I'll go back to the office right now and talk to SSG and Technology and everyone else I need to talk with to put the tap and tail in place.'

'They better be good. He's already nervous.'

'Don't worry about SSG. They are the best.'

That was debatable, Dom thought, but he didn't say. They were good, that was not in doubt, but Dom suspected a few other American agencies had surveillance personnel who could give them a run for their money.

'Again.' Albright pointed a finger at Dom. 'I'm not doing a thing until I get your word you won't interfere. And not your word as a gentleman, because that ship has sailed, but your word as a guy who knows he'll get his ass arrested if I see him anywhere around Ethan Ross. I don't give a shit that your uncle is President. Your dad could be the Pope and I'd still frog-march your ass if you pull any more of your shit.'

Dom stood and extended a hand. 'I promise. I'm out of this. It's up to you guys now.' Albright shook Caruso's hand, reluctantly because he was still annoyed, and he headed out the door on his way to the Hoover Building.

Dom could see it on the FBI special agent's face. Albright knew he was in for a long night.

25

Ethan took a cab to a bar on M Street a few blocks from his house, then walked the rest of the way to his neighborhood. He arrived at a quarter to midnight and stood across the street in Volta Park for several minutes, watching his place from a distance, looking for any surveillance in the cars or windows or trees.

A satellite TV van was parked on Q Street, just north of his place, and this caught his eye and unnerved him. He'd seen enough TV and movies to know FBI surveillance often parked in disguised vans right in front of their target location, and he wondered if inside the dark, still vehicle, three or four men sat at computer banks with headsets on, just waiting for his return.

But after ten minutes shuffling in the dark and cold in the corner of the park, Ethan watched as a man wearing the uniform of the satellite TV company exited the home of a neighbor, chatted with the lady in the doorway for a moment, and then climbed inside the van. He drove off down the street and disappeared.

Satisfied and somewhat surprised that his place was not being watched, Ethan stepped up to his house and entered through the front door. As was his custom, he crossed the dark living room to the security keypad to turn off the alarm before he flipped on the lights in the living room.

But as he got to the keypad he realized his alarm had been deactivated.

Again?

He stood there in silence, a little light from the street-lamps on 34th Street filtering through the blinds and across the floor, but the house was otherwise dark. He took a step toward the lamp on the table by the sofa, then he stopped suddenly. He sensed a presence there in the room with him.

He froze. His voice cracked when he spoke. 'Who . . . who is there?'

'What have you done?' It was Eve. Her voice low and flat. The tone both lamenting and accusatory.

The terror he felt thinking he was about to be arrested by Albright washed away quickly and was replaced by the knowledge that Eve Pang was now suspicious of him. What did she know? What had she told the FBI?

He stepped over to a small lamp on an end table by the wall and flipped it on. There, on his couch, sat Eve Pang. Still dressed for work in a long black skirt and a white blouse. Her hair back in a bun and her cat-eye glasses on her face. He'd rarely seen her when she was dressed for work; invariably she wore her hair down and her contacts in when they went out on a date, and either sweats or his dress shirts when they were in. He found her serious and professional look as disconcerting as her voice.

Without speaking, he sat down on the chair across from her, still wearing his ski jacket and his car keys dangling from his fingers. He smelled alcohol – vodka, he thought – but he didn't see a glass or a bottle, so he guessed she must have consumed a lot for it to be emanating from her skin.

'Where is your car?' he asked.

'I parked in back so you wouldn't know I was here.'

'Why?'

'Where is *your* car?'

Ethan cleared his throat. 'I took a cab.'

'I watched you through the window. No cab.'

'I . . . had a flat tire.'

'Lies! You are lying. You have been lying to me all this time.'

'What? No.'

'The FBI came to talk to me today.'

Ethan nodded. So Albright *had* told the truth. He said, 'They don't have any suspects in this leak case, so they are trying to manufacture one. It won't work. They just picked me because they know you are a security specialist. They think maybe you might be involved somehow. I told them that was crazy.'

'I am involved. Aren't I?'

'Of course not.'

She shook her head, and a single tear dripped from her eye and ran along the inside of the frame of her glasses. 'The FBI man told me how the breach was perpetrated. Someone logged in as the domain administrator from the NSC JWICS portal. Just exactly the insider threat vector I told you about. You got me drunk and . . .' She started crying. Her dispassionate professional visage disappeared completely now. 'You got me drunk all those times. I thought we were having fun. I thought you loved me. I thought that was just what lovers do here in America. But it was all just to make me talk.'

Ethan's initial shock of the moment had given way to a

cold calm. He told himself he could negotiate his way out of this. 'That's not true. The FBI has put this shit in your head. You can't let them make you think those things. They will turn you against me.' Ethan's eyes narrowed. 'What did you tell them?'

She was openly sobbing now. 'I told them they were wrong. I *had* to, didn't I? I can't let them catch you, Ethan. That will destroy everything I have worked so hard for. You have already broken my heart. I will not let you ruin my life. My future.'

'Calm down, Eve. You are being dramatic. I didn't have anything to do with the breach.'

'When I told you about using the domain administrator logon, I didn't tell you about the spot audit record that's done on it. I just didn't think about it. I don't know why. It turns out that was the one mistake the leaker made, and any real computer systems expert who logged on as the domain administrator would have known about it. No . . . the person responsible for the breach had the credentials to get access . . .' She cracked a sad little smile. 'But not the expertise.'

Ethan's jaw clenched tight and he squeezed his car keys till his fingers turned white. 'You don't know what you are talking about.'

She took off her glasses and began wiping her eyes with the tissue in her hand. Ethan could see in her eyes now that she was intoxicated. She said, 'I thought you were smarter than this. Why would you be a traitor? Fools are traitors. Men caught in traps.'

Ethan stood up, trying to control a growing fury.

She continued. 'I know what trap you were caught in.

A trap of your own making. You overestimated your intelligence. You overestimated your importance.'

'I don't have to listen to this,' he said. 'I'm leaving. I'll get a hotel. You can stay here tonight, you are too drunk to go anywhere.'

This took Eve by surprise. She launched to her feet. 'No! You aren't leaving. I'm not finished talking to you.'

But Ethan had already opened his front door and was out on the stoop. She followed him out, grabbed him by the collar.

Ethan saw a lone dark-colored sedan roll up an otherwise dark and empty 34th Street. He turned from it as he pushed Eve back inside roughly, but he faced the sedan again as he headed to the stairs off his porch.

The sedan pulled to a stop in the street right in front of him. The driver's-side window lowered. Ethan assumed some meddlesome neighbor or passerby had seen him shove a girl, and he was about to get yelled at.

He'd yell right back.

But from inside the car he heard, 'Ross!'

Ethan stopped at the top of the steps. Eve charged out of the house and up behind him again, frantic.

'Talk to me, Ethan! Tell me why!' She screamed it through blubbering sobs.

But Ross was not listening. He only saw the gun now, because the driver extended his arm out of the darkened interior and the gun was in his hand and the metal barrel reflected light off the streetlamps. The barrel rose, aimed directly at Ethan, at a distance of just thirty feet.

'Please!' Eve screamed as she grabbed his shoulder from behind.

Ross ducked.

A flash of light from the barrel of the gun, then a hollow snap that echoed up and down the street, no louder than a slammed car door.

Ethan crouched on his stoop, behind him he heard a gasp of surprise, and then a crash on the hardwood floor of his living room, but he didn't turn to look. Instead, he watched the gun barrel disappear back inside the vehicle, and then the sedan accelerated calmly, still heading north on 34th. It disappeared in seconds.

Ethan turned to find Eve Pang on her back on his living room floor. Her hands by her sides. Blood expanding from the center of her chest, reddening her white blouse.

'Eve!' He crawled to her, but only after checking back over his shoulder for the sedan once more. He pulled her farther into the house and shut the front door, then knelt over her. Her eyes were closed, her face slack, her body small and still.

He crawled to the window now, peeked out through the blinds to the street, but all seemed perfectly quiet, as if the neighborhood had no idea there had just been an assassination attempt on a high-ranking White House employee in their midst.

Ross was certain of only two things: one, the bullet that had killed Eve had been meant for him. And two, all his options had run out. He needed to execute the scrape.

He climbed to his feet, took Eve by the arms and dragged her on the hardwood floor, pulling her behind the sofa. He left her there, then found her purse on the peninsula in the kitchen, right next to an open bottle of Grey Goose and a glass of melting ice. He dug through the purse, found her car keys and her house key, then he dug some more, and pulled out her two-part authentication security fob that said *Pang-DDA*. He slipped it into his jacket pocket, locked the front door, and headed out the back of his house to Eve's car.

Ethan arrived at Eve's Bethesda house on foot after parking her car at a restaurant six blocks away and then walking the rest of the way, all the while looking out for strangers on the street. As he had done at his own house an hour earlier, he watched her place from across the road, but when a light rain began to fall he cut his reconnaissance short and entered through the back door, feeling his way through the dark until he found a pink Hello Kitty flashlight Eve kept on top of her refrigerator. He used this to make his way to the ground-floor spare bedroom she used as an office. Her laptop was there, set up like it always was; next to it were a teacup and a bag of cookies. Eve often worked here late into the night when she wasn't spending the night with Ethan.

He put his hand on the cold cup, ran his fingertip around the rim. Ethan was not a sentimental man, but he couldn't help feeling a twinge of sadness about Eve. Still, his mind drifted quickly from this as he considered the attempt on his life that she had had the misfortune of stepping in the way of.

Ethan thought the assassin must have been an employee of one of two possible groups: the CIA or the Israeli Mossad. In the warped sense of justice of both groups he could imagine they would have motive to target him, if they somehow knew what he had done. Ethan wondered if Eve had let something slip earlier in the day during her FBI interview, something that filtered to the spies and assassins Ethan had fought against by stealing the peace flotilla files in the first place. Yes, that must have been what happened.

It comforted him a little to think Eve might have had some hand in her own demise.

It felt as if everyone was out to get him. As if the walls were closing in on all sides. He thought of prison, he thought of psyching, he thought of the assassins out there who might have thought they had succeeded in silencing him, but soon enough would come to the realization that he had survived.

Ethan shook the thoughts out of his head. No time for that now. Now was the time to create value for himself, and to do this, he had to act.

Ethan knew the password to Eve's laptop, having obtained it through social engineering. They'd been cooking dinner one night, using a recipe Eve had found online for Lobster Newberg in puff pastry, and her laptop had been stationed on the island in the middle of the kitchen so they could both follow along. The screensaver came on while Eve was carefully removing the delicate pastries from the oven, her hands were full, and Ethan had seen an opportunity. He'd insisted she unlock her machine that instant because he needed to know, without delay, whether the egg yolks should be beaten before or after adding the brandy.

Without looking up from the oven, Eve had shouted out an eight-digit alphanumeric code that Ethan had used to unlock the screen, then committed to memory long enough to add it as a note on his smartphone when he went to the bathroom. He'd tested it a few days later when she was in the shower, curious as to whether or not she would have changed it after giving it to him. To his pleasure, she had not, and he'd always remembered that he had access to her machine if ever he could find a moment when he was one hundred per cent certain she wouldn't catch him.

Now, as he sat down in front of the laptop and pulled her fob out of his jacket, he told himself he had never been more certain of anything in his life.

He typed in the password and the screen came to life, then he launched the virtual private network access. A few seconds later he was prompted to enter the direct-domain credentials and the current code on Eve's DDA fob.

'Access granted.'

With a sigh of relief he slid the crawler drive into a USB port. It was a self-executing program, and instantly it launched on to Intelink-TS and began looking for specific server locations where high-level intelligence data was stored.

Ethan didn't know how this crawler was created, or who created it, but it seemed to know exactly which servers to access, and how to reach in and pull out the pertinent information.

Outside hackers often execute their exploitations with days, weeks, or even months of virtual reconnaissance, picking through the data to look for critical information. But Ethan didn't have anything like that amount of time. He had hours. Just a few hours, in fact. He assumed Eve would be missed at work in the morning, it wouldn't take long for people to go to her house looking for her, and it wouldn't take long for people to look at her DDA logon history on the virtual private network. Her body would be discovered when entry was made at his house, and that would happen when he didn't show up for work in the morning.

Ethan looked at his watch and saw it was now 1.30 a.m. He knew the transfer rate over the virtual private network would be one hundred megabits per second, a small fraction of the speed on the network itself. Though he had a full terabyte of storage space on his drive, a terabyte of data would take twenty-one hours to download, and he didn't think for a second he had anything like that amount of time. Instead, he decided he'd give himself four hours, that would give him one hundred and fifty gigabytes of top-secret intelligence, and that would just have to do.

He headed downstairs to brew himself some coffee, moving slowly in the dark.

26

Ethan was already sitting on the bench by the cannon in Fort Marcy Park when Gianna Bertoli and Harlan Banfield arrived just before 8 a.m.

As they approached he sat up straighter and looked down at his clothes. They were wrinkled and dirty, he was certain his face was drawn and gaunt, and he could see straight blond hair, hair that he normally kept swept back with molding clay, now hanging in his eyes. He had a black backpack secured on his back, and he wore a Washington Nationals cap on his head and sunglasses he'd bought at a CVS up in Bethesda.

Harlan stepped up to him and shook his hand. 'I saw the chalk mark. Damn, son. It looks like you slept here all night.'

He shook his head back and forth slowly.

Bertoli offered him a hug. Ethan stood up and embraced her, his body heavy with exhaustion. 'They tried to kill me.'

Bertoli gasped while Banfield made a face of disbelief. '*Kill* you? What on earth are you talking about?'

'A man in a car. Last night. He shot at me.' Ethan shrugged. Then he added, 'He missed. He killed Eve instead.'

Banfield grabbed Ethan by the arms. 'Oh my God. How can you be sure? You're not a doctor.'

'Shot through the fucking heart, Harlan. It doesn't take a doctor.'

'Who did it?'

Bertoli answered before Ethan. 'Mossad. I'd bet my life. You are that important.'

Banfield started pacing back and forth. 'Where is her body?'

'On my living room floor.'

'Christ, son!'

'What the hell was I supposed to do? I wasn't going to bury her in the fucking backyard and I couldn't call an ambulance.'

'Yes. Of course not,' said Banfield. He looked to Ross like an old man who just realized he was in way over his head.

'What do I do now?'

Banfield didn't answer. He didn't look like he had a clue. But Gianna emanated an air of calm. She put her hand on his cheek. 'You run, Ethan. You run.'

'Run where?'

Bertoli said, 'It might surprise you to know it, but the Venezuelans have a very good operation here in Washington. Their embassy has been helpful with our efforts in the past. A few times they were able to provide quick and discreet assistance.'

'Venezuela helps American whistleblowers? I never heard about that.'

She gave a half-smile. 'I told you they were good. The incidents never came to light.'

'The Feds didn't find out about them?'

'They discovered the actions and identities of the whistleblowers, yes. But they had their reasons for keeping the incidents quiet. Your case is much the same. If you stay quiet, then *they* will stay quiet. But the key is getting out of the country as soon as you know they are coming for you. If you are still around they will grab you, and no one will hear from you again.'

Ethan looked to Banfield. The older man just nodded gravely. Ethan said, 'The guys who went to Venezuela. Are they still there?'

Bertoli said, 'Last I heard, one was living in Paris. Nicely, I might add. A prominent journalist. I visited him last fall.'

'You're kidding.'

'Another went to Buenos Aires. He married a local down there. A third returned to the U.S. She was given immunity from prosecution in exchange for her leaving government service. She's teaching at a prominent university in South Florida now.' Bertoli smiled. 'A good trade, I should think. Miami is beautiful. But more important, in all these cases the government decided to drop the charges because the whistleblowers had taken more data that they never exploited, and they simply returned that data and agreed to leave government service forever in exchange for the government calling off the chase. Everything stayed quiet.'

Ross reacted as if he had been thrown a lifeline.

'*That's* what I need, Gianna. I don't want my mother thrown into a big scandal. I don't want to be chased around by fucking hit men. I just need this bullshit to blow over.'

She said, 'Venezuela will help you, I'm sure of it, but they won't do it for free. If you had something to offer them, I could contact a friend of theirs and make arrangements.'

Ethan smiled for the first time today. 'I did it. I have it.'

'The scrape?'

'Yes. One hundred and fifty gigs. All categorized and searchable.'

'Oh, Ethan. That is wonderful.'

Ross thought about what gems he could pull from the Intelink-TS scrape that the Venezuelans would find valuable. 'I can get the names of all CIA contracted personnel working in their country. Will that buy me a ticket out of town?'

Bertoli smiled. 'I feel certain it would.'

'I'll give them something to let them know I have the goods they want. But the bulk of it will stay on the drive and encrypted until I am out of the U.S.'

'I think that would be agreeable to them.' Gianna thought for a moment. 'I'll need a few hours to set it up. We will hide you out until then.'

'No,' Ethan said quickly. 'I have something I need to do first. I'll meet up with you two later today.'

'You aren't safe alone.'

'I'll take my chances. I need about four or five hours.'

Bertoli gave Ethan the phone number to a mobile she'd purchased here in D.C. and had not yet activated, and told him to call her as soon as he was ready.

Ethan put the number in his phone, but he looked at Banfield. 'What about you, Harlan?'

Banfield had been silent, but he said, 'This is where you and I say good-bye. I am the local director of the ITP, I won't be handling you when you go abroad.' The small and frumpy man looked whiter than usual. He hadn't recovered since Ethan told him about the assassin, obviously, but he shook Ross's hand and wished him luck. 'Be careful, son,' he said, and Ethan headed back up the trail alone while the other two watched him leave.

Darren Albright shuffled in his seat, annoyed by the delays but energized by the anticipation of action. He checked the time on his mobile phone for the third time in the last ten minutes, and drummed his fingers on the dashboard of the black GMC Yukon while he looked out the window at 1598 34th Street, a two-storey whitewashed row house.

There had been a virtual cavalcade of suspicious events today, and they all led Albright here to the home of National Security Council deputy assistant director Ethan J. Ross.

It all began when Albright learned Ethan Ross called in sick to work this morning. This in itself wasn't noteworthy other than the fact he was now a person of interest in a federal Official Secrets Act investigation. Second, the Special Surveillance Group team that had been covertly waiting for him outside his house had reported no activity by 10 a.m. If Ross was indeed ill, this meant nothing, but Albright's suspicions began to grow that he was not even home.

Around eleven, real alarm bells began ringing when Albright received word that Ross's girlfriend, Eve Pang, an IT expert at Booz Allen Hamilton, had not shown up for a meeting she had scheduled with IT personnel at Joint Base Anacostia-Bolling. She was due in at eight, but since she bounced around to many different remote locations, no one marked her as missing for nearly three hours. Albright himself called her mobile and received no answer, so he sent agents to her place in Bethesda with authorization to force entry if necessary.

The agents kicked in the front door when there was no answer, and inside they found no sign of Ms Pang, and no sign of anything out of the ordinary.

Immediately upon hearing from his men in Bethesda, Albright dropped all other activity on the case and put the full force of his resources into locating Ethan Ross and Eve Pang. At the same time he applied for an order to make entry on Ross's home – Ross wasn't officially missing, so he couldn't kick his door in without a warrant – but while he waited on the warrant he ordered a BOLO be sent out to local D.C. police on both Ross and Pang.

Albright and three special agents arrived at Ross's home at 1 p.m. A pair of SSG surveillance experts had been under cover as landscapers in the park across the street, and they'd notified Albright that they'd seen no signs anyone was home, but at this point the supervisory special agent decided to just go up to the door and knock.

There was no answer.

He walked around the outside of the building, banged on the basement door and the back door, and then returned to his Yukon to wait for the warrant and to monitor the SSG radio traffic while they looked for their missing persons of interest.

A D.C. metro police officer ID'd Ross at 3 p.m. She noticed a man who looked much like the image on the computer screen in her squad car as he climbed out of a cab on Pennsylvania Avenue. He wore sunglasses and a ball cap and carried a black backpack, and to the police officer he looked like a shady character, so she called in the sighting to dispatch. Within five minutes a pair of SSG officers had raced into the area and took up watch on the man. Through the long-range lenses of their cameras they confirmed their target, and they watched as Ross climbed into another taxi.

As the cab rolled down the street, a full sixteen-person SSG follow team converged on it.

Not everyone who works for the FBI, even on operational status, is a special agent. The Special Surveillance Group is an FBI entity charged with investigative support functions for the Bureau, meaning physical surveillance operations. They carry FBI credentials, but they don't have authority to make arrests and they don't carry firearms in the field.

The ranks of the SSG are filled with men and women of all shapes, sizes, colors and backgrounds, because a key component of the work is appearing ordinary, not standing out like a Fed, even to a target who knows full well what a Fed looks like. The surveillance specialists who operate in the follow teams are trained in the ability to remain in the shadows while tailing their subjects in vehicles and on foot.

SSG investigative specialists Beale and Nolan were working together this afternoon, tailing their subject's vehicle as part of the six-vehicle team. The two men were both white males, riding around D.C. in a vehicle together, and this ran the risk of tipping off their target that they were Feds, except for the fact Beale drove a maroon taxi and Nolan was his passenger in the backseat.

Beale was twenty-one years old and had worked for a package-delivery service before landing this job with the FBI. Nolan was forty-six and he'd been a cop in a suburb of Des Moines before deciding he wanted to do something more interesting with his time than ticketing speeders and busting teenage drinkers at high school football games, so he answered an online ad for the FBI, and within months found himself tailing foreign spies throughout the streets of D.C., usually on behalf of the FBI's Counterintelligence Division.

This afternoon's subject, Ethan J. Ross, was different from their average mark. He was American, a relatively high-ranking employee of the National Security Council, and, if Beale and Nolan's brief from special agent Darren Albright was to be believed, he was a potential insider threat to the U.S. intelligence community.

Both SSG men had backpacks in the cab with them containing various articles of clothing, eyeglasses, hats, and other forms of disguise, but rolling around D.C. in a taxi was a great way to blend in, and they had no plans to ditch their car for a foot follow this afternoon. That said, surveillance was always dictated by the person under surveillance, so Beale and Nolan had to be ready to ad-lib if the situation called for it.

The six-vehicle team had picked Ross up ten minutes earlier from the police tip, and now they stayed in a box pattern in the very familiar streets of the capital as Ross's cab meandered through traffic. They drove into Georgetown, where Ross was dropped off in front of the Nike store on M Street – fortunately for the SSG team, one of their vehicles had been passing by at the exact moment Ross climbed out because the delivery van that had been serving as the eye lost sight of him on the previous turn.

Beale and Nolan's vehicle's movements, like the movements of all the cars, trucks, scooters and motorcycles on the team, were directed by an operations hub that maintained radio contact with all the officers via earpieces. Their taxi was several cars out of rotation when Ross left his cab, so they followed orders to move east of the subject's location and park on Thomas Jefferson Street.

They resumed the eye again a few minutes later as he walked south through Georgetown. They took a few pictures of the man with the Nationals cap and the backpack, but they did it from a distance so as not to risk compromise.

'Any guesses as to where he's going?' Nolan asked as he slid the camera back in his bag.

Beale thought for a moment. 'If he's dirty and working with a foreign intel service, he could be heading to any of a dozen embassies around here.'

Nolan said, 'Close up just a little. If it looks like we're going to lose him, they might authorize an in extremis arrest. If we have to bail out to tackle this guy, I don't want to get into a foot chase. This prick looks like a runner.'

Beale said, 'I'd love it if he was a runner. I've been involved in a couple of arrests, but I've never done a foot chase.'

'Kid, you can be my guest. I chased my share of yahoos when I was a cop in Iowa. I'll sit here and watch.'

'Man, I don't believe that. If that dude starts running, you know you'll start hauling ass after him.'

Nolan smiled. 'Yeah. Shit gets in your blood.' He turned serious again. 'Still, tighten up. He looks fast.'

Beale chuckled and brought the taxi a little closer and reported his location to the operations hub on the other end of the radio.

27

Darren Albright sat in his Yukon, staring at Ethan Ross's house just twenty feet away. The damn warrant was taking forever, but to bide his time he had a walkie-talkie in his hand, and with it he listened in on the SSG tail of one of his two persons of interest.

From Albright's mental picture of Ross's movements, it seemed like he was on a dry-cleaning run at the moment, which made him look even more suspicious. One of the agents in the backseat of the Yukon was obviously thinking the same thing, because he mumbled something about maybe moving Ross from person-of-interest status up to suspect status, but before Albright had time to reply, his phone chirped in his pocket. He quickly stowed the walkie-talkie on his hip and answered his phone. 'Yeah? Okay. Good.' He pocketed the phone and turned to the men in the SUV with him. 'Warrant came through. We're good to go. Let's see what's what in that house.'

He climbed out of the SUV and his three agents followed suit. One went around to the back of 1598 34th Street while Albright and the two others took the six steps up to the front door.

He banged on the door once, shouted, 'FBI! Search warrant.'

The three men drew their service weapons, .40-caliber SIG Sauer pistols, and Albright himself kicked at the door. It had been a long time since he'd had the pleasure of a kinetic breach, but he executed it perfectly. The door cracked at the lock and splintered, and it opened fully, setting off a wailing security alarm siren.

Albright ignored the noise and led the men through the door, his gun high in front of him.

But that single step was all it took for him to register a smell he was trained to recognize, even though he'd never quite gotten used to it. 'That's a cadaver,' he said over the sound of the alarm, and then he moved farther inside so that his men could sweep the area.

He found Eve Pang behind the sofa in the middle of the room. Albright was certain she was dead, but he knelt to check her pulse anyway. As the other two agents slipped quietly into the hallway to begin clearing the rest of the house, Albright pulled his walkie-talkie to his mouth. It was already set on the channel that communicated directly with the head of the SSG team following Ross.

He shouted over the siren. 'This is Supervisory Special Agent Albright! I want Ethan Ross picked up right now! Consider him armed and dangerous!'

The terse reply came back instantly: 'Understood.'

Albright stood from the body, hooked his walkie-talkie back on his belt, and shook his head in disbelief. 'Son of a bitch.'

For the third time on this surveillance operation, Nolan and Beale had taken over the eye from one of their colleagues, this time a fifty-year-old woman driving a Vespa. They'd tailed Ross into the promenade of Washington Harbor, a dual-use office building/shopping area with a large public space. Ross was on foot in a pedestrian zone, but they could see him from their vantage point on Thomas Jefferson, so they'd remained in their cab for now. While they parked along the curb, they helped route other cars into the area to control exit points off the promenade, and the operation's hub rushed officers to the ferryboats that left from the harbor for Potomac cruises just in case the subject tried to board.

Beale had positioned his taxi so that he could pick Ross up first if he decided to skirt around the harbor complex and walk back up north into the heart of Georgetown. The concern remained the man would try to slip into an embassy, and Georgetown was loaded with potential places for a spy to run and hide.

Just as Ross slipped out of sight in the promenade, a call came through both men's earpieces. 'Uniform Victor, this is control. Maintain the eye while we move SWAT to your location. Immediate arrest has been authorized, but we are advised subject is now considered armed and dangerous.'

Beale and Nolan were designated Uniform Victor. Beale responded into his headset, 'Roger that. We'll have him again in twenty seconds.' He glanced at his 'passenger' in back. 'This clown doesn't look armed and dangerous.'

Nolan rolled his eyes. 'Everybody's armed and dangerous to SWAT. Otherwise they wouldn't have shit to do.'

'I hear you.'

Fortunately, Beale saw Ethan Ross walking north, back up the hill into Georgetown on 31st. Beale pulled in well behind him, stayed far back, keeping other cars between his cab and the man walking on the sidewalk. Nolan called in to the operation's hub, telling them to put a unit back on M Street, a couple of hundred yards up the hill. It was the next major intersection ahead, and therefore the next decision point for Ross unless he went into a building or turned down a little alleyway.

'Might be taking the towpath,' said Nolan.

Beale said, 'Shit. You're right. If he does, we'll lose the eye here in a second.'

To both men's surprise, however, Ethan Ross made a quick right off 31st Street into a narrow alley that led back over to Thomas Jefferson. Their taxi had been the unit stationed on Thomas Jefferson a couple of minutes before, so they knew there would be no eye on their subject on the far side of that alley.

Beale called it in to control, who replied it would take at least ninety seconds to move a vehicle back on to Thomas Jefferson.

'Shit,' Beale muttered to Nolan. 'Do I follow through the alley?'

Nolan hesitated. Then said, 'Just pull up and take a look from the street. Don't want to get stuck in a one-lane alleyway if we don't have to.'

The cab stopped at the mouth of the alley; in the distance Ross was already more than halfway to Thomas Jefferson.

Beale said, 'We're gonna lose him. He can grab the towpath or head back down to K or up to M or he could –'

'Go!' ordered Nolan.

The cab pulled into the narrow alley just as Ross made a left a hundred yards in front of them.

'I'll call it in,' said Beale. He rolled slowly, keeping his eyes peeled left and right in case Ross had a spotter helping him on his dry-cleaning run. While he drove he touched his finger to his earpiece. 'Operations hub, this is Uniform Victor. We are eastbound to T Jeff. Subject just made a left out of an alley. Still on foot.'

'Roger.' As the hub scrambled to route another vehicle into the area, Beale picked up speed in the little alley, hoping he'd be able to catch a helpful glimpse of Ross before he reached a decision point and disappeared from view. But as he passed the midway point through the alleyway, he had to slow because a pair of big garbage dumpsters were positioned along the wall on his left, cutting his clearance down to less than a foot.

Just as he drew abreast with the cans, a large dusty blue van backed out of a covered parking lot in front of him and stopped just feet from the grille of his cab.

Beale had to slam on his brakes to avoid a collision.

He lowered his window. 'Move it, asshole!'

Nolan looked back over his shoulder and saw a sedan with tinted windows pull into the alleyway behind them. It stopped twenty feet back, blocking the cab in next to the dumpsters.

Beale saw the second car as well, and instantly he knew this was some sort of an ambush.

'I'm ramming them!' Beale slammed the transmission into reverse, because the sedan was smaller, lighter, and a few feet farther away than the van.

'Do it!' urged Nolan.

But before Beale could step on the gas, two men in black masks and black wool coats stepped out from between the dumpsters, just a foot from the driver's side of the taxi. As one, they raised black pistols with long silencers.

Nolan screamed, 'Watch out!'

Behind them the sedan driver leaned on his horn, masking the sound as the two masked men opened fire on the cab, peppering both the driver's-side and the passenger windows with round after round from their suppressed pistols.

The two SSG surveillance officers crumpled on to the seats next to them. The cab rolled back until it came to rest gently against the parked sedan, which was no longer blaring its horn.

Iranian Quds Force operatives Ormand and Kashan quickly slipped their weapons back inside their coats. With no words between the two gunmen, they reached through the broken windows and opened both the front and back doors. They pushed the bloody American bodies farther inside the car and out of their way. Ormand climbed behind the wheel, while Kashan sat in the back. They rolled down the broken windows, cleared away shattered glass from the doors, and watched while Shiraz moved the van out of the way in front of them, and then turned toward Thomas Jefferson.

The cab followed suit behind, making a right at the mouth of the alley.

Behind them, Isfahan climbed out of the sedan with a long device in his hands that looked something like a metal broom. It was a NailHawg magnetic nail sweeper, used by roofers for collecting loose roofing nails in grass.

Quickly and calmly he rolled the device back and forth in the alley where his two colleagues had been standing, and he picked up eleven spent shell casings from their weapons.

He was back in his sedan a moment later, heading down the alley to 31st Street.

Before the four Iranian assassins had even left the neighborhood, Ethan Ross entered in the side door of the Venezuelan embassy two blocks away on 30th Street, completely unaware of what had happened behind him, and completely undetected by either U.S. intelligence or law enforcement.

28

For the first few hours Ethan Ross sat alone in a window-less office on the ground floor of the Venezuelan embassy. He was given coffee and then a snack and finally a meal – Vietnamese food from a restaurant on M Street – and he sat alone at a conference table and ate. All the while – more than five hours in the place – no one interviewed him, interrogated him, or did anything more than peek in on him from time to time to see to his needs. So he sat at the conference table or on a small sofa next to it the entire time, his backpack looped around his arms and hanging off his chest, as if the pack that held his computer and other equipment were an infant.

At around 9 p.m. an attractive woman in her twenties entered the office – Ethan had pegged her earlier as an intelligence officer – and with a smile she invited Gianna Bertoli into the small room. Ethan stood to hug her, not because he needed the Swiss woman's comforting embrace but rather because he knew Gianna would offer a hug.

Ethan was happy for the chance to find out what was going on from someone he trusted. 'Where have you been? How much longer am I going to be sitting here?'

Gianna sat back down at the conference table with him. 'I've been here all day. Mostly upstairs in conference calls with agents here in the embassy, as well as counter-intelligence agents in Caracas.'

'What's taking so long?'

'It was all going smoothly, but then some sort of a problem developed on the streets outside.'

'What sort of problem?'

'Police. A *lot* of police. For the first hour or two the Venezuelans thought they were looking for you. They began to grow concerned about this entire enterprise, thinking if the Americans knew about you already, then they would have a hard time getting you out of the country. They talked of contacting the State Department and turning you over. I insisted that the intelligence you have would make it worth their while, but they remained noncommittal.'

'Bastards.'

'It's okay. It seems whatever is going on here in Georgetown is unrelated to you. The police are looking for a taxi with two occupants, but they aren't providing any more information than that. This placated the Venezuelans, and everything is back on track.'

Just then, the door opened again, and a tall, handsome Latin American man with salt-and-pepper hair entered, trailed by the female intelligence officer Ethan had met earlier. He introduced himself as Arturo, and Ethan determined instantly he was General Intelligence Office, the foreign arm of Venezuelan intelligence. He offered Ross and Bertoli coffee, and another good-looking female brought it in a moment later.

There was a little small talk. Ethan asked questions about the police presence out in the streets, but Arturo knew no more than Gianna had already told him.

Soon the small talk trailed off and Arturo got down to business. 'Now, Mr Ross. We agree to your terms – we will remove you safely from the United States and take you to Caracas, where you will be both protected and free to come and go whenever you wish.' He held up a finger. 'With the provision you provide documentary evidence of all American agents working for the CIA in Venezuela.'

Ethan shook his head. 'No. I will not give you everything.'

'I don't understand.'

'I will give you a portion of what I have.' Ethan smiled. 'But it will be more than enough to keep your organization busy, I promise you that. Once I'm safely in Venezuela, I'll give you the rest.'

The truth was, Ethan had no idea what sources the CIA had in Venezuela. He'd never given it a moment's thought. He felt certain there would be something, however, and even if he had to give every last shred of relevant intelligence to Arturo right now and lie about there being more on the drive, he was going to do whatever it took to get a ticket out of the USA, tonight.

'*Muy bien,*' said Arturo. 'What do you need from us?'

'I need an office with a printer. I will print out the files from my computer.'

Arturo took him down a staircase, to a door off a basement lobby, and he unlocked the door with a key card. With a flourish he bowed and Ethan stepped alone into a small dormitory room, with a computer and a printer on a simple desk against the wall. Arturo closed the door, leaving Ethan alone inside.

He put his laptop on the desk, then pulled the comforter off the bed. He threw the comforter over his head, covering the laptop as well. This way, if there were hidden cameras in the room they wouldn't see him enter his password.

He had the NASCAR drive in his backpack, but he did not retrieve it. Instead, he reached down inside the front of his trousers and felt along his waist, just above his left hip. He pulled a small, flesh-colored moleskin bandage off his skin and then brought it out of his trousers. Stuck to the inside of it was a tiny micro SD card, roughly the size of a fingernail. He pried it from the moleskin and placed it into an adapter from his backpack.

He'd come up with the scheme to hide the scrape on his own, and he'd transferred the files from the NASCAR drive during his several free hours this morning after leaving Fort Marcy Park. Now the NASCAR drive was blank, as was his computer, but both devices were heavily encrypted, so anyone attempting to recover the Intelink-TS files would have no way of knowing Ethan had relocated them to a tiny device he kept hidden on his body.

It wasn't a perfect solution, but Ethan liked feeling that he had some semblance of control over events.

Once his computer read the micro SD card, he entered a series of passwords, and soon he was in. It took three minutes to pull up a massive cataloged database – U.S. top-secret intelligence out of Intelink-TS. He typed some search terms into a wiki-like program, waited an instant for the search engine to do its thing, and then he smiled.

In front of him was a mother lode of intelligence about U.S. assets in Venezuela, all well categorized and easy to sort and read. As he scrolled through page after page of raw intel source documents, he saw there were no names per se, because they were redacted before going on to the network, but the identities of specific agents could be quite easily discerned.

One file relayed the CIA's relationship with the assistant manager of the Caracas office of Conviasa, the state-owned national air carrier of Venezuela. Another file dealt with two concierges at the Gran Meliá Caracas hotel who'd been passing information to Langley for years. A series of documents defined an operation that utilized help from the chief of police of the city of Maracaibo.

Ethan even saw that the assistant deputy minister of Interior and Justice was a CIA agent on the take.

The files went on and on. It took more than an hour, but eventually Ethan pulled up hundreds of documents from CIA files, giving vague but identifiable personalities of thirty-three agents in Venezuela, and he printed them all out. He could have kept working and pulled another fifty or sixty names, but he wanted to save the rest for when he got to Caracas.

He spent several more minutes clearing all his cache on his computer and then signing out and shutting down. When he was finished he took off the comforter, put the drive back in the moleskin, and reattached it to his hip. He threw the backpack on to his shoulder and then left the room, heading back upstairs to the office.

Gianna Bertoli, the GIO officer who had introduced himself as Arturo, and two young female Venezuelans looked up from the sofas where they were sitting. Ethan noticed a pair of young men in suits standing by the elevators in the lobby down the hall now. He assumed they were security, and he appreciated their presence, but he wasn't one hundred per cent certain they weren't here to keep him in as opposed to keeping others out.

Arturo stood from the conference table. 'So, what do you have for us?'

Ethan handed over the printed pages and said, 'A list of twenty-three Venezuelan citizens and ten foreign nationals living in Venezuela who are all in the employ of the Central Intelligence Agency. Thirty-three men and women, mostly in Caracas, who are currently spying on the Venezuelan government.'

One of the women spoke softly: *'Increíble.'*

Arturo started going through the pages silently.

Ethan looked to Bertoli, but he addressed the Venezuelans. 'This is just the tip of the iceberg, believe me. Once I get somewhere safe, I can get you more identities, a list of front companies in Venezuela, CIA informants working at your consular offices all over the world, and information about CIA's reach into Venezuela's oil and banking sectors.' Ethan raised his eyebrows. 'It's really interesting stuff. I should think you would want to see it.'

Arturo nodded gravely. 'I very much do want to see it.' Then he smiled. 'I agree to your terms. We will leave for Caracas at once.'

'Excellent,' said Bertoli.

Dom sat alone in his condo, thinking about going out for a night on the town. He wasn't in the mood for it, really, but this afternoon he'd done little more than sit around, and he felt like getting out.

Adara Sherman had stopped by an hour earlier. Dom didn't answer the door; he knew it was her because, through the blinds, he saw her car parked outside. His place was a mess and he didn't feel like having company, especially company who had dropped in on him only to check him out and evaluate his physical and mental state for his boss, Gerry Hendley.

Dom didn't think either his physical or his mental state should be on display at the moment.

Just as he stood to head into his bedroom to change for a few hours of barhopping, there was a new knock at the door. At first he thought Sherman had returned; he groaned, but figured he might as well let her in and get it over with. But when he looked through the peephole he saw a familiar man wearing a dark blue suit.

He opened the door. 'Albright.'

'Can I come in?'

'Of course.'

Albright didn't sit down; instead, he just stood in Dom's living room, his hands on his hips.

Caruso assumed the special agent brought some news. Albright's body language was all wrong for someone who was going to either gloat or celebrate. No, Dom knew before he said a word, Albright was here because something bad had happened.

'I thought you should know,' he said. 'It looks like you were right about Ethan Ross.'

Dom raised an eyebrow. 'How did you figure that out?'

'His girlfriend.'

'She's in on it?'

'Not looking like it.'

'Why not?'

'Found her body in Ross's living room. Shot once in the

torso. DRT.' Caruso knew DRT was unofficial cop speak meaning 'dead right there.'

Caruso blew out a gasp. 'Who did it? Ross?'

'I don't know. No record of him having a gun . . . but you know how that is. A guy who wants to kill somebody can find a gun easily enough.'

'That's true.'

'We'll investigate all possibilities.'

Dom didn't understand the comment. He asked, 'Where is Ross now?'

'Disappeared.'

Caruso looked at the ceiling in frustration.

'And we've lost a couple of SSG guys during the hunt.'

'What the hell does that mean? Lost?'

'They, and the taxi they were in, vanished about three o'clock this afternoon, just prior to SWAT moving in for an arrest. If Ross killed Pang to silence her, he would have had no compunction about killing to save himself.'

'Yeah.'

'I know what you are thinking, Caruso.'

'I bet you do.'

'You are thinking this is my fault. You are telling yourself if we just grabbed Ross by the throat the first time his name popped up, Pang would still be alive, and my two guys wouldn't be missing.'

Dom did not reply.

'We don't operate under black-ops rules in the FBI. You might have forgotten that, but it's the law.'

'Yeah. I used to be a law-and-order man myself,' Dom said. 'It only gets you so far.'

'That's a dangerous thing to say to me, Caruso.'

'I just think you should have bent the rules a little with this one, Albright. Shaken a little harder.'

Albright kept his hands on his hips, his eyes on Caruso.

Dom softened. He shouldn't have been so hard on the guy. He was doing his best. 'Anything I can do to help?'

'Yes. You can give me your gun. I want to run ballistics on it.'

'*What?*'

'Look. It's just to rule you out. I don't think for a moment the President's nephew murdered Eve Pang, but you are an armed man running wild through the middle of all this shit, so I would be a fool if I didn't at least check off the box that says you're clean.'

Caruso thought about protesting, but he knew that would just make Albright get a warrant and come back. So he stepped to his bookshelf, grabbed his shoulder rig out of its hiding spot, and pulled his Smith & Wesson from its holster. He dropped the magazine out, racked the slide to eject the round in the chamber, and locked the gun open. He handed it to Albright. 'I want a receipt for that.'

Albright closed the slide and slid the empty weapon into his waistband. 'Of course. That is standard operating procedure.'

'You'd know, wouldn't you?'

29

Ethan Ross was spirited out of the Venezuelan embassy at 12:12 a.m., facedown on the floor in the back of an Infiniti sedan, driven out of the garage by the young female intelligence officer, with a security man in the front passenger seat. In the back with Ross, with their feet gently resting on his back, were two male IOs. Ethan lay on his backpack, protecting it and its contents with his body.

The four Venezuelans had been instructed to do everything in their power to avoid losing the American NSC staffer, up to and including initiating high-speed flight from the police in the event there was an attempt to pull them over. A second vehicle, this one a Cadillac Escalade, trailed behind the Infiniti, serving as a chase car, ready to swoop in to take Ross away if necessary.

But the Infiniti was neither tailed nor stopped, and after forty-five minutes of travel it pulled into the hangar of a fixed-base operator at Dulles Airport. Everyone else left the car, but Ethan was told to sit up and wait a few minutes so the others could check the area to make sure they were clear before he walked to the plane.

Ethan climbed off the floor of the car, checking the contents of his backpack even before he stretched his sore muscles. He put his hand around the battery pack for the phone Banfield had instructed him to purchase earlier in the week. He had removed it before heading toward the

Venezuelan embassy the previous afternoon out of an abundance of caution, and now it, and the phone itself, were crammed into the bottom of his backpack.

He suddenly realized this would be his last moment in the United States for an indeterminate amount of time. Gianna promised him his life would get back on track once a deal was reached with the government, but that was before the assassination attempt. Now all bets were off that he could ever come home. He also didn't know what would be waiting for him when he got to Venezuela.

On a whim he snapped the battery back into the phone, powered it up, and dialed his mother's house in San Francisco.

It was 10 p.m. there, and even if Ross hadn't done the math to determine this, he would have been able to figure it out from his mother's voice. She was tired and annoyed and concerned, all at once.

'Who is calling?'

'Mom. It's me.'

'Ethan? Ethan, what's wrong?'

'Nothing. Well . . . I just wanted to call.'

'Why?' Emily Ross was wide awake now. 'What's happened?'

'I . . . everything will be okay. I just wanted to tell you not to worry.'

'Worry about what? I'm worried now! Talk to me.'

The car door opened and the female IO looked at Ethan angrily.

'I have to go. Forget I called. I'll call you tomorrow if I can.'

'Why *wouldn't* you be able to —'

'Love you.' He hung up just as the young woman yanked the phone out of his hand. She removed the battery, and Ethan got out.

He took a moment to get his bearings, and he realized he was standing next to a Beechcraft King Air 350i.

He was not impressed with the aircraft. It was a twin turboprop, not a jet. Ethan's work both at State and in the NSC gave him a lot of experience traveling on smaller jets as he moved around the world, and he couldn't help registering a little disappointment that his escape from the United States would be in a plane that flew slower than he would have liked. Ethan felt his contribution to Venezuela's intelligence services would have earned him an aircraft of higher performance.

The female Venezuelan spy took the phone to Arturo, who was conferring with others near the plane. He stormed back over to Ross by the Infiniti.

Ethan held his hand up. 'Don't worry. No one can trace it. I bought it today in Reston. No one knows I have it. It's not in my name. The call I just made was the only time I used it.'

This placated Arturo somewhat, but the woman said, 'We will have to frisk you before you board the aircraft.'

'The hell you will.'

She looked to Arturo. The older man asked, 'Who did you call?'

'My mom. I just told her I'd call her in a couple of days.'

'You could have compromised this mission, Mr Ross.'

'The only thing compromising this mission, *señor*, is us standing out here in the open.'

Arturo fought with his composure for a moment, then

he just motioned for Ethan to board the plane. He climbed the four steps to the cabin, still lamenting the fact his Venezuelan accomplices couldn't come up with the cash for a last-minute corporate jet charter.

Once Ethan ducked his head into the small but surprisingly well-appointed cabin he saw six others already on board. Another man from the Venezuelan embassy was here, who introduced himself as a cultural attaché and shook Ethan's hand at the door and then took a seat just behind the cockpit, directing Ethan to move to the empty captain's chair in the back of the plane. Ethan knelt and moved to the back and settled into his leather seat, and here he found himself facing Gianna Bertoli. She reached out and squeezed his hand with a smile. 'Are you okay?'

Ethan nodded. He wasn't okay, of course. But there wasn't anything she could do about it right now.

Seated next to her, pressed up to the window, was a small, young-looking man with olive skin and short dark hair. Ross assumed he was Venezuelan at first, although the rest of the intelligence officers in the cabin were in suits and ties and this man was dressed like a college student. He wore blue jeans, a blue flannel shirt with a red T-shirt under it, and Ethan saw a black ski parka tucked under his elbow.

On the table in front of the young man a sub-notebook computer lay open, and he typed on it furiously, not even looking up as Ethan sat down.

Gianna said, 'Ethan, I would like you to meet my good friend Mohammed.'

Mohammed? Ethan thought. Clearly not Venezuelan, then.

Mohammed glanced in Ethan's direction now and offered a hand, smiling nervously. 'I am pleased to meet you.'

Bertoli said, 'Mohammed has been working with us for more than a year now.'

'Really? In what capacity?'

The question was directed at Mohammed, but Gianna answered for him. 'He is one of our best hacktivists. He has been incredibly helpful.'

'Where are you from?'

Mohammed's eyes danced around the cabin, everywhere but on Ethan. He answered, 'Lebanon,' then looked back down.

Ethan nodded. 'And you will be traveling all the way to Venezuela with us?'

'Yes, sir. If that is okay with you.'

Ethan shrugged. The young man seemed odd. Uncomfortable. Ethan couldn't put his finger on it, but despite the Lebanese man's decidedly nonthreatening demeanor, he made Ethan a little uneasy.

Ethan looked to Gianna, and she just smiled back at him. 'We're almost on our way. Your future awaits, Ethan. Please don't worry, I will take care of you.'

The plane's engines fired, and soon they were rolling out of the hangar.

The Beechcraft bounced and bucked on its initial climb out over Virginia, but as it banked to the south the air smoothed out, and by the time they reached their cruising altitude of twenty-five thousand feet, Ethan was drinking a Bloody Mary and picking at a bag of chips.

By his second cocktail his attention returned to the Lebanese computer geek in front of him, and he began asking Mohammed questions to see if the man was, in fact, who he said he was. When Mohammed claimed he received his undergrad at the American University of Beirut, Ethan knew he'd be able to test the man's truthfulness, as he knew several professors there through his work at the NSC. He asked the young man about his studies, and his suspicions were allayed when Mohammed mentioned some familiar names at the university.

Next Ethan asked him about his work as a hacktivist, and even though he seemed a little strange and discomfited, from a computer science standpoint Mohammed had no problem discussing denial-of-service attacks, computer Trojans and worms, and several other technical aspects of computer hacking. Ethan decided the man was what he said he was, a Lebanese computer hacker, which put him somewhat at ease.

As they talked, Ethan noted the young man's edginess in interpersonal communication. In Mohammed, Ethan recognized a unique intellect, and a familiar level of awkwardness that often came with true genius.

Still, Ethan decided there was more there, something Mohammed was keeping to himself.

Gianna Bertoli sat quietly while the two men talked, but when things quieted down an hour or so after leaving D.C., she put her hand on Ethan's knee. 'Ethan, you are not running away. You are removing from the American government their one option to end this on their terms.'

Ethan nodded, but he bristled hearing Bertoli refer to

the FBI as the 'American government.' Hell, he was every bit as much a part of the American government as the G's chasing him. Still, he let it go, and asked Bertoli about how they would approach the U.S. government in an attempt to get his life back.

'Let's get to where we are going today, and we will discuss our plans tomorrow. We aren't safe until we get to Caracas.'

The King Air landed at Miami's Opa-locka Executive Airport to refuel. A customs official working there had a family member back in Venezuela serving in a low but lucrative position in the government, and the customs worker was accustomed to clearing government planes to Caracas without looking over the passengers or their luggage, thereby ensuring both her relative and herself a profitable career.

By 6 a.m. they were back in the air, heading over the Gulf of Mexico.

When they'd been in the air less than an hour, Arturo leaned over Gianna Bertoli, and woke her with a little nudge.

'Hi, Arturo. Is something wrong?'

The Venezuelan addressed Ethan now. 'Mr Ross. The information you have given us has been outstanding.'

Ethan had been staring out over the water as they flew, his mind on his mother mostly. Now he turned to Arturo. 'Of course it has.'

'But in it we see a serious problem.'

'Which is?'

'If we fly you into Caracas right now, there are American

agents who will know. People who need to be rounded up and arrested.'

'Obviously. So get to work on that.'

'Our security services are working as we speak. But with what you have given us, there isn't time to clean up this mess before we land. The Americans have agents in our police, in our security services, in our presidential administration.'

'What are you suggesting?'

'I am suggesting, *señor*, that we go to a safe house in a third country.'

'A safe house? Where?'

'Panama. We can keep you secure there while we clean our organization of American influence. Two or three days at most.'

Ross didn't like it. 'You can't protect me from the U.S. government in Panama.'

Arturo said, 'We can, my friend. Don't worry. Our location is quite secluded and secure. If there is any trouble, we can get you away by aircraft or boat very quickly. We have brought others there over the years.'

'And the Panamanians?'

'They don't bother us.'

Ethan looked at Gianna. She just nodded a little. Ethan turned to Mohammed to see if he had anything to say on the matter, but the baby-faced man was fast asleep.

Arturo said, 'Trust me, *amigo*. With the intelligence you just gave us, going to Caracas would be the worst possible move you can make.'

Ethan looked out of the window. Events were moving

so quickly. 'Okay. But you won't get any more intelligence from me until we reach Caracas.'

'No problem,' Arturo said with a sly smile. 'You have already given my organization all it can handle.' He turned away to talk to the flight crew.

Dom Caruso had spent the evening thinking about Ethan Ross. He'd promised Albright he'd stay out of the way, but within hours of his making that promise, the case had gone off the rails. As far as Dom was concerned, Albright needed some help, despite what Albright might have thought of the situation.

He called David at 8 a.m. 'Did you hear about the murder of Eve Pang?'

'Yes, and the disappearance of the two FBI men along with Ethan Ross. All very unfortunate.'

'Yeah.'

'I am assuming this is the man you told me about yesterday. The person whose name you would not give us.'

'One and the same.'

'We might have been able to help. Our sources say there are no leads as of yet.'

'I'm hearing the same thing,' said Dom.

'Assuming this was not some random act of D.C. crime that the FBI men stumbled into, we have to wonder who else would be so interested in Ross and what he knows that they would take such steps to keep him out of the hands of the American authorities.'

Dom said, 'If we find out where he went, I suspect we'll have the answer to that question.'

'Any progress on that end?' David asked hopefully.

'I'm not in the investigation. Albright has pushed me away. I can only assume they are tracking his mobile phone and know where he went.'

David hesitated, then said, 'His phone hasn't left his home. I'm sure the FBI knows that already.'

Dom asked, 'How the hell do *you* know that?'

'We have some ability to look into the cell phone companies' records.'

'Is this where you tell me Israeli intelligence has hacked into a U.S. business?'

'I'm not telling you anything of the sort.'

'Right.' David was going to be coy about the specifics of Mossad's capabilities, and Dom knew to let it go. At least the Mossad man was talking to him.

David continued. 'Anyway, his phone is still sending a signal to the mobile tower closest to his house.'

Dom rushed over to his laptop and opened it. 'I've got the SIM card number from a secondary phone he was using. He might have that one on him. Can you track it via the number?'

'I don't know, but I can find out. Have you given this to the FBI?'

'No. That would involve some questions I don't want to answer.'

'Ah. I understand completely. I'll look into this and call you when I have something.'

David called Dom less than an hour later and the Mossad officer asked Dom for a person-to-person meeting at 10 a.m.

30

The Beechcraft King Air landed in Bocas del Toro International Airport just after 9 a.m., and it took all Ethan's self-control to keep from pushing past the others to get out of the tight confines of the little cabin and into the open air. Once out on to the hot and humid tarmac, however, he realized he had been more comfortable inside the plane's climate-controlled cabin.

The airstrip was located on the tiny island of Colón, and Ethan had seen on the flight in that the island was part of an archipelago, surrounded on all sides by a multitude of larger islands and cays. All of them were flat and overgrown with tropical vegetation, but Colón airport was surrounded by the ramshackle Bocas Town, with houses and businesses standing just fifty feet on either side of the runway past overgrown grasses and brush that ran along the airport property's fence line. Palm trees blew in the hot breeze, and the smell of gasoline and jungle filled the American's nostrils.

The Beechcraft was met on the already hot tarmac by a twelve-passenger van crewed by a pair of big, severe-faced Latin men Ethan assumed were more Venezuelan intelligence agents. The small amount of luggage from the King Air was transferred to the van, and everyone boarded for the ten-minute drive through dirty and congested Third World streets to the docks.

Except for Arturo. He climbed back aboard the air-craft, intending to continue on to Caracas to help organize the roundup of American spies.

As the van motored through the little town, it was explained to the three non-Venezuelans in the van – Ross, Bertoli, and Mohammed – that the safe house was on the nearby larger but more remote island of Bastimentos. They passed a few police cars and even a truck full of soldiers from the Panamanian Public Forces. This unnerved Ethan, but he recognized he could do little but sit patiently and hope the Venezuelans knew what the hell they were doing, so he just continued looking out the window.

At the docks he saw all manner of boats doing a steady business moving people and products between the neighboring islands and cays, but his sizable entourage walked past the ferryboats and water taxis and instead boarded two large speedboats. Almost immediately they headed off to the southeast over choppy water. They passed just south of Carenero Cay, then turned to bisect a transportation lane full of ferry and cargo traffic, before finally motoring into the calmer waters between Solarte Island and Bastimentos Island.

At first Ethan thought Bastimentos looked completely uninhabited, but as they neared the shore and trolled along it to the south, every few hundred yards he could pick out the metal roof of a building sticking up from the thick jungle.

Within minutes the two boats turned into an inlet and began cruising very slowly. On their left was thick mangrove, but on their right a yellow sandy beach came out of the water and continued into thick palms. As they rounded a bend in the inlet, Ethan expected to see a dilapidated tin shack of some sort, but instead a large white colonial home appeared, surrounded by a huge manicured lawn, some twenty-five yards back from the shoreline. The two-storey building had a wraparound veranda on the first floor, and Ethan saw several men standing there, looking down at the approaching boats.

Around the main building the neat green lawn ran all the way to the sandy water's edge and the jungle on either side of it.

A bald-headed man with a bushy mustache and a tropic-weight suit stood on the dock, waiting for the boats. His smile was wide and inviting, but on either side of him younger, tougher-looking men stood with side-arms on their hips.

In English he said, 'My friends! Welcome.'

Ethan climbed out of the boat ahead of Bertoli and Mohammed, and he shook the bald-headed man's hand.

'My name is Leopoldo. Please, call me Leo.'

'Ethan Ross.'

'Bienvenido a Panamá, Señor Ross.' He shook hands with the other two visitors, and the four of them began walking up the steps to the main house.

'What is this place?' Ross asked.

Leo grinned proudly. 'We think of it as a home away from home. Originally this was the residence of a French businessman in the fruit industry, about a hundred years ago. Then for many years it was a luxury hotel. A friend of the Venezuelan government bought it several years back, and he loans it to us when we need it.' Leo was obviously proud of this place. 'All the comforts of home.

Satellite TV and phones, good Internet, we even have our own chef.' He patted Ethan on his back as if they were old friends. 'You all will be very well taken care of, and I am personally at your service.'

Mohammed interrupted, but softly and apologetically, 'Excuse me, sir. What can you tell us about the security of this location?'

Leo opened his jacket, revealing an MP5 machine pistol. 'Don't worry, my friends. Ten men are dedicated to security here at the compound. Five more of us are also armed and trained. Panamanian police have a gunboat that patrols around here, and they watch out for us as well.'

Mohammed pressed Leo on the plan. 'What if we are somehow discovered by the Americans? How do we get out of here?'

'The boats, of course. Plus there are a couple of trucks in the driveway, always ready for escape. This island is over fifty square kilometers in size, with dirt roads in the jungle. And there are docks on all sides with more boats. There are many ways to get away from here if we need to do so, but nobody can sneak up on us without us knowing about it.'

'Thank you,' said Mohammed.

Ethan found it surprising that the young Lebanese man had the nerve to question the Venezuelans' operation, but Leo didn't seem offended in the least.

The colonial house was large, with a massive two-storey great room and several common areas on the ground floor, and eight bedrooms on the first floor. Several outbuildings sat around a dirty swimming pool and a cracked tennis court and provided more shelter for the guard force of the safe house.

Ethan was given a room in the northeastern corner of the first floor, and an armed but professional-looking silver-haired security man was posted outside.

There was no access to the wraparound veranda from Ethan's room, but through the window he saw monkeys climbing in the trees outside.

He felt protected, more or less, but he was no fool. Despite the assurances of the Venezuelans, he knew if the Americans or the Israelis came for him here, his only chance would be to run for his life.

31

Georgetown Neighborhood Library was a beautiful colonial building in one of the most upscale quarters of Washington, D.C., but it smelled, quite literally, like shit. A homeless man who slept the day away on one of the comfortable chairs had shat himself, and the odor wafted through every inch of the ground floor of the historic building.

The employees, by now quite accustomed to the homeless in their midst, had developed the ability to ignore the smell, but the well-dressed gentleman looking through the racks of the history section could not hide his expression of extreme displeasure.

Dominic Caruso appeared at his side. 'You okay?'

'Fine,' David said, lying through his clenched teeth. 'Shall we go upstairs, and try to get away from the unpleasant smell?'

David led the way up two flights and they found a quiet corner in the second-floor Peabody Room that was both secluded and odor-free.

'Much better,' David said. 'I brought news for you. It is only for you. As far as I know, no one in your government is aware of this right now.'

'Keep talking.'

'We were able to geolocate the SIM card you gave us, and we found the phone.'

Dom winced. 'Let me guess. It wasn't with Ethan Ross.'

'I am afraid not. The phone was in a dumpster behind a 7-Eleven in Reston, Virginia.'

'Damn it. Dead end, then.'

'Not at all. We got a look at the security camera feed inside the 7-Eleven that corresponded with the time the phone was dumped.'

Dominic leaned against the rack of books, crossing his arms. 'And how the hell did you manage that?'

David smiled. 'We've been through this before. Our relationship requires trust, Mr Caruso. And it requires taking things on faith.'

'Right.'

'On the camera we saw Ethan Ross enter the store, alone, and purchase a mobile phone. We figure he tossed his three-day-old phone in the dumpster, then went and grabbed an even fresher one. We used the transaction details from the register to find the bar code information from the packaging of the phone. From this we –'

Dom held a hand up now. 'Wait. What? The Mossad can hack into a 7-Eleven's point-of-sale system?'

David raised his eyebrows but said nothing.

'Okay, I'll stop asking questions.'

The Mossad officer went on. 'From the bar code we were able to pull the SIM number from the phone, and we geolocated it to Dulles Airport. Apparently he took the battery out, but in Dulles he put the battery back in, we got a hit, then he removed the battery again, and we lost the ping. At first that looked like another dead end, but on closer inspection the phone did not go to the main terminal. Instead it pinged from a charter hangar. There was one charter that left around the time the phone was at Dulles.'

'Where did it go?'

'Miami. And then from there it filed a flight plan to Caracas, Venezuela.'

'Caracas,' Dom repeated. 'Do you know who chartered the flight?'

'Yes. A front company for Venezuela's General Intelligence Service.'

Dom scratched his head, utterly confused now. 'Ross is a Middle East expert who gave away secrets that benefited the Palestinians. What the hell does any of this have to do with the Venezuelan government?'

'We do not know. But there is another problem. We had people waiting in Caracas for the flight to land, but the aircraft changed the flight plan in the air and went to Panama.'

Dom leaned his head back against a bookshelf. 'From Panama City they could get on a flight to anywhere.'

'They did not go to Panama City. They went to Bocas del Toro, in the north of the country. A small airport on Isla Colón. They should have landed in the past hour. We weren't able to get anyone to the airport fast enough to look for them.'

'Any idea why they flew to Bocas del Toro?'

'None.'

Dom thought it over. The Panamanian government and the Venezuelan government were not exactly engaged in a shooting war, but the two nations did have an adversarial relationship. Dom could imagine no reason Venezuelan intelligence would sneak an American spy out of the United

States and drop him off in the middle of the Panamanian jungle.

Dom left the library with a promise to call David soon. Neither of the men knew what their next step would be in the Ethan Ross hunt, but Dom knew where he would find more information.

As he walked back to his motorcycle in the lot behind the library, he called Gerry Hendley, and asked him if he could find out what the CIA knew about Venezuelan operations in Bocas del Toro, Panáma. Gerry was quite understandably confused by the request, but he promised to call one of his contacts on the seventh floor of Langley and get right back to him.

Thirty minutes later, Dom was back in his Lincoln Circle condo when his phone chirped. He saw it was Hendley on the other end.

'Tell me you've got something, Gerry.'

Gerry spoke in his characteristic southern drawl. 'I've got something, but I have no idea what good it will do you. My contacts at CIA gave me three locations in Bocas del Toro they say have been pegged in some shape or form to the Venezuelan security services. That's GIO, the General Intelligence Office, and GCIO, General Counterintelligence Office.'

'Let me have them.'

'There is a hotel in Bocas Town that was bought by a couple of ex–GIO boys from Caracas a few months back. I've got the address.'

'In the town itself? No, that doesn't sound like what I'm looking for. What else?'

'A pilot for a puddle-jumper service at the airport has been identified as a Venezuelan asset.'

'Damn,' Dom said. He thought it possible Ross was put on yet another airplane in Bocas and flown somewhere even more remote than Bocas del Toro. But the more he thought of it, the less it rang true. They were flying in a King Air 350i, an airplane that didn't need a particularly long field for landing. They wouldn't have to change planes to go to a remote airport.

Dom said, 'What's the third lead?'

'For the third they couldn't give me an address. They gave me the longitude and latitude. Apparently, it's a large old colonial building on a tropical island a few miles' boat ride from Bocas del Toro itself. It's owned by a family tied to the Bolivian government in power in Caracas.'

Dom knew instantly this lead was a much better prospect than the first two. 'Give me the coordinates.' Gerry did so, and Dom typed them into EagleView on his laptop.

Looking over the satellite map of the property, he thought it could possibly be used as a safe house for the Venezuelan security services. It was secluded, with good views of both a narrow inlet and a dirt road that headed to the southern part of the island. 'Yeah,' he muttered to himself. Then Dom said, 'Gerry, sorry, but I need to call you right back.'

Dom dialed David and checked his watch while the phone rang. As soon as the other man answered, the American said, 'I think I know where Ross is.'

'Where?'

'Before I tell you, I want assurances you won't get in my way. You offered me logistical help. That's what I want.'

'Agreed.'

'He's going to be in a safe house run by Venezuelan intelligence on a tropical island near Bocas del Toro, Panama.'

'I see. Do you have any idea what he is doing there?'

'None at all. I'm speculating, but perhaps he gave the Venezuelans some intelligence in exchange for safe passage out of the country. I don't know what intelligence, nor do I know why they wouldn't just take him directly to Caracas.'

'But you want to go down there to look for him? Alone?'

'Yes.'

'What is it you hope to accomplish?'

'I'm going to get proof he's there, and get some intel on the location.'

'And then?'

'And then maybe you can send a team of Shayetet Thirteen commandos to kill him. It's Panama. It's not D.C. Surely you won't have any qualms about smoking this guy on a jungle island in Central America for what he did to the Yacobys.'

David replied coldly. 'We would do it with great pleasure.'

'But David, just so there is no misunderstanding. If I get down there and happen to find an opportunity . . . I'm going to kill him myself.'

'Even better,' David replied. 'What do you need from me?'

'Guns. In Bocas, waiting for me when I get there.'

David whistled. 'Our operation in Panama is very limited. But I'll see what I can do.'

Dom redialed Gerry Hendley next, and greeted him with a request that did not take the ex–South Carolina senator completely by surprise. 'I would like to ask permission to leave the country for a few days.'

'Let me guess. You want to go to Panama.'

'Good guess.'

'The reason for this impromptu vacation?'

'Venezuelan intelligence has Ethan Ross. This has been established by my contact in the Mossad. They took him there to Bocas, likely to that colonial building in the jungle.'

Gerry said, 'If the Venezuelans have him, why the hell isn't he in Venezuela?'

'That's the question of the hour. Haven't figured that out yet.'

'What do you plan on doing once you get there?'

'I plan on evaluating the security situation around him. And then liaising with Mossad.'

'Why don't you communicate what you know with the FBI?'

'Right now it's less what I know and more what I think I know. I can't prove anything yet.'

Dom hadn't said anything about either taking a shot at Ross himself or arranging for Israeli Special Forces to do the hit, but Gerry was no fool, and he knew what his man had been going through since India. He filled in the blanks and said, 'You know killing Ross won't bring the Yacobys back. What you are planning is simple vengeance. Nothing more.'

Dom said, 'I know.'

After a moment, Gerry sighed. 'Fair enough. You

understand this operation you are undertaking is in no way sanctioned by The Campus or the United States government.'

Dom wanted to say, 'That's the whole idea,' but instead he just said, 'I do.'

'Having said that, I'm not letting you go down there without support. What do you need from me?'

'I appreciate it, but I'm not going to expose our operation in this endeavor. I'll get the support I need.'

Before Gerry could respond, there was a loud banging at the door that even Gerry heard over the phone. Dom looked up quickly, then his eyes narrowed. He said, 'On the topic of assistance, have you been sending Adara Sherman to check up on me?'

'Is there any point in me denying it?'

'I was hoping it was the fact she'd finally noticed my good looks and charm.'

Gerry chuckled. 'Nope. In fact, it's the opposite. She told me you looked like hell and were acting even darker and more brooding than usual, which for you is saying something. So I've asked her to watch over you.' A pause. 'I guess if you've been out running around with foreign agents on a one-man vengeance mission, she hasn't done a terribly good job.'

'She's done fine. I've been working full-time to avoid her. She's here now.' Dom looked at the door suddenly. 'Gerry, I need to call you back again.'

Gerry seemed surprised, but he recovered quickly. 'Uh, sure. All right. Stay in touch.'

Dom opened the door, Adara stood in front of him wearing blue jeans, winter boots, and a thick coat. Her blond hair was hidden under a knit cap, but the cap did nothing to hide the perturbed expression on her face. 'You do realize, Caruso, that I've got other things I could be doing with my time.'

'Of course. Come on in.'

She entered, looked around at Dom's messy condo, and then opened his refrigerator like she owned the place. It was all but empty, as were the cupboards she checked. She lifted a bottle of Maker's Mark off the kitchen table and saw that it was almost empty. She turned back to Dom and gave him a disapproving look. She said, 'I'm going to clean up around here, and then I'm going shopping. You need some food, some real food. You're going to bitch about it, but it's going to happen anyway, so you might as well go somewhere and mope while I do what I'm going to do.'

Dom shook his head vehemently. 'Appreciated, but not necessary, Sherman. I'm actually going out of town. Today. I promise I'll call you when I get back in town.'

Adara Sherman did not bat an eye. 'Actually, *that* won't be necessary.'

Dom's eyebrows rose. Maybe these wellness checks were finally over. 'Really? Why not?'

'Because I'm going with you.'

'No. This is OCONUS. Outside the continental United States.'

She sighed. Annoyed. 'You don't think I know what OCONUS means?'

Dom fought a groan. He didn't have time for this. He needed to get on a plane ASAP. 'Look, this will be a recon op, okayed by Gerry but not exactly sanctioned, and very

325

possibly dangerous. I'm sorry, but I can't take responsibility for you.'

'Of course you can't. I'm worried you can't take responsibility for yourself, so *I'm* going along to watch over *you*.'

Dom started to protest some more, but he stopped himself. 'Hang on a second. Do you know anything about boats?'

She rolled her eyes. 'I was in the Navy, Caruso.'

'I don't mean battleships. I mean something small. Fast enough on open water, but something that won't stick out.'

Sherman said, 'Two things. One, the U.S. Navy doesn't have battleships anymore. And two, where would this boat be operating and what would it be transporting?'

'An archipelago in Panama, and I need it to transport me and some scuba gear.'

'That's it?'

After a shrug, Dom said, 'Maybe a gun.'

The attractive blonde did not hesitate. 'Okay. You'll want a shallow draft, something small, twenty to thirty feet long, I'd say. Maybe a ski boat. MasterCraft makes some great ones I'm very familiar with. Of course, it all depends on what's available down there.'

Dom had already returned to his computer, and now he was pulling up flights for today. 'Okay. You win, you can come along. Go home and pack a bag, then meet me at Dulles in an hour. There's a 1 p.m. flight. If you haul ass we can just make it and be in Panama City by five. We can find air transport to Bocas del Toro when we get there.'

Adara didn't move. 'My passport is in my purse, and I have a three-day carry-on in the trunk of my car. Part of working for Gerry Hendley. On call twenty-four-seven. I can buy anything else I need en route or once there.'

Dom was duly impressed. Even he and the other operators of The Campus bitched if they didn't get at least a couple hours' prep time before traveling OCONUS.

'There's just one problem,' Sherman added. '*You* have dark hair, dark eyes, tan skin. You can fit in down in Panama as long as you don't open your mouth. I, on the other hand, have short blond hair and gray eyes. I'd fit in better on the moon than in Central America.'

Dom laughed. 'You'll be my hot but overly controlling girlfriend. Trust me, Sherman, *nobody* who meets you is going to second-guess that cover story for a second.'

'Not after I give you a black eye, they won't.'

32

Gianna, Ethan and Mohammed lunched at a table set up by the poorly maintained swimming pool in the back of the large colonial home. Guards wandered the property or watched over them from the veranda.

All three ate grilled sea bass, and Gianna and Ethan drank Chilean pinot grigio, while Mohammed sipped orange juice. He remained glued to his laptop, though Ethan had no idea what the young man could possibly be working on.

The Venezuelan intelligence officer Leo had spent the entire morning since their arrival with his guests, but just before lunch he retreated for a conference call with Caracas.

Between healthy sips of wine Ethan asked, 'What's the next step?'

'Harlan and I will connect via Cryptocat this afternoon. He's reaching out to his sources to see what is known in the FBI investigation into Eve's death.'

'That's it?'

'Really, for right now, there is little more for us to do but wait and try to relax.'

Ethan was not going to relax, this he knew for certain. He topped off his glass of wine, ignoring Bertoli's.

Gianna said, 'There is some news out of Washington. As I was dressing for lunch in my room I watched

CNN. I can't see how it is related to your case, but it is very distressing, nonetheless.'

'What is it?'

'The bodies of two FBI employees were found floating in the Potomac River.'

Ethan's eyes widened in shock. 'Wait . . . they can't think I had anything to do with it, can they?'

Mohammed just took a sip of orange juice.

Bertoli said, 'I don't imagine they really think it, but I can't say they won't use it. It's bad timing. I know how the Americans operate. They will be looking for other crimes to charge you with. Maybe these two men died in a robbery or something, and they want to blame you. Maybe there *are* no dead men, and this is all some ploy to charge you with a murder.'

Mohammed spoke without looking up. 'Murder of a federal law enforcement officer in America is punishable by death.'

Ethan put his head down on the table. Bertoli rubbed the back of his neck while Mohammed calmly picked up his knife and cut into his sea bass.

Dom and Adara flew a Copa Airlines flight out of Dulles at 1 p.m., and they worked quietly together on their surveillance plan during the entire five-hour flight down. They made a list of gear they would need to find, and they passed an iPad back and forth with an EagleView map of the area.

They landed in Panama City and immediately climbed aboard an Air Panama Fokker 50 that would take them to Bocas del Toro. The fifty-seater was filled with locals mostly, but a few tourists were on the flight, as well, so Sherman didn't feel like she stuck out too much.

They touched down on the hot runway at Bocas del Toro Isla Colón International Airport a little after 6.30 p.m. As they stepped off the plane and on to the broken tarmac of the little airfield, Dominic shouldered his backpack. Adara did the same with her pack; then she reached out and took Dom's hand and held it as they walked toward the tiny terminal building. Dom didn't make a comment about this, but just before they passed through the door toward the cabstand, Adara leaned close to him. 'Couple of guys standing around the terminal who might be spotters. Can't be too careful.'

'No, you sure can't.' He put his arm around her and led her toward a waiting taxi.

Their hotel was the aptly named Hotel Bocas del Toro. It was positioned on the eastern tip of the island in the heart of downtown Bocas, so close to the shore a portion of the three-storey colonial-style building actually hung over the water. Dom and Adara took a room on the second floor that faced Carenero Cay, an impossibly green slice of land sticking out of impossibly blue water with rusty tin roofs sticking out of the trees.

They dropped their bags on a table and looked around at the small room. Neither made mention of the one bed as they headed out to the balcony and surveyed the neighborhood from the second floor. Once outside, Adara leaned toward Dom, so quickly it startled him and so closely he thought she was going to kiss him. Instead, she said, 'Should we assume we're being listened to?'

Dom cracked a little smile. 'No. Not here. We're okay.'

'Gerry told all of us in the flight crew that when we were working we should assume every hotel is bugged and to act accordingly.'

'The only bugs in this place are the centipedes on the wall.'

Sherman turned and looked at the wall just inches behind her. A prehistoric-looking insect the length of a Magic Marker crawled along next to the French doors between the balcony and the room. Adara turned her nose up a little, but otherwise ignored it.

Dom said, 'Aren't you supposed to freak out or something?'

'Because I am female?'

Not only did Dom not answer, but he regretted asking the question in the first place.

Adara said, 'I was in Afghanistan. We had camel spiders the size of dinner plates climbing around our latrine. Bugs don't faze me.'

'Then this place is going to feel like the Ritz.'

Dominic called David on his satellite phone, and the Mossad officer passed on an address on the far side of Colón Island and told Dom he had a meeting there with a local Mossad contact, but not until 11 p.m. As soon as the call ended, Dom and Adara went downstairs and headed to the nearby docks. Here they split up; Adara's job was to find a boat available for rent, and Dom's task was to purchase the scuba gear and other equipment he would need for his surveillance tomorrow.

Dom walked into and then back out of two dive shops. At the first one they didn't have any equipment of the quality he required, and at the second he did find top-of-the-line equipment that would suit his needs, but there was a significant problem. The buoyancy-control device – the vest a diver wears that holds his tank and other equipment and helps control his buoyancy in the water – came only in red or bright purple. Dom was no slave to fashion, but he suspected swimming into harm's way wearing a big brightly colored vest might not afford him the low-profile infiltration he was looking for.

The third dive shop, however, had exactly what he needed. He rented a pair of full oxygen tanks, a three-millimeter neoprene wetsuit, a black BCD, a weight belt, a regulator, fins, a mask, and a dive knife with an ankle sheath.

He paid an extra fifty dollars in U.S. currency to have the equipment delivered to his hotel, and then he went off in search of other gear. He found a little camping store that catered to sea kayakers who set up camps on the beaches of the little uninhabited islands around the archipelago, and here he bought a canteen, rope, a waterproof backpack, plastic bags, binoculars, and a dozen other odds and ends that he thought might come in handy while he did surveillance on the potential Venezuelan safe house.

When Dom had everything he needed, all packed in the waterproof backpack, he returned to the hotel. Adara was already sitting on the balcony with a cold Balboa beer in her hand, studying nautical charts of the area she'd bought at the boat rental shop. Dom looked over the maps. To him it looked like a complicated mess of channels and splotchy, misshapen spits of land, all crisscrossed with lines and numbers.

'Can you read that?'

'Child's play,' she said as she motioned to a cooler on the balcony. Dom pulled another beer out and sat down next to her.

'Want to see the boat?' she asked.

'You got us a boat already?'

'I can do more than pass out peanuts on a plane, you know.'

'I do know. Where is it?'

'Look down. Black hull, white body.'

Dom looked off the balcony and saw the boat bobbing in a slip along the hotel dock, three stories below. It was a MasterCraft MariStar 235; it was not large at twenty-five feet, but big enough for the two of them and all the gear, and the perfect size for going into the inlets around the Venezuelan safe house if they needed to.

'Is it fast?' Dom asked.

Adara didn't look up from the charts. 'Those are 350-horsepower engines. They'll put out enough power for our needs. It's a ski boat, so it won't win any races with a real speedboat, but it won't stick out either. I've seen a half-dozen just like it in the water around here in the past hour.'

Dom nodded in approval, and then the two of them began looking over the charts together to start working on an infiltration plan.

With a few hours to kill before their 11 p.m. meeting with David's local Mossad contact, the two Americans walked down to a restaurant on the water to grab dinner. It was a slow night at the Ultimo Refugio, and they found a secluded table on the open back deck. They both ordered beers and fried fish, and for the first half-hour they did their best to keep the conversation off the operation that would commence at first light tomorrow.

Finally, Adara said, 'This is going to sound like a cliché to say this, but someone needs to say it to you, because I don't think you're going to figure it out on your own. Killing this guy won't bring that family in India back.'

Dom nodded. 'I've been told.'

'But you'll do it anyway.'

'If I can.'

Adara sipped her beer slowly. Dom could see she wanted to say something, but she was trying to decide if it would be her place to do so.

'What?'

'You have survivor's guilt. About the Yacobys and about Brian.'

Dom shook his head. 'No, I don't. I know I did my best, both in India and in Libya.'

'It doesn't have anything to do with what you did. It has to do with the randomness of it all. The fact you survived an incident, and others didn't.' She looked at him. 'Your brother. The Yacoby children.'

'Survivor's guilt.' Dom said it softly. 'Makes me sound like a head case.'

'You're not crazy. It's perfectly natural. You don't understand why you are here and they aren't. You think it's unfair that you won the roll of the dice.'

Yes. Dom realized this was exactly what he had been thinking ever since Brian was killed. The feelings had subsided a little in the past two years, but after India they had come back twice as hard.

'Are you a shrink, too, Sherman?'

She shook her head with a smile. 'No. Not at all.'

'Then how were you able to diagnose me?'

'Because I have the same thing, and I've had it longer than you.'

'Something happened over there in Afghanistan? When you were a corpsman?'

She nodded. 'A lot of somethings.' Before Dom could ask anything else, she said, 'Can we just leave it at that?'

'Yeah. Sure. I understand.'

There was uncomfortable silence between them for a few minutes. Both ordered more drinks. Dom asked, 'How did you get linked up with The Campus?'

'A patient.'

'A patient?'

'A young oh-one.'

'What's an oh-one?'

'Sorry. A Marine second lieutenant. I was a Navy corpsman assigned to a Marine Combat Engineer Battalion in the Korangal Valley. An oh-one from a rifle platoon nearby took an AK round to the head. I was the first corpsman to him. He was bleeding out and I managed to stop the bleeding.'

Dominic tipped his glass to her. 'Good for you. You saved his life.'

Adara looked away, out at the placid water. The sunset was behind them, but the channel glowed from the last rays of the day. 'No. No happy ending, I'm afraid. He made it back stateside, but he died anyway.'

'Shit. I'm sorry. What did he have to do with The Campus?'

'The lieutenant's dad was a colonel. He sent me an e-mail a month or so after his son died, told me how grateful he was that his boy had been able to come home and die among his family.' She smiled, still looking at the moonlit channel. 'I guess if you look hard enough you can find a silver lining in almost everything. Anyway, we stayed in touch over the years. He retired and went to work for MITRE Corp on a top-secret government contract. When I got out of the Navy he offered me a job. I was going to go to nursing school, but his offer was pretty good. I got vetted, got my top-secret clearance, and then he took me to Maryland and introduced me to Gerry Hendley. The job was working on the Hendley Associates aircraft.'

'Do you regret not going to nursing school?'

'I'll still go. One day. Besides . . .' She smiled at Dom across the table. 'You and the other guys are giving me a lot of real-world practical training. Every one of you has managed to get hurt.'

Dom chuckled. 'It's the only way you'll give us any attention.'

It was a joke, but Adara gave him a serious look. 'Do me a favor. Try not to get hurt down here.'

An unfriendly parrot perched on the railing next to their table. Adara fed the bird a couple of pieces of fish, but that only made it more annoying, so Dom shooed the bird away.

'I'll do my best. And I promise I'll keep you out of danger.'

Dom ordered a third round.

'Are you trying to get me drunk?'

'I'm trying to get *me* drunk. You are just collateral damage.'

Adara tipped her little glass to Caruso. 'That's a great line. Does that work on the girls around D.C.?'

Dom chugged his beer. 'Not really.'

'If you have a hangover in the morning, it's going to make your job a lot harder.'

Dom said, 'Four beers isn't going to kick my ass.'

'Four?' They'd had only three.

Dom looked at his watch. 'We have time.'

33

Just before 11 p.m. a belching taxi took them through Bocas Town, past rusty tin-roofed shacks and beat-up but brightly painted Victorian and colonial buildings. Street vendors selling handmade junk appeared at the windows of the taxi, no doubt triggered by Adara Sherman's shock of blonde hair that announced the presence of a tourist.

The taxi dropped them off at an address David had provided earlier, on the northwestern edge of the town, and the two Americans stood alone in the street in front of a small supermarket for a few minutes, unsure if they should go in or wait outside. Before they could decide, an old two-door hatchback parked in an alley across the street flashed its lights, and after a look between them, Dom and Adara began walking toward it.

A woman in her forties climbed out from behind the wheel as the Americans approached. She introduced herself only as Maria. Dom and Adara shook her hand, but they offered no introductions at all.

Dom was on guard, he looked around the alley, deciding it was secluded enough for a clandestine transaction such as this, but it was hardly a safe place to hang out for very long. He had the titanium diving knife strapped to his calf, but otherwise he was unarmed. This woman looked incredibly nervous, and that, along with the unsecure location, made Dom more than a little edgy himself.

Maria lit a cigarette, then offered one to the two Americans, who both declined. She said, 'I'm sorry. I'm a little tense. I got the call this afternoon. Normally, when they need something ... Well, it's been years since they've needed something. And it wasn't anything like this.'

Adara Sherman was confused, but Dom understood.

'You are Sayan, right?'

'Yes, of course. You don't think I do this sort of thing for a living, do you?'

Sayan were volunteers for Mossad, local assistants, not formal employees of the organization, but Jews living around the world ready to be called upon to perform duties on behalf of the Israeli spy service. Sayan could be doctors or shopkeepers or travel agents or truck drivers, they were normally people motivated by their duty to the nation of Israel.

Dom recognized that her anxious mannerisms were due to the fact she'd probably been pulled off her job as a lawyer or a town administrator or something similar and then sent out to procure weapons for a couple of foreign operatives. Looking at her in this light, Dom decided her anxiety was perfectly reasonable.

Adara said, 'Don't worry, Maria. You are doing great. We appreciate your help.'

Dom tried to get the meeting back on track. He didn't want to stand here in this dark lot any longer than he had to. 'You brought some things for us?'

She lifted the hatchback, revealing a large external-frame backpack. Dom opened it and pulled out a beat-up-looking M9 Beretta pistol, U.S. Army issue, and an M16 rifle that had been partially disassembled to fit inside. The rifle was U.S. military issue, as well, but Dom could tell it was very old. The military didn't use this version of the M16 any longer and hadn't in years. 'Did you get these guns from a museum?'

Maria smoked nervously behind him. 'The request was highly unusual. I did my best. We are a little island. Not many opportunities to –'

Adara said, 'These will be just fine. What about ammunition?'

Maria cocked her head. 'The bullets are already in the guns.'

Adara looked at Dom, then asked, '*Spare* ammunition?'

'What? I'm sorry. That was not specified. As I said, it wasn't easy getting these guns.'

Dom checked the magazines in the weapons. 'Both weapons are fully loaded. Ball ammo.' He ejected a round from each and looked them over in the interior light in the back of the vehicle. 'Really *old* ball ammo. U.S. military. But the cartridges seem to be in good condition.'

Dom inspected the guns over a little more. 'Oh, wow. These are from the war.'

'*What* war?' Adara asked.

'The U.S. invasion. Nineteen eighty-nine. Jesus, lady. That was a quarter-century ago.'

The Sayan looked more annoyed than embarrassed. 'I'm sure they work fine. Lots of security guards in supermarkets and banks use American guns. Again, I was given just hours to accomplish this task. I don't just sit down here waiting to be called on by Tel Aviv to buy illegal weapons.'

'We understand,' said Adara. Her voice was considerably softer and more conciliatory than Dom had made his.

'There is some synthetic motor oil in the boat. We can clean and lube these tonight.'

Dom slid everything back into the pack, and he hoisted it on his shoulder. While he did this the Panamanian woman eyed Adara suspiciously. 'I'm sorry, but I have to say. You don't look like Mossad.'

Adara just smiled. 'And *that*, Maria, is the key to my success.'

They made it back to the hotel before midnight. Dom wanted to grab another drink in the tiny and empty lobby bar, but Adara talked him out of it, insisting they needed to clean the guns and get some sleep before tomorrow's operation.

In the room, Adara stripped and lubed the M16 while Dom worked on the Beretta M9. Dom didn't have much experience with this particular pistol, but it broke down and operated similarly to almost all of the other semi-autos he shot, both with the FBI and in his clandestine work with The Campus.

Adara, on the other hand, had been issued an M9 in the Navy, but in Afghanistan she'd carried an M16 not altogether unlike the one she now cleaned. This model in front of her was the A2, and she'd shot the A4, but internally they looked virtually identical.

After the weapons were ready for action, Adara excused herself and disappeared into the bathroom for a few minutes. She came out wearing a gray T-shirt with NAVY written across the chest, and a pair of sweatpants with VIRGINIA in orange running down the left leg. Her short hair was in a ponytail, and she wore eyeglasses, which Dom found extremely appealing.

He also stole a few glances at her body as she got ready for bed; then he went into the bathroom to change.

Five minutes later Dom came out wearing plain black boxers and a plain white tank top. Adara had all the lights off except for a single lamp by the bed.

She said, 'I've got an alarm set for oh-five-thirty.'

'Sounds good,' said Dom, and he began walking toward his side of the bed.

Adara raised an eyebrow, and Dom noticed the gesture. He smiled confidently. 'Don't worry, Sherman, I'm a gentleman.'

She returned his smile, then said, 'Glad to hear it,' before grabbing a pillow off the bed and tossing it on the wicker sofa. 'I saw a blanket in the closet. I'd shake it for bugs if I were you.'

Dom stood in the middle of the room for a moment. He looked at the good-looking blonde on the big bed. And then he looked at the uninviting sofa. 'Really?'

Adara nodded. 'Really. Night, Caruso.'

Dom grabbed the blanket out of the closet, gave it a few shakes, and headed for the couch as Adara Sherman flipped off the lamp by the bed.

'Night, Sherman.'

Adara and Dom headed to the dock at 6.30 a.m. A cool early-morning rain shower kept the streets even emptier than they would have normally been at this time of day. They carried full backpacks and more gear in bags under their arms, but it still took two trips to the boat to get everything loaded.

Once on board Dom pulled the pieces of the M16 out

of the backpack Maria gave him and assembled the rifle, which he stowed in a large cooler under the row of seats at the boat's stern.

Adara was surprised. 'You aren't taking the rifle with you to your hide site?'

'I wish I could, but with everything else I am hauling, a forty-inch-long, ten-pound M16 is going to be more than I can deal with. I'll just take the pistol. You keep the rifle on board the boat in case you've got to come pick me up in a hurry.'

'There is another option,' she said.

'I'm all ears.'

'I can leave you in the water at the waypoint we decided on, then head around to the other side of the island. I'll find a secluded place to drop anchor, then I can make my way to you overland with the rifle. It might take me a few hours, but I'll get it done.'

Dom shook his head. 'I appreciate the spirit, Sherman, but I'd rather have you and this boat together at all times. There are a lot of unknowns on this operation, so I'm not giving up the option to run away.'

Adara fired the engines of the MasterCraft at 7 a.m. Even though a light rain continued to fall, boat traffic in the channel was picking up. Small cargo vessels running between the islands, ferries, fishing boats, dive boats heading out to fuel up for the day, it seemed to Dom that every third vessel around Colón Island was already out of its slip and on the water.

Adara stood at the helm and piloted the boat with confidence. Once they left the transportation lanes she pushed the throttle forward and the two 5.7-liter engines churned up more of the dirty canal water, the stern lowered deeper, and the bow rose as the twenty-five-foot vessel picked up speed.

Dom sat on the deck at the stern and donned his scuba gear, then he checked and rechecked the rest of the equipment he'd be taking on to the island with him. His backpack was fully laden with water and gear, enough to last him forty-eight hours if necessary, and he'd wrapped all the items inside the waterproof pack in a layer of garbage bags to keep everything dry while diving.

It was a ten-minute run across the channel before Adara cut speed and began trolling along Bastimentos Island. There were a few little eco-lodges on the shoreline, but the farther south they traveled, the less development they saw. They approached the mouth of a wide inlet. The water was calm other than the effect of the raindrops on the surface. She consulted with a printout from Eagle-View a few times to check the distance to the Venezuelan compound so she would be sure she didn't get any closer than she had planned.

When they were close to Caruso's planned ingression point, Adara cut all power. The light rain had picked up to a driving downpour. Adara wore a baseball cap that kept water out of her eyes, but otherwise she was soaked. Dom, on the other hand, was all suited up and ready to go diving, so the rain was inconsequential to him.

He said, 'Head straight back to the hotel, but be ready to come pick me up at all times.'

'I'll gas up and stay close to the boat. If you call for extraction, I can be back in the area in less than twenty-five minutes.'

'Good. I will check in every other hour by sat phone. If I miss two checks, bring the boat back here and try to raise me on the walkie-talkie. If that doesn't work, I'll have to swim out to you. Whatever happens, I don't want you landing this boat and coming ashore yourself. Are we clear about that?'

'Fine. But if things get dicey and you want to rethink that plan, just let me know.'

Dom attached his backpack to a piece of rope tied around his waist, then donned his mask and sat on the portside edge of the boat. He put on his fins, slipped the regulator's second stage in his mouth, and held on to his mask to keep it in place. With a nod to Adara Sherman he rolled backward, his fins flipped up in the air as he disappeared over the side. Once in the water he gave Adara an 'okay' signal and let some air out of his vest; then he disappeared below the surface.

Adara waited for a few minutes, then started the boat's engines and turned back for Bocas Town.

Dom wore a belt with twenty-five pounds of lead weights to counter the buoyancy of both his wetsuit and BCD, as well as his watertight bag of gear. With the weights he descended easily to a depth of thirty feet. There he pumped air into his vest to give himself just enough buoyancy to glide over the sandy and grassy bottom. He swam into the center channel of the inlet so that the bubbles from his regulator would not be visible from shore. With the rain he felt confident it would be hard to detect a single diver from the surface, but he was alone, with no easy avenue of escape if he was discovered, so he didn't plan on taking any unnecessary chances.

He swam to the east, keeping just above the seagrass on the surface of the brackish inlet, using the compass built into his watch to orient his route to the Venezuelan safe house. The current was with him, and he found himself moving much faster than he'd expected. After only twenty minutes he chanced a slow ascent to the surface. He was right where he wanted to be, so he went back down, left the center of the channel, and headed to shore.

He remained near the bottom all the way to the shore, pushing through tall grasses, spooking fish that kicked up sand, and then negotiating his way through thick mangrove under the surface. When he thought he was in position, he lifted his head out of the water slowly and looked around in all directions. He quickly realized he'd made a miscalculation.

He'd arrived at the shore, and it looked much as it did in the EagleView image, but there was a problem. The mangrove was so thick on this part of the shoreline, Dom knew he wouldn't be able to get through it without a chain saw.

He took a moment to try and pick another location to come ashore. After a minute he saw a tiny cove ahead that might have dipped deep enough into the mangrove to allow Dom to fight his way through, so he put the second stage of his regulator back into his mouth and went back under the water.

He swam to the middle of the inlet, again to prevent his bubbles from being obvious to anyone on the shore, but as he arrived he heard the unmistakable sound of a boat's engine.

He stopped where he was, hovering twenty-five feet

below the surface, rising and falling slowly as he took breaths from his tank that filled his lungs and made him more buoyant and then blew them out again.

He saw the hull of the boat now, directly overhead and trolling slowly. He put it at about thirty feet. It was hard to discern anything about the type of craft from his view below it, but as he watched for a few moments he got the impression the objective of those on the boat was some sort of a patrol. They didn't seem to be fishing, because it was moving through the channel, and they certainly weren't hauling cargo or ferrying people, because of their slow speed.

Dom worried the boat was somehow tied to the Venezuelan safe house, and he knew if his concerns were valid, getting out of the area in a hurry was going to be even more difficult than he'd imagined.

Fifteen minutes after the trolling boat disappeared, Dom returned to the shore less than two hundred yards from the edge of the lawn that encircled the Venezuelan safe house. He ended up infiltrating a little closer to the target than he would have liked, but after seeing how dense the jungle was around here he decided to chance it, not wanting to risk spending the entire day moving into position.

As soon as he was out of the water and into the trees, he took off all his scuba gear, closed his tank to preserve the remaining air, and hid everything under thick ferns that grew below the canopy of crabwood and guariuba trees. From his pack he pulled a dark brown shirt and camouflage pants, and a pair of black sneakers. Very little of the rain made it through the trees down to him, but he hoped the heavy cloud cover would continue throughout the day to keep him cool. He stuck the M9 pistol into his waistband, slipped the backpack on to his back, and checked his location with his GPS. He added a waypoint to the device's computer, pinpointing the exact location where he had stowed his scuba gear, fully expecting to exfil from the target the same way he'd ingressed.

Before he began moving toward his intended hide site he heard the rumbling of a boat again passing through the inlet. He dropped down on his belly and moved behind the ferns, then peeked between them. In front of him he saw a thirty-foot Panamanian police boat with four men on board, and a .50-caliber machine gun jutting from the bow. From its size and its speed Dom felt certain this was the vessel he'd swum below earlier. Now it was back – the boat seemed to be on a regular patrol and not hunting for anything in particular, but Dom didn't like the fact that it happened to be cruising around this narrow inlet. He could swim under the patrol boat with no problem if he had to escape, but in case Adara needed to retrieve him from the shore for some reason, he knew the police in the bigger, faster and much more heavily armed boat could pose a serious problem.

Once the patrol boat had moved on up the inlet, Dom turned and left the bank, pushing his way through the thick foliage. He moved purposefully but without rushing, doing his best to keep an eye out for snakes and spiders and other creatures that could ruin his day.

This was a typical tropical rainforest. Ferns and flowering plants along the ground, proliferating in the wet air and low light below a triple canopy of oak and guava and sandbox trees. The way forward was arduous, but at least the ground was flat and only moist, as opposed to muddy. Dom made good progress, and took special care to check his GPS repeatedly to avoid accidentally popping out of the jungle and stumbling into the Venezuelans.

It took him an hour and twenty minutes to travel two hundred yards, but by 9.45 a.m. Dom caught his first glimpse, through the rainforest, of the back of the big colonial-style Venezuelan safe house.

He stopped, lowered himself down to his hands and knees, and found a fair hiding spot at the edge of the tree line. He secreted himself and his gear tight against the trunk of an oak tree surrounded by viny epiphyte and wild fern, and he slid his brown pack in front of his body to disrupt his outline. Only when he was comfortable that he was secure in his location did he pull out his binoculars and scan the property in front of him.

The rain had stopped and the sun had come out, cooking the water in the air and making for oppressive humidity, especially here on the floor of the rainforest. Dom had trouble focusing his optics through the haze, but after some work he saw two big old black Ford Expeditions parked on a dirt drive and facing away from the main house. Dom knew there was no paved road system on this island, but from EagleView he'd seen a few crisscrossing dirt tracks running through the jungle.

Two men stood at the dock that jutted out into the inlet. Next to them, a pair of white speedboats bobbed in the water. The men wore light khaki shorts and linen shirts, but Dom could see big black Heckler & Koch G3 rifles hanging from their shoulders. Another pair of men strolled the grounds in the distance, and they also wore G3s.

Dom felt certain there would be a lot more than four armed guards, but he had only a three-quarters view of the rear of the property.

On the far side of the colonial mansion and only barely in view from his position in the trees to the east, he saw a kennel with large dogs inside. He thought they were German shepherds or Belgian Malinois; either way, he was certain they were part of the property's defense.

His initial scan of the windows of the building had turned up no signs of Ethan Ross, but from the defensive posture of the location, he had a strong suspicion the Venezuelans felt the need to protect *something* inside the house.

He checked in with Adara on the satellite phone, swatted at some bugs crawling up and down his arms, drank some warm water from his canteen, and settled in to his hide. He fully expected to be here at least twenty-four hours, so he tried to make himself as comfortable as possible in his hide site next to the oak tree.

34

The Russian Navy's *Admiral Chabanenko* was a modern Udaloy II class anti-submarine warfare destroyer, so the 163-meter-long vessel drew a lot of attention from the locals as it dropped anchor in the harbor at the Pacific Nicaraguan port of San Juan del Sur. The ship had just arrived for a three-day call, another stop in a friendly nation during its five-month cruise of the southern Western Hemisphere.

The sailors on board the *Admiral Chabanenko* could barely contain their excitement at the prospect of a liberty call. Even though no one expected much from the sleepy Third World port, the sailors also knew they couldn't be choosy, and a couple of days of booze, women, fresh food and terra firma, in that order, sounded good to everyone afforded shore leave. Plus, their money would go further here in Nicaragua than it had in Buenos Aires or even Caracas. The rumors of beers costing only fifteen córdobas – about twenty rubles – sounded particularly inviting to the poorly paid Russian sailors, who would spend a minimum of four times that amount at a European port of call.

An hour before the first of the *Admiral Chabanenko* crew disembarked for the frivolity ashore, a secure radio call came for the leader of a six-man unit of Russian naval Spetsnaz on board. The first lieutenant had been packing his weekend bag to go ashore with his men, but instead he ran up to the marine operations center to take the call.

As a Spetsnaz commando, the first lieutenant was actually a member of the GRU, military intelligence, so he was not completely surprised to learn the voice on the other end of the radio was a GRU captain lieutenant, but when he was transferred to an FSB general in Moscow to be given orders for an in extremis mission, he was thoroughly shocked. And he was doubly astonished by the orders themselves. He and his men had trained for all manner of operations, but the first lieutenant had never executed anything like the mission the FSB general ordered him to undertake immediately.

Less than three hours after the radio call came through, the first lieutenant and his five men had dressed in civilian clothes and were rolling duffel bags toward the helipad on the rear of the *Admiral Chabanenko*. While other sailors still on board watched with curiosity, the Spetsnaz unit climbed aboard the destroyer's own Kamov Ka-32 helicopter and lifted off into the evening sky over the port of San Juan del Sur.

Their flight to the military air base near Managua took only an hour, and there they were briefed by an FSB officer who had just arrived from Caracas. This briefing took another hour, and then the men were ordered to finish planning their mission and wait for a green light from Moscow.

It was not until 4 a.m. local time when the green light came, and as soon as the first lieutenant knew the mission was a go, he and his team boarded a civilian Cessna Caravan owned by a front company affiliated with Nicaraguan intelligence. They had already stowed all their gear on board, which was not easy, because each man had nearly sixty pounds of kit, so the cabin of the ten-seat plane was packed full of men and matériel. Still, the aircraft rose into the dark skies over sleeping Managua and banked to the south.

While this was all going on, a second contingent of Russian nationals was on the water, having departed Maracaibo, Venezuela, in the late afternoon. These men were Russian intelligence agents, FSB, and they had received a phone call every bit as surprising as the naval Spetsnaz first lieutenant's afternoon radio communication.

The FSB operatives in Maracaibo's orders were to secure a fast yacht and immediately sail across the choppy waters of the Caribbean Sea at best possible speed to the northwest. Their destination was the same as that of the commandos coming via air from the north; an archipelago in northern Panama called Bocas del Toro.

Neither the GRU commandos nor the FSB operations officers knew that the FSB rezident in Caracas had initiated the entire chain of events the day before. He had been told by friendly officials in Venezuela's General Counterintelligence Office that the federal police would begin rounding up men and women across the city. It was explained that an American traitor had given the Venezuelan embassy in Washington a list of thirty-three names of CIA agents in Venezuela, in exchange for quick and safe passage out of the United States. Further, the GCIO executive relayed with excitement that the traitor soon intended to pass a second list of names, those of spies working against Venezuela in its embassies abroad.

When the FSB man in Caracas contacted the Russian embassy in Moscow seeking confirmation of this wild story, he was told the FSB had just learned through a highly placed intelligence source in the U.S. government that the American FBI was looking for a National Security Council staff member named Ethan Ross who had just fled the country, possibly after murdering his girlfriend and a pair of FBI agents who had been pursuing him. Also, rumors were circulating that he was on the run with a large digital cache of top-secret documents.

At first the FSB man in Caracas was skeptical; this sounded like some sort of American disinformation campaign. How could one man walk out of Washington with such a treasure trove of intelligence? But the GCIO officer showed Ethan Ross's list of Venezuelan spies to the FSB rezident, and the Russian knew he was dealing with a real intelligence leak. Although the actual names of the agents weren't listed – they were given code names – the files described positions held, job titles, relationships with known personalities, and other recognizable aspects, so the agent's true identities were easy to discern. The Russian immediately recognized some of the positions as legitimate spies for America that the FSB had already identified but left in place.

The rezident was on the phone with Moscow within moments of getting this confirmation, and he was ordered by FSB leadership to pressure the Venezuelans to hand over the entire intelligence scrape as soon as the American was in Caracas. The rezident himself suggested to the GCIO that they inject the American with SP-117, a Russian-developed 'truth serum' drug that would, in theory, anyway, ensure he gave up the password for his data, but the Venezuelans rebuked the Russians, claiming the American would be kept at a safe house in Panama until the arrests were complete and the time was right to bring him into the country.

The FSB knew any American traitor with intelligence on his person of the nature this man allegedly had was a rapidly depreciating asset. The Americans would come after him hard and fast, they would find him in days if not hours, and they would do what they needed to do to close the compromise. The FSB rezident in Caracas conferred urgently over secure comms with Lubyanka, the FSB's headquarters in Moscow, and the decision was made to obtain the files via active measures. Executing the operation in Panama would be diplomatically preferable to doing it in Venezuela, and fooling the Venezuelans into thinking the Russian commandos sent on the mission were, in fact, Americans would be better still.

The FSB rezident thought it to be something of a miracle that this decision had been rendered in only twenty-four hours, but by the time the green light came for the Spetsnaz commandos in Managua, one thing was clear: the Russians were coming for Ethan Ross, they wanted the man and his files, and they planned on leaving no trace back to Moscow of their act.

It had been a long and dismal day for Dominic Caruso. He'd avoided a cruel sunburn by staying under the edge of the rainforest canopy tucked inside a large fern, but he felt like he'd come damn close to heat exhaustion during the afternoon. He'd been bitten by ants and mosquitoes and crawled on by spiders and stared at by a sloth and a howler monkey.

And shortly before dusk this evening he'd had an experience that he knew would someday bring laughs from the rest of his team of operatives at The Campus.

A toucan had actually shat on his back from its perch in the oak above him. At the time, a two-man guard patrol had been nearby on the lawn, so Dominic just lay there and took the splatter. When he finally did get a chance to try and wipe it off he saw he was covered in red, as if the bird had been eating a steady diet of wild berries.

Dom would have laughed himself, had he been in the mood. But he wasn't, because through all today's effort and misery he had yet to see any hint of Ethan Ross.

Just before dusk he did see one man who did not look like he belonged here at the mansion. A small, dark-complexioned individual who wore blue jeans in the ninety-degree heat stood on the veranda for several minutes talking on a mobile phone. Through the binoculars Dom made out short hair and a very young-looking face, and he put the man at no older than twenty-five.

Dom pulled out a camera and took a few long-range shots, but the distance and the fading light made them all but worthless. After a lengthy phone call the small man returned to the cool of the house and shut the door behind him.

Dominic decided to change his position after six hours without any sighting of anyone other than the small man and the guard force. He left the majority of his gear in his hide – after pinpointing it with a GPS waypoint – and began moving laterally to the west toward the back of the property.

He found a new temporary hide with a view of the swimming pool and the wraparound balcony at the rear of the house. When he was sure he was well hidden in deep tropical shrubs under the canopy of the rainforest, he pulled out his binoculars and scanned the windows. Unlike in the front, several of the curtains here were open, and he could see one man moving around, back and forth, on the first floor.

Probably another guard, Dom determined, but he liked this position nonetheless and decided to wait until dark when there would be a better view inside the lighted rooms and hallways of the property.

Shortly before ten-thirty in the evening, a breeze picked up and Dom smelled the approach of rain in the air. He decided he'd go back to his original hide site; it had better coverage, and he had a light poncho stored in his backpack he could use in the case of a serious downpour. But just as he put down his binoculars he saw movement on the veranda. Quickly he brought the glasses back to his eyes, and he saw a blond-haired man with a wineglass in his hand, standing against the railing and looking out over the swimming pool. He clutched what looked like a closed laptop computer under his arm.

Dom scanned the man up and down. He couldn't really make out his face because he was standing out of the light. 'Is that you, Ross?' he whispered to himself. It was impossible to be certain at eighty yards' distance, even with the binoculars.

He grabbed his camera and got a few inconclusive shots, then he took more pictures when a female with long and curly black hair came through the French doors behind the blond man. She carried a glass in one hand and a wine bottle in the other. Even at a distance, Dom could detect a wide smile on her face. She hugged the blond-haired man, awkwardly, because her hands were full, and the man just continued looking out over the back of the property like she wasn't there.

Dom willed the blond-haired man to step back into the light and face in his direction. Eventually a large man in a cream-colored suit and with a brown mustache stepped out on to the veranda, and with his gesticulations Dom could tell the man was beckoning the others back indoors. He focused the binoculars on the blond, who finally did turn back to the French doors and step through them while talking to the big man in the cream-colored suit. As he did this, he walked into the light and faced the rainforest on the eastern side of the property. There, eighty yards away and invisible in the darkness beyond the lawn, Dominic Caruso lay under a fern with binoculars to his eyes.

It was Ross.

Softly, Dom said, 'Nice to see you again, asshole. You think you're safe here? You might be safe from Albright, you might even be safe from me. But you aren't safe from Shayetet Thirteen.'

Ethan Ross disappeared behind the doors and the light on the veranda snapped off.

35

Dominic made it back to his primary hide site just before midnight. He planned on calling David to let him know that he had positively identified Ross, but the rain clouds had completely obscured the moon and taken every bit of the natural light Dominic planned on using to traverse the jungle. Instead, he found the only way he could move was by keeping dangerously close to the lawn of the safe house. Even though the main house's lights didn't reach all the way to the rainforest on the edge, some ambient light made it this far, so Dom used the faint glow to find his way back toward the water and his hide.

Now back in place and secure, he pulled out his sat phone, ready to call in Israeli Special Forces. But before he could make the call, the phone vibrated in his hand and the low-light screen came alive with one word: *ALBRIGHT*.

This was interesting. Albright calling *him*? Dom answered in a voice just above a whisper. 'Actually, Darren, this is kind of a bad time.'

The line hissed and crackled. Dom assumed the rain clouds were interfering with his signal. Albright's tone was sharp despite the distortion. 'That is interesting. A couple of days ago you were bugging the shit out of me, and now you've suddenly found something better to do. Well, I won't keep you, I just thought I would let you know before you see it on the news.'

'Let me know *what*?'

'Ethan Ross has stolen something in the neighborhood of six hundred and eighty thousand files out of Intelink-TS. Sensitive compartmented intelligence documents relating to CIA assets all over the world.'

'What the hell are you talking about?'

'He perpetrated a one-hundred-fifty-gig intel scrape the day before yesterday. He used Eve Pang's credentials and logged on to a virtual private network, used some sort of a crawler that knew just where to go and what to look for. Forensics is still trying to reconstruct the breach so we can figure out exactly what he has, but it has been characterized to me as, and I'm quoting the techs here, "pretty much everything."'

'Oh, God.'

'The two missing SSG guys turned up floating in the Potomac riddled with bullet holes. And a body that was shot up and torched in a Richmond hotel room the other day has been ID'd as another government IT guy. An ex–NSA employee named Phillip McKell. This murder looks like it is somehow related.'

Dom just laid his head on the wet ground. 'This keeps getting bigger, doesn't it?'

'You're damn right it does. And that's not the worst of it,' Albright continued. 'Now it looks like Ross has run off to Venezuela.'

Dom lifted his head and cleared his throat softly. 'Why do you say that?'

'Our CIA liaison has come to us at FBI to let us know that Agency proxy assets in Caracas are getting snatched off the street. We're talking about somewhere around two dozen, just in the past forty-eight hours.'

That's it, Dom thought. Payback to the Venezuelans to get him out of the country. Before he could say anything, Albright continued.

'We checked some static cams we have set up to monitor the Venezuelan embassy on Thomas Jefferson here in D.C., and we see Ross walking into a side door the day before yesterday, right about the time the surveillance officers went missing. We figure he gave Venezuela intel from the scrape so they would help get him out of town. In the process, either Ross or the Venezuelans killed Phillip McKell, Eve Pang and two FBI surveillance officers. We've got to assume he's down in Caracas right now.'

Dominic's brain executed a multitude of calculations in the next few seconds. He tabulated all the pros and cons, and decided to tell Albright *almost* everything he knew. 'I've got some intel you can use.'

'I kinda hoped you might.'

Dom said, 'Ross is in Panama. Bocas del Toro Province. An island called Bastimentos.'

If Albright expected that Caruso might have something for him, he certainly didn't expect *this*. 'I beg your pardon?'

'He is under the protection of Venezuelan intelligence officers. He's being held at a safe house about a half-hour boat ride from the airport.'

After several seconds with nothing but the pops and cracks of the sat-phone connection, Albright replied, 'If you don't tell me how you know this, I am going to make the very small and very reasonable leap that you are, in fact, working with Ethan Ross.'

'You know that is asinine.'

'Probably so. But I'm going to fuck with you anyhow. You are impeding my investigation.'

'Damn it, Albright, I just told you where your suspect is hiding. That is exactly the *opposite* of impeding your investigation.' Dom took a calming breath. Did his best to look at it through Albright's eyes. 'I know because the Israelis told me.'

'*What* Israelis?'

'The guys who want Ross for his role in Arik Yacoby's death.'

'Any chance I could sit down with these Israelis and have a little friendly chat?'

'I doubt it. Anyway, they have me at the tip of the spear right now. I know more than they do.'

'How is that?'

'I've got eyes on the safe house as we speak.'

Albright's tone turned even darker and more accusatory. 'You are in Panama?'

'Yep.'

'You are in pretty fucking deep, aren't you, Caruso?'

'Hey, man, no law against a private citizen taking a trip down to sunny Central America.' As he said it, the rain began to fall again.

'Don't bullshit me. You're down there with your spook friends with a plan to kill Ross.'

'I keep telling you. No spook friends. I am down here with a hot blonde who could kick both our asses, but she's no spook.' Dom cracked a half-smile, wiping water from his eyes as he did so. 'She's just a stewardess.'

Albright obviously didn't know what to make of this comment, but he did not, for a moment, think it was true. He was fixated on the fact Caruso might be on a kill mission. 'Listen to me very, very carefully. Whatever you and your friends have planned for Ross . . . this is a game changer. Ethan Ross very likely has the scrape with him right this minute. You kill him, and we might lose access to it. It's out there in the wind somewhere, and we *have* to get it back.'

Dom said, 'He's got a laptop with him. I saw it.'

'That might be it, then. If not that, it could be on a portable hard drive.'

'How do you know he hasn't already handed it off to someone?'

'We *don't* know. But this last-minute scrape wasn't designed to go unnoticed. It has all the markings of some-one trying to give himself a bargaining position. To steal data because he knew we were on to him so he'd have something to barter with. We think he'll keep it with him at all times. He knows computers and has the expertise to encrypt the files to where they are worthless to anyone else without his password.'

Dom wanted to kill the son of a bitch in that house lit up across the dark lawn, or at least help the Israelis do it, but he knew now that killing Ross without getting the scrape back would endanger the lives of American assets all over the world.

Fuck. Things just got complicated.

He understood the ramifications of that type of intelligence product loose in the wind. He'd play by Albright's rules.

'Okay. I'll hang tight where I am and help you guys get it back. I'll text you the coordinates as soon as we're off the phone. How long till you are down here?'

'I'll get a fly team from HRT together and get the paperwork in motion. It's four-plus hours in the air direct with fixed-wing to Panama City. We'll need to meet up with helos that can take us to his actual location. It might be after dawn before we get there.'

'I'll keep an eye out till then,' Dom said.

'Not alone you won't. We'll get you some support. We're friendly with the Panamanian Public Forces, I can make a call and –'

'Look, it's your show, but I wouldn't do that.'

'And why not?'

'I've seen Panamanian police patrol boats cruising up and down the waterway by this safe house all day long. I think it's possible the local cops are getting paid by Venezuelans to keep an eye out.'

Albright understood the quandary. 'Shit. And even if we talk to the federal cops, there's no way to be sure they won't let the wrong thing slip to the local cops, and Ross might well disappear again.'

'Bingo,' said Dom. 'Maybe you guys should just haul ass down here and raid this place. I haven't seen more than a half-dozen guards outside. I assume there are at least that number inside, but if you come in with enough shock and awe first thing tomorrow when everyone is half asleep you can wrap up Ethan Ross and his scrape.'

Albright said, 'It would make me feel better if you went ahead and admitted you did have some other spook friends with you.'

'There are no other guys, Albright.'

The FBI man sighed. 'I'll send special agents from the FBI office in Panama City your way. It's just a couple of guys who investigate bank fraud, but I want Bureau control of your operation.'

Dom said, 'I have no idea what kind of time we have. The Venezuelans might move him any minute.'

'It's important that you and your guys keep eyes on him and do *not* try to take him yourselves.'

Dom sighed. He was tired of repeating himself that he wasn't down here with the CIA. He said, 'Okay, I'll pass the word down to the rest of my brigade to stand fast.'

'Smart-ass,' Albright mumbled before hanging up.

Dom's phone rang moments later, he looked down and recognized David's number. The D.C.-based Mossad officer would be calling for an update, hoping his American confederate had made a positive ID of the target so he could send down a team of shooters on a vengeance mission. The Mossad's interests were clear and unchanged, they wanted Ethan Ross's head on a pike, but Dominic's mission had changed with the call from Albright. He didn't even see how he could tell David, an agent of a foreign nation, about the intelligence scrape. Israel was an ally of the United States, so maybe the CIA would notify them at some point, but Caruso knew it sure as hell wasn't his call to make.

He did not answer his phone. David would be pissed,

but right now there was nothing Dom could do about that.

He shifted position in his hide and moved the fern a little in the process. He reached up to stop the stems and leaves from moving, and as he did he heard a noise nearby.

Dom froze, but after twenty seconds of holding his breath he saw the source of the noise in the dark. A pair of howler monkeys moved along the lawn in front of him, not forty feet away. Either they didn't see him or they didn't care that a human being was lying in the brush at the edge of the trees.

Once he relaxed his nerves with a few sips of water from his canteen, he realized it was time to check in with Sherman. Even though it was midnight, she answered on the first ring; Dom was continually impressed with her abilities as a supporting agent.

He told her about seeing Ross and about getting the call from Albright that meant this tropical island would soon be running with hyped-up and pissed-off American federal law enforcement officers.

Adara said, 'You want me to start heading that way?'

'No. I'm going to keep eyes on the compound all night.'

'It's midnight now. There are still a few boats moving between the islands. If I don't get you now, you run the risk of getting stuck there. If you call me for an extraction at 3 a.m. or some other time in the middle of the night, I'll be the only boat on the water. The Venezuelans will hear me coming for miles, or the Panamanian police will stop me. A blonde tourist cruising alone in the middle of the night is going to draw some attention that neither of us wants.'

'I understand. HRT will be here in the morning, and I need to give them real-time intelligence on the area. I'm on my own till the Feds get here. Then I'll have you come and pick me up.'

'Roger that,' said Adara, and Dom hung up. He lay there surrounded by the flora and fauna of Central America, hoping like hell nothing larger than a mosquito would dine on him this evening while he kept tabs on the American traitor tucked in and comfortable in the big house across the lawn.

36

It was still dark at 6 a.m., although the rain clouds had moved on and faint moonlight filtered down to Bastimentos Island. Dom rubbed his eyes, slowly realizing he had fallen asleep for a few minutes, though it hadn't been long enough to provide him any real comfort. His position happened to be right in the habitat of a group of small colorful frogs, and throughout the night the hopping creatures in the ferns by his face or on the ground in front of his backpack startled him and ensured he'd stayed awake the vast majority of the time.

He lifted his binos off the ground next to him, wiped condensation off all four lenses with a rag, and then brought them up to his eyes to scan the area. He saw a pair of guards on the far side of the property; their flashlight beams made them obvious even at a distance. There was no movement inside the building other than a couple of patrolling guards he could see through the windows just inside the main door at ground level.

An aircraft passed high above, and Dom realized it had been the faint engine hum that had roused him. Dom couldn't see the plane with the thick canopy directly overhead, but he could hear the drone of a single-engine turboprop and guessed it was probably about five thousand feet above ground.

He kept scanning the house; his eyes were impossibly tired, but he did his best to focus.

As he scanned, he was surprised by the sudden crack of a tree branch on his left. It wasn't close to his position, but it was loud enough to stick out among the other sounds. Chirping frogs fell silent with the noise. A moment later, a second breaking tree branch followed, and then a quick succession of rustling leaves and more cracks of breaking limbs came from another part of the jungle, also on his left.

Dom pulled the M9 pistol from his hip and then he tucked himself lower under the fern, unsure what was happening thirty or forty yards off his left shoulder.

Before he could ponder the question, a figure appeared on the lawn in front of him, and above the figure, the silhouette of a de-forming parachute. The dark canopy covered the man, and Dom watched as another figure dropped from the sky not twenty yards away from the first man, just outside of the lights of the house.

Dom almost launched to his feet in surprise.

Now another crash in the trees, this time to his right. From the noise, Dom concluded another jumper had landed short of his intended landing zone and was now hanging from one of the oaks or yellow trees here in the rainforest.

Dogs began barking in the kennel on the far side of the house now, and then two more figures landed on the darkened lawn, and they collected their chutes in their arms and then followed the others back into the trees.

That made a total of six men that Dom had seen or

heard falling from the sky, all in the space of no more than ten seconds. They had all pulled back into the edge of the rainforest, and were now likely stowing their chutes and preparing their gear somewhere very close to his position.

Holy shit, Dom thought. Could it be the FBI Hostage Rescue Team? Albright hadn't said a damn thing about an airborne mission on the compound, but Dom couldn't rule it out. He'd love to check with Darren right now, but he wasn't about to make a phone call with a crew of unknowns around him. Even if they *were* FBI and aware he was here and providing overwatch on the property, Dom knew announcing his presence in the middle of a bunch of itchy trigger fingers wouldn't end well for him.

No way. Dom decided he would lie right here and watch.

Surely, he told himself, this had to be the FBI. *Who the hell else could it be?*

Mossad? No. David had called Dom a half-dozen times in the past few hours, and Dom had not called back yet. He didn't think it likely Mossad would launch its own mission against this location without any reconnaissance from the man they knew they had on the ground.

A pair of flashlight beams emanating from the driveway illuminated the lawn. This would be the two-man guard team Dom had seen patrolling the perimeter all night long. From the casual sway of the beams, the Venezuelans didn't seem to be too worried about the dogs alerting to something in the jungle, but they were coming this way nonetheless. Dom assumed the men had heard noises, but considering the prevalence of monkeys, sloths, toucans, and other wildlife large enough to rustle the trees, the guards would be dulled into complacency, no matter what official threat level their leadership had imposed for the safe house.

Dom caught glimpses of the approaching men at first due to the flashlight beams in his face, but when they passed his position, moving closer to the water, the beams tracked away and Dom could clearly make out the men behind the lights. The two Venezuelans had taken their G3 rifles off their shoulders and they held them one-handed, with the lights in the other. Again, to Dominic these guys didn't look like they were ready for a fight.

But those six men in the trees would be ready, Dom had no doubt. And as soon as the two guards passed, Dom saw a second pair of dark figures moving behind them. He could discern no weapons in their hands, but they closed on the armed guards quickly and quietly, and as one they took them by the necks from the rear, spun them, disarmed them, and silenced them with a series of blindingly fast strikes to the torso and face.

The two guards crumpled into a single heap on the dark lawn, and Dom knew from the damage inflicted on vital parts of their body, they were dead. The mysterious killers then dragged the men and their weapons back into the trees to the right of Dom's hideout.

Dom had seen the entire fight from twenty yards away, and even though not a word had been spoken, even though Dom could not see the faces of the men who'd just parachuted on to the island, and even though the men wore no insignia or recognizable uniforms, Dom knew who they were, because he knew the fighting style. The two men had employed an efficient and lethal flowing attack against the guards that was not dissimilar to Krav Maga, but it was distinct enough for Dom to recognize it. It was Systema, and it was a style developed in Russia and used by Russian special mission units.

Things around here just got *even more* complicated, because Spetsnaz had dropped from the sky.

A minute later, Dom saw the six silhouettes moving across the lawn to the west, closer to the trucks and the swimming pool. He made out the distinctive shape of the Heckler & Koch MP7 Personal Defense Weapon in each man's hand, and the men, of course, moved like a para-military force, covering and advancing in pairs. But they weren't heading directly to the colonial mansion just yet. It looked to Dom as if that they would not attack the house immediately; instead, they disappeared up the driveway. Dom thought they were going to do a little recon themselves to get a feel for the situation inside by finding cover near the pool house and watching the building from there.

He tried to call Albright, but got no answer. Dom assumed he was on the aircraft heading down and couldn't get a signal at the moment. And even if the FBI agents from Panama City were already here in the area, that wouldn't do him much good, since they were financial crimes experts and not paramilitary trained like HRT, and they would probably be in Bocas Town, where even if they could secure a boat it would still take them a half-hour to get here.

Whatever was about to happen would be over in much less than a half-hour. Dom recognized he was on his own.

Well, he thought, *not exactly.*

He called Adara.

She answered quickly. 'It's only been an hour since last check-in. Is something wrong?'

'It's more than wrong. It's all about to turn into a battle zone over here.'

'I'm moving to the boat. Keep talking.'

Dom said, 'Don't head this way yet. Just be ready by the boat if I need you.'

'But –'

'No buts. Stay right there till I call for you.'

'What's going on?'

Dom told her about the Russian Spetsnaz troops and their killing of the guards. He explained he thought they'd probably move toward the house soon, and when they did, they would take Ethan Ross and his intelligence scrape with hundreds of thousands of documents detailing the thousands of paid agents for U.S. intelligence around the world.

'Yeah,' Adara agreed. 'The Russians would love to get their hands on that, and killing a few Venezuelans to pull off an intelligence coup of that magnitude would be no big deal to them at all.'

Twice more Dom had to tell Adara to stand fast at the dockside hotel. She was champing at the bit to come in support of him, but Dom didn't even know what he was going to do yet. The last thing he wanted was to have to watch over her.

Dom strained through his binos for any glimpse of the dark figures near the pool house around the side of the house, but he saw nothing but blackness. He figured the next time he would be aware of the Russians' presence was when he saw the flashes of the MP7s in the windows of the colonial mansion.

He saw it as almost a fait accompli that these half-dozen Russian commandos would take Ross. They would have some avenue of escape already set up; Dom assumed there was a boat to get them off the island or maybe even a helo inbound to the property. They would all be long gone from the scene before Albright and his HRT arrived on-site.

He slammed his fist into the ground, his body desperate to expel some of the frustration building up as he lay there thinking about losing the man responsible for the Yacobys' deaths to a nation that would use him and his intelligence to ruin the CIA.

'No,' he said softly. He could *not* let this happen.

Dom decided he knew only one thing for sure: Ethan Ross in the hands of the Venezuelans was *not good*, but it was a whole lot *less bad* than Ethan Ross in the hands of the Russians. No question that more damage could be done to America by Moscow's spies.

Dom knew he couldn't stop the Russians, but he could give the Venezuelans a heads-up. He would have to reveal himself and then suffer the consequences, which likely meant taking fire from the Russians and the Venezuelans, but he decided he would much rather have Ross and his scrape in the Venezuelans' hands than the Russians' hands.

He called Adara back, and as soon as the call was connected he said, 'Remember when I told you I would keep you out of danger?'

'Is this the part where you tell me you were lying?'

'Of course not. This is the part where I tell you I was mistaken.'

'I'll forgive you, if you forgive me for ignoring your instructions. I'm on the water and on the way to you already.'

'Good. Stay on the boat. I'll come to you.' He thought for a moment. What if he could actually get his hands on Ross? It sounded implausible, but he expected an incredible amount of chaos in that house in the next few minutes, and the prospect of taking advantage of the confusion and somehow taking control of Ross and his scrape seemed like it might be worth the risk. He said, 'If I get really lucky I'll have a guest with me.'

'*Ross?* You're actually going after Ross?'

'I can dream, can't I?' Dom hung up, then climbed to his knees and began working on a plan, all the while still utterly bewildered by the fact he was about to go into battle partially on the side of an American traitor and the enemy intelligence agency that spirited him out of the United States.

'Crazy,' he said softly, and then he broke into a low sprint across the dark lawn.

37

As Dom moved low and fast across the property, the barking of the dogs on the far side of the house seemed to grow louder, even though there was no way they could see him in their kennels. Two men standing on the veranda ringing the first floor shone flashlights all around the lawn facing the inlet and the dock, but Dom moved laterally to avoid them, and he ran on to the side of the house near the driveway. More men shone their lights at the back of the property; Dom could see the beams raking across the pool area and the vehicles, and as he ran he wondered if the Russian paramilitaries hiding somewhere back there might find themselves spotlighted by the guards on the veranda before attacking the building.

Dom made it to the side of the big colonial house. He pressed his body flush with the cool wall, and then began moving along the wall through thick, flowering hedges. He came to a darkened window, chanced a look inside, and saw nothing but black on his first glance.

He stood to the side of the window, waited a moment, then looked again.

It took a few seconds for his eyes to pick up any features inside, but soon he realized the room was some sort of a storage area. Banquet tables were stacked high against the far wall, sporting equipment, small soccer goals, a croquet set, and several balls in net bags hung from hooks on the wall.

The door to the room was closed. He tried the window but found it securely locked. He thought about breaking one of the panes near the lock, but just as he prepared to use the butt of the Beretta to do this, he stopped, took his flashlight and flicked it quickly on the little room, his eyes locked on the ceiling near the window.

Yep, as he expected, a glass-break sensor jutted an inch from the ceiling. If he smashed the windowpane, sirens would blare all over the property.

As he turned away to look for another point of entry, a sudden crackle of gunfire echoed off the trees of the rain-forest and all over the lawn. It had come from the rear of the property, near the pool, and Dom knew this meant the Venezuelans and the Russians were engaged in a firefight.

Alarms started blaring throughout the house. Dom took advantage of this by turning back to the window-pane and smashing it with the grip of his pistol. In seconds he had the lock open and the window lifted high enough for him to enter.

Ethan Ross woke from an alcohol-aided sleep and leapt to his feet with the loud crackling sounds. He thought it might have been gunfire, but he'd never been around actual shooting, and he'd expected it to sound like it did on television. He stuck his head out the door of his bedroom, on guard but more curious than afraid, but almost instantly he panicked when the sirens began blaring. A guard stood close to his door, but the man had turned away to look over the mezzanine down at the main room of the mansion.

'What's going on?' Ethan shouted, but the man did not respond. He knew just enough Spanish to ask, *'Qué pasa?'*

'No sé,' the man shouted back. He had his big black gun against his shoulder and he waved it around at the first floor below.

Just then Mohammed came running around the corner in his stocking feet. He made a beeline straight to Ross, passing Gianna Bertoli with utter indifference as she came out of her room with a robe held around her shoulders.

Ethan noticed Mohammed had a mobile phone in one hand and his computer in the other. He'd left his shoes, but he hadn't left his computer or his phone.

Mohammed shouted, 'The Americans are here! We have to leave!'

Ethan turned and ran back into his room. He tried to shut the door, but Mohammed was right on his heels and followed him in. 'Get the drive! Do you have the drive?'

Ethan looked toward his laptop, and Mohammed caught the look. 'It's on the computer?'

Ethan didn't answer. The drive was still attached with moleskin to his hip, but he snatched the laptop off the table, threw it into his backpack, and slung it over his back.

When they raced back out on to the mezzanine, Ethan saw the Venezuelan intelligence chief Leo had arrived with two more of his men, making a total of four armed Venezuelans. Leo wore a sweatshirt and cotton pants, but he carried a machine pistol in one hand and a walkie-talkie in the other. 'Quickly, come with me! I have a man in a truck waiting for us by the kennels. The Americans will expect us to try for the Expeditions on the other side of the house. We must hurry.'

Mohammed asked, 'How many attackers?'

'I don't know!' shouted Leo, but he led the way with his weapon out in front of him.

The procession moved down the rear stairwell, and then out into a long gallery that ran the length of the back of the house. Leo turned to the left and the others began following, but as they passed an archway that led to the large main room of the home, automatic gunfire erupted from the dark. One of the Venezuelan guards spun dead to the wooden gallery floor, and Leo and the other three fired back into the room as they ran past the archway and out of the line of fire.

Mohammed and Gianna were ahead of Ethan, so they made it across the kill zone, but Ethan had hesitated, and now he found himself alone between the stairs and the archway, afraid to move forward and join the others. As Mohammed shouted at him, urging him to catch up, Ethan instead turned away and began running in the opposite direction down the gallery, past the stairs and toward the kitchen.

Behind him at the archway the gunfire increased.

He rounded the corner into the kitchen now. A row of dim lights ran under the shelves over the counter, giving the room a glow, and with this light Ethan could see a fig-ure standing in the middle of the room, not twenty feet in front of him. He was a white man in wet brown clothing and a scruffy beard. His sleeves were rolled up and his forearms were covered in mud. He held a black pistol in his hand, and he pointed it straight at Ethan.

Ethan stopped. Raised his hands quickly.

'You got it with you?' The man spoke English.

Ethan was too terrified to answer. Behind him, on the far side of the gallery, multiple automatic weapons barked back and forth at one another.

'You got the scrape?'

'I . . . I . . .'

The man pulled the hammer back on his pistol. 'I'm not asking again!'

'I've got it!'

'You're coming with me.'

'Who . . . who are . . . no!'

The man with the gun raised the weapon suddenly and fired. Ethan screamed, dropped to the ground, his hands still above his head. Behind him, a GIO officer had run into the room with a G3 rifle shouldered, but the American in the brown shirt shot him dead as he entered.

A second Venezuelan entered the kitchen, his rifle firing as he came through the door. Ethan rolled on to his side in the fetal position, screaming at the top of his lungs, but he kept his eyes open and he saw the American in the brown shirt run to his left, chased across the kitchen by flashing sparks and bullet holes that tore into the stove and refrigerator and tiled backsplash over the oven. The American dove through the air, his pistol still in his hand, and he executed a complete forward roll on the floor to get through the doorway to the dining room.

'Ethan!' The scream came from behind, and Ross looked

back to see Mohammed crouched low in the doorway next to the Venezuelan with the rifle. Mohammed's hand was out, beckoning Ethan to crawl out of the kitchen. 'Come on!'

The American in the brown shirt ducked his head back around from the dining room. The Venezuelan shot at him, but the American returned fire with the pistol, firing several rounds, then he retreated again around the corner.

Ethan looked at the Venezuelan. He'd been shot in the left shin, just below the knee, and now he lay on the ground, grabbing at his leg, with the rifle on the floor next to him.

Mohammed dove on the rifle, lifted it up toward the dining room entrance, and fired several rounds. Even with all the chaos, Ethan was surprised the small Lebanese computer geek knew how to shoot a gun.

Mohammed shouted, 'Ethan! Come!'

Ethan climbed to his hands and knees and crawled out of the dim kitchen. He found his feet and started running through the main room of the house, but Mohammed caught up with him from behind. 'No! Not that way. You are going toward the other Americans.'

On cue, more gunfire snapped at the back of the house. Glass shattered, and men shouted.

'Run!' Mohammed commanded, and Ethan found himself following the Lebanese man's instructions. Together they ran through the main room of the house, which had been the center of the battle just a minute earlier. Now, however, much of the gunfire seemed to be upstairs. As

Ethan ran he tripped over the body of a dead man, fell to the floor, and lay there exhausted and terrorized.

'Get up!' Mohammed shouted, and he pulled Ethan to his feet, then pushed him forward.

They found a broken window in a library on the ground floor near the back of the house, and Mohammed used the barrel of the rifle to push out enough glass to climb through. Ethan followed, both men found themselves outside in a hedge near the pool that rimmed the building, and Mohammed scanned all around for any movement.

Just then Leo and Gianna rushed out the French doors that led to the pool area. Leo had been shot, blood ran from his shoulder down the length of his body, and even in the dim decorative lighting around the pool deck Ethan could see the man's face had gone white.

He staggered past his guests, holding a walkie-talkie in his hands and calling out to members of his guard force.

No one was replying, but there was definitely still a fire-fight raging on the first floor.

Leo made it to the two Expeditions in the drive, then he spun around and lifted his small machine pistol high. He began scanning the first-floor veranda for threats while still calling on his walkie-talkie.

Gianna, Mohammed and Ethan ran to him.

Ethan said, 'The Expeditions! Do you have keys?'

'Get in the black one!'

In the dark both SUVs looked black, but once Ethan got closer he realized one was dark green. He climbed into the backseat of the black Expedition, and Gianna moved in next to him. Mohammed took the front passenger seat, and Leo got behind the wheel and started the truck.

They lurched off down the muddy driveway, heading away from the inlet and into the trees.

'Where are we going?' Ethan asked, looking over his shoulder to make sure no one was following.

Leo's voice was weak. 'We can go to the docks on the east side, where we have boats. The Panamanian police boats will support us once on the water.' He coughed. 'Please sit quietly.'

This sounded like as good a plan as any to Ethan, and he found himself astonished to have made it away from the Americans. His hands shook violently.

Gianna noticed this. She must have been going through her own panic at present, but she hugged him to comfort him nonetheless.

Four Naval Spetsnaz commandos burst out the French doors to the pool area and ran toward the remaining Ford Expedition in the driveway. They had been fighting the last of the resistance upstairs when one of their number saw the taillights of an SUV at the far edge of the lawn, racing into the jungle, and the lieutenant ordered the members of his team still in the fight to take off in pursuit.

Two Russians lay dead. One man had been killed on the back patio as he tried to pick a window lock for a stealthy entrance. A passing guard saw the movement and opened fire, and this caught the rest of the team still outside the house in the open. They'd fought their way inside, killed several Venezuelans in the process, but their attempts to take the American had been delayed and, at least temporarily, thwarted.

A second Russian commando was felled in the archway to the gallery. The Venezuelans had put up a surprising defense, and now, as the four men raced to the remaining vehicle parked in the driveway, the lieutenant feared this operation was falling apart around him.

He'd wanted helicopters for this job, he'd pressed for them right up until the minute he and his team climbed aboard the Cessna Caravan with their parachutes, but the FSB was running the op, and they demanded Ross be taken to a yacht moored on the eastern edge of the island. Russian helos would be too overt, they had said, any pictures or sightings of the birds would prove they weren't American, and the entire mission was to be constructed as a deniable operation. The lieutenant suggested using Nicaraguan helicopters, but the FSB had patiently explained this would do nothing to convince the world America had invaded Panama, *again*, this time to recover a loose-lipped employee. Then the FSB impatiently told the commando leader to stop worrying about their end of the mission and to start worrying about his own end of the mission.

The lieutenant dove into the front passenger seat of the Expedition, and one of his men opened the driver's-side door and leapt behind the wheel. They had already hot-wired the vehicle to use in their getaway. It was the lieutenant's one piece of good fortune that Ross and his entourage had run off in the other Ford, leaving the one prepped by Spetsnaz behind. The Expedition kicked mud and rock and water into the air and shot down the drive in pursuit of the American and his confederates.

*

Dominic Caruso raced around the front of the house on to the driveway, his pistol arcing left and right and up and down as he ran.

In the distance he saw a Ford Expedition moving into the trees, and he raised his weapon to fire at it, but from behind he heard a shout: *'Alto!' Stop!*

Dom froze, raised his hands, and dropped the pistol into the mud. Turning around slowly, he saw a Venezuelan guard with a G3 rifle on his shoulder walking across the patio near the pool, approaching rapidly. He shouted at Dom, no doubt they were commands of some sort, but Dom couldn't understand. The man was alone, a little more amped up than Caruso would have liked, considering he had a finger pressed against the trigger of his rifle and the muzzle pointed directly at his target's head.

The gun flicked to the left. Dom assumed that meant he was supposed to head back through the French doors. He kept his hands high, then turned to walk back to the house, complying with the gestures of the guard, if not his exact wishes.

The guard started following him, his rifle still pointed at Dom's back.

Dom took a couple of steps toward the house and then slowed suddenly but did not stop. He hoped the man would keep walking and actually touch him in the back with the rifle. He had no such luck, but the Venezuelan did say something, and Dom used the sound of the man's voice to picture the location of both the man and his gun.

Dom spun, his right arm coming up, and he knocked the G3 sideways as a flash and the cacophonous report of a gunshot echoed across the lawn. He launched forward at the man, struck him in the chin, and the Venezuelan tumbled on to the driveway, rolling backward three hundred and sixty degrees. Dom leapt for the rifle, but as he did he realized his opponent was lying directly on top of the Beretta pistol in the mud.

Dom lifted the G3 as quickly as possible and pointed it at the Venezuelan, who had just climbed to his knees and wrapped his hands around the Beretta. Dom aimed at the kneeling man's chest and pulled the trigger.

The G3 went 'click' in Dom's hand.

The Venezuelan's eyes widened and he quickly lifted the pistol to aim at the American's face. At a distance of less than fifteen feet, he couldn't miss.

Dom shut his eyes as the boom of a gunshot echoed off the colonial mansion behind him.

38

Dom opened his eyes when he heard the thud of a man falling on to his back on the gravel driveway.

The Venezuelan was dead, the Beretta dangling from the trigger finger of his slack right hand.

Dom spun around and looked out at the lawn near the water behind him. Adara Sherman stood with her M16 held high up to her sightline. Her black knit cap hid her blond hair, and she wore a black zip-up raincoat, but her Virginia sweatpants gave her away.

She lowered the gun and approached while Dom felt his knees weaken. It was just now setting in how close he'd come to having his ticket punched by some government gunman in Central America.

Dom fought the urge to fall over, then dropped the empty G3 on the ground and turned to pick the Beretta out of the dead man's hand. As he did so, Adara Sherman shined a flashlight on him. 'You're hit!'

Dom looked quickly down at his body, feeling over his chest and arms. 'Where?'

'Your back.'

Dom reached behind and rubbed his free hand on his shirt. He breathed out a long sigh. 'A bird shat on me.'

'That looks like blood.'

'I think he was eating berries or something.'

'Oh. Okay.'

Dom had the pistol now, and he shoved it into his pants.

Adara scanned her rifle around the front of the house, looking for any more targets. There was no sound, as if everyone inside was dead. She said, 'The boat is only a couple of hundred yards east. I tied up next to a little beach. There's a footpath through the trees. Let's go.'

'I've got to go forward, not back.'

Adara kept scanning. 'Really?'

'The Russians took off in pursuit of Ross. I can't let them get the scrape and the password.'

'Okay,' she said. 'This is your op. Lead the way.'

'We need a vehicle.'

'Over by the kennels there is a truck with a dead guy behind the wheel. It's running.'

'Good. You grab that and bring it back here. I'm going in the house to get a weapon.'

Adara took off around the front of the house.

Ethan Ross kept checking out the back window of the Expedition, but even though dawn had lightened the sky a little, he could see nothing under the thick jungle canopy. The road, while muddy and narrow, was in surprisingly good repair, and as they wound up a series of hills the Expedition's V8 engine roared with power, giving the three passengers confidence that the attack would soon be far behind them.

Mohammed spoke on his phone; he kept the words hushed, although Ethan doubted anyone in the truck spoke Arabic. Ethan closed his eyes for a moment, trying his best to force himself to pick out some of the words. He was by no means fluent in the language, but had spent some time in the Middle East and learned some words and phrases. He was getting nowhere with Mohammed's quick, soft conversation.

Suddenly Mohammed began shouting. Ethan thought he was yelling into the phone, but almost immediately he saw that the young Lebanese man was screaming at Leo.

Ethan leaned forward and he understood the reason for Mohammed's agitation.

Leo's eyes were closed, his head hung down, and his hands had dropped from the steering wheel into his lap. He was breathing in short wheezes, and he appeared to be unconscious.

'Fuck!' Ethan shouted. 'Get the wheel!'

Mohammed dropped his cell phone and grabbed the steering wheel, but he was unable to get his foot on the brake across the center console of the vehicle. He looked ahead, steered with his left hand, and passed his G3 rifle to Ethan.

'Take the gun! Push on the brake! Hurry!'

Ethan did as Mohammed instructed, he pushed over half his body through the space between the front seat and jammed the barrel of the rifle between Leo's legs, and after a few misses he found the foot pedal and pressed down.

The Expedition skidded to a lurching stop in the middle of the dirt road, just before a sharp turn to the right.

Mohammed was able to put the vehicle into park, then

he leapt out, moved around to the other side, and opened the door. He yanked the Venezuelan intelligence officer out and let him fall in the mud. Leo groaned as he hit the ground but did not move.

Mohammed climbed behind the wheel. Both Gianna and Ethan knew the man was still alive, but neither said anything to Mohammed about leaving him bleeding to death on a jungle road. They were both more concerned about their own predicament.

Ethan still held the rifle in his hands, and he climbed into the front passenger seat.

Mohammed retrieved his phone and started talking. Again, softly and in Arabic.

Ethan shouted at him, 'We can't stay here! Where are we going? We don't even know where Leo was taking us. The Americans might be just behind us!'

Mohammed looked to Ethan. 'See if there is a map in the glove box.'

Ethan found a weathered map of the entire archipelago in the glove compartment, and hand-drawn lines over the island of Bastimentos indicated the road system. Mohammed took it from Ethan's hand and began looking it over carefully.

'Hurry up,' Ethan shouted, and he looked back over his shoulder, certain the Americans were closing fast.

A faint hint of sunrise in the east glowed as Dom climbed into the driver's side of a large and very old flatbed farm truck. Adara moved over to the passenger side, and she rested her M16 muzzle-down between her legs.

Dom ground the old gears as he got the vehicle

moving, but it became immediately obvious the truck was built to haul big items around the island, not to chase down other vehicles.

Adara registered his disapproval. 'The Maserati dealership was closed. This was the best I could do.'

'The Russians are in a four-wheel-drive Ford SUV. They are going to catch up to Ross.'

Adara reached into her jacket. 'I brought the EagleView printout of the island. I'll see if we can figure out where they are going and find a shortcut.'

Dom had turned pessimistic about their prospect for stopping the Russians from capturing Ross. His plan to grab the American traitor himself was only a distant fantasy now. 'A shortcut? This thing won't float or fly, so there's not going to be a shortcut.'

'You may be right. But the good news is this road continues on for the next five miles. Then it keeps going to the west, but there is a turnoff that leads to the south. We just have to be close enough to them to see which direction they are going. They can't be more than a mile and a half ahead.'

'We won't catch them before the turn. We'll have to guess which way they went.'

Adara looked closer at the satellite picture. 'Hang on a second. There is a levee up ahead. It should be dry and flat and solid enough for this truck. It connects to the road on the other side of some twists and turns. If we take it and don't get stuck, we'll make up some time.'

Dom thought it over. 'We're desperate. I'll give it a shot. Lead me to it.'

*

Mohammed folded the map and stuck it under his leg, then he put the Expedition in gear and started driving with the phone to his ear. The tires had just begun rolling when the headlight beams from a vehicle on the road behind filled up the cab.

'The Americans!' Gianna shouted.

Mohammed floored the truck, spinning the tires, but he picked up speed quickly.

The vehicle behind couldn't be more than two hundred yards back, and it was closing fast.

Dom was astonished that they'd both found the levee in the dark, and negotiated its distance without crashing. Twice Dom almost rolled the truck off the side and into the jungle when his wheels got too near the edge and the wet earth began to give way.

Now they were back on the main road, and Dom flipped off the headlights as he made the turn. A hundred yards ahead or so they caught occasional glimpses of brake lights.

Dom said, 'That's got to be the Russians. No way we got between the two SUVs.'

Adara looked back but saw nothing. The light was getting better by the minute now, but under all the vegetation it was still too early in the morning to know for certain whether or not a dark-colored truck could be running without headlights behind them. After a minute like this, however, they came up a hill and out of the trees. Adara leaned her head all the way out of the Expedition to scan the road; a quarter-mile of it was visible for a split second before they made a turn.

'Nobody. Those are the Russians in front of us. I don't know how far ahead Ross is, but he can't be too far.'

Just then the Expedition made a hard right turn and took off to the south.

Adara said, 'If they knew to make that turn, they must have Ross in sight ahead.'

Caruso banged his hand on the steering wheel. 'The Russians will catch him, and they have some sort of extraction plan on this island. A helo or a boat. We're gonna lose him.'

'I can try to shoot out the Russians' tires,' Adara said.

Dom glanced at her for an instant. 'Can you make that shot in this light, at this distance, in this moving vehicle?'

'Probably not. Can you?'

'Nope.' Another sigh. 'Any more shortcut levees on that map?'

'Nothing. The road straightens out here to the south for a while before going crazy again in the hills, about one mile ahead.'

Dom flattened the gas pedal to the floor, taking advantage of the straight road and the gentle downward slope. As a result he had the Russians no more than eighty yards ahead now. There was no indication they knew they were being pursued. Dom presumed they were completely focused on their own pursuit.

'You're catching them!' Adara said.

'Just on this stretch. We won't catch them before the turns come, and their vehicle is faster than ours.'

'Not on the turns.'

Dom looked at her quickly, then his eyes went back to

the road. 'What do you mean? They can corner twice as fast as we can, plus I have to downshift.'

'You don't have to downshift if we don't plan on turning.'

Dom looked at the speedometer. He was going fifty, and this was the absolute top speed of the truck. 'If you've got an idea, I need to hear it.'

Adara put her finger on the map. 'A half-mile ahead is a hairpin to the right at the bottom of this hill. There is nowhere for them to turn off before we get there.'

'So?'

'They'll have to slow down to nothing to make that turn. They'll *have* to. But we keep on going full tilt down the hill. We can catch up to them.'

'But . . . how do we stop?' As he asked the question he thought he knew the answer.

'We stop when we slam into them. We just plow right into the passenger side on the turn and knock them off the road.'

'Holy shit,' Dom muttered. 'What's the terrain like on the far side of the hairpin?'

'It's jungle. This whole island is jungle, Dom.'

'I know that. I want to know if we're going to go tumbling down a hill if I miss the truck.'

She looked at the image. 'It's difficult to tell on the sat photo.'

Dom sighed. 'Try really hard, Sherman. Play like our lives depend on it.'

She gave it another glance. 'It's not a cliff or anything like that. It's just rainforest. Maybe descending away.'

'If I don't time it right, we're going to shoot off the road and into the jungle at more than sixty miles an hour.'

'Then time it right.'

Dom shrugged. 'Okay. Let's do it.'

Sherman reached over and tightened Caruso's seat belt, then she did the same with her own.

Dom said, 'After we crash, we're going to have to get out and shoot those guys.'

'I know.' Adara then asked, 'How much ammo do you have?'

'I have an MP7 I got off a dead Russian. Thirty rounds. I've got a few rounds in the pistol.'

Adara clutched her M16. She'd fired only one round, so she knew she had twenty-nine left. 'We might run out of ammo in the gunfight, but at least we don't have to worry about reloading.'

Dom chuckled through the tension as he fixed all his attention on the vehicle ahead. 'Lucky us.'

The four Russian Naval Spetsnaz men readied their weapons in the rear Expedition. They'd closed to within thirty yards of Ethan Ross and his protection detail, and the driver told his lieutenant he would be able to overtake them in the next series of turns. He watched the SUV in front of them fishtail through a hard muddy turn to the right that hairpinned down a hill to the west, so the driver slowed his own vehicle down in plenty of time to make the turn.

One of the two men in the backseat yelled out, 'Vehicle behind us!' and then he and his mate in the back spun around and raised their weapons, pointing them at the rear window and the truck beyond it. The green Expedition began its turn to the right, and the vehicle was fully in the curve, when a burst of rounds from the pair of HKs in the backseat blew out the glass.

'He's not slowing down!' shouted one of the Spetsnaz men.

'Watch out!' screamed the other, just as the big dark truck slammed broadside into the Expedition. The SUV crumpled and spun, the front end whipped all the way back around and hit the side of the truck, and it rolled backward into the dense jungle. The flatbed jolted hard to the left with the impact, the front tires left the road, and it ripped through the trees just feet away from the Russians' SUV.

39

Ethan had been trying to keep his eyes on the truck chasing them, but he'd turned away for a moment when suddenly the headlights shining on him turned to the right. Ethan looked back and in the dim morning glow he saw mud and leaves and other debris kicked up in the jungle at the turn, as if the tropical vegetation had swallowed the Americans' vehicle whole. 'They crashed! The Americans just crashed making that turn!'

Bertoli stared back in shock with her hands to her mouth.

Mohammed took a turn himself, this one to the left. He tried to look back over his shoulder, but he saw nothing. 'Good. That is good,' he said, then he switched back to Arabic and continued talking in his mobile phone.

The smell of radiator fluid mixed with the earthy scent of the jungle. Dominic felt a sticky wetness on his face from his hairline all the way down to his neck. There was next to no light here in the cab of the truck; they'd come to rest upright, somewhere off the road in the rainforest. The hood of the truck was smashed and up in the windscreen, and there was broken glass all around.

Before he checked on what he assumed was a gaping wound to his head, he looked to his right to see if Adara was okay. But he couldn't see her. A fat and lush ficus tree had crashed through the windscreen, and now all Dom could see next to him were leaves and broken branches. He reached out through the greenery and felt for Adara. He grasped her left shoulder and was glad to feel movement; she was in the process of unbuckling her seat belt.

'You okay?' he asked. As he spoke, he reached to his face and he was relieved to find the source of the dampness there. A large wet palm frond covered the entire left side of his head. He pulled it off and then unsnapped his own belt.

Adara didn't answer. Dom grabbed the small HK MP7 Personal Defense Weapon he'd jammed between his seat and the door, and turned to find Sherman. In the low light and thick wreckage of foliage he had a hard time pushing his way toward her, but before he could even call out to her again, she shouted at the top of her lungs.

'Contact right!' Sherman opened fire with her M16 through the passenger-side window.

Dom didn't hesitate. He opened his door and climbed out, then stood on his seat. Looking over the roof, he scanned the impossibly thick jungle on Sherman's side of the truck. He didn't see anything at first, but then muzzle flashes erupted in the thick undergrowth forty feet away.

Dom snapped the fire selector switch to fully automatic, and he began spraying bursts at the sources of fire. Between bursts he shouted, 'Bail out! My side!'

He'd fired more than half a magazine in six three-round bursts before he felt Adara move past his feet and then drop out of the truck and on to the jungle floor. He turned and leapt off behind her, and as he did so he saw her yank her rifle off the ground and point it toward the rear of the flatbed truck. In the wasted space of torn trees, flattened undergrowth and uprooted plants, Dom saw a man spin around the back of the truck with a weapon high at his shoulder.

Adara Sherman shot the man before Dom got his gun up. Blood blasted from the man's skull and splattered on the greenery all around, and he dropped facedown into the brush.

Dom grabbed Sherman by the shoulder and pulled her with him, and they moved away from the vehicle, deeper into the jungle, in the opposite direction of any surviving Russians. As they retreated they fired a few rounds in the general direction of the threats, covering their withdrawal.

Within moments they backed up into a rusty corrugated shack. It looked like it must have been some sort of storage shed; maybe a farm had been here before the rainforest reclaimed the area. Dom and Adara moved around to the back of the shed, doing their best to find cover from any Russians remaining in the jungle around them.

They both knelt down, Dom covering one side of the shed and Adara the other. Back-to-back, Sherman said, 'You okay?'

'Yeah. You?'

'Good enough. There could still be a couple –'

Dom reached back and squeezed her arm, silencing her immediately. He heard movement in the jungle around his side of the shed, still several feet away but approaching quickly.

He unseated the magazine in the grip of his MP7 and

checked. He had only three rounds remaining. He replaced it and whispered to Adara, 'Ammo?'

He heard her drop her mag, check it, and then click it back into place. 'Two.'

Dom pulled the Beretta from his pants and handed it back to her. She took it without looking. He said, 'Count to ten and empty the Beretta into the trees.'

'Roger.'

Dom rose, moved to the edge of the shed and peered around carefully. He saw nothing but thick jungle ahead, so he moved around the corner, then up to the southeastern corner. He stopped here, readied his weapon on his shoulder, and waited.

Soon he heard Sherman open fire with the handgun. He hoped this would flush out anyone in the trees near the crashed vehicles, get them to return fire. With luck he would see the muzzle flashes and engage them by surprise.

But as he spun around the corner of the little shed he was surprised to see a pair of men, themselves using the shed for concealment. As Sherman fired on the other side of the dilapidated building, one man lifted his weapon to fire through the rusty tin walls. The second man peered around the corner toward the source of fire, not fifteen feet away.

Dom knew Sherman was a sitting duck. She had no idea these guys were here on the opposite side of the shack. He shot the first man just as he fired through the tin. The Russian wore body armor, and he absorbed the hit and spun toward Caruso, just feet away. Dom shot him twice more, the third round taking him in the jaw and killing him instantly, but Dom knew he was out of ammunition.

As the last remaining Russian spun his MP7 around to Caruso, he leapt back around the corner of the tin shack, landing hard on his back in the overgrowth.

Dom screamed, 'Sherman! Hit the deck!'

The Russian opened fire on the shack, spraying copper-jacketed lead into it to kill the two threats around opposite corners.

Dom felt bullets snapping just over his head, and from the sounds of cracking branches around him he could tell the man was sweeping his fire back and forth, trying to gun down Adara as well.

For an instant Dom had no idea what to do, but then he remembered the diving knife. He reached to his right ankle, pulled the titanium blade from its sheath there, and when the Russian stopped firing to reload his automatic weapon, Dom leapt to his feet. All around him leaves fell from the trees and bushes, all victims of the heavy gunfire the jungle had just endured.

Dom raced around the corner of the tin wall, now pocked like Swiss cheese, and he caught the Russian just as he'd chambered his weapon with a fresh round from a fresh magazine. Dom dove for the man, who spun toward the movement, but Dom collided with him before he could get his gun up, and both men crashed into the brush. The Russian fought back for a short moment, but Dom drove the knife handle-deep into the man's stomach below his body armor, and the fight stopped.

When the last Russian lay dead under him, Dom shouted for Sherman between pants. 'Adara? Adara? You okay?'

He fought his way up to his knees, pushed off the tin

shack to hurry around to check on his partner. 'Coming around! Don't shoot!'

Dom saw Adara rolling on the ground, her arms and legs flailing. He assumed she'd been hit, but at least she was moving.

'Adara!' he knelt down to her. 'Lie still! Where are you hit?'

She kept flailing. 'I'm not hit. You told me to get down, so I dove for the deck. Landed on a damn anthill.' She reached under her black parka. 'Little bastards got inside my jacket.'

A wave of relief washed over Caruso, and he couldn't help laughing.

The Black Ford Expedition drove off the dirt road and right down the middle of an empty sandy beach at the southern tip of Bastimentos Island. Before Ethan or Gianna could ask what he was doing, Mohammed skidded to a violent stop at the water's edge.

He said, 'Everyone out. Quickly, please.'

Ethan looked out to sea. There, in the calm waters just fifty yards from the shoreline, a blue and white single-engine de Havilland Beaver floatplane approached slowly, its propeller spinning just fast enough to give it some forward motion in the water.

Mohammed said, 'Please. We must hurry to the plane.'

'Whose plane is that?' Ethan asked. When no one answered, he looked to Bertoli, and quickly he recognized she didn't have a clue where the hell the young hacker Mohammed managed to score an airplane, either. But he climbed out of the Expedition and followed Mohammed into the water, and now he counted four men with the aircraft. One sat in the pilot's left seat, and another man, presumably the copilot, sat on his right. Another climbed out of the cabin and stood on the float closest to the beach, and another jumped out of the other side, into the knee-deep water, and he began wading behind the float-plane, avoiding the propeller on his way to the shore.

The two men outside the aircraft were tough-looking and olive-skinned, with short haircuts and khaki shirts and pants. Ethan looked to see if the men were carrying guns – at any other time a gun would have uneased him, but right now he would have been happy to see that the people here to rescue him had some way to fight off the Americans who still might be only minutes behind them.

He saw no weapons on them, but wondered if they had something concealed. They certainly looked like some sort of security force.

Despite a list of misgivings a mile long, Ross took off his backpack and held it over his head. Then he followed Bertoli and Mohammed and crashed through the water on the way to the plane. He took the hand of one of the olive-complexioned men, who pulled him up and ushered him into the back of the cramped cabin without a word.

Within seconds the Beaver's engine roared; the interior of the aircraft rattled and shook as if it could fall to pieces, but the machine picked up speed and lifted off into the cool dawn.

Mohammed Mehdi Mobasheri placed a headset over his ears and brought the microphone to his mouth. The leader of the Quds Force men with him, Shiraz, did the same next to him, right behind the pilot's seat.

Mohammed was careful to speak in Arabic, in case Ethan Ross could hear any of his words. He knew Ross didn't speak the language, even though the Middle East was his specialty at NSC.

Mohammed said, 'Good work.'

'Thank you. We will have a jet waiting for us in San Salvador. We can be in Tehran in less than twenty hours.'

Mohammed shook his head. 'There is nowhere I would rather go, but we're not finished yet. We'll go to El Salvador, and then the woman will tell us where to go from there.'

Shiraz stared back in disbelief. 'Why are you letting her make the decisions?'

'We want the intelligence on the drive, and we can torture the American to give us his passwords. My first choice would be to throw her out of the plane now and make him decrypt the files. But Bertoli's organization is helpful to us. We will go back with her to Switzerland and spend the next few days working with her on Ross. We will persuade him to give us the information so we can categorize it or redact critical information so we can publish a portion.'

'I don't know, boss,' said Shiraz. 'I like your first idea better. The woman complicates things.'

Mohammed nodded. 'Agreed. They have the tendency to do that. If she becomes too much trouble, forcibly removing Ross from the protection of the ITP will be the easiest part of this entire operation.'

Shiraz nodded. 'I'll await that order.'

*

Adara Sherman and Dominic Caruso made their way back on to the dirt road a few minutes after engaging the Russians. They were a hundred yards away from where the firefight had taken place. They'd seen no evidence any Russians were still alive, but they didn't know how many had been in the Expedition in the first place, so they couldn't be certain. As they began walking south on the road, both of them stopped to watch a floatplane fly overhead, ascending into the early morning.

Dom had pulled an MP7 from one of the dead men, and now he pointed it at the aircraft, placing its holographic red-dot sight on the single engine.

But he did not fire.

Instead, he just muttered, 'If I shoot it down, it won't be Ross. It will be a group of nuns down here on a mission trip. But since I didn't shoot it down . . . I'd bet money we just watched Ethan Ross slip away.'

The plane disappeared to the north.

Adara started walking again. She was still picking ants out of her clothing. 'Do you think those were Venezuelans?'

Dom said, 'Don't know. At least it wasn't the Russians.'

'Might have been another group,' said Adara.

'This shit is getting complicated. We kept Ross out of the hands of the Russians, but for all we know, whoever has him now is even worse.'

'What do we do now?'

Dom sighed. 'We go home.'

40

Special Agent Darren Albright returned empty-handed from Panama late in the afternoon. His FBI jet landed at Reagan National, and the rest of his team, mainly Hostage Rescue Team members, left for their homes around the D.C. area, mostly in Maryland and Virginia.

Albright, however, climbed in his FBI-issued Yukon and drove into the District. He parked in a loading zone in front of a residential building near Logan Circle, tossed his FBI parking decal on the dashboard, and took the elevator to a condo on the fifth floor.

Dominic Caruso opened the door to his place. If he was surprised to see Albright, he didn't show it. 'You made it back fast. Come on in.'

Albright followed Caruso to his messy living room, then sat in the leather chair while Caruso plopped down on the sofa.

Albright said, 'I've been trying to get in touch with you.'

'Sorry about that. Lost my sat phone this morning.'

'You made it back quickly yourself.'

'Just got home. First plane out of Bocas. First plane out of Panama City.'

'You hurt?'

''Bout a hundred and fifty bug bites. Does that count?'

'Considering what went down? Not really.' Albright

added, 'I saw you tried to call me before the Russians hit the safe house.'

Dom nodded. 'They dropped out of the damn sky.'

'We heard. Panamanian police interviewed witnesses. Sounds like there was quite a show this morning. I'd love for you to tell me what you saw.'

'When did you guys get there?'

'We were ninety minutes out when the shooting started. We arrived on scene after the Panamanian police. Didn't go in. We found out through embassy channels that there were no Americans present. We had concerns Ross might have left his stolen documents behind but –'

'He didn't.'

Albright cocked his head. 'You know this how?'

'He had the scrape with him right before he left the house.' Albright raised an eyebrow, so Dom answered the next question before it was posed. 'He told me.'

'Wait. You *talked* to Ross?'

'Briefly. I almost had him in hand.'

'But?'

'Shit happens. He got away.'

'No idea where he went?'

'Didn't see the tail number of the floatplane. Don't imagine they filed a flight plan. Did you learn anything from the Panamanians about the aircraft?'

Albright just shook his head. To Dom, the FBI special agent looked like a man at the end of his rope. He'd probably not slept three hours in a row since getting the case more than a week earlier, and now it looked like he'd hit a dead end. 'Nothing.'

'So what happens next?'

'I keep hunting for him. I've got a criminal complaint with his name on it. Violation of U.S. Code Title Eighteen. Section 798. Theft of government property, unauthorized communication of national defense information, and willful communication of classified communications intelligence to an unauthorized person. He's wanted for questioning in four murders as well. He'd go on the Ten Most Wanted List, but I am sure CIA will lobby to keep this somewhat quiet. The Bureau will push back because of Nolan and Beale, our two SSG guys. Interdepartmental bullshit aside, any way you slice it, Ethan Ross is now America's most wanted.'

He added, 'I guess your uncle the President could just drone-kill the son of a bitch, but we'd still have to find him first.'

Dom dreaded the answer he might get, but he asked the next question anyway. 'Why don't you guys just offer him immunity for the breach if he returns the scrape and comes back to deal with the murder investigation?'

'I imagine the offer will be made if we can prove he hasn't leaked the scrape to a foreign power.'

'Obviously he *did* leak it. You told me Venezuela is arresting agents en masse.'

'That's small ball considering what's in his possession.'

Dom asked, 'Do you really think they might extend immunity to him for giving it all back?'

'I'm a law-and-order guy, as you've mentioned before. I'd like to try him, convict him, and give him the needle for killing Nolan and Beale. Still, decisions like that are far above my pay grade. The CIA might press for immunity, depending on what he has.'

Caruso told himself that if Ross received immunity by the Justice Department, he'd find him and kill him himself. It was easy to say, but harder to do. The guy could be anywhere in the world right now.

Minutes after Albright left, Gerry Hendley called. Dom had been expecting a call, because he knew Sherman would call Hendley as soon as she headed back to her place. Dom wasn't bothered by this. Adara had kicked ass in Panama, and if his only price for all her help was that she was keeping their employer apprised of his mental state, then so be it.

And to Hendley's credit, he did nothing to hide the fact that Sherman served as his surrogate eyes and ears. 'I spoke with Adara. She gave me a pretty detailed after-action report on your exploits in Panama.'

'I figured she would. I guess she told you I let Ross slip away.'

'She didn't characterize it like that. She says the deck was stacked against you, and you did your best.'

'I am sick and tired of doing my best. It doesn't matter. Ross is still out there somewhere.'

'I've been reaching out to my contacts in the intelligence community to find out just what level of threat his information poses.'

Dom asked, 'How big is this? Has the CIA given you specifics yet?'

Hendley said, 'It's potentially ruinous. Over one hundred and fifty gigs' worth of docs. Most top-secret. Local agent information vacuumed from case officer reports. Front companies listed by name. Affiliate and liaison intelligence services.'

'Names of agents?'

'No, but plenty in there to ID them. If these files make it into the wrong hands, the entire U.S. intelligence community will take a devastating hit.'

Gerry continued. 'We can't say this is the biggest intelligence leak in U.S. history. That was a couple of years back when the Chinese took forty terabytes of DoD files. But this is the leak that will get more people killed in the intelligence community than anything we've faced. *Ever.* Think about it. Virtually every agent on CIA's payroll. That doesn't just expose thousands of foreigners around the world. Anyone who has access to this intel can dig into those foreign agents and find out who they met with, and that will lead them to larger networks. It will also lead them back to their American case officers.'

Gerry exhaled into the phone. 'If Ross's leak makes it into the hands of a foreign power, the ramifications will reverberate for decades. The agency will have to bring in a new generation of case officers and recruit a new generation of foreign assets. That has never happened.

'The United States will suffer greatly in these down years. It will be devastating.'

Caruso rubbed his eyes. 'We have to plug the leak. There is no other alternative.'

'The FBI, State, and the U.S. intelligence community are doing everything they can. Your uncle has made it the priority it needs to be to get attention.'

Dom said, 'I'm not doing everything I can. I need to get back out there, Gerry.'

'You want to continue your involvement in this matter, don't you?'

'Damn right I do. I want to see this all the way to the end.'

'There's probably some speech I could give you about not making this personal.'

Dom half rolled his eyes. 'Yeah. If it will make you feel better, I'll sit here while you give me that speech.'

'No need. But I do need to let you know the rest of The Campus is operational again.'

This surprised Caruso. 'They are working on getting the data back?'

'Negative. It's another situation entirely. They are on their way to Asia right now.'

'Tell me about it.'

'No. You are deployed on your own operation. When you are ready to rejoin your team, I'll read you into their op.'

'But –'

'Dominic, at this point you don't have a need to know. You are running solo. Stay that way until you are ready to integrate back into The Campus fully.'

Dom grumbled out a 'Yes, sir,' and the call ended a moment later.

Dom was both angry and frustrated, but he had the presence of mind to realize he did retain some control. If he could somehow affect the outcome of the Ross investigation, he could move on and rejoin his unit. To that end, he went back to his laptop and opened up his IBM i2 Analyst's Notebook software. He began wading through the data findings of all the intel he recorded from Ethan Ross's home. He'd loaded it in his computer days earlier, but the data points hadn't led to any real pattern analysis conclusion. To find anything in the treasure trove he knew he would need to add some more context, otherwise he would have to run down every lead, every name off every phone number, or every connection between all the disparate data points. That wasn't a job for a man alone on his couch, that was a job for the FBI.

The only problem with this was the fact Dom knew Albright would throw him in jail if he somehow managed to produce hundreds of pieces of intel from Ross's house. The FBI would have access to the same information that Dom now had, so he didn't feel too bad about keeping it to himself.

As he looked through the data, more than eight thousand items in all, he focused on the handwritten addresses and phone numbers. He began highlighting numbers, searching on a graph for any link analysis or trends with that number. He didn't have the ability to trace any phones other than simple Internet searches, but this ruled out the vast majority of all numbers. Still, there were several phone numbers that had no known relation to any other bits of data. They weren't restaurants, NSC or White House employees, or known friends or relatives of Ethan Ross.

Dom wondered if answers were staring him in the face, but all this information was more overwhelming than it was elucidating.

He decided to change his strategy. He pulled up the photographs of the three pill bottles he'd found in Ross's kitchen. He enlarged the images, then enlarged them again, and soon he was on the Internet looking at PillID. com. He typed in the shape, color and markings of each tablet, and within five minutes he had identified all three drugs.

Clonazepam, glycopyrrolate and sertraline. He wasn't familiar with any of the medications, but as soon as he started researching them, he realized these were the meds the polygraph examiner Finn had suspected Ross of taking.

If Ethan did not have a prescription of his own for these meds himself, it was reasonable to conclude someone had given them to him, and not beyond the realm of possibilities that that person was aware of his need to defeat the FBI polygraph.

Dom realized he needed to find the doctor who had prescribed all three meds, somewhere in the forty-eight or so hours between Ross's learning he would be polygraphed and the actual exam.

These weren't ironclad times, of course. Ethan could have had these pills for months or years, they could have been sitting around since his last routine poly, but Dom knew the forty-eight-hour parameter was the most likely.

Dom had no way to find the doctor on his own. He knew he could either contact Albright, and quite possibly get tossed in jail for breaking and entering, or reach out to David at the Mossad. The Israeli had shown his organization had the ability to get answers. Dom didn't know how they were doing it, although he suspected they were getting help from key members of the U.S. intelligence community.

He decided on David, although he didn't know if the Mossad man would be much help. The two men had not spoken since Dom went radio silent in Panama.

David answered his phone after several rings, and his greeting told Dom that all would not be forgiven easily. 'You have demonstrated to me that you do not contact me to provide me with help, so I can only assume you need something.'

'Yeah. I'm sorry about yesterday.'

'I thought we had an agreement about Panama.'

'Facts on the ground changed quickly.'

'We know about the digital breach Mr Ross made.'

Dom assumed he would have heard about the scrape. He said, 'I hope you understand that I wasn't in a position to discuss that with you at the time.'

'That's fair. But you handled the situation poorly. I am disinclined to help you now.'

Dom said, 'I have a piece of evidence that might lead us to Ethan Ross.'

David chuckled, but there was coldness to it. '*Us*, Mr Caruso?'

'Well . . . me. Look, I want to help U.S. intelligence get the files back. I'm not sure what you know about the scope of the breach, but I'm sure your organization can see that it's in Israel's best interests as well.'

'Go on.'

'If I find Ross, I would love to kill him myself, but killing him won't get the data back. I'll bring in the FBI. I have no choice. I know you want vengeance –'

'We both want vengeance. But vengeance can wait. We agree with your assessment. Getting the data back is paramount. How can we help you?'

Dom told David about the pills, and his theory they

were prescribed between Monday and Wednesday of the previous week. David said he'd see what he could find.

The return call came in only thirty-five minutes. Dom was astonished how fast it had been. He answered with, 'You have got to be kidding.'

He could hear David smiling when he talked. 'Whoever obtained these medicines was very clever. They did not use the same doctor for all three.'

'How can we know the meds are related to Ross if they didn't come from the same doctor?'

'The clonazepam and sertraline are very common anti-anxiety drugs, and they are often prescribed together. But in a one-hundred-mile radius of Washington, D.C., only three doctors prescribed glycopyrrolate between Monday and Wednesday of last week. It's not a common medication.'

'Okay. Give me the three names. I'll check them out.'

'No need. Two of the doctors are dermatologists. It is a medicine for excessive sweating, so that is quite understandable. The third doctor, however, is a heart surgeon in downtown D.C.'

'A heart surgeon? That sounds fishy.'

'Indeed.'

David gave Dom the man's name and number. Dom plugged the information into his Analyst's Notebook, but was frustrated to see no connections to any data points there.

'Nothing,' he said.

David replied, 'I can e-mail you his call logs for that time period.'

Dom's eyebrows rose. 'That might be helpful.'

Within minutes Caruso's eight-thousand-point file on Ross had an additional three hundred and twelve pieces of forensic evidence, all phone calls going to and from a cardiac surgeon in downtown D.C., both his office and his mobile phone. After loading it into his Analyst's Notebook, Dom clicked on a visualization tool that would show him any interconnection between data in Ross's home and the surgeon.

A graphic came up on his screen, and when he highlighted it he saw an image of a Post-it note, and on it a handwritten phone number that Ross had left sticking out of a magazine lying on a coffee table on the back porch.

David had been waiting on the other end of the line. 'Anything?'

'One more number to trace.'

'Give it to me.'

Dom read it out, there was a pause of less than a minute, and then a reply. 'That is the mobile phone belonging to Harlan R. Banfield of Washington, D.C. He is a reporter, used to work for the *Post*.'

'Bingo,' said Dom. A journalist had arranged for Ross to beat the FBI polygraph. Dom wondered what else the man had done.

41

Harlan Banfield stepped off the elevator into his parking garage, tired from a full, stressful day. He walked to his Volkswagen in the corner, and while doing so, he told himself he was getting too old to work so late in the evening. The garage was four-fifths empty; he figured he was the only person in the building putting in twelve-hour days.

He'd taken a few steps toward the elevator when he noticed the shape of a man standing in the darkness between two cars off his right. He thought of Ethan; this was just a few yards away from where the NSC whistleblower had appeared from the dark the week before, starting this entire traumatic episode for the sixty-six-year-old journalist.

But where Ethan had merely stepped into the light, this figure stormed forward out of the dark, charging at Banfield.

The man grabbed Banfield by the coat and slammed him up against a cement support column, then yanked him around behind the column, hiding him from anyone else who might come out of the elevators.

Banfield was too breathless to scream, but when he saw the gun, just a squat black pistol his attacker produced from inside his coat, he managed a small cry of alarm that emanated from the back of his throat.

The man slammed Banfield again into the column, his

head against the cold concrete by the attacker's forearm, and the gun disappeared from view.

But Banfield knew where it went. He felt a hard metal object press against his crotch.

The attacker was face-to-face with him now. He wore a mask, and Banfield could see nothing of the man's eyes even though they were just inches away from his, because the light was so bad here in the corner of the underground lot.

'Who are you?' Banfield tried to put power into his words, but they came out in a hollow vibrato.

The masked man said, 'I'm the guy who's going to blow your fuckin' nuts off if you don't tell me what I want to know.'

'Wh-what do you want?'

'Ethan Ross. Start talking.'

'Ethan Ross? Who's that?'

Banfield could see the man's mouth, and realized he was grinning. 'That's how you're going to play it?' He jabbed the barrel of the gun harder against Banfield's manhood. 'This is how *I'm* going to play it.'

'Wait! Please.'

'I'm not going to wait. I'm going to shoot you. I've got to prove to you I'm not fucking around, don't I?'

'No! I know you are serious. I know who you work for. You are CIA.'

'Not even close, asshole. Those pussies over at Langley have rules. I'm calling my own shots.'

'Christ almighty. *You.* You were the one who killed Eve Pang. And the FBI men.'

The masked man cocked his head. 'What are you talking about? Ross killed them.'

'*Ross?* No. That's ridiculous. Ross couldn't hurt a fly. It was you.'

The man in the mask seemed confused for a moment, but he recovered. He jammed the gun in tighter between Banfield's legs.

Banfield said, 'I'll . . . I'll tell you whatever you want to know.'

'Where is he?'

'I swear I have no idea.'

'That sucks for you.' The man pulled the hammer back on the pistol. The click echoed around the parking garage.

'Wait! I can find out.'

'How?'

'I have a secure messaging service on my computer. I can check with someone.'

'Jitsi? ChatSecure? Cryptocat?'

Banfield nodded. 'Cryptocat.'

'Who is your contact?'

Banfield shut his eyes. He hesitated, but only for an instant. 'The head of the ITP.'

'Give me a name.'

'Bertoli. Gianna Bertoli.'

'You are going to contact her, right now, and you are going to find out what they did with Ross.'

Banfield nodded his head.

Dominic Caruso took Banfield upstairs to his office at gunpoint. He had to remove his mask for this, he couldn't be sure they wouldn't pass others on the way, and walking through a downtown D.C. office building with a black neoprene balaclava would pretty much ensure the police would arrive en masse.

But he stayed behind Banfield, nudging him with the gun in his pocket.

Dom hadn't fired this gun in years, and he sure hoped he didn't have to test it. It was a Walther PPK his brother, Brian, had given him as a gift when he graduated from the FBI Academy. It was more a show gun than anything, but right now Dom's Smith was somewhere under the control of Darren Albright, so he'd pulled his Walther out of his gun safe, cleaned, lubed and loaded it with .380 hollow-point ammunition, and then rushed over to Banfield's place of work.

In the elevator ride up Dom saw the older man positioning himself to catch the reflection of his attacker in the polished metal doors. Dom just said, 'Head down, or I'll shoot you through the kneecaps when we get to your office.'

Banfield looked down the rest of the way.

Inside the tiny one-room office, Banfield made his way to his computer at his desk and logged on. His hands shook while he typed; Dom stood behind him and held the pistol to the back of his head. 'Any chance I could get you to move that gun just a little?'

'No chance at all.'

'It makes me nervous.'

'You *should* be nervous. Fear is a reasonable reaction for you right about now. I'll be honest. If I were you, I'd be scared shitless.'

Banfield did his best to concentrate on what he was doing. Finally, he initiated the chat.

The relief he felt when Bertoli answered on the other end of the Cryptocat connection was blunted by the angry and armed man behind him.

The man said, 'If I even suspect you of trying to tip her off, you won't live to see the sunrise. I'll kill you right here, right now.'

Harlan held his quivering fingers over the keyboard. 'I wouldn't think about it.'

'Of course you would think about it. You are thinking about it right now. But if you *do* it, if you try one little thing, you die slow and nasty. I won't ask you if you understand, because I see it in your eyes. You *do* understand. You were a foreign correspondent. I know you've been to some of those Third World shitholes where they've made torturing people into an art. Well, guess what, asshole? I have, too.'

'Who . . . who *are* you?'

'I'm that thing you've always known was out there. In the shadows. Except I'm not out there. I'm here, with a gun pressed to your head.'

Banfield only uttered a hoarse 'Dear God.'

'Relax. I'll slip away quietly and let you live if you just make a series of correct decisions over the next few minutes. But I will kill you if you give me any cause to do so.'

Harlan was certain this man was one of the operatives he'd spent the last several years trying to uncover. A group deeper and darker than the CIA, working here within America's borders, against journalists and others that would reveal the existence of the shadow government.

The man behind said, 'Find out where he is.'

Harlan typed.

I wanted to make sure you are okay.

I am fine.

And our friend?

He is fine.

Anything I can do?

Not at this time. Thank you.

Banfield hesitated a long time, then typed: *I need to know if I am safe here. If there is any exposure to me.*

Why would there be?

Banfield looked up at Caruso. 'I don't know what to say.'

Caruso told Banfield what to write, and he typed.

The FBI has been in his house. Can you ask Ethan if there was anything that could lead the FBI back to me? He called me on my primary cell phone once, many months ago. Any chance he wrote the number down? If so, I might still have time to leave town.

Banfield finished typing and then his finger moved to the Enter key. But before he could depress it, Dom reached down and snatched the older man's hand back.

Banfield was startled. 'What's wrong?'

Dom stared into Banfield's eyes, a hard cruel glare. '*Ethan?* Above you called him "our friend." That was early on. You were scared. You've done what I've asked, so you relaxed a little, and now you are trying to tip her off. You don't call him Ethan in your comms to Gianna, do you?' Banfield did not answer, but his face twitched. Dom said, 'No. You wouldn't. Not Ross, either. You just call him "our friend," don't you?'

Banfield nodded.

'If you are lying, I will fail in my mission. If I fail in my mission, I will have a lot of free time. Plenty of time to find you.'

'I swear it.'

'Fix the message and send it.'

Banfield did so, and there was a long pause.

And then a reply.

He says he might have written your number down. He doesn't remember. I think you should get out of town.

'Does that tell you where he is?' Dom asked.

'It does. Ethan Ross is in Geneva.'

'You are sure?'

'Absolutely. The world HQ of ITP is Gianna's home right there in the city.'

'And she'd take him there?'

'She has support from local government, other European nations with consulate or UN offices there. It is safe ground.'

'You have an address?'

'No.'

Dom lifted the gun again.

'Not an address. But they work out of the University of Geneva!'

'Good enough.'

Dom watched while Banfield ended the chat and logged off.

'It's your lucky day, Banfield. You don't die.'

Dom ripped the computer out of the wall and picked it up. 'I'm taking this with me as collateral to ensure your silence. And if, at any time, I find out you communicated with Ross or anyone in the ITP, one of my colleagues will come for you, and my colleagues aren't nearly as much fun to be around as I am.'

'I won't talk. I swear it.'

Dom left Banfield alone and shaking in his small office.

42

The Four Seasons Hotel des Bergues in Geneva sits overlooking the Rhône River next to the Mont Blanc Bridge. From her sixth-floor suite, Gianna Bertoli gazed out at the view, a cup of coffee in her hand and a placid smile on her face.

Switzerland felt so much more secure and civilized than Panama. Even more than Washington, D.C. She was glad to have the experiences of those cities behind her. In all her time with the ITP she'd never done anything at all 'in the field,' and now she doubted very much she ever would again.

It was good to be home in Geneva, safe among friends.

She turned away from the view, stepped off the balcony, and sat back down with Ethan. He'd just poured himself his first cup of coffee of the day, and she regarded him while he sipped.

He looked terrible, as if he had aged a decade in the week she had been around him. Even though he had a suite as large and comfortable as hers just across the hall, it was obvious he hadn't slept – she saw veins in his eyes, dark circles under them – and his hands seemed to have developed a tremor she hadn't noticed before.

'Ethan, why don't you have some orange juice? You need the vitamins.'

He sipped coffee with a jittery hand and ignored her

comment. 'When we got here last night we had the entire floor to ourselves. This morning there were a dozen people moving luggage into their rooms. Who are all these people?'

'Colleagues with ITP. I've called everyone in Europe here. A show of force, let's say. They are staying four or five to a suite. By the end of the day we will have twenty-five friends close by. Journalists, hacktivists, attorneys, human rights proponents, university professors.'

Ethan put his cup down. 'And they all know about me?'

'No. Absolutely not. None of them do. They know I am here, and I invited them. When we arrived from Panama I decided we needed to wrap ourselves in the organization. It is best for you right now. We have the entire floor to ourselves.'

'Not exactly. I noticed Mohammed had more men with him. There are the four who pulled us out of Panama, and now two more guys that look just as dangerous as the first four have shown up.'

'Yes, I know.'

'Who are they?'

Gianna said, 'Mohammed told me they were friends of his who could help us with security.'

'Why does a computer hacker have friends who can provide security?'

'As I understand it, they are part of his organization.'

'His *Lebanese* organization?'

Gianna sipped coffee. 'Yes. Why do you say it like that?'

'The four on the plane. They were speaking Arabic,' Ethan said. 'But did you hear what they called each other?'

'I did not understand them.'

'Shiraz, Isfahan, Kashan, Ormand. They are cities in Iran. I don't know about Mohammed, but those guys are Iranian.'

Gianna shook her head. 'I've been to his offices in Beirut. I know who he is. I don't know about the other men. What does it matter? They saved us from the American assassins. I, for one, am grateful.'

'We don't even know the men who attacked us in Panama were Americans.'

'Who else could they be? Who else wants you dead? The Israelis *maybe*, but does it really matter? We know they work together.'

Ethan conceded the point. 'The question remains, what do I do now?'

'I'd like to talk to you about just that. I hope you will listen to me, and continue to put your trust in me.'

The two of them spent the morning discussing Ethan's future, and by 11 a.m., Ethan had reluctantly agreed to Gianna's plan. He went back to his suite, and soon Gianna knocked on Mohammed's door. She found him working in his room, on his phone with his laptop in front of him. Four of his six colleagues were there as well, but they were just sitting around.

Gianna did not have the impression they were computer hackers themselves.

She sat with Mohammed at a table just inside his closed balcony. She said, 'I have spoken to Ethan, and together we have come to a decision. The Americans have gone to great lengths to kill him. There will be no détente. He realizes this now. The only way he can save himself is to get out in the open.'

Mohammed did not understand. 'What does that mean, "out in the open"?'

Gianna said, 'Ethan and I have decided we will go public. Very public.'

Mohammed shook his head with an apologetic smile. 'You can't do that.'

'We will hold a press conference here in the hotel, tomorrow at noon. I will reveal myself as director of the Project. This is of no consequence to me, as I will not return to the field. I prefer to remain here in Geneva, and to work as a figurehead promoting our work. Ethan will detail the events that brought him here, including America's attempts to kill him, both on the streets of Washington and in Panama.' Gianna smiled. 'By the Tuesday news cycle both the work of the Project and the crimes of America will be on the lips of every journalist in Europe.'

Mohammed stood, crossed around the table and in front of the Swiss woman. 'Gianna, that is a very bad idea.'

She put her hand on his shoulder. He looked at it awkwardly, and she pulled it away. Recovering quickly, she said, 'Don't take this the wrong way, but publicity is not your area of expertise. We will make an announcement that Ross was a prisoner of conscience working for the American government. He was chased out of the country by assassins, assassins who killed his girlfriend, and then he was pursued by the Americans in Central America. Once we go public like this, he will be safe. He will be surrounded by people here in Europe who will protect him,

428

and the Americans won't dare try anything once the word gets out.'

Mohammed banged his fist on the table. 'And the data in his possession? Our entire objective was to get control of that data. Have you forgotten?'

'Relax. Of course I haven't forgotten. Your plan was brilliant, and it worked almost flawlessly. When you told me you had software that could raid the U.S. government's top-secret databases, I knew Ethan Ross could serve as our inside man, if only we created a situation desperate enough for him. But we never counted on people dying in the process.'

Mohammed did not reply.

Bertoli's chest heaved. 'It's ironic, isn't it? In our efforts to portray America as a lawless nation, we have found ourselves surprised by their capacity for lawlessness.'

'Nothing has surprised me to date, Gianna. Except for the astonishing fact you want to tell the entire world about Ross. I'm sorry, but the moment you do that we will be swept to the side as the world's intelligence agencies begin to muscle in. The Four Seasons will be crawling with spies from all over the planet. They will all have their sights on Ross and his data.'

'We will protect him. Hotel security will protect him. The canton police will protect him. When we go public with the news of the assassinations and their attack in Panama, America will be embarrassed, and we will capitalize on that. Ethan will, in his own time, allow the ITP access to the cache.'

'When America learns he is here, we won't have any time!'

The Swiss woman cocked her head slightly. 'You do want to help the ITP, yes? Your allegiance is to us, is it not?'

Mohammed said, 'Of course. Why do you ask?'

'Ethan seems to think you are working for Iranian intelligence. I told him this was crazy, I've been aware of your operation in Lebanon for years. But I have to admit, you are acting strangely now, as if you have some other objective for the American files.'

He took a calming breath before saying, 'I simply believe you are making a mistake.'

Bertoli eyed the small man across the table for a long moment. Finally, she replied, 'The decision is made. We've notified the media.'

Mohammed stood and stormed out of his suite without another word.

Ethan Ross sat at dinner in a private banquet room in the Four Seasons, surrounded by more than two dozen prominent hacktivists, human rights lawyers, journalists, and other hangers-on of Gianna Bertoli and the ITP. A ring of security officers, all provided by the hotel, stood just outside the door to the banquet room.

While the American NSC employee had made no statement today – that would come tomorrow – the ITP members present had been putting the pieces together themselves. This American in their midst obviously came from Washington. Bertoli's major announcement would detail who he was and what exactly he had done. Bertoli herself had leaked out a little to some of her guests. It was

Publicity 101: she knew she needed to create a buzz before tomorrow's big reveal.

Wine and champagne flowed throughout the meal, any excuse was a good excuse for a celebration among the members of the Project on those few occasions when they all got together, but tonight's revelry seemed to be in keeping with the magnitude of Bertoli's coming announcement.

Mohammed was noticeably absent tonight. He'd been on his telephone all day. Ethan had seen him in the lobby, up on the sixth floor, and even standing out on his balcony. His colleagues stayed close to him at all times, almost like some sort of bodyguard detail.

Throughout dinner, the toasts and the revelry, Ethan sat quietly, his misgivings growing by the minute. The celebratory nature of the evening seemed out of phase with everything that had happened.

And more than this, he had another concern. He just couldn't shake the sensation that this entire affair had been orchestrated to lead him to this point. Like he had been coaxed and prodded and manipulated into the decisions he had made, the actions he had taken, the path he had traveled.

The sense of being a pawn ran completely counter to his self-image, but the dinner party convinced him the International Transparency Project stood to gain mightily from his misfortune. That said, he hadn't met a single person in the ITP, Bertoli included, who he thought capable of pulling his strings the way they had been pulled to cause all of this. He could not help wondering if some other entity was involved.

It was too much to contemplate, so he didn't. Ethan reached for the closest bottle of champagne and filled his water glass with it, telling himself he needed to relax to be able to think clearly in order to deal with what was still to come. He'd get shit-faced drunk tonight, and tomorrow he would deal with tomorrow.

43

Dominic Caruso and Adara Sherman arrived in Geneva, Switzerland, at 7.40 a.m. on a nonstop United flight from Dulles. They didn't rent a car at the airport; instead they took a cab directly to the Hôtel St-Gervais in the city center, then checked in to a deluxe room on the third floor.

Initially they planned on hunting for Ross and Bertoli here in Geneva for as long as it took, but their hunt was greatly simplified when word came from Gerry Hendley that the ITP would be holding a major press conference at the Four Seasons at noon. It was obvious the conference would involve Ross, and Dom planned on being there so he could tail him from the hotel.

To that end, Adara walked a couple of blocks to rent a four-door BMW sedan that would blend in here in luxurious Geneva, and Dom left the hotel to go to a nearby motorcycle shop, where he rented a fully gassed BMW F 800 GS, a helmet, and a dark gray one-piece thermal motorcycle suit. He and Adara thought it a near certainty they would have to do some vehicle surveillance, so they wanted to have two vehicles to spread their coverage.

There was an immediate snag in this plan, however. All the talk on the local news was of a late winter storm brewing in the mountains to the south of Geneva, forecast to hit the city by midday. Dom wasn't crazy about biking through a blizzard, so he considered renting a second car, instead of a bike, but he stuck with the bike and told himself if the weather turned too bad he could park it and grab a four-wheeled vehicle instead.

An hour later he and Adara met back at their hotel room. She had scoped out the Four Seasons on her way back from the rental car office and offered to draw Dom a map of the interior, but he decided he'd drive over for a look himself. Dom had no plans to go inside the building, once the press arrived for the conference, so he headed off immediately.

Light snow began falling as he parked in a lot next to the Church of the Holy Trinity, just a block from the Four Seasons. He walked over to the hotel and noticed several satellite trucks out front already. He ducked in a side entrance and started walking around the ground floor.

He wanted to get a feel for where Ross might go after the press conference. He pictured the American being shuffled out a side exit into a waiting vehicle, but from Dom's limited view of the banquet hall from his vantage point in the lobby, he decided it was just as likely he would come right out the front of the building and on to the street there.

Dom worried he'd have a hard time knowing where to station himself for static overwatch outside, but while he thought about it his satellite phone chirped in his pocket. He grabbed it and saw it was Gerry Hendley.

'Hey, Gerry. It's about 4 a.m. in D.C., isn't it?'

'Don't remind me. Listen up. Just heard from my contact at Justice. Your friend Albright is there, in Geneva, and he has been given a green light to arrest Ross.'

Dom was impressed, but still incredulous. 'I hope he doesn't expect it to be easy.'

'I guess not. He's got an HRT team with him, as well as a surveillance unit. They are going in hard and fast.'

'Did the Swiss give them the okay to do this?'

'Negative. FBI is going to try and snatch him out from under the Swiss. The concern is the scrape. Even if it falls into Swiss hands, it won't be secure. They are an ally, but we can't say they don't have people in their midst who would misuse the data. We have to take it off the playing field. We can kiss and make up with the Swiss after the fact.'

'When is it going to happen?'

'It's imminent, from what I can tell. Right there at the Four Seasons, before the press confab. It's the only time they know where he will be with certainty, and the last chance to get him before this all goes public.'

Dom looked around the lobby. For all he knew, there could be FBI surveillance teams in the building. 'I guess I'd better get out of here before Albright shows up.'

'That sounds like a good idea, son.'

Caruso left the hotel immediately, then headed back to the parking lot. He stood next to his bike and looked to the sky. Even through the snowfall, he could see massive gray thunderheads hanging over the mountains to the south. He called Adara and asked her to head to the lobby of the Four Seasons and to keep him posted about what was going on.

Ethan put on a suit he'd bought that morning in the men's store in the lobby of the hotel. He tied his tie, and while he did so he looked at himself in the bathroom mirror.

Ethan was narcissistic, but he retained enough realism to recognize that he looked like shit. His eyes were sunken and rimmed with dark circles, his cheeks sallow from poor sleep and worse diet.

He took a minute with his hair, but finally he gave up and sat down on the edge of his bed. He bent over, covering his head with his hands. He remained motionless for over a minute, and moved only when there was a knock at his door.

Gianna stepped in a moment later, sat next to him and reached to hug him, but Ethan pushed her away.

'What is wrong? We have to be in the conference room in fifteen minutes. Mohammed's men will escort us down.'

Ross shook his head. 'I can't do it.'

'What do you mean?'

'I'm not going public. I want to reach out to the FBI before we have the press conference. I'll tell them I'll turn over the drive. They aren't going to offer immunity . . . but they might –'

'No. You can't do that.'

'Of course I can. I want to go home. It was never my intention to be a spy for the Iranians.'

Gianna shook her head. 'I told you. Mohammed is Lebanese. And Mohammed works for me.'

'Are you really that naive?'

Ross had worked with the ITP, in part, because he felt he was more intelligent than those he worked around in the government. Suddenly it hit him that he was more intelligent than the ITP, and the effects of this realization were devastating.

Gianna sighed slowly, and stepped closer to Ethan.

'Look. He always told me he was Lebanese. As I said, I've been to his office. But if he is Iranian, what does it matter?'

Ethan just muttered, 'I've got to get out of here.'

Bertoli addressed Ross as if he were one of her underlings now. 'Let me tell you how things work. The best hacker groups in the world are in China. Next best are in Russia. Then come the Iranians. They are better than the private groups here in Europe.'

'Why don't you work with the Chinese or Russians?'

'The Chinese work for their state. We do collaborate with the Russians, on occasion, but they are just in it for the money.'

'And the Iranians? What are they in it for?'

'They are in it for the same reasons we are.'

'To damage the West?'

She shrugged. 'If you like.'

'You are a fool. Mohammed and his group are under direct orders from Tehran. He doesn't work for you. You work for him!'

'That's ridiculous.'

'Let me ask you this. When you got my intelligence about the peace flotilla attack four months ago, did you give it to Mohammed?'

She hesitated. 'We needed them to unpack the compressed files and redact any names. That is a time-consuming process. Mohammed took care of it.'

Ross understood everything now. His career in the National Security Council went a long way to helping him put the pieces together of a truly brilliant and diabolical scheme.

'Mohammed played me all the way through. Through you he learned about Yacoby, he knew the Palestinians would go after him, and they knew this would reveal your whistleblower in U.S. intelligence. All it took was something that would make me run . . .' He thought for a moment. 'Like an assassination attempt.'

The door to Ethan's suite opened. Standing there in the doorway were Shiraz and Isfahan, leather coats fat with stowed weapons under their arms. Another man appeared in the hall and entered the room behind them. It was Mohammed, but it took Gianna and Ethan seconds to realize this. Gone was his awkward demeanor and college-student clothes. In its place he wore a suit and tie, he stood taller, his shoulders were back, and he appeared utterly confident. 'Well done, Ethan. You have it exactly right so far, but let me expand on it for you.'

Ethan looked around. 'You've bugged my room?'

Mohammed smiled, held his hands up in apology. He said, 'My initial vision for this operation was too narrow.

'I had access to an IT professional at NSA, and I knew I could persuade him to build the crawler we needed to get the secure data, but I did not have the inside man I needed to put the crawler on the network. When Gianna gave me the flotilla files to work on, I saw that whoever passed this intel from NSC might well have access to much more. A great deal of vital information about America and its assets around the world. I couldn't find this person on my own, so I had to draw him, or her, out into the open. The way to do that was to give the information about Yacoby to the Palestinians.

'I knew they would act. I even helped coordinate the

action in India, bringing the Palestinians and the cell of Yemenis together.

'I knew it would be clear the American data leak led to the attack. There would be an investigation. I was getting the Americans to do the work for me, you see. Once the man at NSC was drawn out, I knew Gianna would reach out to him. I knew she would offer him protection.' He smiled. 'And I knew I had to be there, in the middle of it all.'

He turned to Bertoli. 'I could not be certain you would be able to get him out of the U.S. That was a very weak link in my scheme. But after consulting with colleagues in Tehran I was given approval to go myself to America to assist.

'We found out his name from Banfield, we put surveillance on him ourselves. But it would do no good for us to take him. We could have done it, though it would have been a dangerous exposure. But he had to take the data first. To commit the scrape.'

Mohammed smiled. 'My friend Gianna was complicit in this. I told her about the crawler, she thought she could use her power of persuasion to get you to download the files, but to her surprise, you were not as easy to manipulate as she had hoped.'

He looked at Ross. 'So I increased the pressure. We made it obvious you were being followed, but still you were stubborn. You wouldn't download the files. So we had to get even more serious.'

Ethan understood. 'Eve. You murdered her. It wasn't an assassination attempt on me. You were trying to scare me.'

Mohammed smiled. 'You *were* scared, weren't you? You

actually ducked and made shooting her easy. It was beneficial. She was suspicious of you. Had she lived, she might have tipped off the FBI and gotten you arrested. That would have been unfortunate for us. I also knew you needed her credentials to access the virtual private network to get on the CIA's network remotely. I put the chances at fifty per cent that you would just lose your mind when she died and not go through with the scrape. But I underestimated your cunning.'

Ethan mumbled, 'She wasn't going to turn me in.'

Mohammed shrugged. 'Then I overestimated her patriotism. Anyway, it all turned out perfectly.'

'You used me,' Ross mumbled.

'A vulnerable asset is a valuable asset.'

'You used *me*!' Gianna shouted it in fury.

Mohammed pointed in her face. 'Of course I used *you*! You were easy to use. You knew I had the crawler, and you knew you had to get Ethan to install it. But you were helpless in that regard. I made him scrape the files.'

'And now what will you do?' asked Ethan.

'I wanted to kidnap you after Panama and bring you to Tehran, but my leadership demanded I preserve my relationship with ITP if at all possible. I thought it was possible. I thought we could come back here, Gianna and I could work on you for a few days, wear you down, persuade you to give up the password to your intelligence scrape.

'But that was not to be. You insisted on going public, drawing attention to yourself, at which point the Americans would kidnap or kill you. I can't wait around for someone else to show up and take the breach that I worked so long and hard to create. I am going to take it myself. Now.' He motioned to Shiraz, who walked over to the laptop computer on the table. The Quds Force man opened the lid, then turned back to Ross.

Mohammed said, 'I assume the files are on the computer. You wouldn't have left them on the crawler drive. We need the passwords, please.'

'What will you do with the information?'

'We will take the information back to Iran. Of course.'

Ethan shook his head. 'I'm not going to tell you anything.'

Mohammed smiled. It was sinister, more so because it was completely out of place with the personality of the man Ethan had been around for the past several days. As if his body had been taken over by another being.

The Iranian said, 'Of course you say that now. Let's see what you say when I am through with you.'

Suddenly Kashan spun into the doorway, entering the room at a run. He said something in Farsi that Ross couldn't understand, but it was telling that the men weren't troubling themselves with Arabic any longer. There was no pretense but that they were agents from Tehran.

Mohammed's face went from calm confidence to obvious alarm. 'The FBI is here. Outside.' He motioned toward the door. 'We are leaving now.'

Bertoli said, 'Where are you taking us?'

'We must hurry.' He was emphatic. Brusque. 'We'll go downstairs to the parking garage. Now.'

Shiraz stuffed the laptop into the backpack, slipped it on to his back. Isfahan looked out the doorway, checking up and down the hall.

Ross wondered where the other Iranians were, but he did not ask.

'I'm not going anywhere with you. I'm staying right here.'

Isfahan and Shiraz pointed silenced pistols at Ethan and Gianna. In seconds everyone was moving toward the stairs.

44

Mohammed Mobasheri and two other members of his team led Ross and Bertoli through the underground garage quickly and professionally. They had the air of a close protection detail, although the two Westerners with them were most definitely prisoners.

Gianna Bertoli said, 'We should stay in the hotel and let the police deal with them. The Swiss government won't let the Americans take Ethan. They have no authority.'

Mobasheri shook his head as he walked. 'The FBI will break down every door in the building to get to our friend.'

'So we are leaving the hotel?' Bertoli asked.

'Correct.'

'But it's freezing outside.'

'Your coats, as well as the rest of your luggage, have already been removed from your rooms and will be brought to you immediately.'

'What? Your people have been through my things?' Gianna's voice echoed in the parking garage. Her tone was caustic with the breach of her privacy.

Mobasheri conferred in Farsi with someone on his phone.

Ross asked, 'You don't think the FBI will have people outside?'

The Iranian took the phone from his ear. 'The FBI is watching the exits of the hotel. But where we are going there is no hotel exit. I assure you, I have your safekeeping under control. I need you. Keep walking.'

They stepped into a narrow stairwell that was clearly not part of the Four Seasons property and they ascended to street level. When one of the Iranians arrived at a door, he opened it slowly, and he looked out before indicating to the others they should follow.

Ross thought he would find himself on one of the streets outside the hotel, but instead he saw they were in a long narrow courtyard area chock-full of construction. The Four Seasons was actually connected to an entire block of five- to eight-storey buildings, and this paved area was closed for renovations. The inner walls of the apartments and office buildings here had all been covered with green mesh to keep the windows safe from the ongoing construction, and there was little activity in any of the office buildings.

Ross suddenly felt the uncomfortable sensation of solitude. He'd quickly moved from a hotel floor with dozens of people around to here, completely isolated other than a small group around him he did not trust.

They continued through the outdoor construction area. There was little snowfall here because of the high buildings and the wind. It was clear to Ross the Iranians had set this escape plan up earlier, although he couldn't guess how they could have known to do so. He expected now they would all head to the street and hail taxis, although he wondered if Mohammed had some other trick up his sleeve.

For the first time he tried to directly resist the Iranians.

He stopped walking, and he reached out and took Gianna by the arm to stop her as well.

'Listen to me, Mohammed. I'm not taking another fucking step. You aren't getting the intelligence. I want to stay here.'

Mobasheri barely broke stride. He nodded to the man on Ross's left, who slammed his fist into the back of the American's shoulder, knocking him forward and off balance. As soon as he was able to turn around in hopes of defending himself from another strike, Ethan saw the Iranian had produced a black pistol, and although the man held it at hip level, it was pointed directly at Ross's chest.

Gianna started to scream, but a second man put his arm around her neck and covered her mouth with his hand. He pulled her onward in a headlock.

In English, Mobasheri said, 'I ask everyone to keep moving, please.'

Ethan Ross turned with his hands raised to ward off any follow-on blows, and he resumed walking through the quiet courtyard.

Caruso would have given six months of his Campus salary to be in the Four Seasons when Darren Albright and the HRT studs took Ross down. He was certain there would be video taken of the event, and it would play in a constant loop on the cable channels back home for a long time. The video might cause problems; he was damn sure the UN and the EU and God knows who else would have an aneurism when they saw it, especially if Albright and company had to go in loud in the posh European hotel.

The video will be cool, he told himself, but it would be so much better to be in there watching firsthand, so he could see the color drain out of that prick Ross's face when he realized the rest of his life would be spent in a ten-by-twelve can in a supermax prison.

But Dom knew he couldn't be inside. He had to keep his own face out of the constant video loop, and he sure as hell didn't want Albright to know he was here. He was already thinking about the after-effects of this operation, and he didn't need a guy like Albright any more curious about him and his organization than he already was.

So Dom went back to his bike parked in the lot in front of the Church of the Holy Trinity, and he zipped his jacket tightly and slipped on his helmet. It was snowing heavily now, but he fired up his BMW F 800 GS and drove slowly back toward the hotel, hoping to at least get a glimpse of the tail end of the arrest, protected from both hotel surveillance cameras and the FBI's watchful eyes by the tinted visor of his helmet.

He motored slowly back through the snowfall, along with the light traffic, staying in the turning lane to make a left in front of the hotel. When he made the turn he noticed three silver SUVs parked across the street along the Rhône River. He thought it likely the vans belonged to the tactical team, and this was confirmed a moment later when he saw men behind the wheels who looked like they had been sent by Central Casting. Short-cropped military haircuts, muscular necks disappearing into nondescript dark coveralls, and black watch caps.

Dom smiled inside his helmet. The takedown was going on right now in the building on his left. Catching

Ethan Ross wouldn't bring anything approaching the closure he needed to get over the Yacobys' deaths, but it was a hell of a lot better than nothing. Plus, it would dam up the most dangerous leak to the U.S. intelligence community in history.

Dom wanted to park right here by the vans to watch the action, but he saw no movement at the front of the Four Seasons, and he decided he had a couple of minutes before Ross was frog-marched out. He didn't want to draw any attention to himself, so he stayed in traffic, making the decision to circle the block to eat up some time.

He made a left on Rue du Mont-Blanc, and here he saw four more FBI men watching the street. They were across from the hotel, standing in two groups of two, and obviously aware there were exits through some shops at the street here that also had doors that led to the lobby of the hotel.

Good, thought Dom. HRT wasn't just going to bum-rush the conference, they were prepared with surveillance in case Ross tried to squirt out another exit.

He made another left on to Rue de Cendrier. This was the end of the block, and he looked for FBI back here, but he saw no one. He presumed this meant the stores here, a luxury eyeglass shop and a men's clothing shop, didn't have access to the hotel, which was on the other side of the block.

The fat snowflakes made it hard to see more than a hundred yards, but as he reached the corner and prepared to make a left, ahead of him he saw a large white panel van rolling toward him. His first thought was that the HRT was even bigger than he'd thought. If they had come in three vehicles they could haul as many as thirty-six people.

That didn't sound right. He wondered if Albright had authority to make arrests other than just Ross; perhaps this white van was a paddy wagon with which the FBI would haul in all the major players of the ITP.

No, Dom decided. It was going to be tough enough for Albright to get away with the American citizen and get him across the bridge to the U.S. consulate. The arrest itself was going to create a massive international incident. Hauling in Swiss citizens, Italian citizens, German citizens. *No,* Dom thought. No way in hell Albright would have the authority to pull off something like that.

He discounted the large vehicle approaching as a coincidence and turned left on Place Kleberg, and immediately he picked out a group of FBI surveillance cars parked near an employee entrance to the hotel and the ramp that went down to a loading bay and the underground parking garage. Their engines were running and there were multiple men in each vehicle.

They had been easy to spot, but Dom cut the guys some slack. At this stage of the arrest the security teams cordoning off the area weren't worried about maintaining a low profile. They had to be ready to block the exits and support the triggermen inside the hotel if necessary.

Dom passed the vehicles by the ramp to the parking lot and headed back around toward the front of the hotel, hoping Albright and his men would hurry up and end this thing.

*

Mohammed Mobasheri was in the lead of the group when they arrived at the end of the narrow courtyard. He pushed through a long cut in the green mesh that covered the buildings, then held open a door for the others.

This room was a small and simple office and storage facility for the groundskeeper of the property. A tiny work desk was on one wall, and all around the ten-by-ten-foot room were shelves with equipment, tools, coiled extension cords, and other odds and ends. Against the wall were snow shovels and a gas-powered snowblower on wheels.

At the far end of the little space was another of Mobasheri's men. He had a sledgehammer in his hand, and from the looks of it he'd apparently just knocked an impressive hole through the plaster and cinder-block wall. It was three feet high by a foot and a half wide, and it would just accommodate the procession if they passed through it slowly and carefully.

As the Iranian put the sledgehammer on the ground and redonned his black jacket, Mobasheri extended a hand toward the black hole.

'Ms Bertoli, if you will?'

'Where are you taking –'

'Move!' His shout exploded in the small maintenance room.

Bertoli, Ross and the Iranians all climbed through the ragged portal and into the narrow and dark warehouse space at the back of a men's clothing store. They took a moment to brush off dust and bits of plaster, then continued out on to the sales floor.

The light from the windows at the front of the shop

was muted, it was an overcast day with a snowstorm blowing through, after all, but as soon as Ross neared the front door he saw a white panel truck pull up outside.

This was their ride out of here, that much was plain.

But a ride to where? Ross had no idea.

His first inclination was to make a run for it the second he got out on the street. He was fast enough, and even though he wasn't dressed for the cold, this was downtown Geneva. It wasn't like he was up in the mountains. All he had to do was find a cop or an FBI agent or any public space or, just maybe, he could run right into the entrance of the first embassy he came across.

Surely to God the Iranians wouldn't shoot him in the back if he made a break for it.

As they neared the entrance, Mobasheri stopped Ross by touching his arm softly.

'Clothes. Quickly, I want you to change your clothes.'

Ethan looked around. The store was full of Lacoste clothing. Some of it was skiwear, so he grabbed some thick nylon pants and put them on, then looked for a heavy sweater.

While he did this Gianna Bertoli had grown uncharacteristically silent. It was clear to Ross she realized that she had completely lost control of the situation, and she was scared. Her concern only gave Ethan more incentive to try to get away from these men.

In seconds he had changed all his clothing, even slipping on a pair of rubber boots.

Mobasheri gave him a satisfied nod, and then one of the Iranian Quds men unlocked the glass door of the clothing store.

Ethan's heart pounded, and he gulped the warm air of the shop. This was his chance.

By his second loop around the block, Dom was convinced something had gone wrong on the inside of the hotel. He knew the HRT guys would want to enter the conference quickly and use speed and surprise to overwhelm their target and his security. Every single minute they sat around inside that building was one more minute where some security guard or cop in attendance could throw a wrench into the works.

And just then, as if on cue, Dominic heard sirens coming from the direction of the bridge over the Rhône.

The local police were on the way, and Dom hoped like hell Albright could effect his takedown and get the fuck out of there before men with guns and questions showed up to find out what the hell the dozen or so American guys in coveralls were doing milling about the five-star hotel.

Just as Dom made his left turn on to Rue de Cendrier, the far side of the block from the hotel entrance, he noticed the white van again. It had pulled to the curb next to a men's clothing shop.

Dom looked back over his left shoulder for the FBI surveillance unit on the street on Rue du Mont-Blanc. He could see their cars through the snow, but they were fifty yards away and facing the opposite direction.

Dom slowed, then braked suddenly when he saw the door to the darkened clothing store open and Ethan Ross appear. He was just a step ahead of a group of several other men and one woman, but unlike the rest of the group, Ross was running like hell.

'No, no, no!' Dom mumbled in astonishment.

Ethan took flight as soon as he was outside, sprinting to the right of the door, trying to make it around the front of the van. He clearly surprised Mohammed and his men, because he managed to get ten feet of separation on the sidewalk in just a few bounds. The snow on the sidewalk had been ankle-deep, and when he landed in the street he slipped a little on the compact, icy surface. He managed to right himself and keep going.

He was nearly past the front grille of the white van when the driver put the vehicle in gear and stomped on the accelerator. The van lurched forward and delivered a glancing but powerful blow to the fleeing American, hitting him on his left side, spinning him through the air, and upending him.

Ross crashed to the ground on his back, not fifty feet in front of Caruso.

Holy shit!' Dom shouted into his motorcycle helmet.

His first inclination was to race over to Ross, either to scoop him up and make a run for it or to run him down a second time, but three men surrounded his prostrate form in the snow-covered street. They rolled him on to his stomach, then yanked him back up to his feet roughly.

Dom just sat on his rumbling BMW motorcycle as the group moved as a unit around Ross. They pushed and pulled him back on to the sidewalk and into the side of the van, and then the vehicle rolled off in Dom's direction.

Caruso let it pass, then watched it from over his shoulder as it made a left on Rue du Mont-Blanc.

When it had completely disappeared from view Caruso revved his engine, snapped his bike into gear, and spun on the snow. He burned a one-hundred-and-eighty-degree turn in place and took off in pursuit of the American traitor.

45

Ethan lay on his back in the rear of the van; next to him Gianna Bertoli sat with her coat wrapped around her. True to his word, Mobasheri had packed up her luggage, and it, along with Ross's, sat by the back door of the vehicle. She'd pulled her coat off as soon as she'd climbed inside, and now she sat next to Ethan but she didn't render him any aid, as she was consumed by her own thoughts and worries.

Ethan's hip and his back and his arm hurt from the impacts from the truck and the hard-packed snow in the street. He didn't think anything had been broken, but he wasn't sure.

Mohammed was sitting in the middle row of seats. He turned and looked back at Ethan. 'Are you okay?' The concern in his voice seemed genuine.

'You could have fucking killed me!'

Mohammed smiled, spun around forward, and said something in Farsi to the others. Instantly two men leapt on top of Ethan and began pulling at his clothing.

'What are you doing?'

'You ran away, but you didn't have your computer. The scrape is not on the computer, is it? You have a drive on you.'

'No!' he screamed.

It took them a minute. They stripped him down to nothing, rummaged through his clothes as he lay naked and fetal. One man pulled his arms away from him and another his legs; they were ready to begin a body-cavity search, but Ethan shouted to stop them.

'Okay! Okay!' He reached to his hip and tore off the moleskin patch. It was passed up the van to Mohammed, who pried the microdrive off the adhesive.

He nodded appreciatively. 'Well done, Ethan. Well done. The computer was just a decoy.'

Ethan pulled his clothes back on. While he did so, he said to Mohammed, 'You are Quds Force, aren't you?'

'I am Revolutionary Guard. On a mission by order of the Supreme Leader. These men are Quds Force.'

'Where are we going?' Bertoli shouted the question. She'd been forgotten in the corner of the van.

Mohammed seemed to weigh whether or not to respond for a moment. Finally, he said, 'You see what happens if you try to escape, yes?'

Both Bertoli and Ross nodded.

'We are going to Genoa.'

'Genoa, *Italy*?' Bertoli was confused. 'What's in Genoa?'

Mohammed smiled. 'A boat that will take us to Libya.'

Bertoli began shouting a string of obscenities, making it crystal clear she had no desire to go to Libya. Ross, on the other hand, tried a different tactic.

'It's got to be four, five hours to Genoa. We'll never make it before the Americans figure out where we are.'

Mohammed waved away the comment. 'Let me worry about that, Mr Ross. You need to worry about what we are going to ask of you when we get where we are going.'

Ross knew what they wanted. They wanted the password. He told himself he would never give it to them, but thinking about the lengths they would go to force him to reveal his password made him close his eyes and shudder.

Dom Caruso was a skilled motorcyclist, but he'd never before raced a road bike on icy streets while his helmet visor was half covered with wet snowfall.

And on top of all this, he had to break his concentration to make a phone call.

For the first few minutes of his tail on the van, they traveled through the narrow, winding streets of downtown Geneva, with intersections every hundred yards and large buildings that obstructed his view. He couldn't make it to the phone in his pack, he had to give all his attention to not losing his quarry.

Finally, the road straightened out some and Dom backed off a hundred yards to stay out of sight in the snow. It took a moment to get his hand under his butt to pull his glove off, but he managed, careful to keep his glove in place while he dialed his phone.

After four rings Dom heard a recording in his earpiece. 'You've reached Supervisory Special Agent Darren Albright. I am unavailable at this time. Please leave a detailed message. Good day.'

'Fuck.'

The state-of-the-art Bluetooth headset in his ear, and the sound-dampening effects of the helmet made the call relatively clear, but still Dom had to all but shout over his bike's engine. 'Albright, it's me! Ross, Bertoli and several armed subjects are in a white twelve-passenger van heading . . . I guess this must be south. We crossed the

Pont du Mont-Blanc and are on – hold up while I pass a sign – we're on Route du Malagnon. I need HRT on them quick before they get to wherever they're going. Call me back.'

He disconnected the call.

Dom had to tighten up on the van again as it entered a hilly section in a southwestern neighborhood, and then he backed off when it took the wide and straight Rue Blanche. He almost lost it once in the snowstorm, but he pressed his luck and closed, and this paid off, because he caught sight of the white vehicle just as it took an access ramp for the highway.

They got on the A40, which Dom thought was good news, because he knew it would have been impossible to stick on the van much longer without being spotted as it traveled up and down city streets. But the bad news was there were fewer cars and trucks on the highway and Caruso was certain he stood out more now. As the vehicle picked up speed it blended in with the snow much better than his black bike, dark gray riding suit, and black helmet, but he concentrated on keeping as far back as he could and retaining as much of his vision as possible by wiping his visor with the left forearm of his suit every twenty seconds or so.

Dom could not be sure Darren Albright would pick up his message in time to catch up with Ross. The Swiss police might have already detained the FBI team, or else simply delayed them, which, as far as Dom was concerned, would be just as bad.

So he called Adara, who answered on the first ring. 'Where are you? I came back to the Four Seasons. This place is crawling with police.'

Dom explained where he was.

'What can I do?'

'Call Gerry and get the name of the CIA station chiefs in Geneva, Milan and Lyon. They are the closest cities with stations. Then get those people on the phone. If you can't get the COSs, find the DCOSs. Whoever you can get, tell them the situation.'

Adara hesitated. 'Right. Just so I know . . . what, exactly, *is* the situation?'

'Good question. First, don't tell them who you are or who I am. Just say Ethan Ross is traveling southeast on the A40 in a white van. Tag number Golf Echo, three, eight, niner, seven, seven, two. Destination unknown. He's got a half-dozen or so armed subjects with him, possibly Palestinians, but I'm just guessing.'

'Okay. They might want me to establish my bona fides somehow.'

'Tell them you work for Darren Albright, FBI CID. If those station chiefs are worth a damn they'll move mountains to get that intel back from Ross. They'll check into the tipster later.'

'I'm on it,' Adara said, and Dom disconnected the phone and struggled to get his glove back on.

For nearly fifteen minutes, Caruso drove through the snow alone, with a faint view of the van's taillights. The pounding in his heart, adrenaline from the early stages of the chase, was dissipating and only the motorcycle's drone remained.

His headset chirped in his ear, startling him. He accepted

the call by pulling off his glove again and pressing a button on his phone with his thumb.

'Albright?'

'What the fuck, Caruso? You're *here*? In Geneva?'

'Actually, I'm outside the city, rolling through the Alps. Still headed southeast.'

'What are you doing in Switzerland?'

'Right now, I'm tailing your target. What are you doing still in Geneva?'

'One of my teams got held up by the canton police. We think Ross was tipped off by locals somehow, and that's why they were ready for us.'

'Wouldn't doubt it.'

Albright asked, 'How many are with you?'

'How many *what*?'

'How many men on your team?'

'*Team?* There is no team. I'm flying solo. It's just me. I'm on a BMW bike, chasing this bastard through a snowstorm.'

'Bullshit. I know you are running an agency operation.'

'Tell you what, when you catch up, you'll see I'm alone, and then you can snag Ross and take all the glory.'

'I'm en route with five men. The other trucks are headed north to pull off the police.'

Dom passed through the small hamlet of Bonneville, but he was still on the A40 and Ross showed no hint of exiting the highway here. Dom gave Albright this information and Albright put Caruso on hold for some time so he could confer with his team. After a few minutes he came back on the line. 'Okay, looks like you are ten minutes ahead of us, tops. They are heading straight into the mountains. With this shitty weather we're not going to be able to call up air transport, but that's actually good news. Ross and his people won't be flying out of here. If you can keep up with them and lead us to them we'll catch up, and we'll fight them on the ground and end this thing today.'

Dom had considered the weather and come to the same conclusion. No helicopter pilot in the world would risk flying in this shit.

'Any clue where they are going?' he asked.

'In a few minutes they'll be over the French border in Chamonix. From there it's a right turn into the Italian Alps. I don't know how that helps them, maybe they've got a safe house. Maybe they just need a bolt-hole till the weather passes and they can fly out.'

Caruso said, 'If they exit the highway, it's going to be impossible for me to stay with them for long.'

'Understood. We're closing fast. I'll call you when I can see you.'

Caruso added one more thing. 'There's something you don't know. At this point, Ross is unwitting in all this. I saw him try to make a run for it. The armed guys have him, and maybe Bertoli, at gunpoint.'

Albright responded without hesitation. 'That complicates things for Ross, but not for me. When we go in for the arrest I am treating everyone as hostile.'

Dom nodded in his helmet as he drove. 'Can't say I blame you there.'

46

As Caruso and Albright suspected, Ross and his kidnappers left the highway in the French border town of Chamonix, and turned on to a road that led to the Mont Blanc Tunnel, a 7.2-mile passage under Mont Blanc, the highest mountain in Europe. On the other side was Italy.

Dom quickly called Albright back and informed him of this before entering the tunnel, where his phone promptly became useless to him.

Inside the Mont Blanc Tunnel, Dom immediately dropped almost a mile back from the white van so he wouldn't be detected. When he exited the tunnel into Italy ten minutes later, he returned to the poor visibility of the snowstorm, and he could no longer see Ross's vehicle ahead of him. He floored the bike to try to close the distance between himself and his target, and he tried to call Albright back to update him, but Dom found himself alternately in the basin of a narrow valley or racing through one of many more tunnels cut into the mountainsides, so he remained out of comms with the FBI team behind him.

Fortunately, he caught a glimpse of the van in the distance, and he locked on to its taillights a few hundred yards away and concentrated on keeping a fixed distance.

After traveling more than ten miles into Italy, the van pulled off the A5 and on to the SS26, a two-lane winding road that worked its way through the foothills on the northern wall of the valley.

Soon after, Dom's headset chirped in his ear.

'Albright?'

'Yeah. Okay, we're right behind you. Saw your taillight as you turned on to the SS26. Ross is still in front of you?'

'He's a quarter-mile ahead, tops.'

Albright said, 'I want you to pull off at the next exit and shoot ahead of him through the town of Saint Maurice. That will get you out of our line of fire and ahead, in case we blow the felony stop and he squirts free.'

'Understood,' Dom said. 'I'll go through the town and wait on the road ahead until I hear back from you.'

Albright said, 'You're armed, right?'

'Negative. I hope he doesn't squirt, because I won't be able to stop him. Good luck.'

'Yep.' Albright hung up.

Albright and his five men traveled three to a vehicle in a pair of identical silver Ford Expeditions. They'd spent the last several minutes racing into and out of nearly a dozen mountain tunnels, where they sped up to over one hundred miles an hour, before slowing back down to fifty when they came out of the tunnels on to the slick roads. This tactic had allowed them to catch up to the fleeing American traitor, and now they could see his vehicle just fifty yards ahead as they entered yet another tunnel.

Albright's driver asked, 'Want to do it in a tunnel or on the open road?'

Albright said, 'Open road. As shitty as the weather is,

462

we can use it to get up on their ass undetected, and use the poor road conditions to help with the stop.'

'Roger that.'

Albright ordered the other Expedition to initiate the stop, so the agent driving the other truck waited until they left the tunnel and he was obscured in the storm, then he began advancing on the target vehicle.

In both Expeditions the men clutched their short-barreled M4 carbines or, in Albright's case, he put his hand on the grip of his SIG pistol in his waistband, and they readied themselves for the high-risk felony stop just a few seconds away.

Ethan Ross had spent the last several minutes with his eyes fixed on Mohammed. The Iranian sat with his phone pressed to his ear almost constantly. He was conferring with someone, it sounded like it was Arabic and not Farsi, but Ross could not be sure.

Ross didn't speak either language, but he had understood one thing Mohammed had said. After several loud, almost angry outbursts, the Iranian said an unmistakable phrase in English.

'Track my iPhone.'

Ross and Bertoli exchanged confused glances.

While Mohammed barked into his mobile phone, the driver of the van looked into the rearview mirror and shouted an alarm. Again Ross had no understanding of what was being said, but he pieced it together when all the Iranians swiveled their heads around and looked behind them. Ross followed suit, and he saw a silver SUV racing up from behind in the left lane.

Ross assumed it was nothing more than a crazy driver ignoring the awful conditions, but the Iranians began reaching for their weapons in their coats.

Ross ducked down in his seat, still keeping his eyes out the window, and still expecting the vehicle to pass. But to his horror the silver SUV merged quickly into the van's lane. The right-front quarter panel of the Ford truck made contact with the left-rear quarter of the van briefly, knocking it gently.

And that was all it took. The driver of the van shouted and Ross realized the man had lost control. The nose of the van angled to the left and the rear tires slid to the right. Soon everyone inside was grabbing on to something or someone, and the van began skating sideways on the two-lane road at over fifty miles an hour. Ross slammed into Bertoli as the van skidded one hundred and eighty degrees; it showed no sign of slowing as it left the road and impacted a guardrail, then scraped along and shot backward.

At the end of the guardrail the van left the road and slid slowly backward down a thirty-foot-long snow-covered hill. It stopped in a drift and teetered, finally tipping over, crashing down on its side in a foot of snow.

Ross ended up on top of Gianna Bertoli in the back of the van. Mohammed and three Quds men were pressed together in front of them, and in the front, the driver and the passenger were still strapped in their seats.

Quickly men clambered over one another to get out through the driver's-side doors. One after another they rolled off the side of the van and they dropped into the snow, taking cover behind the hood and the roof.

Ross heard the back door of the van open behind him, and then he felt hands on his jacket, his belt, and even in his hair. Two men pulled him roughly out and into the snow. He screamed in pain as his hair was wrenched nearly out of the scalp.

For a brief moment he lay alone on his back by the rear of the van. From his position he had a view of the road above him, and he saw two silver Ford Expeditions parked there. Several men appeared; they crouched with rifles pointed down in his direction.

Even though Ross lay on his back, he raised his hands high in the air.

Just then someone grabbed him by his ankles and pulled him around the roof of the van, removing him from the line of fire.

He looked around quickly. Gianna was sitting in the snow with her back against the van's roof. She seemed dazed, and a black-and-blue bruise that covered her right cheek and eye socket told him she'd been injured in the crash of the van.

The Iranian men in the ski jackets were all around. The two who had pulled him around the van joined up with the others; they knelt or squatted low behind the van, and they all held black pistols in their hands. They swiveled their heads back and forth between the road above them and Mohammed, down here behind the van on his knees.

Ross looked at Mohammed now and realized the Iranian was, incredibly, still talking on his telephone.

What the fuck?

Just then he heard the squawk of a bullhorn. 'Ethan Ross! Can you hear me?'

Ross answered instinctively. 'Yes!'

'Tell your men to put down their weapons!'

Ross was confused. He looked around him. MY MEN? 'They aren't *my* men! I'm a prisoner!'

The amplified voice said, 'I want to see guns in the snow, now!'

Bertoli crawled frantically over to Mohammed, grabbing at his arm and pulling the phone away from his ear. 'We must surrender! My friends here in Italy will protect us! Please, don't do anything –'

Mohammed backhanded her with enough force to knock her on to her back, and he kept talking into his phone.

From above, the man with the loudspeaker said, 'I need you to comply immediately or we will be forced to –'

Mohammed shouted something in Farsi, and then, with no hesitation, his six men stepped out on either side of the van and opened fire uphill at the men in the road.

Ross cowered into the fetal position and covered his ears. He closed his eyes. Hot brass ejected from the pistols and landed all around him.

Gunfire from above boomed louder than the pistols.

Within five seconds Ross felt a blow to his head. He opened his eyes and saw that an Iranian had fallen on top of him. He was dead where he fell, his black-clad leg and ski boot lying atop Ross.

A man on the far side of the toppled van dropped to his knees and his pistol tumbled free. He clutched at his throat and Ethan watched as a geyser of blood spurted through his fingers. He let out a garbled cry, and then another spray of blood exploded out the back of his head.

He flopped on to his back in the snow as the men next to him kept firing.

Darren Albright positioned himself at the rear axle of one of the Expeditions, keeping the vehicle between himself and the Iranians shooting. He had his SIG pistol in his hand, but the five HRT men were laying down withering fire on the armed men below.

After thirty seconds of incessant shooting, there was a break in the gunfire. Albright saw that one of the HRT men had been hit, but he'd been dragged back to cover by another agent, and he appeared to be only lightly wounded. The others expertly moved wide on both sides of the road. Albright knew they would try to hit the men below from the flanks simultaneously. He covered their movement with his pistol, ready to lay down fire on anything that appeared from behind the toppled van.

Albright was the first to hear the noise. He cocked his head and looked up to the sky as the faint but unmistakable thumping of a helicopter's rotors filled the air. In this weather the helo was a surreal sound, and within seconds every last member of the FBI Hostage Rescue Team followed Albright's gaze into the sky. The snowfall was heavy and constant; it seemed as if the clouds were no more than twenty feet above the ground.

Albright brought his radio to his mouth. 'That helo does *not* belong to us. Who the fuck is flying in this –'

A blue-and-white helicopter appeared out of the gray soup just over the highway, less than a hundred yards away. It skimmed twenty feet off the road surface and closed on the two SUVs, and it pivoted ninety degrees, revealing an open sliding side door. Figures were visible moving inside. Like something from a nightmare, Albright saw flashes come from the helo's interior, and he heard the quick staccato sounds of automatic gunfire.

The first SUV on the road shook on its chassis as copper-jacketed lead tore through its aluminum skin.

An FBI agent near Albright swung his weapon up toward the new threat, but he immediately spasmed and fell, blood erupting from his legs and lower torso and splattering across the snow-streaked highway.

Albright dove for the deck and shouted into his mike. 'Engage that fucking helo!'

47

A cell of six Hezbollah operators from Lyon, France, sat strapped inside the Eurocopter EC145 that streaked sideways over the snowswept Italian highway. Five men were in the back, firing down on the Americans on the road with their mishmash of automatic weapons, while one man sat in the copilot's seat and held his CZ nine-millimeter pistol to the head of the pilot.

His name was Ajiz, he was the leader of this cell and the oldest at twenty-four, and he had been in near-constant communication with the Iranian Revolutionary Guards officer running this operation for most of the past twenty-four hours.

From the moment Mohammed Mobasheri arrived in Geneva and saw the welcome reception of ITP members, he decided he might need to snatch Ross out of the hands of the ITP to satisfy his mission parameters. To do this, he began planning a way to effect the abduction. He was well aware the weather would be turning bad – the winter storm was all over the news because it was coming so late in the season – but he didn't think he could take Ross overland all the way to the Mediterranean, a five-hour drive.

Mohammed knew he needed a helicopter and a pilot, and with the approaching storm he decided he would need the best pilot available to travel in the miserable winter conditions. He did some Google research the previous afternoon and found a private helicopter rescue company that operated in the area. Their helos were responsible for plucking injured climbers off Mont Blanc, as well as other mountains in the Graian Alps, so he decided they would be best suited to the horrible conditions coming. He ordered the Lyon cell of Hezbollah men to hijack a helicopter and a pilot from the service and to have it meet him on the road outside Geneva.

More research showed Mobasheri that he could mask the flight of the helicopter on radar if it flew low through the Alps, so he made the decision to move the transfer of Ross from the van to the helicopter to somewhere in the Aosta Valley, the nearest suitable location.

The six Hezbollah operatives had arrived at the hangar of Mont Blanc Copter Services at ten o'clock that morning. Flight operations had been canceled because of the snowstorm, but the staff lived on the mountain, so they showed up to do paperwork and routine maintenance. There was no security on the property, just a secretary at a desk, three maintenance men, two pilots, and a receptionist.

Ajiz and his team took the entire staff at gunpoint into an office, where he demanded to know which of the two pilots had more experience. Neither man spoke up, but a photograph on the receptionist's desk told Ajiz what he needed to know. Claudette, the thirty-year-old receptionist, was the daughter of the fifty-six-year-old pilot named Henri. The Hezbollah cell commander knew instantly he could use this to his advantage.

The French pilot told the young Middle Easterners that

they were mad if they thought anyone could fly in such poor visibility.

The honest truth was no one in the Lyon cell wanted to fly in this weather any more than the Frenchman did, but they had their orders from Mohammed, and they knew failing to carry them out would mean a certain death sentence back in Lebanon for themselves and their families.

The French pilot and his daughter were pulled into the hangar and the others were lashed with tie-down chains and locked together in a supply room off the hangar with padlocks from the storage doors. They weren't killed, because Mohammed had passed orders on to Ajiz mandating that he keep them alive. He knew the pilot would need the incentive of believing he would be left alive at the end of the operation.

Killing the others would tip him off that even his total compliance would not save him and his daughter.

Ajiz ordered the pilot to fuel and preflight the largest craft in the hangar, a blue Eurocopter EC 145, then he, his daughter, and the six Hezbollah operators from Lyon rolled it out into the heavy snow on a trailer.

The pilot begged the armed men to reconsider, telling them they would all likely slam into a mountain before they accomplished whatever the hell it was they were planning. Ajiz just strapped in beside him and waved his gun while Claudette was placed in the back in the middle of the rest of the Lyon cell. Ajiz put on his headset and told the Frenchman they would be heading somewhere down in the valley, and he'd provide him more information soon.

The helicopter lifted off into the gray. The pilot used

his instruments and his radar and his GPS to pick his way forward slowly between the peaks of the mountains, certain they were all going to die, but aware he'd saved his colleagues back in the hangar, and desperately trying to come up with a way to somehow save his daughter as well.

The flight was miserable and stressful for all involved, but Ajiz was in comms with Mohammed for most of the flight, and this made things ever more difficult. The pilot flew much slower than Mohammed demanded, but Henri refused to fly faster, even with a CZ pistol jabbed in his neck.

By using a locator app from Mobasheri's iPhone, Ajiz was able to direct the pilot to the van on the road, although the iPhone signal was intermittent as the phone entered and exited tunnels.

When the helo reached an altitude of only twenty-five feet above the highway, the pilot could see both the ground and any wires along the road, and this gave him the confidence to pick up speed.

Mobasheri contacted Ajiz seconds after the van crashed down the hill. He told the Lyon cell leader they were under attack, and he ordered the men in the helo to engage the Americans and the vehicles on the road.

Seconds later the two silver SUVs appeared one hundred yards in front of the helicopter. Ajiz ordered the pilot to turn sideways so the men could shoot out of the side door. Henri feigned trouble with the task, but the butt of an AK-47 rifle to the side of Claudette's head showed him that he needed to comply. As he flew perpendicular to the highway Henri heard the heavy gunfire coming out of the cabin of his aircraft. He ducked down as low as he could, and hoped his daughter would be able to do the same behind him.

A minute earlier, Dominic Caruso raced through the rustic village of Villair as fast as he could without sliding his big bike into the side of a stone house or crashing through a wooden fence. Off his right shoulder and a thousand yards away he could hear the rolling echoes of gunfire from both M4 rifles and handguns, and he hurried to get back on the road and get his own weapon into the fray.

When he was still several hundred yards away from the SS26 he backed off on the throttle for a moment, because he thought he heard a helicopter overhead. It seemed unlikely, impossible really, as there were high hills on both sides of the road here that disappeared into the clouds just feet above his head.

The sound disappeared and he all but dismissed it, but suddenly a new barrage of even more intense gunfire erupted from the site of the FBI traffic stop to the north. It seemed several more guns had entered the fight, and the only explanation Caruso had for it was that somehow the Iranians had managed to show up with reinforcements from the air.

He rolled on to the SS26, turned west toward the gunfight, opened the throttle on his BMW bike, and leaned down behind his little windscreen. He flew headlong through the snowstorm with no idea what he would encounter when he arrived at the battle.

Supervisory Special Agent Darren Albright pressed himself tight against the frozen highway. There was no cover from the helicopter above him, so all he could do was fire on it with his pistol and attempt to make himself as small a target as possible out here in the open.

Another man from the HRT went down just feet away, and bits of road kicked up around him.

The helicopter made a slow pass over the road, still flying sideways. Albright dumped an entire magazine from his pistol at the threat, then he scooped up the fallen tactical officer's rifle. The helo spun around quickly to come back for another pass, and Albright flipped the fire selector switch on the rifle to semi-automatic. He aimed at the tail rotor of the aircraft and squeezed off a carefully aimed round. Then a second, then a third.

After another shot at the tail rotor, Darren knew he had to take cover behind the SUV on his right, because the blue helo was heading right for him. He lowered the rifle and started to run, but out of the corner of his eye he saw a man on the hill by the side of the road. It was one of the men from the van, and Albright spun his rifle toward him just as the gunman got him in the sights of his pistol.

Albright felt the blow to his right shoulder, well above his body armor, and his gun flew out of his hand. A second round hit his vest, but the third shot slammed into his pelvis, breaking it and buckling the FBI man on to the highway. He fell on his back, his eyes to the sky as the helicopter flew directly overhead on another gun run.

Inside the Eurocopter, two of the Lyon cell men were dead, shot by FBI HRT men and still strapped in their seats with their heads bobbing along with the movements of the aircraft. A third man had been hit in the right hand, but he continued firing on the road below with his left hand, until he and the others saw the Iranians move up the hill to the road and walk between the human forms lying still there.

Ajiz ordered the pilot to land, and Henri did as he was told.

As the helicopter touched down, Mohammed Mobasheri climbed to his feet behind the van at the bottom of the hill. He pointed his pistol toward Ethan Ross, who remained on the frozen ground in the fetal position.

'Move!' Mobasheri ordered.

Ethan stood slowly, his hands in the air, and Gianna Bertoli stood up with him. Together they walked up the hill with Mohammed bringing up the rear.

The French pilot looked to Ajiz while they sat parked on the highway. Through his headset he said, 'I want to speak to my daughter.'

'Why?'

'She knows the highway down here. She can help us get away. I only fly up on the mountains.'

Ajiz looked over his shoulder. The woman's wrists were bound with the straps cut from one of the seats, and she was buckled into another seat. There was blood across her face, but it was blood from one of the dead Hezbollah men and not her own. She sat next to a headset on the wall behind her. He motioned with his pistol for her to put the headset on.

She did so, and before she could say anything, Henri

spoke to her in Italian. Henri and his daughter were French, but they both knew Italian. He could only pray the Middle Eastern man next to him did not know the language.

'When we leave I will fly low over the mountains. If you can do it . . . you must get out.'

'But what about you?'

'These men won't let us live. Believe me. I want you to survive. I will try to survive myself, but only if you are safe.'

'I can't leave you –'

He snapped at her. Ajiz glanced at him, but assumed they were arguing about the route through the valley. 'Then we both die today. *Please*, Claudette. You are the one who can give us both a chance.'

Their eyes met, she nodded slightly, and then they discussed the route they would take to the south.

The stretch of SS26 near the idling helicopter was a scattered scene of bodies, blood and damaged vehicles. Four or five civilian vehicles had stopped in each lane; the drivers had missed the shooting and saw merely what they at first perceived to be a horrific automobile accident and a rescue helicopter. The rotor wash of the helicopter blew the already whipping snow into a blinding torrent and added to the chaos and confusion. Only the first car facing in each direction saw the guns and the fact the men standing were doing nothing for the men lying in the road.

The four Quds Force operatives still alive climbed into the helicopter after unfastening the two dead Lebanese men from the Lyon cell and letting their bodies fall out on to the frozen highway.

Ross boarded as ordered. He was shoved into a seat in the back and strapped down.

Mobasheri himself was in the back of the group boarding. As the men loaded up, he realized there would not be enough room for everyone. He pushed past Gianna Bertoli as she tried to board, and she was happy to let him take the final place, thinking he would let her go.

But as soon as he took his seat Mohammed turned to Gianna. Over the booming rotor noise, he shouted, 'Unfortunately for you, I need Ross, and I need these men. I no longer have any use for you or ITP.'

His pistol rose quickly and he shot her through the forehead at a distance of six feet. Her head snapped back, her curly black hair flew over her face, and she dropped on to her back on the highway.

Ross saw the Swiss woman die, he screamed in shock, and the helicopter lifted off into the snow.

48

As Dominic raced to the scene he heard the low-flying helicopter churning the air right over his head. He looked up, but he could make out only a slight lightening in the clouds from the aircraft's running lights as it flew by. He still couldn't imagine how in the hell anyone could get airborne in these conditions.

Within seconds he was driving his bike through the after-effects of the battle. There were bodies lying motionless on the road. He passed the unmistakable form of Gianna Bertoli; she was on her back and snow had already blown across her jacket, dusting it with white.

He found Albright lying on his side by one of the shot-up silver Expeditions. Dom parked the BMW and ran to the man, rolled him on to his back.

Albright was alive, but there was blood everywhere. He'd been shot in the shoulder and the hip; he groaned in agony, but he was conscious. He reached out to grab for his mobile phone, which had been knocked several feet away in the gunfight.

Dom scooped it up and handed it to him. 'Is Ross gone?'

Albright nodded. He grunted in pain again, then said, 'Helicopter.'

'I still hear it. It's heading southwest.'

'Farsi.'

'What's that?'

'They were speaking Farsi. They're Iranians.'

'That figures,' said Caruso.

'We've got to let the Italians know,' Albright said, and groaned.

Dom pulled a med kit out of the closest vehicle and returned to Albright, who was dialing a number on the phone with his bloody fingers.

Dom knelt to treat the man's wounds, but Albright waved him off. 'Check the others first.'

Mohammed Mobasheri was not satisfied with the pilot's performance: they seemed to be flying too slow, though it was difficult to be certain in the near-whiteout conditions.

The Iranian put on a headset and crawled between the Lyon cell men just behind the pilot's seat. 'Go faster!' He looked to Ajiz in the copilot's seat, and the Hezbollah man waved his pistol in the man's face.

The pilot did not seem to notice. He was covered in sweat and his eyes were locked on the multifunction display in front of him, worry evident on his face.

Ajiz, who had been flying alongside the man for a half-hour, noticed a change in the man's behavior.

'What is it?'

'A problem.'

Mohammed held his own pistol to the pilot's head. 'You lie! You will fly this helicopter south. To Genoa.'

The pilot spoke into his mike. 'It's the tail rotor.'

'What is wrong –'

'It's not responding properly.'

Mobasheri screamed at the man. 'No! You are lying!'

He struck the pilot in the head, but the man did not react, so carefully was he watching his gauges. After several more seconds, Henri said, 'It's getting worse!'

Henri did feel an abnormal oscillation in the tail rotor, but he was not, in fact, losing control. He used the opportunity to bank to the right, following the moving map display in front of him to fly along the snowy ridgeline at the top of the valley.

He decreased altitude and lowered his speed. The Middle Easterner next to him screamed at him, and the man between the seats behind him shouted as well, but Henri focused on what he was doing. Just as he arrived at the top of the ridgeline, he shouted into his headset.

'Claudette!'

Behind him, Henri's daughter took her opportunity. She unhooked her seat belt, dove on to the blond-haired man by the back door, then she kicked her legs out over the side. Shiraz recognized what she was doing, he lunged for her, desperate to take hold of any part of her clothing. The coiled wires of his headset pulled tight just as he got his hand on the cuff of her ski jacket, but gravity was stronger than his grip, and she was out of the helicopter, disappearing over the side.

The other men in the back saw the movement, but they were too late to do anything more than lean out over the side and watch her disappear into snowy trees. Her fall was no more than fifty feet, with hundreds of branches to slow her before she hit the powdered drift on the ground.

She would break bones and lie in pain for hours, but she would survive.

Henri turned back around in his seat when he heard the shouting in Farsi. As he turned he prayed he would not see his daughter in the cabin, but at first he could not be sure. He saw nothing but arms and legs and the blurred motion of angry men crawling over one another. More screams in his headset told him the men remained agitated, so he had reason to hope, but he could not see the seats directly behind him. It was possible Claudette had been moved. It was not until the men on the starboard side looked down into the trees below, shock and anger and even some fear registering on their faces, that he knew she had done it.

His beautiful, brilliant, brave daughter had *fucking* done it!

His heart had been pounding in terror unceasingly for the last hour, but now it pounded with a father's pride.

Henri turned back to the windscreen in front, and he flew the helo over the peak, picking up speed as fast as he could. The little winding valley disappeared below him, and these men would never be able to find it again. Claudette was, if not safe, then at least safe from these murderous terrorists.

Now he steeled himself to be as brave as his little girl. He turned to his right and eyed the man called Ajiz, then looked over his shoulder at the little man with the boyish face. They called him Mohammed. He appeared to Henri to be truly the least likely in the group to be in charge of anything, much less these brutes. Mohammed had been focused on the activity in the back. He shouted what were obviously admonitions at his men, only two of whom were wearing headsets and able to hear him.

Now Mohammed stopped talking suddenly, and he spun his head to the pilot.

Henri stared back at him, a thin, determined smile on his lips.

The Iranian's eyes widened. He shouted, *'Non!'*

Henri's smile grew with the terror evident on Mohammed's face. *'Oui,'* he said, grinning now.

Henri turned back to the windscreen, and sucked in a chest full of air, and he slammed the cyclic forward, while pushing the collective to the floor.

The Eurocopter pitched down and dove toward the undulating landscape hundreds of feet below. Mohammed screamed in sheer terror, while Henri closed his eyes and found himself at peace, thinking about how damn lucky he had been to have lived his life in such a beautiful place as this mountain.

Mohammed looked away from the pilot toward a sudden darkness that filled the right half of the windscreen in front of him. A craggy mountain wall was directly in the path of the Eurocopter, a violent jolt from behind told all on board that the tail rotor had struck the rock face. The rotor disintegrated and the helo spun hard to the left. The main rotor dug into trees and the aircraft slammed into a forested hillside and tumbled down.

Dom had found two Americans still alive in addition to Albright, though both men were badly injured. Several cars full of civilians had appeared at the scene with their own medical kits, and they began treating the wounds to the best of their abilities. Caruso had just returned to

Albright and knelt down to help him when he heard a sound to the southeast.

It was far in the distance but unmistakable. It was the low muffled thump of an impact.

The faint but persistent rotor noise of the distant helicopter stopped abruptly.

He stood up quickly and spun toward the noise. 'They crashed! The helo just went down!'

Albright was holding the phone to his ear and gauze against his bloody hip. He'd heard the noise, too. He looked at Caruso. 'Go get that asshole. I can treat myself.'

'You sure?'

Albright shouted now. 'Go!'

The FBI special agent put down his phone and lifted his pistol for Dom to take. But Caruso ignored it. Instead, he scooped up one of the dead HRT member's carbines and dropped the magazine to check the round count. It was fully loaded with thirty rounds, and there was a 3.5-power scope on the rail.

Dom ran back to his motorcycle without another word.

49

Mobasheri found himself facedown with his forehead buried in snow and his body lying on a broken Plexiglas windscreen. He pushed himself up, rising slowly to his knees, and he shook his head to fight the daze from the crash. Looking himself over he saw that his coat was torn the length of the right arm, and he felt a gash above his elbow.

Somehow he had managed to end up outside the torn fuselage of the helo. The wind blew into his face, snow melted in his hair.

At first he thought it was nighttime, the light was poor, but a quick look around showed him the helicopter had come down in a heavy forest on the hillside. High trees blocked off much of the light above.

There was no fire, which surprised Mohammed, but he remembered learning in his brief military training long ago that helicopters' gas tanks are designed to resist puncture and rarely explode like they do in the movies.

His mind recycled back to his mission, and he felt inside his coat for Ross's microdrive. It was there, right in the zipped pocket where he'd left it, so he looked to the left and right searching for Ethan Ross. He found him still strapped into his seat and suspended sideways in the twisting wreckage. Blood dripped off the American's forehead, but his eyes were open and he looked around in confusion, and a wash of relief muted Mobasheri's pain.

The Iranian crawled over to Ross, pushing his way back into the wreckage to get to him. While he moved closer he saw that some of his men were moving, either unbuckling themselves from their seats or already out of the twisted EC145, crawling through the snow.

Others lay limp, arms and legs askew.

Mohammed unfastened the American's harness and Ross slid down a few feet, crumpling slowly into a mass of twisted metal and wires.

'Get up!'

Ross's unfixed eyes and pasty white skin gave Mohammed the impression that mild shock had set in, but he did as he was told. As soon as he put weight on his legs to stand, however, he cried out and dropped back to the ground.

Mohammed looked down and saw plainly that Ross's right leg was broken four inches above the ankle.

The Iranian screamed in frustration. *'Madhar jendeh!' Motherfucker!*

He began calling out to the men around him. He didn't know who was alive and who was dead, and he didn't ask who had been injured or incapacitated. He just ordered his people to drag the American from the wreckage.

When he finally separated himself from the chaos of the interior of the shredded helicopter, he was able to take stock of his situation. He'd lost one of his Quds Force operatives; it was Kashan, and he was hanging upside down in a nearby tree with a branch impaling his lower torso. And one of the Lyon men was caught in the wreckage and near death, unconscious and breathing shallowly.

But three Quds and three Hezbollah remained, including Ajiz, who had also been thrown out the door of the helicopter into the trees but was not badly hurt and had been the first man on his feet.

Mohammed joined Shiraz and Ajiz on the hillside a few feet from the wreckage, and together the three of them surveyed the crash site. The location looked impossibly remote. They were on a steep, forested incline, with no sign of a road or of any man-made structure in any direction, although they could not see very far. They were surrounded by pines, all of which save for the ones involved in the crash site had over a foot of snow on their branches.

As there was no fire, only steam from the hot engines' contact with the snow threatened to reveal their position, and since the storm continued and the isolated hillside was completely enshrouded in clouds, Mohammed thought it likely the wreckage would stay hidden until the sky cleared.

Mohammed trudged and climbed to get around to the front of the helicopter, where he looked through the windscreen. The pilot was alive but bloodied and badly wounded, half buried under snow and earth and the front of the helo.

It was no matter, Mohammed didn't need him anymore.

Ross was the big problem. He ordered two of his men to heave the American out of the snow and move him. He told them – in Farsi, of course – that he didn't care if the man was in agony, he just needed to get out of the area.

Three minutes after impact, Mohammed, his men and his prisoner were moving away from the crash site, albeit painfully slowly. Before he himself left the scene, Mobasheri walked back over toward the pilot, drawing his pistol as he did so.

The Frenchman knew about Genoa, so he had to die.

Dominic raced his bike to the southwest for almost ten minutes, making the transition to smaller and smaller roads as he progressed up into the rugged foothills of the Italian Alps. He passed through the town of Pondel, but it was virtually deserted, and other than a smell of wood smoke and a few cars in front of a local market he detected no signs of life. He spent a minute skidding and sliding on snow-covered streets as he tried to pick his way through the village toward the location of the impact, but soon he was progressing again into the forest.

He was doing little more than guessing where he was going, but it was an educated guess. He based the location of the crash on the direction in which the helo was traveling when it flew over him, as well as the general location of the sounds of the crash.

The road ended at a sheer hiking trail, and Dom revved the engine on the big street bike and launched up the trail, but after no more than twenty yards or so he realized this had not been one of his better ideas. He spun out on the first turn, lost his balance, and fell ungracefully off the bike and into the low brush by the trail.

He decided to leave the bike behind, so he ripped his

helmet off his head and began running upward, the M4 rifle still hanging off his back.

He followed the winding trail, sucked the thin cold air, fighting the desire to slow or to rest, even for a moment. The trail led him to the south, but he felt like he was veering away from where he had heard the crash. Just as he stopped to consider changing directions, he heard the distinctive report of a pistol firing a single round.

Dom left the trail and began climbing through the trees, following the direction of the gunshot.

Mobasheri and his entourage traveled through the woods for several minutes, first uphill, but once they made it through a tiny forested draw, they saw a narrow valley in front of them. It was below the low-hanging clouds, and they could look out a few hundred yards before everything faded to white.

In the near distance, maybe two hundred yards from where they stood in the draw, one of Mohammed's men noticed a cluster of slate rooftops, barely visible in the vapor and snow. They set out for them immediately, Mohammed leading the way.

Behind them, far away on the other side of the valley, sirens blared as emergency vehicles roamed the roads looking for a downed helicopter that had been reported by locals.

Once they were down the hill and in the bottom of the valley, thick pine trees obscured their view for some time, and Mohammed could only guess if he was going in the right direction. But the slow-moving procession came out of the trees on to a one-lane paved road; then they followed it as it wound around.

Finally, Mohammed saw a chalet through a quick break in the snowfall and he thought it was a gift from Allah. It looked like the winter cabin for a wealthy family, but there were no signs that anyone was home at present.

He said, 'There! We go there!'

Shiraz kicked in a ground-floor window, crawled through, and then opened a side door for the others. It was a small house, but the open-concept floor plan meant the entire downstairs was one large room.

The home was very modern for a mountain chalet, with electric lighting, new appliances, and a desk in the corner with a large-screen Mac computer.

Mohammed posted two of the Hezbollah men outside as security, and he ordered his three Quds officers to help the hobbled and dazed Ethan Ross to a chair in front of the fireplace. Once Ross was in the chair, Mohammed took Ajiz to the far side of the room.

'The American is slowing us down. I don't need him, I need the password in his head. As soon as I get it, we are leaving.'

'There were some other buildings up the road. I can go look for a vehicle.'

'Do that.'

After Ajiz left the chalet, Mohammed pulled his own chair up in front of Ross. The American was in agony, his broken leg was swollen and throbbing, and it was sickening for Mohammed to look at.

Mohammed took the microdrive out of his coat and

handed it to Shiraz. He put it in an SD adapter and plugged it into the port of the computer on the desk. He brought up the password-protection screen of the crawler database, and then he looked to his commander from the Revolutionary Guards.

Mohammed, in turn, looked at Ethan. 'Let's not waste time. You know what I need. Provide me with the password to the encrypted files, and we will leave you right here. You will be safe.'

Ross wiped tears from his face with the cuff of his coat. He shook his head weakly.

Mohammed put his foot above Ross's broken leg, and he held it there. 'I can't take you with me. Even if we find a car we won't make it out of the country carrying a wounded American with us. I am out of options. I either get the password right now, or . . .' Mohammed put his shoe on Ross's foot. 'Actually, there is no other choice.' He pressed down, and Ross began to scream and thrash on the chair.

Mohammed called two of his men over. Ormand and Isfahan stepped behind Ross and they held him in place, twisting his arms behind his back to do so.

Ross screamed in agony, but Mohammed shouted over him. 'Give me the password and it stops!'

'I can't do it!' he shouted, hysterical from the pain.

Mohammed took his foot off the broken bones and sat back in the chair for a moment. 'You are stronger than I anticipated.' With a shrug, he said something in Farsi. Shiraz rushed into the kitchen. He found a bottle of red wine and, after conferring with Mohammed for a moment, he shattered the end of the bottle against the stove. Wine poured on to the floor, and the broken, jagged-edged bottle emptied. He brought it over to the living area and handed it to Mohammed, before returning to the computer at the desk.

Ross's eyes rounded in fear and tears dripped to the floor as he shook his head back and forth. His voice was just a whimper. 'Please, no. God, please, no.'

Mohammed sat in front of him with the broken bottle.

'I know something about pain, Mr Ross. The broken leg hurts, but the shin is not a major nerve center, and the swollen tissue provides a very slight numbing effect on the area that works against my interests.

'Unfortunately for you, I have seen torture firsthand. My father was something of an expert. He was trained by the state, but he was not above practising on his children.' When Mohammed smiled, he looked insane to Ethan, especially in light of what he'd just said. 'I know that which is most effective.'

He addressed the men behind Ross. 'Stand him up, and lower his trousers.'

'No!' Ross screamed.

The men did as instructed. Ross could put weight only on his left leg, but he thrashed, desperate to pull free of the two men behind him. But his struggle was in vain. After a half-minute he stood there with his trousers and underwear down at his ankles, and Mohammed in front of him with the crude torture device in his hand.

'Physically and psychologically, what I will do to you now is the worst that can be done to a man. My father never did this to me.' He smiled, but his eyes were narrow as he thought of his past. 'But he threatened it more than once. Only the suggestion was necessary. I did what was asked of me. And now you can do the same. You can avoid this very easily. Just take a moment and think about how unfortunate it would be for you if I shred your genitals, and *then* you reveal the password. That would be an unnecessary waste, would it not?'

Ethan began sobbing, and Mohammed sighed in exhausted frustration.

50

Caruso never saw the wreckage of the helicopter. He passed it in the trees fifty yards on his right, but as he climbed through the woods he came across the tracks of several men, along with streaks of blood in the snow, and he followed the tracks into a draw between two hilltops. Here not only could he look out into a small valley, but he could also see that Ross and his entourage had done the same, as the tracks and bloodstains indicated they had paused here.

Dom used the scope of his rifle to scan a row of roofs he saw in the distance. They looked like chalets arranged in the woods along a road, but he could see nothing more than that. He thought it likely the Iranians holding Ross would head for the buildings in hopes of finding transportation out of the area, and the prospect of them getting away forced Caruso to pick up the pace. He all but ran down the hill, into the trees and toward the road, and while he did so he attempted to call Adara. He was not terribly surprised to find he had no service here, so he pocketed his phone and told himself he was the only one between the Iranians and their complete and unfettered access to the intelligence scrape.

It took Caruso just a few minutes to arrive at the road, and he crossed it carefully, then entered the trees to approach the first chalet unseen.

The trees ended just twenty yards from the side of the house, but Dom stayed back another twenty-five yards to remain deep within the tree line. He saw a man sitting on the steps in the front of the wooden building with a Kalashnikov resting on his knees. He was olive-complexioned, wearing a gray ski jacket and blue jeans, and he looked young and fit, but from the way he handled his weapon, not terribly well trained. Dom had seen the men around Ross, and this guy was definitely not part of that crew.

Part of the reinforcements from the helo, Dom guessed.

He got eyes on the second sentry just seconds later. The man held an HK MP5 submachine gun, and he stood out of the wind, squatting next to a woodpile facing the woods behind the house.

Dom moved to a position where he could see into a large window on the side of the house near the driveway. He used his rifle's scope to peer inside the chalet. The lights were on and through the 3.5 magnification afforded him by the ACOG battle sight on the rail of the M4, he could see one of the men sitting at a computer screen at a desk. To his left was movement. Dom shifted his focus to it, and there in front of him was Ethan Ross.

The American was being held up by two men, they had his arms up high behind him in a stress position. His trousers were down to his ankles.

Dom withdrew his eye from the scope in surprise.

Focusing again, he saw another subject, this man stood in front of Ross and spoke to him – from his animated demeanor, Dom thought the man might have been shouting.

This man Dominic recognized. He'd seen him on the veranda of the Venezuelan safe house in Panama.

And then he saw what was happening. The Iranian held a broken bottle in his right hand. Low at Ross's crotch.

'Oh, God,' Caruso muttered.

Caruso quickly shifted his rifle to position it next to the thin trunk of a pine, then he used his forearm to make a solid shooting platform, nesting the rifle in the crook of his arm and holding the pine with his left hand. He placed the red chevron reticule in his scope on the small man's forehead.

Dom realized that as soon as he fired a single round, the two men outside, right in front of him really, would know he was here, and they would be able to engage him from two directions.

Shit, Dom thought. He found himself at a ridiculous tactical disadvantage. All his training told him to back into the trees and disengage, but he knew he didn't have that option.

He had to end this, even though he had a strong suspicion that the moment he fired his rifle, shit would start to go wrong.

Mohammed stepped forward with the broken wine bottle.

Ethan screamed; spit shot from his mouth and snot dripped from his nose.

'No! Please, no!' Sobbing, he said, 'I will tell you!'

'What is the password?'

'I will tell you when we get to Iran.'

Mohammed shook his head. 'Our journey together

must end now, Ethan. That is my decision. You only get to decide if you will live, or if you will keep your manhood.'

'I have other information. Get me to Iran and I will tell you –'

Mobasheri shook his head. 'You have no power to negotiate, because I know you will tell me what I need.' He slipped the broken wine bottle between Ethan's legs.

Caruso held his finger on the trigger, but he did not fire. He took his eye out of the scope again and counted off targets. He saw six in total. Two outside, and four inside. If he shot the man with the broken bottle he could quickly engage the two men outside, maybe he'd get both of them, maybe he'd get only one. Even if he got both, however, that would still leave two men inside with Ross, and there was no way in hell they wouldn't be ready if Dom came in after them.

They still had access to Ethan, so they still had access to his information.

From fifty yards away he heard a bloodcurdling scream. He quickly looked back into the scope and saw the Iranian torturing Ross with the bottle.

Quickly he lined the reticule up on his target's head. He took a full breath and blew it out halfway.

And then he pressed the trigger.

Mohammed leaned into Ethan's face while he cut, screaming at him to talk.

Ethan did talk. Through frantic cries he shouted, 'I'll tell you!'

496

Mohammed pulled the bottle away, and just as he did Ross lunged forward at him, yanked out of the restraining arms behind him, tumbled on to Mohammed, and knocked him to the floor.

Mobasheri thought Ethan was attacking him, but as he landed on his back on the wood floor he felt the hot blood splashing on his face. It dripped into his eyes. He had no idea what was going on, he knew Ross's hands hadn't come up when he lunged forward, so he thought maybe the American had somehow managed to bite him.

The three other men in the room began shouting in Farsi and Arabic, the shouts garbled and panicked.

Mohammed brought the broken bottle up to strike Ross with it, but instead he scrambled out from under the American on the floor, pushed him to the side, and saw the incredible amount of blood covering both men.

Ross's eyes were wide open.

Only then did the words shouted by his men make sense.

'Sniper!'

Ross was dead. Shot through the back of the head. How the bullet had not penetrated all the way through and killed Mobasheri as well he had no idea.

The crackle of automatic weapons fire erupted outside at both the front and the back of the chalet. Mohammed dropped back to his hands and knees, rushed over to the computer on the desk, and retrieved the microdrive and the adapter. He stuffed them into his jacket and ran low and fast for the front door.

*

Dom had called it – shit went wrong almost immediately. After he shot Ethan Ross in the head, determining it to be the least worst option, he'd pivoted to get an angle on one of the men outside the house. Just as he lined the man up in his sights, gunfire from the other sentry tore through the trees just feet above Dom's head. Dom shot the man with the AK dead at the front door, but the man in back with the MP5 had impressive aim, and branches all around Dom began snapping off trees. He dropped to the ground, nine-millimeter bullets coming so close he felt the over-pressure of them as they parted the cold air near his face.

He all but buried himself in the snow until the man stopped to change his magazine. Dom rose to his knees and fired several rounds at the man with the MP5, striking him in the stomach and knocking him into the snow. By now someone else was firing, and Dom thought it might be coming from the kitchen window. He turned and crawled through the trees for fifty feet or so, rose and aimed his rifle at the house behind him. He squeezed off three rounds without having a target in his sights in an attempt to make some noise and slow down anyone coming after him.

His gunfire was met with multiple weapons chattering back in his direction, and he hit the ground again and then crawled for cover.

Mohammed Mobasheri stood in the doorway to the chalet. One Hezbollah man from the Lyon cell lay dead in front of him, shot multiple times in the chest. Isfahan had already leapt off the porch and started to run off after the retreating sniper, but Mohammed stopped him with a shout. He didn't want his small team to split up; there would be a lot more police crawling around here soon enough, and he knew they needed to be gone by then.

His entire operation had been derailed by the bullet to the back of Ethan Ross's head. He had been making quick changes to his plan since the moment he stepped off the plane in Washington last week, and he'd rolled with the punches, but he'd never anticipated losing any chance to obtain the password from Ross.

All he could do at this point was to get himself back to Iran with the microdrive full of CIA intelligence, and leave it to machines to crack the encryption. He'd been told it might take months or even years to do this with brute-force computer decryption techniques, but now that the only other option was lying dead on the floor in the house behind him, he saw no choice but to escape from Europe with the drive and begin the arduous process.

Ajiz rolled up the short driveway behind the wheel of a red Mercedes 4Matic SUV. Mohammed ordered everyone into the vehicle, and Ajiz remained at the wheel. As they pulled out of the drive of the chalet, leaving Ross's body behind, Mohammed began programming the GPS in the car to get them out of these fucking hills and down to Genoa as fast as possible.

It took Dom a minute or two to realize it, which was understandable, considering his focus had been on not getting shot, but soon he came to the conclusion there was no one chasing him through the trees.

He stumbled back out on to a road, ran across to the

other side, and then dove into a small gully. He swung the black M4 around and scanned the way from which he had just come. Through his scope, through the trees on the other side of the road, he saw a red SUV – it looked like one of those boxy Mercedes – pulling up the driveway of the chalet. He couldn't see people at this distance, even through the scope, so he knew he wouldn't be shooting at the vehicle. His chest heaved and vapor shot out of his mouth in cadence with his panting. He forced himself to hold his breath so he could listen for the telltale sounds of pursuit, but he heard nothing more than the hiss of snowfall and the whine of a drifting wind through the pines. In the distance the singsong sirens of emergency vehicles came and went. They sounded like they were a half-mile away or more, nowhere in this valley, and Dom thought it likely they hadn't even made it to the site of the helicopter crash.

He took a moment to dial Adara again, keeping his eyes peeled while he did so. There was no service. He fought an urge to throw his fucking phone into the snow, but instead he just jammed it back into his jacket and continued to scan and heave while he lay there on his chest.

He'd killed Ethan Ross, that was just now sinking in. He didn't think he'd had much of a choice, and considering what Ross had in store for him at the hands of the Iranian with the broken bottle, Dom felt he'd done the bastard a favor. He'd say a bullet to the brain was more than the American NSC man deserved, but he'd realized at some point in this entire affair that Ethan Ross, though responsible for the deaths of the Yacobys, was little more than a bit player in the entire event.

A fool in over his head.

He didn't feel bad about killing the American traitor, but he didn't feel as great about it as he thought he would when he had been seeking vengeance.

Dom wondered what the Iranians would do now. He didn't think Ross had given them the decryption key before he died. If he had it seemed unlikely they would have taken the time during their escape to break into a house just to cut up their prisoner's genitalia. No, they were torturing him for the password. But just because they didn't have it, brute-force decryption – plugging the encrypted drive into a computer, then throwing tens of millions of possible passwords at it – was also an option. It would be time-consuming, but Dom knew, with enough time and effort, Iranian intelligence could still penetrate the breach and reveal its secrets.

Caruso also knew enough about intelligence and counter-intelligence to know that the CIA would have to operate under the assumption that all the data on the drive had been compromised. This would result in operations stopping cold, profitable ties with agents being severed, facilities closed and moved, and case officers recalled. It would be a disaster even if the breach was never actually fully exploited by the opposition.

The red SUV backed out of the chalet and sped off in the opposite direction.

Dom stood and climbed out of his one-piece motorcycle suit. It was restricting his movement, and he knew he was going to have to run. The bike was somewhere back in the valley, a quarter of a mile in the opposite direction. Wearing only a pair of jeans and a sweatshirt, he hefted his gun and sprinted back across the street. He was outnumbered by at least five to one, but he saw no alternative – he had to go after the drive.

As he ran, he heard the voice of Arik Yacoby in his head.

'C'mon, D. Soldier on.'

51

Dominic made it to the chalet a minute after the Iranians left, but he kept running. He considered looking for a landline phone inside, but he knew if he didn't find one the Mercedes would be long gone in the time it took him to check. He sprinted first through the yards of the other winter chalets on the winding street, and then on the snow-covered paved road. He knew it would be impossible to catch up with the fleeing vehicle, but without an intelligent plan, action seemed like his only recourse.

On the other side of the first bend in the road, just a hundred yards or so beyond the chalet where Ethan Ross's body now lay, he saw that the thick trees gave way to a wide-open windswept hill alongside the road. He was able to look out here over the valley, and he thought it possible he might get a sat phone signal here as well. Just as he reached for the phone tucked into his waistband, the earpiece in his ear chirped. He took the call by touching it.

'Adara?'

'Yeah, it's me. I've been calling you for a half-hour! Where are you?'

'In Italy. In some mountains. That's about all I know.'

'Well, I'm en route, so if you can be more precise, call me back. In the meantime, I can conference you in with the deputy chief of CIA station Milan. He's been working the phones dealing with your situation for twenty or thirty minutes, but he needs to talk to you.'

Dominic was winded from running and talking at the same time, but he kept running and said, 'Put him through.'

There was a full minute of nothing on the line. Dom caught another look over the valley and noticed the road ahead wound back and forth in a series of tight switchbacks to maximize the number of little vacation chalets the developers here could cram on the hillside. Dom left the road, ran between a pair of wooden cabins on his left, then started tearing down a forested hill, hoping he could catch up to the Mercedes by running straight down the hill.

Suddenly a booming and annoyed-sounding voice came into his ear. 'Who's this?'

'Deputy Director, I'm an FBI special agent involved in the Intelink-TS counterintelligence case in Geneva. Are you aware of the situation?'

'Yes. I spoke with the woman who patched me through to you. I know *what* you are, I am asking for your name.'

'I'm afraid I can't give you that.'

'Why the hell not?'

Dom kept running. He stumbled over a bicycle buried in the snow in the backyard of a chalet, but in seconds he was up and running again, speaking between pants as he reached the next paved stretch of the switchback road and continued across it. 'Look, my name is Jones. Will that work?'

'No, it won't. FBI doesn't mask their identity, so that tells me you aren't from the Bureau. Before we go any further, I need to know who you work for.'

'If you need to know who I work for, then we won't be going any further.'

There was a pause. Dom covered twenty yards before the man spoke again. 'You're one of those, huh?'

'I'm the only guy who knows what the hell is going on over here, so that might be good for something.'

The DCOS took a moment, but finally he said, 'Okay. I understand you are in pursuit of Ross and an unknown group of actors.'

Dom shook his head while he ran. 'Ross is dead. Iranian intelligence officers have his data. I don't know if they have the decryption key they need to get into it, but I'm sure they have the drive itself. They are in a red Mercedes SUV heading south.'

'Shit. What's your location?'

'I'm about a half to three-quarters of a mile south of where the helo went down. That was a couple of miles south of the SS26 highway. Does that help you?'

'Yes, I know where the local emergency crews are responding to the crash. I've got some help on the way to you.'

'Agency help?'

'Negative. I'm in Milan and I have no armed assets close. I'm sending you U.S. Army help. It turns out a group from the 173rd Airborne Brigade Combat team is in your AO right now. They are based in Vicenza, but a rifle platoon is doing some alpine training in the foothills south of the SS26. I was able to get routed right through to their CO, and he ordered them to load into trucks and head in your direction. I'll call them back and tell them about the Mercedes coming down the road.'

Dom slowed, then started walking. He couldn't believe his luck. 'A platoon of infantry! Are you kidding? That's perfect.'

'Well, not exactly perfect. There is *one* problem.'

'What's the problem?' As far as he was concerned, they could wrap this up in minutes.

The deputy COS began explaining the situation, and before he finished talking, Dom had broken into a frantic sprint once again. He continued down the hill as fast as he could.

Twenty-three-year-old First Lieutenant D. J. Dower slammed his radio back in its cradle in the cab of the truck and ordered his driver to make a hard left at the next intersection. The whiteout conditions that they'd experienced earlier in the day had improved greatly, but he could still barely see the turnoff that led up the hill toward the neighborhood of luxury chalets to the north.

Dower still wasn't quite sure what the hell was going on, but he did know that whatever it was, it was 'real world' and not part of their training.

And D. J. Dower had never done *anything* 'real world.'

He and his platoon had been eating chow over a campfire in their bivouac after a long morning of training when he was contacted by a colonel at U.S. Army Garrison Vicenza, told to leave all their gear except their small arms, load up into their three M939 five-ton trucks, and move out to the south. Ten minutes later, just after they were on the road, a second radio call came through, this by a man patched through from Vicenza. He gave no information about himself, but he asked Lieutenant Dower about the number of troops in his platoon, and then told him there was a national security situation in his AO.

Dower didn't get it. The area he was heading for was wild snow-covered hills and fancy vacation villas. This wasn't exactly western Pakistan.

The unidentified man on the brigade network channel told the lieutenant that he and his men would have to move as a blocking force to stop a red Mercedes SUV descending one of the hills just south of their location.

D. J. Dower coughed nervously. 'Uh, be advised, we have no live ammunition.'

'I understand that. You are going to have to improvise.'

Dower looked at his first officer, behind the wheel, who just looked back at him. After a moment the lieutenant said, 'Improvise with what, sir?'

'Son, you'll have to be scary. You've got thirty-four armed and uniformed soldiers. That's an imposing sight. Make the most out of it.'

'Yes, sir,' Dower said. 'The occupants of the Mercedes. Are they armed?'

'Heavily. Not going to sugarcoat it, son. I'm throwing you in a shitty situation.'

A second radio call from the same man two minutes later pinpointed an intersection at the bottom of a high hill. A winding road through a field led away from the intersection and up into the trees, where it snaked back and forth for several miles around entire neighborhoods of small but luxurious wood chalets.

Dower ordered the trucks to stop and to block the entire intersection, and then he gave the order over his radio for everyone to dismount.

Bravo platoon's M4 carbines and M249 light machine guns all wore BFAs, blank firing adapters. They were screw-on bright red metal plugs that attached to the muzzles of their rifles so that the low-pressure blank rounds would properly cycle the weapons.

With the BFAs in place, all thirty-four guns could fire loud blanks that made them sound like they were lethal weapons. But with the BFAs in place, all thirty-four firearms were obviously nothing more than nonlethal props. The red plugs were visible at one hundred yards.

As they moved into position, Dower told his men that their assignment was to stop a carload of armed opposition from escaping. He was certain every single one of the thirty-four men with him said some sort of a curse. Most cussed loud enough to be heard, and the rest just bitched under their breath. And the first lieutenant couldn't say he blamed them. They were pissed at him for the order he gave, and he was pissed at the man who gave him the order.

Nevertheless, Dower and his men would do their job.

They spread out in front of the trucks, and Dower had to shout to be heard. 'Everybody with an M4, I want you in a cordon on the road with me. The six of you that have LMGs, I want you on overwatch on that rise behind the trucks. Out of view from the road.'

The Bravo LMG operator, a nineteen-year-old Hispanic American named Chacon, said, 'Overwatch, sir?'

'Yeah. We'll take our BFAs off so we look legit. If the

bad guys start shooting at us, I want all six of you rocking full auto with the LMGs. All we've got is attitude and noise, so we're going to use as much of both as we can.'

Dower knew his only chance was for the armed men heading his way to consider their situation hopeless, because if they decided to fight, Dower and his men were pretty much dead. Quickly he and his men unscrewed their BFAs from their rifles and hid them in cargo pockets. Then they waited on the frigid road, all eyes up the hill.

52

The red Mercedes SUV appeared out of the forest, two hundred yards away. It continued down the hill for several seconds, as if the driver did not see three five-ton trucks parked in the middle of the two-lane road with more than two dozen infantrymen holding weapons high in the air. But finally the driver realized his predicament, and he slid to a stop fifty yards from the roadblock.

Then he just sat there, parked in the middle of the road. Dower stood front and center in the roadblock, closest to the SUV. He felt like a matador staring down a bull.

His first officer stood just behind him. He shouted to his platoon, 'That's right, men! Guns high and pissed-off faces. Nobody fucks with Third Platoon!'

After twenty seconds, the Mercedes backed up and turned around. It started racing up the road.

Dower said, 'LMGs . . . Give them something to run from!'

All six light machine-gunners fired their weapons fully automatic. Even though blank rounds weren't quite as loud as actual live ammo, it sounded real enough. The incredible noise bounced off the tree line, and Lieutenant Dower knew the men in the Mercedes would think they were taking fire from behind.

The red vehicle disappeared into the forest up the hill.

Dower's Charlie squad leader asked, 'We ain't chasin' it, are we?'

Dower didn't know for sure, he hadn't been given instructions on what to do if the armed men retreated, but he wasn't going to let his men see any indecision. 'Fuck, yeah, we are! Load up!'

Dom was exhausted. He'd covered well over a mile, almost all of it downhill in deep snow.

He'd fallen on his face a half-dozen times, but still he ran like hell. He knew the men on the road somewhere below him were essentially defenseless, and they would be going up against several armed and motivated killers. Dom had a loaded weapon, he just needed to bring it to the fight before it was too late.

He stumbled down on to the wet blacktop – this was the fifth switchback he'd crossed – and just as he started crossing the road he heard several fully automatic light machine guns firing somewhere down in the valley. His heart sank, worrying the men were firing blanks against a half-dozen trained Iranian operatives.

But right when he got to the middle of the road, racing to the snow on the other side, the red Mercedes SUV squealed around the turn on his left, heading up toward him.

He was only seventy feet away.

The driver saw him. Dom was just a man in jeans and a sweatshirt and dark hair and a beard, but he held an American carbine rifle in his hand. The Mercedes accelerated, Dom swung his rifle toward the threat, flipped the fire selector switch to fully automatic, and blasted the SUV as it neared.

He saw the windshield explode and the metal hood rip with pockmarks of bullet holes, and smoke and steam spray out from shredded hoses in the engine compartment, but the vehicle kept coming. Dom dove off the road and tumbled into the snow, just barely missing the grille as it passed.

He rolled to his knees and opened fire on the Mercedes from behind, but after a few rounds his gun clicked.

He was out of ammo.

The SUV launched off the road and went airborne, then slammed into a tall pine tree, shaking hundreds of pounds of snow free and sending it crashing down on to the roof of the red vehicle.

Dom leapt to his feet, the adrenaline of the moment overtook his exhaustion, and he ran to the crash.

Mohammed Mehdi Mobasheri opened the front passenger-side door and rolled out into the snow. He was covered in blood, but he knew it came from Ajiz in the driver's seat. The Lebanese Hezbollah cell leader from Lyon had taken a round to the throat and another to the forehead, and now the entire front seat of the Mercedes was as red as the exterior paint job.

Lying stunned in the cold snow, Mohammed first felt for Ethan Ross's microdrive. It was right where he had left it inside his jacket. Then he got his hands around the pistol in his waistband and pulled it free.

Behind him he heard a shout, then a series of grunts and impacts. Men in hand-to-hand combat, just feet from where he lay. He pushed up to his hands and knees, and began swinging the pistol around to aim it at the threat, but just as his gun found a man in its sights, the man kicked at the pistol, knocking it out of Mohammed's hand and up into the air. It landed somewhere in the snow far behind him.

A bearded man with wild eyes grabbed Mohammed by the collar of his jacket and lifted him, threw him on to the hood of the Mercedes. The Iranian looked around for support from his Quds men, but through the smashed windshield he saw Shiraz dead in the car, and Isfahan on the ground in the snow.

'Where is the scrape?' The man spoke English. That was no surprise, although the fact he was alone, and seemingly unarmed, did seem peculiar.

'Where is the *fucking* scrape?' The man shouted, then he slammed Mohammed's head into the hood. The young Revolutionary Guards officer started to reach into his jacket, but the American grabbed his wrist and reached into the pocket instead. He pulled out the drive and looked at it.

'Is this it?'

Mobasheri nodded.

'This is all of it?'

Another nod. Mohammed closed his eyes. He had failed.

'Everybody had to die for this little thing?'

Mohammed opened his eyes, eyeing the strange man curiously. He said, 'Yes. They did. Of course. We are at war with the West.' He shrugged a little. 'You just do not know it.'

*

Dominic Caruso wrapped his strong hands around the thin man's neck, and he started to squeeze. He knew he could strangle him easily, he could do it as quickly or as slowly as he wanted. And he thought he might do just that. The rage in him – pushing out through the exhaustion, outlasting the cold and the pain, overwhelming the sadness of the loss of those who did not survive – the rage was a pure and powerful force, and Dom almost gave in to it.

As he tightened his grip he heard a rumbling noise. At first he thought it was the Iranian's throat emitting a low gurgle as his windpipe was crushed. He ignored it for a moment, concentrating on his task, and soon three large U.S.-Army-green trucks pulled up behind him and stopped. Men leapt out and ran over, they enveloped the scene, checking the dead and wounded, pulling men out of the car and securing weapons.

All through it, Dom kept the pressure up on the small man's neck. The Iranian was turning blue in the face, his mouth was open, and his fat tongue poked out an inch.

Dom watched him with fascination for a moment. He wondered how long it would take for him –

'Sir?'

– to die.

'Sir?'

Dom relaxed his grip. The Iranian on the hood of the Mercedes sucked in a desperate chest full of air.

'Sir?'

Dom turned around. An African American first lieutenant stood with his rifle pointing at him.

'Step away!'

Dom said, 'You're gonna shoot me with your blanks?'

The young officer said, 'If you know we've got blanks, you must be one of the good guys.'

Dom shrugged and let go of the Iranian's neck. 'Yeah. I guess I am.'

'Sir, we are ordered to secure this scene.'

Dom nodded distractedly. Then said, 'Good. Start by securing this little fucker. He might have weapons on him. I suggest you strip him down to nothing and hog-tie him. He's a hell of a lot more dangerous than he looks.'

'Yes, sir.'

Dower ordered his men to take the still gasping man off the hood of the SUV and cut his clothes off with their combat knives. They pulled him into the street, and Mohammed screamed in terror while they went to work on him.

Dom took Dower away from the rest of the group. Sirens in the distance seemed to grow by the second.

'I'm FBI,' Dom said, but he offered no identification. 'Here's the deal, Lieutenant. In a few minutes half of Italy is going to be here. I need to be gone when that happens. It wouldn't hurt if you and the prisoner were gone, too.'

The young junior officer just nodded.

Dom reached into his pocket and handed him the microdrive. 'This little thing is what all this is about. That's all you need to know. A guy from CIA is going to show up at your barracks at Vicenza pretty soon. Hell, he might beat you back there. He's going to want you to hand this over. If you do that, you and your platoon probably have some pretty big attaboys coming your way. If you lose it, your career is over.'

Dower's hand closed over the device.

'Take the prisoner back, too. If I take him with me, he'll turn up in a shallow grave, and he might be worth something to somebody.'

'We'll take him.' Dower looked around at the dead bodies. 'Can I ask who those men are?' He hesitated, still looking at the bodies in the snow. 'I mean . . . who they *were*?'

Dom shrugged. This young man and the others had just risked their lives. They deserved some information about what this was all about. 'They are all Iranian spies. They've killed innocent people on four continents in the past week. And today, you boys stopped them.'

Dower's chest heaved with pride. But even so, he said, 'I do believe *you* stopped them, sir.' He smiled. 'But I'm not going to deny we might have helped a little bit.'

Dom smiled, slapped the young man on the shoulder, turned, and headed back into the trees.

Epilogue

Adara Sherman picked Caruso up twenty minutes later from the driveway of an unoccupied mountain chalet. Dom had been hiding behind a woodshed as Italian police cars raced by, but when she arrived he ran across the driveway, climbed into her rented BMW, then laid himself gingerly in the passenger seat and lowered it flat.

Adara had the BMW turned around and leaving the area again in seconds.

They passed dozens more emergency vehicles rolling through the valley, they even heard a helo in the air, though the weather was likely still below minimums. Adara concentrated on the road, but after only a few minutes of rolling in silence, Sherman looked down at Dom and thought he might have passed out.

Adara said, 'Caruso? Caruso? Talk to me. Are you injured?'

Dom just nodded slowly.

Her eyes widened. 'You're hit? Where are you hit?'

'I'm going to need you to evaluate me. See how bad it is.'

'Okay. I'm pulling over.'

'No. Keep going. We'll get out of here, back on the highway, head back to the northwest.'

'You sure you can hang on?'

Dom nodded. Coughed a little. His eyes closed.

'Just keep talking to me, okay?'

'I'll . . . I'll try.'

They drove for a full minute before Adara said, 'When you came up to the car on the drive, I didn't think you were hurt. You looked tired, yeah, but not wounded.'

'It's bad, Sherman. I told you.'

'Okay,' she said. Then, 'Where, exactly, were you hit? I don't see blood.'

Dom fought a little smile now. Adara missed it. 'Look. You're the medic, not me. You'll have to check me out. There's a hotel I passed on the way down. It looked really nice. A steak restaurant off the lobby. I say we check in for the night, order a couple of bottles of champagne.' One of Dom's eyes cracked open and looked over at Adara quickly, then it closed again. 'For medicinal purposes, only, of course.' He coughed, making a show of it now. 'And then you give me a complete physical.'

Now both eyes opened slowly, and he found Adara behind the wheel, staring down at him. A little smile crossed her lips, but she seemed to be fighting it.

'You're an asshole. You had me worried.'

Dom said, 'It's about ten more miles. Near the border.' He smiled. 'I'll try to hang on till then.'

Adara just drove now, looking out at the road. After a long moment she said, 'My first inclination is to say no, to drop you off at the next bus stop I see, and to go home without you.'

Dom pushed the button to move his seat back into the upright position now. He said, 'I'm holding out hope for your second inclination.'

Adara nodded. 'Gerry *will* want me to sign off on you

before you return to duty. Maybe we should start that process with a complete physical.'

Dom shrugged. 'Okay. Sure. Let's do it for Gerry.'

Adara said, 'But I'll warn you now. It won't be easy. You will have to prove to me you are in peak condition.'

'I'll give it my all, Sherman.'

The black BMW drove on through a brightening afternoon, the light snow tapering to nothing and the clouds above curling up and away as the last winter storm of the season moved off to the east.

He just wanted a decent book to read ...

Not too much to ask, is it? It was in 1935 when Allen Lane, Managing Director of Bodley Head Publishers, stood on a platform at Exeter railway station looking for something good to read on his journey back to London. His choice was limited to popular magazines and poor-quality paperbacks – the same choice faced every day by the vast majority of readers, few of whom could afford hardbacks. Lane's disappointment and subsequent anger at the range of books generally available led him to found a company – and change the world.

'We believed in the existence in this country of a vast reading public for intelligent books at a low price, and staked everything on it'
Sir Allen Lane, 1902–1970, founder of Penguin Books

The quality paperback had arrived – and not just in bookshops. Lane was adamant that his Penguins should appear in chain stores and tobacconists, and should cost no more than a packet of cigarettes.

Reading habits (and cigarette prices) have changed since 1935, but Penguin still believes in publishing the best books for everybody to enjoy. We still believe that good design costs no more than bad design, and we still believe that quality books published passionately and responsibly make the world a better place.

So wherever you see the little bird – whether it's on a piece of prize-winning literary fiction or a celebrity autobiography, political tour de force or historical masterpiece, a serial-killer thriller, reference book, world classic or a piece of pure escapism – you can bet that it represents the very best that the genre has to offer.

Whatever you like to read – trust Penguin.